ABSINTHE
OF THE
HEART

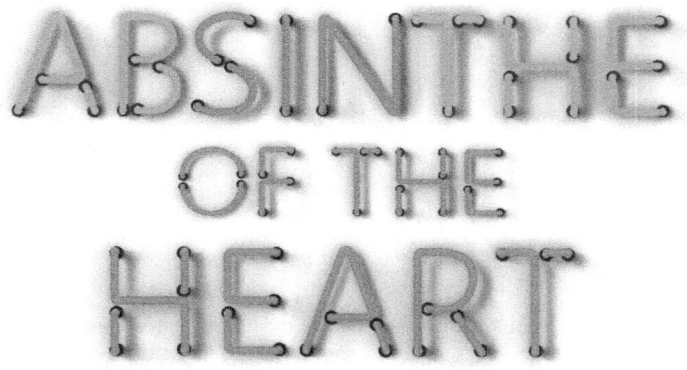

ABSINTHE OF THE HEART

BOOK ONE

International Bestselling Author

MONICA JAMES

Cover Design by Perfect Pear Creative Covers
Editing by Toni Rakestraw of Rakestraw Book Design & Editing 4 Indies
Interior Design and Formatting by

www.emtippettsbookdesigns.com

CreateSpace Independent Publishing platform

Follow me on:
monicajamesbooks.blogspot.com

Dedication

For my sister.

PROLOGUE

1977

"**M**ommy, this sweater itches," griped Delores Brooks as she tugged at the collar of her prickly pullover.

"I know, baby. Mommy is sorry, but it's part of the uniform." Elsa tightened the blue ribbons in her daughter's pigtails one more time. She had to look perfect.

Delores chewed at the corner of her mouth as best she could because her missing two front teeth prohibited her habit, making it almost impossible to do. She was nervous, but she didn't let it show. She knew how much this meant to her mother.

Crouching to level her daughter with her emerald gaze, she brushed away any imperfections that might reveal just who Delores really was. "Do you remember what I told you?"

Delores's hooded eyes widened as she peered around, watching with interest as her fellow pupils were walked to the white gates by their parents. They looked so different from Delores's mom. They wore designer suits and expensive furs, their gold jewelry and different color diamonds illustrating to the world just who they were. In their social circles, they ate people like Delores and Elsa for breakfast. They looked down their nose jobs at people like them, who didn't have fifty dollars to their name.

They didn't belong here, and the rich folk knew it. They only had to take one look at Elsa's thrift store outfit to know where the Brooks stood in the greater scheme of things. But with Elsa's mother passing and leaving her only daughter a small fortune, Delores now had the opportunity to attend one of the most elite, private elementary schools in California. This institute was a feeder to Harvard-Westlake, where Delores would be attending after she finished the sixth grade. God rest her soul, if it wasn't for Alene's passing, then Delores would be attending her first day of kindergarten at the public school close to home. Elsa had no problems with that reality. It was good enough for her.

However, it was Alene's dying wish that her only granddaughter got the best education she couldn't provide for her daughter. Alene and her husband, Bram, were Dutch immigrants who came to America to better their life. And they did, for the most part, until Bram ran off with a waitress and left his family to fend for themselves. Alene did the best she could. She worked three jobs to look after her daughter, but times were tough.

Elsa was *that* kid in school. No one wanted to play with her because she wore hand-me-down clothes and lived off food stamps, but she never cared. She got pregnant when she was nineteen and married her high school sweetheart six months later. Life wasn't easy, but she and Tyler made it work. Life was good back then, but things…they change.

"Mommy, why are you crying?"

Elsa quickly wiped away her tears, not wanting her nostalgia to ruin her daughter's first day at school. "I'm just so happy. Look at you in your uniform. You're such a big girl."

Delores smiled, peering down at her white shirt and navy pinafore dress. She'd never owned such shiny shoes before. She was certain she could see her reflection in the gleam. The sweater still itched, but she resisted the urge to scratch.

"Delores—" Elsa turned serious, lowering her voice "— what did Mommy tell you?"

They'd practiced this speech a thousand times before, so Delores knew it by heart. "My name is Delores Brooks, and I live in Bel Air." Elsa nodded, relieved her daughter could recite the lie with ease.

The truth would eventually unravel, but all Elsa wanted was for Delores to be on equal ground with her peers as long as she could before they judged and ostracized her for being different—for being poor.

"Why do I have to lie?" Delores's innocence broke Elsa's

heart. Her sweet, naïve daughter would soon figure out why.

"It's to protect you, baby," she replied, brushing the silken hair from Delores's brow. "I love you so much. You're my little angel. Never forget it."

"I love you too, Mommy. Is Daddy coming to pick me up?"

Elsa's heart didn't just break; it shattered into a million unrepairable pieces. She barely held it together, knowing one mishap would taint her daughter's future forever. "No, I told you…Daddy is with Grandma Alene."

"In heaven?" Delores asked, not fully grasping the concept. Delores saw the casket, but how could Elsa explain to a five-year-old her father died of leukemia? He was the healthiest man Elsa knew. His life insurance would take care of them for a little while, but if Elsa had her way, she'd give back every penny if it meant he would still be alive.

"Yes, baby, in heaven. That's right. It's just you and me."

Delores could see the tears in her mother's eyes, but she still didn't understand why her mother cried herself to sleep at night. She learned, however, that whenever she mentioned her father, her mother went to bed early, taking a bottle of pills with her.

She didn't want her mother to be sad, so she adjusted her backpack and smiled. "I can walk myself inside. I'll be okay. I'm a big girl now."

When tears welled in her mother's eyes, Delores feared she'd said the wrong thing. But Elsa nodded, wiping both hands down her exhausted face. She felt so much older than twenty-four. One could be excused for thinking Elsa was dropping off her younger sister at school. Life certainly hadn't turned out the way Elsa thought it would. And that was the reason she was here. She wanted a better life for her daughter. And if lying was the sacrifice she had to make, then so be it.

"I'll be here at three o'clock."

Delores nodded, ignoring the butterflies in her belly because like her mother said, it's only them now and she had to be strong for her mom. Elsa placed a gentle kiss on her cheek, lingering and savoring the sweetness her daughter emanated. She knew she was destined for great things.

Observing the daunting gates, Delores took a big breath. "Don't cry, Mommy." Her tiny fingers reached out to brush the fallen tears from her cheeks. "Daddy is watching over me. So is Grandma Alene."

Elsa sniffled, standing before she broke down. "Have a-a good day, baby."

"You too." Delores turned, an excitement suddenly bubbling within. She'd never had many friends. Living in East L.A., in a neighborhood which was commonly known as the "hood" because it literally was a hood, her mom rarely let her play outside unsupervised.

Her home was a small, two-bedroom house which had seen better days. After a while, Delores got used to the sirens and gunshots. They became background noise which helped her fall asleep.

But she pushed those thoughts far from her mind because the noises she heard right now were sounds she didn't hear too often—kids' jubilant laughter, the gentle hum of expensive cars' motors idling by the curb, and people talking in hushed tones, not a hint of vulgarity slipping into their conversations. She could get used to those sounds.

Climbing the three steps, she chewed on her lip, wondering which way to go. A pretty lady holding a brown clipboard to her chest made eye contact with Delores. Her gentle smile and bright pink earrings instantly made her feel at ease.

"Hello there. Is this your first day?"

Delores knew her mother was watching, poised and ready to run to her daughter's aid if there was a hint of trouble. She didn't want to be the cause of any more tears, so she pulled back her small shoulders and nodded.

"Y-yes." She cleared her throat. "My name is Delores Brooks, and I live in Bel Air." It rolled off her tongue so freely, she almost believed the lie herself.

"Hello, Delores. My name is Miss Jackson. I'm your teacher." She bent at the waist, clutching the clipboard to her chest. "I'll show you where to put your bag." Delores smiled. She was extremely proud of herself.

Miss Jackson gestured for Delores to follow, signaling with her hand. She didn't look back, only forward as she marched behind, taking in the sights and sounds. St. Martin's Elementary was everything and more. The high buildings were painted a pristine white, far whiter than anything Delores had ever seen before. There were no cracks in the exterior. No uneven surfaces for one to trip over and break an arm. The yard was clean. The football field was a lush green. The playground was outfitted with equipment which looked brand new. Delores's feet itched as she was desperate to take off in a dead sprint and see how high that swing could take her.

But she followed, absorbing and cataloguing everything, knowing there was plenty of time to play later.

Miss Jackson turned over her shoulder, ensuring Delores was keeping up. She liked her already. "Our room is just up on the left." She nodded, gripping the straps of her backpack, her tiny fingers trembling in anticipation.

When they turned the corner, Delores stopped in her tracks, unable to process what she was seeing fast enough. Children her age ran and laughed with their peers, playing tag or maneuvering a silver spring down a set of stairs. Delores watched in awe, as she'd never seen anything like it before.

"That's a Slinky," Miss Jackson gently explained.

Although she was being kind, Delores remembered her mother's warning to act as if she belongs. She shouldn't draw attention to the fact she's in a secondhand uniform, or that she's only here because two people she loved dearly died and left their money to better her life.

"I know, Miss Jackson. I have three," she said, accenting her claim with a slight scoff. Miss Jackson didn't say anything, but it was clear she could see through Delores's lies.

Miss Jackson led the way into a small room where a dozen or so wooden hooks were attached to the wall. Some hooks had blue schoolbags dangling off the ends, their zippers undone, revealing different colored lunchboxes and drink bottles inside.

"You can hang your bag here." Miss Jackson pointed at a hook at the end and smiled. Just as she was about to say something else, a loud bang was followed by an ear-piercing shrill. There was no mistaking the sound of someone falling over. Miss Jackson's lovely face turned troubled, and she quickly brushed past Delores to see what the commotion was all about.

Delores exhaled, thankful to be alone. All this pretending was exhausting. She didn't understand why she couldn't just tell everyone the truth. Surely, they wouldn't judge her because her mother didn't drive a fancy car, or she didn't live in a mansion in the hills.

She placed her bag on the hook and decided to take off her prickly sweater. Once she'd hung up her things, she straightened out her dress, and satisfied she looked just like everybody else, she exited the coatroom with a rush of confidence. To fit in, she needed to make friends, and she couldn't wait to find her first best friend. They would be inseparable, just like Bert and Ernie.

The thought was too exciting for words; however, Delores was stopped dead in her tracks when she saw a group of girls form a tight circle around something. At first, she had no idea what they were doing, but when she heard them giggling and noticed them pointing, she realized a blonde little girl was the center of their mockery.

The scrawny girl was crying, her large blue eyes streaming with tears. Delores had no idea why she was so sad but wondered why the group of girls wasn't asking if she was okay. If anything, they appeared to be making her cry harder.

"Crybaby! Crybaby!" one of the taller girls chanted, egging her two other followers on. This only made the blonde girl sob louder.

Delores hated bullies. She'd seen enough of them in her neighborhood, riding their bikes around as if they owned the place. Her mother had taught her to stick up for what was right, and what she was seeing this minute was anything but right.

She didn't think twice before she marched over, tapping the taller girl on the arm. "Excuse me?"

"What do you want?" the girl said, turning around and glaring at her.

Delores gulped. She was suddenly frightened that she'd bitten off more than she could chew. But remembering her mother's words and her father's strength each time he went to the hospital, she swallowed down her fears. "Stop being so mean to that girl." She pointed at the little girl who was shaking, tears still cascading down her cheeks. She saw her backpack lying on the ground, opened, the contents spilling onto the cement.

"Why? She deserves it. Her mom is a gold digger; my

mommy said so," the taller girl said, as if that warranted her cruel behavior. None of them even understood what a gold digger was, but sadly, hate bred hate.

"Well, whatever her mom is doesn't give you the right to be so mean to her. Leave her alone."

The blonde girl's snivels stopped swiftly, and she stared wide-eyed, mouth slightly parted. She looked as surprised as Delores felt. This surge of confidence had come out of nowhere, and she suddenly felt like her hero, Wonder Woman.

The tall girl, who seemed to be the leader of the mean girls, narrowed her eyes. She was already a little brat with training wheels on. "What are you going to do about it?"

Delores wasn't intimated by her. "I'll tell Miss Jackson."

"Who's Miss Jackson?" the girl smugly countered.

"Our teacher," Delores replied, not missing a beat. "I don't think she'll be happy to know she has a bunch of bullies in her class."

The girls' faces paled, as they didn't want to get into trouble on the first day of school. Delores stood her ground, waiting for them to reply. This could go either way. She held her breath, waiting. She exhaled when the girls looked at one another and decided to pick on somebody else.

They shoved past her, almost knocking her to the floor. "Nice dress, by the way," the tall girl mocked. Delores didn't understand until she noticed the logo on her uniform was different from everyone else's. "That was the logo from a hundred years ago. Where did you buy your dress? From the Salvation Army?"

Delores's cheeks burst into flames. Her mom was going to be so angry with her. She just wanted her to fit in, but Delores had brought unnecessary attention to herself and her secondhand clothes. The girls thankfully left, bored by the schoolyard antics already.

Delores felt sick to her stomach. She had no doubt the word would spread about her, and by lunchtime, everyone would know she was the poor kid who didn't belong.

A small voice made her remember why she was standing out here in the first place. "Th-thank you." She turned to see the blonde girl tugging at her plaited pigtail. "I'm Kayla Sinclair. I live in Beverly Hills."

Delores waved, ignoring the knot in her belly. "I'm Delores Brooks, and I live in…" But she abruptly paused, unable to bear another lie. Kayla waited for her to continue. There was something about her. Delores felt a kinship with her and lying to her suddenly felt like the worst thing she could do.

Hoping her mother forgave her, she started again. "I'm Delores Brooks, and I live in the hood." She couldn't pronounce her suburb, but she knew all the kids referred to their neighborhood this way.

She waited for disgust, maybe even a scream, but she got neither. Kayla pursed her rosy lips and nodded. "Groovy. Do you wanna be my best friend?"

Delores gasped, a breath whooshing from her lungs. Did she just have a lapse in hearing? But when Kayla smiled a matching toothless grin, Delores knew she'd found the Bert to her Ernie.

She nodded happily, squealing when Kayla threw her arms around her and hugged her tightly.

Delores never imagined having a best friend would feel that extraordinary. She had visions of them drinking soda by the beach and playing with their dolls. They would be best friends forever.

As both girls went to work picking up Kayla's spilled possessions and talking about the latest shows on TV, Delores didn't realize that her kindness had set off a chain reaction which would affect so many people's lives forever.

Some for the good, but mostly…for the bad.

1988

"Delores, seriously, stop. You're going to ace the test," Kayla stated as she flopped onto Delores's single mattress, belly first.

Delores giggled at her best friend's melodramatics. "You're just saying that so I'll come to this stupid party with you."

Kayla's ears pricked up at the mere mention of Bobby Ferris's party. Bobby was the star quarterback at their school, Harvard-Westlake, and Kayla had been crushing on him since the third grade. He was tall, dark, and handsome, everything a quarterback should be. All the girls wanted a piece of him, but he didn't seem to be interested in anyone.

But Kayla was planning on changing that tonight, and she needed her best friend by her side to ensure she didn't get cold feet.

"Please, Dee, please come with me. How can I win Bobby over without my wingman?" She propped herself on her knees and interlaced her hands together, praying Delores would say yes.

Delores had never been able to say no to her best friend. They'd been inseparable since they were five-years-old. Even when Kayla was old enough to understand where Delores lived, and even when her mother forbade them to be friends, she never turned her back on her. She didn't care that she was dirt poor, or that her mother bounced from guy to guy; all she cared about was that she and Delores remained best friends forever.

Kayla never cared that she was rich—far richer than any of her classmates—because money couldn't buy happiness, and every moment spent with Delores made her happy. They did everything typical sixteen-year-old girls did. They listened to music, went to the movies, and talked about boys. Well, Kayla talked about Bobby, while Delores just rolled her eyes and laughed.

Delores would never tell Kayla, as their friendship meant more to her than some stupid boy, but she too had a crush on Bobby since forever. She hadn't told Kayla, but after school, while she was waiting for Kayla to finish art class, Bobby had stopped by her locker and asked if she was coming to his party tonight. Delores had never been good around guys, so she nervously squeaked out a maybe. Bobby smiled and said he really hoped he'd see her there.

There was no mention of Kayla, and that troubled Delores.

No question about it, Kayla was the better looking of the two. She was blonde, tanned, big busted, and had legs that reached the heavens. Delores was more the girl next door type. Long brown hair, probably too thin for her five-foot-five frame, and far too many freckles sprinkled across her pale skin.

They really couldn't be more opposite.

But Bobby had asked *her* if she were coming, not Kayla, and Delores couldn't help but wonder why. That curiosity was the reason Delores finally caved. "Fine, you win."

Kayla squeaked in excitement, jumping from the bed and hugging her best friend tightly. "Thank you, thank you, thank you! We're going to have so much fun."

Delores half smiled, hoping the decision wouldn't come back to bite her in the ass. "Okay, give me five minutes and we can go."

As she packed up her books, she noticed Kayla hunt through her enormous overnight bag. It wasn't uncommon for her to bring over various outfits, as Kayla stayed over at Delores's house at least twice a week. With Delores's mom working most nights, or shacking up with her latest squeeze, the girls had the house to themselves most days. They sometimes pretended they were roommates, living off campus and surviving in the big, bad world together.

"Here, you can wear this." Kayla tossed a gold dress at Delores, who scrunched up her nose.

"Where's the rest of it?" she teased, holding it up to her body and wondering if there was a tiered matching skirt. She was so not wearing it.

"Don't be such a stick in the mud. I'm sure Ralphie would just love to see you in, or out of it," Kayla said, shimmying out of her acid-washed jeans and short tank. She slipped into a turquoise leather skirt suit with a bright pink tank which showed off her toned, tanned midriff.

Ralphie Arrington was in Delores's advanced math class. He was cute in a nerdy kind of way, but Delores had no interest in him whatsoever.

Kayla had been trying to set them up for months, but neither was interested. Delores had seen the way Ralphie looked at Kayla. Kayla, of course, didn't notice because all she was interested in was Bobby. Delores hoped he didn't break her heart.

Delores watched Kayla tease up her long blonde hair, making her appear like a lioness ready to pounce. As she puckered her bright pink lips and smacked them together, she looked at Delores's reflection in the mirror. "I'm going to lose my V-card tonight, Dee."

"*What*?" Delores was left speechless. Most girls had offered up their virginity to Bobby, and what sixteen-year-old boy wouldn't be thrilled at virgins throwing themselves at him willingly? But Kayla and Delores promised each other that when the time was right, they'd lose their virginity to the person they loved.

Kayla's ploys to snare Bobby hadn't worked, so now she was pulling out the big guns. This night was sure to end in tears.

"Yes, it's happening," she confirmed, slipping on a pair of white lace fingerless gloves. All Delores could do was hope Bobby was too drunk to notice her best friend's advances.

As they caught a cab to Bobby's mansion in the Hollywood Hills, Delores tried fruitlessly to persuade Kayla to change her mind. But she knew her friend was just as stubborn as she was. Her mind was set and nothing would stand in her way. Once this night was over, one of them would no longer be a virgin.

Delores wished she'd said no, because as they trudged up the steep driveway toward the towering manor, she had an unsettling feeling sink to the bottom of her stomach. There were so many kids here. Delores was certain half the school had turned up.

Bon Jovi's "Bad Medicine" blared loudly inside—an omen of things to come even though Delores hoped that wasn't the case. Both girls entered the open front door, pausing in the grand foyer to take in the beauty. Bobby's father was loaded; he was some Texan tycoon. She had no idea what exactly he did, but from the looks of this house, he was successful.

"Let's get a drink," Kayla shouted into Delores's ear to be heard over the loud music. Delores nodded, needing the Dutch courage to help calm her nerves.

Kayla made no secret that she was scouring the crowd for Bobby. She looked beautiful, but she always did. She was the beauty while Delores was the brains—as many people had said—and Delores was fine with that. She was happy to sit on the sidelines and watch her friend sparkle in the spotlight. That was why their friendship worked. There was no jealousy, no competition between them.

So when Bobby sauntered down the white spiral staircase and headed straight for Delores, she quickly turned her back and nudged Kayla in the ribs so she was the center of his world, not her. Kayla quickly lowered the already low neckline of her tank and ran a hand seductively down her side.

"Hey," Bobby said, and Delores squashed down the butterflies. They had no right to be there.

"Hey, Bobby," Kayla replied, her voice low, seductive. "Cool party."

"Thanks," he replied loosely. "Hi, Dee."

Delores closed her eyes and cursed her choice to come here. She should have said no. But she was here now. Turning slowly, she tried not to gag on air when connecting with Bobby's mesmerizing hazel eyes. He looked far older than sixteen, his bulging biceps and facial hair rivaling most of their male teachers. He was a complete rebel with a silver stud in his left ear, and a leather jacket complemented his ripped, bleached jeans.

Not wanting Kayla to clue onto her panic, she smiled. "Hi." Bobby licked his full bottom lip, and the sight shot a surge through Delores.

She knew Kayla was about three seconds from uncovering her secret, so without a second thought, when she saw Ralphie in a Hawaiian shirt a few feet away, she excused herself quickly and ran to his side.

The move was completely chicken shit, but she'd rather that than lose her best friend over a boy. "Hi, Ralphie!" she shouted, a little too loudly.

Ralphie jolted, not expecting the company, but smiled when he saw Delores. "Hey, Dee. You here alone?" He stood on his tippy-toes, no doubt hunting the crowd for Kayla.

"No, Kayla is here. She's talking to Bobby." Delores pointed at where Kayla was inching closer and closer to Bobby, who seemed to be combing the crowd, uninterested in her blatant attempts to seduce him.

"Oh." The disappointment was clear on Ralphie's face, and Delores couldn't help but feel sorry for him. She knew the feeling all too well.

"Wanna get a drink?" Ralphie nodded, appearing thankful they both could drown their sorrows in a bottle of beer.

Twenty minutes later, they were sitting poolside, watching

their fellow classmates' unsuccessful attempts at hooking up. It seemed with the alcohol flowing freely, everyone's guards were down, and before the night was through, Delores had a feeling a lot of V-cards might be checked at the door.

The view from up here was beautiful. There was nothing like seeing the City of Angels from this high up. The bright lights extended as far as the eye could see, and Delores couldn't help but feel blessed she was able to witness such a sight. If it weren't for her mother's sacrifice and her father and grandmother's deaths, then she couldn't help but wonder where she would be. Everything did happen for a reason. She pondered on the reason why she helped Kayla on that first day of school. Would it amount to something life changing? She rather thought it already had.

"Hey, are you all right?" Ralphie asked, breaking Delores's trance.

Shaking her head, she discreetly wiped away her tears. "Yes, fine. I think I'm a little buzzed from the beer."

Ralphie nodded, stealing a peek into Delores's almost empty red cup. "Hey, you're out. I'll grab us a couple more."

Delores knew she should have said no, as she was already wasted, but numbing the pain seemed the only way to deal with what Kayla was probably doing with Bobby right now.

Once Ralphie was gone, Kayla's familiar scent of raspberry and cream caught the warm breeze, and Delores turned to her left, surprised to see her friend. "What are you doing here?

I thought you'd be shacked up with Bobby." She wiggled her eyebrows, hoping Kayla didn't see through her façade.

Kayla swayed. She was obviously buzzed too. "He said he was going upstairs. He'll be back down in a minute. I really like him, Dee, and I think he likes me too."

Delores swallowed past the lump in her throat. "Of course, he likes you. What's not to like?"

Kayla grinned, clapping her hands in excitement. "How's Ralphie?" she teased, her voice dripping with innuendo.

"He's fine. He's just gone to get us a drink."

"I'm sure he has," she mocked, cackling loudly when Delores rolled her eyes.

"Ooh, Dee, tonight is perfect. You. Me. We're invincible. Promise me we will name our kids after the places we visit when we're older and traveling the world together." She slipped her arm around her friend, drawing her to her side.

Delores's stomach turned at the mention of kids, as she knew what had to happen for that to come about. But quashing down the urge to puke, she nodded. "Deal. I think I'll name my daughter...Holland."

"Holland?" Kayla questioned with a laugh.

"Yes, I want to visit where my Grandma Alene lived. She's the reason why I'm even here. It seems fitting I name my future child after her."

Her explanation appeased Kayla, and Kayla pondered what she'd be naming her future offspring. "Okay then...I'll name my son London."

Now it was Delores's turn to laugh. "Why London?"

Kayla cocked a hand to her hip, feigning horror that Delores didn't know why. "Um, hello, fashion capital of the world."

Both girls burst into laughter, everything falling into place.

"Okay, it's settled then." Delores raised her near empty cup to salute Kayla's bottle of Budweiser. "To Holland Brooks..."

"And to London Sinclair," Kayla concluded as they clinked drinks. "It goes without saying they're betrothed the moment they're born. They have no say in the matter because it'll officially make us a family."

Delores raised the cup to her lips and smiled. Regardless of their marital status, they did not intend to change their maiden names. It was modern and progressive. They also felt their children should bear their surnames, seeing as they did all the hard work. "We're already family, Kay."

Kayla nodded, tears filling her eyes. "Sisters for life."

"Sisters for life," Delores confirmed, drinking to their toast happily.

However, once the beer hit Delores's empty stomach, she felt the distinctive sensation that she was about to be sick. "Dee, are you okay?" Kayla asked, her eyes growing wide with concern.

Delores didn't have time to reply. She simply shook her head and covered her mouth, running through the throngs of people, hoping she'd make it to a bathroom in time. She took a wild guess and charged up the stairs, thankful when she saw a line outside the closest door to the right. When it opened, Delores shoved past the girl in line, who called out angrily, but Delores could apologize to her after she was done puking up her guts.

She slammed and locked the door, running to the toilet and throwing up. She'd not eaten much today, but it still felt good to heave up all the booze she'd consumed. After ten minutes, she felt remotely better, but her head felt like a ten-piece brass band was playing the American anthem on a loop.

She needed to lie down.

Once she washed her hands and splashed some cold water on her face, she noticed a tube of toothpaste sitting on the basin. She helped herself, using her finger as a makeshift toothbrush. She felt semi-human.

Smoothing out the snags from her wavy hair, she decided to tell Kayla she was ready to call it a night. She hated to be a Debbie Downer, but she resembled roadkill.

Once she opened the door, she apologized to the girl she rudely cut in front of, who huffed and shoved past her. Out here in the brightly lit hallway, Delores's head suddenly felt worse. If she could lie down for a few minutes, she'd feel a lot better.

Not really knowing where she was going, she ventured down the corridor and took a left. This place was like a maze. She opened the last door, and thankfully, it was dark inside. She slipped out of her sneakers and fell face first onto the queen size bed. The silk comforter was so incredibly soft against her heated skin. A sigh left her parted lips as she nuzzled deeper into the blankets, the musky perfume wrapping her in a restful bubble.

Her eyes were closed for mere seconds, when they suddenly popped open because she realized where she'd smelled this comforting fragrance before.

"Dee?"

Shooting upright, she moaned and raised a hand to her brow. Her eyes strained to see in the dark, but she'd know that voice anywhere. "I'm s-sorry, Bobby. I didn't know this was your room. I'll go." When she attempted to shift however, the room began to spin, and she knew moving wouldn't be happening anytime soon.

"It's okay. You can stay. I'm glad you're here."

"You are?" she asked, wishing she could see him to make sure this was really happening.

"Yes," he replied, his footsteps sounding against the carpet, alerting her he was moving closer to where she sat.

She should move, she *needed* to move, *now*, but she was suddenly rooted to the spot. "C-can you turn on a light?" she asked in a whisper.

The room was gently lit when Bobby switched on the bedside lamp. It took her eyes a moment to adjust, but when they did, a wheeze left her because Bobby was breathtaking. His dark hair was tousled, his eyes slightly glassy from the buzz the beer had given him no doubt—he took her breath away.

"I-I should go." Even though her intentions were pure, her body betrayed her, and she stayed where she was.

Bobby sauntered over to the bed, watching her, not speaking a word. The way he looked at her, hungry and full of fire, stirred something in her she wished she could douse, but couldn't. "Bobby, I-I…." But she didn't know what she was trying to say.

Bobby ran a hand through his hair, his bicep flexing with the movement. "I like you, Dee."

"You what?" she gasped. "W-what about Kayla?"

"I like her, but…she's not you," he replied so matter-of-factly.

Delores had always lived in Kayla's shadow, and it never bothered her, not in the slightest. But she felt wicked, beyond sinful that Bobby Ferris wanted her and not Kayla. She felt so out of place, being here in her ripped jeans and flannel shirt, as she looked nothing like the girls who went to her school. This was the star quarterback, the guy every girl wanted, and he wanted her.

That thought was incredibly intoxicating and had her doing something she'd never done before. When he slipped off his white t-shirt and stood before her topless with a silent invitation, she let go and forgot that Kayla Sinclair existed.

Delores stared at Bobby's huge, muscled body. She'd never seen a guy topless this close before. Of their own accord, her eyes descended to the front of Bobby's pants. They were tight enough that she could see his very noticeable hard-on.

A yearning began to burn between her legs.

He was on her before she had a chance to think twice about her decision, not that she would, because kissing Bobby and feeling him against her was unlike anything she'd ever felt before. Her skin was set alight, but suddenly, kissing wasn't enough. She wanted more.

Their hands grabbed at one another desperately, clothes falling wherever they landed as the need to be naked and pressed against the other was all that mattered. Bobby's red-hot erection nudged at her slick entrance.

She should have felt disgusting for doing this to her best friend, but she didn't—she had never felt more alive.

"Are you sure?" Bobby asked, looking into her eyes as he was suspended, naked, above her.

She bit her lip, a habit she'd had since she was a child. This was her last chance to do the right thing. But why did doing the right thing feel so wrong? Closing her eyes, she nodded, knowing this decision would change her life forever.

She heard Bobby open a drawer and then the rumple of foil. Once he was suited up, he kissed her gently, coaxing her to relax. But she didn't need much coaxing when she felt him slip inside her, breaking down all her reservations.

She lost herself in the moment, focusing on nothing but the feel of him, owning something that would always belong to him. He treated her with care.

They both came undone with a loud, well-sated scream.

As they laid in the afterglow, Delores knew she should feel guilt for what she had just done. But she didn't. Bobby kissed her brow and asked if she was okay, and she was. She knew once she sobered up and the first light of dawn peeked over the valley, it would be a different story, but for now, everything was absolutely perfect.

"…Dee?"

Kayla felt a knife slice straight through her heart when she saw something she'd never thought she'd ever see. Her best friend in bed, naked, with the boy she'd had a crush on for years. Kayla was betrayed, and hurt, but most of all, she felt stupid because she was actually worried about her best friend.

Ralphie had helped her search the house high and low, afraid someone might have taken advantage of her drunken state. But it appears the only person who'd been taken for a ride was Kayla, forever believing her friendship with Delores was real.

"Let me explain!" Delores shrieked, but her naked form was all the clarification Kayla needed.

The final straw was when Bobby put his arm lovingly around Delores, comforting *her*. He should comfort Kayla because her friend was no better than her mother—a dirty, bedhopping whore.

"Never speak to me ever again!" Kayla shouted, unable to keep the tears away.

"Kay, no, please!" Delores pleaded, but Kayla had seen and heard enough.

She ran down the hallway, needing to escape this nightmare before she broke down. This was beyond words. She wished this were a dream, but it wasn't. She officially had no one. Her mother and father barely cared if she was alive or not. They might be rich in possessions, but when it came to love, they were far more impoverished than Delores would ever be. Delores was her only friend, her family, and now, she was all alone.

"Hey, it's okay," Ralphie said, stroking her bicep and softly drawing her into his arms. It felt nice that someone cared about her. And after what she'd just witnessed, that was all she wanted—someone to take care of her.

Ralphie's mouth fell slack when Kayla pressed her frantic lips to his. This was the last thing he'd ever expected, especially after what just happened, but the feel of Kayla's body twisting and writhing against him was just too much. He'd lusted after this girl for years and only dreamed of them ever entwining this way. He knew why she was doing it, but he just didn't care.

When she pulled him into the bathroom and locked the door, any shred of second-guessing was long gone. When she slipped out of her outfit, completely bare beneath, he vowed to treat her like the queen she was. It was a flurry of hands and clothes, and before long, they were both naked. Kayla straddled Ralphie, who sat on the toilet seat, rubbing his eyes to ensure this was really happening.

"I don't have any protection," he said, still a lick of sense left.

She lowered herself, gasping when she felt Ralphie nudging at her, eager to take away something that should never have been his. "I don't care," she gasped, lowering herself onto him, her eyes bulging from the foreign intrusion.

She locked her arms around his nape and began rocking, each painful inch she took etching away at whatever love she had left for Delores. "I just want to forget," she declared, sobbing at the pain tearing down below. And sobbing at the pain carving through her heart. "Please...just make me forget."

Ralphie knew what this was, and he knew he should stop, but he couldn't. He secured his hands around her waist and promised to make her forget. And she did. For a split second in time, she forgot that life as she knew it would forever be changed.

What was done could never be undone, and what they'd all done would never be forgotten...or forgiven, for generations to come.

1

2004

"Would you look at that ass?" gushes my best friend, Annabelle Greene.

Peering up from my math calculus homework, I roll my eyes and almost gag when I see who she's referring to. "Belle, please, for the love of god, give me some warning when you're referring to *that* asshole. I now have to wash my eyes out...with bleach." Belle cackles beside me, knowing that talking about *him* will leave me crankier than a bear with a sore head.

She slides her huge black sunglasses down her nose with her pointer finger and peers over the top of them, licking her glossy red lips. "Too bad he's such an asshole because he's so... fucking...hot." Her pause for emphasis makes me want to knock some sense into her.

"Ugh!" I cover my ears and sing "Naughty Girl" by Beyoncé

at the top of my lungs. I know she's doing this is rile me up because she thinks it's simply hilarious that, while almost every girl at our school, Harvard-Westlake, would happily drop their panties the moment he enters a room, I loathe the star quarterback with every fiber of my body.

But I'm not like every girl, and for that, I'm glad.

When I think I'm asshole-free, I remove my hands, but hold up my finger in warning. Belle giggles, hands raised in surrender. "Holland Brooks-Ferris, you're the only girl who wouldn't think twice if Sin got run over by a bus."

I can't help but raise my eyes to the heavens once again. "Please, *Sin*? Who does he think he is? Some character out of *The Sopranos*. That name is a reflection of what an utter Neanderthal he is. Besides, his surname is actually Arrington, but apparently, that's not cool enough for him, and he goes by his mom's surname instead. And you're right, I wouldn't, because I'd be driving the bus."

Belle's light laughter catches the warm summer breeze. "Okay, sorry, I meant London. London Sinclair-Arrington," she clarifies with a smirk

"Oh, really? That's his name? I didn't know," I quip, which is an outright lie.

Sadly for me, I've had the misfortune of knowing London Sinclair since he tripped me over and stole my lunch the first day of kindergarten. I wish the torture ended there, but he's been a constant thorn in my side since that first day, going out of his way to make my life hell.

It's no secret we're archenemies, and it's pretty safe to say we've hated one another from day one.

I begged my mom and dad to change schools, but they both said it was the best school in town. They're just biased because this is where they went, and fell in love. I shudder at the thought. Parents and love—it's not a combination any sixteen-year-old girl wants to think about.

London, Sin, or whatever alias he wants to go by, is in full gear, practicing for the big game on Saturday night. His confident swagger and the way he holds himself with such an air of arrogance makes me want to slam my head against this thick textbook in hopes of rendering myself unconscious.

The Sin Skanks as I like to call them huddle together on the bottom step of the bleachers, stroking the quarterback's already huge, inflated ego by batting their eyelashes and cheering him on with ridiculous glittery signs they made in art class.

They'd better not sneeze or move in the wrong way because I'm pretty certain with one sudden movement, we'll be seeing who's a real blonde or not. The thought is enough to lose my lunch over.

London charges forward, demonstrating his sheer strength and size as he mows down anyone in his way. He doesn't care who it is; it could be his grandma—all he cares about is winning.

As he ducks and weaves, he scores a touchdown, which incites an almost riot from the skanks down below. Belle and I are on the top of the bleachers, but his overbearing arrogance almost knocks me from my high perch.

He rips off his white helmet, pointing cockily to his legion of fans. Ugh, I hate his guts.

I continue with my math problem, which is far more entertaining, but Belle's swooning is near palpable, so I risk a glance his way, wondering what exactly she's so wrapped up in.

His dirty blond hair is longer on top with shorter sides, a lot longer than you'd expect a jock's hair to be. It's always mussed from him running his long fingers through it, as he knows it drives all the girls, except me, wild. Even though I can't see them from this distance, I know from them staring holes straight through me that beneath that tousled bed hair lies a set of the stormiest blue gray eyes I have ever seen. They're the kind of blue that reminds you of the clearest cerulean sea, but they can also suck you into a punishing storm seconds later.

His nose is evenly sloped and slightly upturned, adding to the air of arrogance he constantly carries on his broad, muscular shoulders. His jawline is chiseled and always brushed with a dark, heavy scruff, which makes him look so much older than sixteen.

His body is taut, muscled, and absolutely imposing, standing at six-foot-four. The way he holds himself, he knows he's been gifted in the looks department. Too bad his virtues got lost in the mail.

He's everything you'd expect a quarterback to be—attractive, rich, and so full of himself, he believes his own bullshit.

I narrow my eyes, watching the way the red jersey clings to his upper torso. He's certainly grown from the scrawny little brat who cut off one of my pigtails in the second grade. Too bad he didn't grow a brain as well.

Lost in visions of our turbulent past, I don't notice him looking at me until it's too late. He's seen me staring, and even from up here, I can see that trademark cocky, dimpled smirk. I hate that grin. I've slapped it from his face a handful of times.

As he runs forward, his bulging arms swinging by his side, he points at me before blowing a kiss. The skanks turn briskly to see who dared steal their limelight, but they have absolutely nothing to worry about. I am not interested in *anything* London Sinclair has to offer. Not wanting him to think I've gone soft, I raise *my* finger—the middle one, that is—before blowing my own kiss with it.

I can see his perfect white teeth flash me a smile from up here.

Screw…him.

As Belle ties back her long blonde hair, she muses aloud, "I wonder what his favorite drink is, because whatever it is has made him big and strong."

"Blue Cherry Gatorade," I reply without pause.

She pauses from primping and arches a sculptured brow. "That's right; you're a walking encyclopedia when it comes to Sin," she teases, just how she always does.

"I've made a point to know my enemy. It's smart business," I explain, scoffing when a groupie runs to the sidelines to offer London a towel.

"Are you looking at Sin...voluntarily?" Belle asks, feigning horror with a hand pressed to her chest.

"Don't be ridiculous," I counter, suddenly feeling hot. But I was, and I hate myself for even giving him a sliver of satisfaction. I need to get out of here because London's arrogance is suffocating. Besides, I need to study.

Belle breaks her ogling and peers up at me. "Hitting the library?"

I nod. "Yes. I have to finish that history paper."

"Holl, you'll ace this, just as you always do."

Her confidence in me is reassuring, but if I want to get into Stanford, I need perfect grades. Unlike most of the kids who go here, I have to work hard for my education. I don't have a trust fund. Nor do I have Mommy and Daddy forking out hundreds and thousands of dollars easily.

My father, Bobby Ferris, comes from money. My grandfather was a Texan oil tycoon. He came to Los Angeles after he struck it big, wanting to capitalize on his good fortune. Before my mother, Delores Brooks, met my father, she was doing it rough. She was poorer than poor, but thanks to my father, her life changed.

We lived in an extravagant mansion in the Hollywood Hills where my neighbors were famous actors and people of "importance." It was all superficial nonsense, so when my grandfather made a bad investment and our lives changed forever, I didn't think twice when we were forced to sell and move to a less luxurious part of Los Angeles.

Instead of a six-bedroom mansion, we live in a two-bedroom home where our neighbors are your average, working-class American families who drive hybrids instead of Hummers. Both my mother and father work honest jobs so they can pay the bills, but to the rich and richer, we may as well be white trash. My grandfather is seen as a con artist because he went to prison for embezzlement, and my mom, she's an apparent gold digger, which is ridiculous, because if she were, why would she still be married to my dad? And my dad, he's seen as having no balls because he remained faithful to his family.

My soiled history is something London Sinclair ensures I don't forget.

We were doomed to hate one another, seeing as my mom and his mom are arch nemeses, which is ironic, considering they were once best friends. I don't know the full story, but it had something to do with some party where both London and I were conceived. My dad used protection, but apparently, some things are meant to be.

London is older than me by two days, but from the way he behaves, all superior and almighty, you'd think it was ten years.

Long story short— London's mom, Kayla, only stays with his dad, Ralphie, because he makes the rich look poor. She's still secretly crushing on my dad, which is so gross on all accounts, and is waiting in the wings, ready to sabotage my parents' marriage any chance she gets. London hates me because, well, I think it's pretty obvious why. I'm a symbol of their love, flaunting what they did to her.

I get that he's protective of his mom, but she is a crazy bitch who needs to back off.

My mom's reputation has been long ruined thanks to Kayla Sinclair. But my father doesn't care. And I love him for that. I love them both for it.

"Where have you gone this time?" Belle quips. I'm known to get lost in my head from time to time. Everyone calls me a dreamer, but I like to consider myself a thinker.

"Just thinking about how I won't make it tonight." Before she can guilt trip me, I stop her. "Belle, I have to work at six, and then I have a bunch of homework I have to catch up on. There is no way I can go, and besides, some kid is always throwing some party. I promise I'll go to the next one."

Belle's lower lip quivers dramatically, and I can't help but laugh. "Don't make that face." I point at her, which only encourages her to pout further. She's my Achilles' heel. She always has been.

Belle's family pretends she doesn't exist, and although that's the consensus for the majority of my peers, Belle is the only one who cares. She is desperately seeking love and affection from wherever she can find it. Some call her needy or clingy, while I see someone who just wants to find her tribe. "Okay, fine, fine, I'll see if I can swing by." I throw my hands up in defeat as she cheers victoriously.

I should have known she was trouble when I caught her eating glue in the first grade. "I'll be there around ten. You know where it is. Haunted Hollows?"

Shaking my head at the ridiculous name, I pull my lips into a thin line. "Yes, I know where it is. Why can't our classmates be normal and have parties inside their over-the-top homes instead of outside in the dark, where the potential to fall to one's death is not implausible?"

Belle shrugs, but the glint in her hazel eyes reveal she's up for the challenge. "It'll be fun. A campfire, toasting marshmallows, telling ghost stories under the full moon." Sometimes, she really is naïve.

A laugh escapes me. "I doubt any of that will happen. We're not in Girl Scouts anymore. Try a bonfire, toasting beers, and singling out which girls they want to bone under the full moon."

Belle squeaks, and I don't know if it's in horror or excitement. Unlike Belle, I'm proud that my chastity belt is still under lock and key. She's desperate to lose the big V to any meathead jock, while I'm desperate to graduate with my dignity intact. Again, I blame this need for affection on Belle's parents, who barely remember their daughter's name.

"I'll see you later." I bend down and hug her tightly.

"Don't work too hard," she singsongs, pulling out a nail file from her Prada bag. Pointing it at me, she smirks. "Save your energy for tonight. Sin will be there. I'm sure you'll be at one another's throats all night."

I curl my lip in disgust. Even his name makes me want to hurl. "If only my hands could squeeze around his throat and I wouldn't go to jail for a very long time for it." I sigh with mock sorrow. She cackles loudly, but I'm half serious.

I bid her farewell, ready to tackle this paper on World War II. Lost in thought, my guard is down, which is a very, *very* bad thing when London Sinclair is around. I amble down the stairs, not taking in my surroundings until it's too late. I know better. This is a total rookie move, one which costs me dearly.

"Watch out!" Belle's warning comes after the event because before I know it, I feel like I've been whacked in the face with a baseball bat.

The force of the hit propels me backward, and I fall onto my ass, the steel of the bleachers making me see stars. It takes me a moment to catch my breath.

"Oh my god, Holl, are you all right?"

Shaking my head, it takes a second for my vision to clear, but when it does, I see what or *who* was the cause of me dropping like a sack of potatoes.

London stands at the bottom of the bleachers, an amused grin tugging at his lips. Off to my left is the reason he looks happier than a pig in shit. His stupid ball. He threw his fucking ball…into my face.

What in the actual hell?

With the world still spinning, I gather my bearings as best I can and jump up, ready to kill him. I sway to the right, but steady myself by holding the aisle chairs as I charge down the stairs. London stands his ground, arms folded across his chest, challenging me.

This…means…war.

"You son of a bitch!" I scream, not caring that the shriek just split my skull into two.

London laughs that arrogant, throaty chuckle. "You should know," he states with a carefree shrug.

How *dare* he.

I forget my pain and quicken my rampage, intent on making him pay. I leap down the bottom step, scrambling toward him, and catch him off guard when I shove at his steel chest. I'm surprised when he actually budges. It may only be an inch, but it's a victorious inch nonetheless.

"Sorry, I didn't see you there," he quips, laughing when I scream in pure rage.

"Fuck you!" I push at him once more. The adrenaline soars through my veins, intent on payback like he's not seen before.

My victory dance lasts only a few seconds, before he stops humoring me and snares both my wrists in his large hands. I notice they're calloused, but I shake such nonsense from my head. "You'd like that," he states, continuing to chuckle at my fruitless attempts to bring him down.

I flail around like a madwoman, attempting to pry myself free, but he's so strong; his fingers are like manacles around my wrists. I glare up at him, not allowing his towering frame to intimidate my petite five-foot-three stature. "In your dreams, you pig!"

His strong jaw clenches as he lowers his heated face inches from mine. He's trying to intimidate me, but all he's doing is making me angrier. "Oh, Princess..." His voice is low, his blue eyes wild. "You make a guest appearance in my dreams quite often."

"Good. I hope I give you nightmares," I bite back, still struggling with him, but he matches me, move for move. To onlookers, it may appear like we're caught in a clumsy, synchronized dance because although I'm fighting with all my might, he's barely broken out in a sweat.

His tongue sweeps out to wet his bowed, upper lip, and the action suddenly leaves me winded. His hot breath bathes my flustered cheeks, and the fact I'm wondering what cologne he's wearing because he smells absolutely *amazing* kicks me in the solar plexus and shakes some sense into me, because I should *not* be smelling him—ever.

What the *fuck* is wrong with me?

I obviously have a concussion or maybe even brain damage because when a smirk tugs at the corner of his pink lips, I actually feel myself growing lax.

"No, you're the stuff wet dreams are made of," he counters

confidently, his voice dropping to an octave that should be illegal.

A strangled wheeze escapes my parted lips because this entire conversation has given me literal whiplash. His admission is laced with an undertone of desire, but the fact I can feel my eye turning blacker by the minute completely contradicts his words.

Either way, I need to remember just who this is, and how he's made my life utter hell. With that as my driving force, I quash down this alien Holland who could stare into those tumultuous eyes for hours, and draw out the sane me, the one who can play this asshole at his own game.

It works for so many others, so I decide to try it on for size.

I know I'm not his type, as his "type" is blonde, big busted, and about as sharp as a bowling ball. But I'm not exactly chicken liver either. I'm dark-haired, light-eyed, and have a lean yet curvy body.

Surrendering completely, I blink once, feigning innocence as best I can. I'm certain he's going to see straight through me, but am surprised when a winded gasp escapes him. I push out my decent sized chest and relish in triumph when his eyes drift to the goods I'm offering.

His fingers are still locked around my wrists, but the fact I've stopped struggling has him loosening his hold.

I bite my lip theatrically, feeling a complete fool, but his sudden interest eggs me on. "Wasting all that talent in your sleep…that's a real shame." My comment has caught him completely off guard, but I try not to gloat—not yet.

His chest begins to rise and fall, his nostrils flaring from the deep, steadying breaths he's taking. The sun beaming down around us draws out the small number of lighter blond strands in his hair, something I've not noticed or cared about in the past. I don't remember ever being this close to him before, so I take a moment to study just why so many girls want London Sinclair.

His runway looks can't be denied. He's all angular and chiseled with perfect bed hair and a dimpled smile, but beneath that perfect exterior lies such imperfection, I suddenly wonder what secrets he's guarding.

But to know my enemy, I need to become him. I need to become the conceited, arrogant asshole who doesn't give a shit about anyone but himself.

"Why? You want to lend a hand?" he asks, the Sin I know shining brighter than ever before. He makes hating him so easy. Maybe that was the plan all along.

"You couldn't handle my hands," I purr. It's unbelievable how easy he's fallen for this temptress act. What a chump.

"Is that a challenge?" he poses, tonguing his cheek with a smirk.

I shrug coyly, my lips parted, my eyes doe. "Let me go and find out."

I can see him weighing my proposition. We've bantered

and bickered our entire lives, but this, this is new. I'm woman enough to admit that some sort of weird tension is currently thrumming through my veins, but I peg it down to a punch of adrenaline, knowing that I've won.

At this moment, I know why they call him Sin. He's radiating it from every inch of his hardened body. He's cocky and arrogant, and call me crazy, but that's why I think every man and his dog wants a piece of that sin.

Epic looks combined with a rebellious attitude make London Sinclair the ultimate bad boy every girl wants to subdue. But little do they know, he's one beast that'll never be tamed.

He releases me slowly, but not before skimming his finger over my thrashing pulse. The tempo betrays my response to him—the utter contempt I feel, laced with a small sliver of something else.

"So, now that you're free…what are you going to do?"

I smirk, my innocence suddenly replaced with one hundred percent bitch. He reads me like a book, but it's too late. Shame on him for thinking I'm like all the other girls.

"This," I reply. The sound of my palm connecting with his cheek gives me a satisfaction beyond words. The sting in my hand also adds to the delight.

His palm shoots up to his reddening cheek, his jaw moving from side to side. His surprise that I can hit that hard is clearly evident, and my insides do a little happy dance in pride.

"Touché," he spits, still rubbing his cheek.

"Just so you know—" I level him with my gaze "—the next time, I'm coming for your balls."

He has the gall to smirk. "Me and my balls can't wait, Princess." To accent his point, he grabs his crotch and winks.

"You're fucking disgusting."

"And you're a smart-mouthed princess." His attention flicks to the tattered copy of *Romeo and Juliet* I'm holding. "Shakespeare? It shouldn't surprise me you connect with a headstrong pain in the ass who led poor, defenseless Romeo to his death."

Yawning theatrically, I roll my eyes. "Bored now. There are only so many minutes in my day I can handle dumb, and you've just taken up all of them. Have fun with your harem of skanks and STD-riddled bros." I don't check my sarcasm at the door. "I have no idea why you choose to hang out with these deadbeats with not an original thought between them. Your GPA is perfect, but hanging around these losers definitely says something about your IQ." He appears stunned that I'm in on his little secret.

London by no means is your typical meathead jock. He's smart—like super smart. But I've always thought he's embarrassed by his academic prowess, as if being an A-grade student will ruin his bad boy reputation somehow.

"Maybe I could teach you a thing or two?" he taunts, as I haven't made my obsessive studying a secret.

"Please…the only thing you can teach me is how to catch Chlamydia."

London looks slightly amused, but mostly, he looks like he wants to rip off my arms and beat me to a bloody pulp with them. With that as my powerhouse, I brush past the stunned bystanders, sporting my black eye with pride.

"In and out," I mumble to myself for the umpteenth time.

Thanks to the fact I look like I've gone ten rounds with Mike Tyson, I've had to come home after work in an attempt to conceal my blackening eye.

I iced it as best as I could at work, but running between the front desk and snack bar at Paradisco Roller Rink made it nearly impossible to tend to anything but the party of fifteen kids jacked up on Cherry Coke and cake.

I've worked there for just over a year, and most days, I loved the disco theme, paired with the roller-skating experience. But tonight, the techno music, bright neon fluorescent lights, and the piercing screams of kids just added to my headache.

I closed up right at nine, desperate to come home and crawl into bed. Sadly, when I checked my voice messages and heard Belle's slurred message, asking when I was coming, I knew I had no other choice but to go down and make sure she was all right.

I wanted to go home first to change and cover my black eye because if I turn up at this party sporting a shiner, then no doubt tomorrow, school will be rife with rumors about how my white trash parents beat me. That, of course, is untrue, but the truth doesn't seem to matter to the rich kids who have nothing better to do than make up rumors to add excitement to their perfect, cushy worlds.

I'm hoping my mom and dad are out because I don't want to explain what happened today. Since I was young, they've known of London's constant attitude toward me. They spoke to our teachers, who spoke to London's parents, but thanks to their history, nothing was ever solved.

London's parents blamed mine, saying they raised a crybaby, while my parents were quick to defend, saying they raised a psychopath. All in all, it just went back and forth, each parent pointing fingers and playing the blame game, while I suffered at the hands of London, who seemed to thrive on conjuring up creative ways to torment me.

I thought it would stop as we got older, but it's only gotten worse. Just when I think he's grown bored, he goes and does some fucked-up bullshit like today. I can't wait to get the hell out of this town. It's my dream to graduate top of my class and go to Stanford. I know we can't afford it, so to achieve this, I have to get a scholarship. And to get a scholarship, I have to ensure my nose stays clean and my grades are infallible.

So it goes without saying, I can't sport a black eye.

I enter through the backdoor softly, shushing Suzie, our family Labrador, by tossing her a treat off the kitchen counter.

She happily runs with it and settles into her bed without a sound. Pausing, I listen carefully, letting out a breath when I hear the house is quiet.

Just in case my parents are locked away in their room, I slip out of my tattered Converse sneakers and tiptoe down the carpeted hallway. My room is the last on the left. I hold my breath as I sneak past my parents' room, only exhaling when I close the door behind me.

I hate lying to them, but if they see me, then the twenty questions will start, and once they find out who gave me the black eye, it'll be on. My dad will go down to London's father's work, hurling abuse, and he'll be escorted off the premises by security, just like a thousand times before. He will be looked at like the white trash they all think he is, and London's father will have grounds to add fuel to this already out of control fire.

London's dad is the brains and money behind designing some new cell phone, which is apparently going to take over the world. He has over four hundred employees working for him, and in the world of technology, he may as well be God.

My father works at an accounting firm downtown. He may be a god to his clients, but to the rich and powerful, he's a bug they could easily squash without even lifting a finger. But that doesn't matter to him, because he would go above and beyond to protect me and my mom. In high school, he was a big deal. Star quarterback who could have amounted to so much, but that wasn't the path his future was to take. He had me young and married my mom, and not once have I heard him gripe about his heydays and what he could have achieved if he hadn't become a father at seventeen.

My parents are remarkable people, and I would do anything to save them heartache.

Not daring to turn on the light, I move around my small room with ease. The full moon streaming in from my window is all the light I need. I change into a pair of flared jeans which once belonged to my mom, a purple silk floaty tank, and top it off with a navy blazer. I slip in my drop earrings and rearrange the silver name necklace I'm already wearing. It's inspired by none other than Carrie Bradshaw.

My long, wavy brown hair falls past my shoulders. I usually wear it down, but decide to sweep it to the side in a low bun. My long bangs are the perfect shield to partially conceal my eye. But I know it'll need layers of makeup to hide the bruising.

Hunting through my drawers, I find some liquid foundation I got for free at the mall and crouch low to get into the right light. Peering into the cracked mirror on the wall, I cake on several layers until it's almost hidden—almost. I'll just have to ensure I talk at arm's length and not rub my eye.

My notched dresser has seen better days, but from one of the supports that holds a few cheap necklaces hangs a pair of rose-tinted shades Belle left behind. I've always thought that wearing sunglasses in the dark was a total tool move, but in times of crises, one has to think on their feet.

I've always been a no-frills kind of girl, but now I feel ridiculous with a face full of foundation and no eye makeup to go with it. I rummage through my dresser drawer once more and find an eye shadow palette. I apply a frosted silver shade, and even in the dull moonlight, I can see my bright emerald eyes pop. Not that that matters, seeing as I'll be wearing shades. I finish off with some mascara and eyeliner.

Peering back from the mirror, I purse my lips, impressed. Who would have thought I could pull off looking like a girl?

Snatching my Smackers strawberry gloss from the messy dresser, I place it and the sunglasses, along with my keys and wallet, into my handbag. I know I won't look like all the popular girls, but that's okay. I'm happy with wearing my own vintage style with pride.

Shutting the door as quietly as I opened it, I tiptoe slowly, still afraid my mom and dad will catch me sneaking out. I give Suzie a quick pat before I slip back into my sneakers and run down the rickety back steps.

I breathe out a sigh of relief, but that soon transforms into a strangled wheeze when a set of headlights turn down my small driveway. I could run toward my beat-up Honda and pretend I was never here, but the fact I'm caught like a deer in the headlights roots my feet to the ground.

My parents' Mercedes has seen better days. It's one of the only things leftover from our "rich" life. My dad insisted we sell and downgrade, but my mom knew how much he loved the thing.

I admire my parents' love for each other and often wonder if I'll ever find that sort of connection with another person. I doubt it'll happen here, however, because everyone knows who I am and the stigma associated with my name.

I've kissed one guy. Lincoln O'Toole. He's a nice enough boy. He's on the football team and popular with all the girls. But the few times we've made out have been secret, and once the deed is done, he acts like he doesn't know my name.

I know he's embarrassed to be caught with me, so I can't help but wonder why he keeps coming back for more. I should tell him to hit the road because I know I'm better than being kissed in the dark. Just this once, I want to be kissed in the light. No stolen or drunk kisses.

The only hope I have is to leave this small-minded community behind and make a name for myself elsewhere. Away from the rich, poor, mean, and judgmental because leaving this town means I get a clean slate.

The prospect is too tempting. It's the only thing that keeps me going.

As my parents pull up beside my car and switch off the engine, I give them a small wave before quickly hunting through my bag and slipping on my shades. I try to act cool, but the fact I'm wearing sunglasses at night and moving my weight from foot to foot is a sure sign I'm up to no good.

"Hello, Sweetie," my mom says as she exits the car.

My mother is absolutely beautiful. She can make the simplest outfit look like the latest trend from Milan. Even though she's in jeans and a plain pink tank, the way she holds herself with such elegance and poise has me hoping I look that good when I'm her age.

My dad steps from the car, looking just as stunning as my mom. I can imagine them turning heads when they were my age. Not only for the fact that they're absolutely magical together, but because my mom stayed at school while pregnant with me.

"Hey." I wave quickly. "I was just going out." That's my out to jump into my car and not look back, but I should have known it wouldn't be that easy.

"Too grown-up to give your mother a kiss?" she teases, pointing at her cheek. I sigh playfully, but amble over to where she stands.

I kiss her quickly, her familiar floral perfume spreading a sense of calm over me. "You look nice."

She brushes her hands down her top. "Thank you. Your father and I got free movie tickets to see *The Day After Tomorrow*. The lead actor is a real hunk. Jake someone." She nudges me in the ribs with a grin.

My father clears his throat melodramatically, while I pretend to gag myself with my finger. "I'm sure he'll be a one-hit wonder. And besides, no one uses the term 'hunk' anymore," I say, using air quotes, which elicits a muffled laugh from my dad.

"Oh, sorry, I'm not up with the lingo of today's youth. I'll have you know, in my day, hunk was an acceptable word to use for the opposite sex. For example, your father was a real hunk," she adds, giving him a look which is reserved for their eyes only.

He primps up his collar smugly.

"Mom! Gross!" I'm suddenly glad I'm wearing sunglasses. Both my parents burst into fits of laughter.

"Where are you off to?" Dad asks, locking the car and rounding the hood.

Settling my nerves, I reply nonchalantly, "Just going to a party a kid from school organized. No big deal. Belle is already there."

My father's brows knit together. He doesn't buy my indifferent act. "Will there be alcohol?"

"I'm pretty sure you know the answer to that." I don't see the point in being coy.

"Oh, leave her, Bobby. She can't be any worse than we were at her age." Mom swoops to the rescue when she sees my father's reservations.

He really can't argue with her, considering I'm sixteen and still a virgin. "Okay, fine. But make sure you're home by curfew."

"Yes, sir." I mock salute, and he smirks.

Just when I think I'm home free, my mom steps in front of me, blocking my road to freedom. "I know I may not be up with the lingo of today, but I certainly know your tastes in clothing and wearing sunglasses at nighttime is not one of them."

She folds her arms across her chest, cocking her head in interest. I suddenly wish she saw the world through these rose-tinted glasses because it would make my life so much easier.

"They're Belle's. She left them in my car. I keep forgetting to give them to her, so I figure if I wear them, I won't forget to give them back." I take a deep breath, betraying my nerves.

My mother looks at my father, silently asking if he believes my story. I gulp, running my sweaty palms down my thighs.

He looks at me, as if weighing up my story. I can tell by his slightly cocked left eyebrow that he doesn't believe a word. "Holland, don't lie to us."

"I'm not!" I beseech. My shrill cements my guilt.

Just as I'm about to plead my case, he walks over to my car and tugs at the handle. It's locked. "I thought you said she left them inside your car."

Busted.

Before I can backtrack, my father outstretches his palm and gestures with his fingers that I'm to give him the glasses. *The makeup will conceal it*, I reason. It gives me the confidence I need to slip off the glasses and place them into his palm with a huff.

"See, my eyes aren't bloodshot; I'm not on drugs, if that's what you're worried about," I smartly state, but soon regret my smugness.

"You may not be on drugs, but you're…fighting now? Who gave you that black eye?" Dad says, shaking his head.

"*What?*" Mom gasps, running over and pinching my chin between her fingers to look at my face.

I pull out of her grasp, turning my cheek. "It's fine. I'm not fighting. It was just a misunderstanding." I need to put this fire out before it explodes into a shitstorm.

"Misunderstanding with whom?"

"Holland?" my mom implores. "Who did this to you?"

Biting my lip, I avert my gaze. I may as well have skywritten who.

"That son of a bitch," my dad mumbles murderously. It doesn't take a rocket scientist to figure out who.

"L-London did this to you?" My mom's falter stabs at my heart. This is exactly the reason why I didn't want to tell them. The physical pain is nothing compared to the emotional pain I'm putting them through right now.

"Yes," I finally reply in a whisper.

The air is stagnant for a few seconds before it detonates into a fiery mess. "I'm going to kill that little bastard!"

"Bobby, no! We can't."

"No, Dee, this is it," my father spits, not interested in playing nice. "We can't allow this to continue. He's now *hitting* our daughter. What's next? I'm going to the police!"

"Dad, no, stop!" I yell, latching onto his forearm to keep him from unlocking the car. His whole body is trembling with anger, and all I want to do is ease his pain. "He didn't hit me. He threw a football at...me." I close my eyes for the briefest of seconds, as that doesn't exactly support my case either.

"And that makes it any better?" he counters heatedly.

"No, of course not, but you can't involve the police. You know any more scandal linked to our name will ruin my chances at a scholarship. I'm almost home free. Please, just let me deal with this," I beg, hoping he sees reason.

"Holland…you're my daughter. What do you expect me to do?" His eyes turn soft, the love for me reflected deeply within.

Rubbing his forearm, I hope he sees reason. "I expect you to trust me, Dad. Trust that you raised me right and that I know what I'm doing. London Sinclair is just a speed bump, he's not a roadblock. I'm almost out of there. I can deal with him, but what I can't deal with is losing my dreams because of him."

My father's chest deflates, but he's still livid. He wants to protect his little girl from the big bad world, but he can't shelter me forever.

"Are you sure, Holland?" I'm surprised when my mother speaks.

"Yes, Mom. I'm sure."

My parents have raised me to stand up for who I am, and what I believe in. And what I believe in is my future. It's the only thing that matters to me, and I won't allow a high school bully to get the better of me.

After a tense few minutes, my father's shoulders sag, and he nods. "Okay, fine. We trust you, but if he lays so much as a finger on you, I will break every bone in his body."

A shiver passes through me because I believe him. "Thank you." I stand on tippy-toes to hug him, never feeling more loved and protected than I do right now. My mom sniffs, a sure sign she's holding back her tears. I know what she's thinking. She's said it more times than I can count—her sins have cost me dearly.

As usual, London Sinclair has caused my family pain. Leaving this town can't come soon enough.

2

park my car half a mile down the road, needing the fresh air to clear my head.

I left my parents clinging to one another as they bid farewell to their only child. Their worry was painted on their faces, but they did as I asked and trusted that I have this under control.

I meant what I said. London and the masses of kids who look down their noses at me because I don't fit into their social circle mean nothing to me. I stopped caring what other people thought about me long ago.

I'm proud of my heritage. My ancestors worked hard to provide for their families, and being a blue-collar citizen is something I'll never hide.

The infamous Hollywood sign is my compass; it's been all

of ours. It's what we've sought out when we've been lost. Visitors travel from places high and low to get a glimpse of something that should symbolize freedom. Its significance, however, gives us a false sense of hope that dreams can come true. When I look upon it, all I see is the desperate need to better oneself because people like me don't belong here.

There is always a buzz in the summertime air. Living in Los Angeles is a constant whirlwind of excitement, but something is truly magical about the hot summer nights, and tonight is no exception. Walking in the opposite direction of the tourist friendly trails, I slip under a linked fence, ignoring the no trespassing sign.

We've been coming out here since we were kids. It's been a popular hangout for decades, thanks to the breathtaking sights that Los Angeles has to offer. The City of Angels looks so small from up here, one can't be blamed for forgetting the huge impact this city has on so many people. People's dreams are made here, but for some, dreams come here to die.

Hiking higher up the rocky terrain, I wonder where I'll be in ten years. Will I still be here, climbing this mountain and feeling beyond insignificant when I look out into the sea of lights and broken dreams?

I refuse to believe that.

My dream is to graduate at the top of my class and move to New York City, where I will become a well-respected attorney, representing the blue collars of this world and fighting for what's right. Los Angeles is where I was born, but I'll be damned if it's where I'll die.

"American Idiot" by Green Day catches on the warm breeze, alerting me to the fact that the party is in full swing. The riotous screams of girls can also be heard, mixed with the deep, raucous rumble of boys. No doubt everyone is intoxicated and out of control.

I can only hope Belle isn't too wasted because she has a tendency to go wandering when she is. I've found her in some strange places, and I'm hoping tonight isn't one of those nights.

Once I pass the trademark, hollowed-out sycamore tree— which looks eerie to the unsuspecting and is how this place got its name—I'm instantly hit with the waft of pot and beer. I'm not in the mood to socialize, but I amble the rest of the way, cringing when a classmate, Helen Tharp, rushes past me in nothing but a skimpy bikini.

Last I checked, there was no need to wear a bikini, as there's not a drop of water in sight, but hey, when in Rome…

A blazing bonfire burns brightly, providing the light I need to witness a sight I've seen far too often. About a hundred kids are swaying to the music, red cups held high in the air as they drown a dozen or so brain cells.

Hyper color beer bongs are being passed between eager classmates, uncaring the liquid is soiling their designer clothes. There is far too much Abercrombie and Herve Leger for my taste.

Swallowing down my revulsion, I peer around for Belle. No surprise, she's nowhere to be seen. My classmates don't hide their surprise, but mostly, they appear disgusted at seeing me here. I don't fit in and being here is breaking some ridiculous rule. The preppy girls whisper behind their hands, laughing at my cheap clothes as they check me out from head to toe.

As they see it, I'm the girl from the wrong side of the hills. I have no right to be here. I haven't earned my stripes to be seen in public with their Chanel and Jimmy Choos.

But not everyone is a complete asshole, and when I see Chloe Helm, a classmate, walking around alone, sipping from a plastic cup, I breathe a sigh of relief. "Hey, Chloe."

Her warm eyes light up the moment she sees me. She seems happy to see a friend because, just like me, Chloe isn't one of the "beautiful people." She's "overweight" according to the wafer-thin girls, but when I look at her, all I see is someone who likes me for me. "Hey! Did you just get here?"

I nod. "Yeah. What did I miss?"

"Oh, you know just the usual. Catfights, testosterone-fueled arguments, and people making out in the bushes. Just a normal night here in the Valley of Crazy." I laugh at the nickname us "normal" kids have dubbed the place we live.

"Have you seen Belle?"

She scrunches up her button nose. "I saw her like an hour ago with Lincoln and a bunch of boys from the football team. She was pretty wasted."

My stomach drops. "Was Sin with her?"

She nods, her cheeks turning red at the mere mention of his name. I ignore the need to slap some sense into her.

"Shit," I curse under my breath. This is so typical of Belle. "Where did they go?"

"To the abandoned zoo, I think."

I shake my head. She knows better, but I have no doubt her quest to check in her V-card is the reason she's acted so recklessly. "Thanks, Chloe." I take off in the direction of where she went.

"Hey, wait up, I'll come too." I don't have time to argue.

Onlookers whisper among themselves, wondering what the commotion is about, but they can all go to hell. All that matters is finding my best friend and stopping her from making the biggest mistake of her life.

I climb up the rocky terrain, a billion horrible thoughts weighing down each step I take. What if I'm too late? What if it's dog pack mentality, and Belle is the bone? I push such thoughts out of my mind and focus on finding my friend.

Chloe and I run track together, so we reach the abandoned zoo in less than twenty minutes. But now that we're here, the problem is where is Belle? I don't have a cell phone—it's not a luxury I can afford—but it's times such as these I wish I had more than two pennies to my name.

"Chloe, can I use your phone?" Chloe nods and hunts in her back pocket.

I dial Belle, but all I'm greeted with is her voicemail. Knowing her all too well, I bet she's let the battery go dead.

Peering around, the darkness seems bigger, vacant. The thick shrubbery and low-hanging branches make it almost impossible to see. I've been here a handful of times but never in the dark. I can't maneuver my way through this rocky landscape from memory, so I'll have to trust my gut.

"Let's split up," I suggest while the whites of Chloe's eyes are illuminated under the moonlight.

"Are you crazy? This is how every horror movie starts. Two girls, alone in the woods…" She shivers, rubbing her arms, snapping her head from left to right.

"Don't worry." She almost looks relieved until I conclude with, "You're rich. They'll hold you for ransom and just torture and kill me." She pales, and I can't help but laugh.

"I'll just stay here."

"Okay. Keep trying Belle," I order, passing her back her cell. I wouldn't blame Chloe if she took off the way we came. I leave her clutching her phone, using the light from the screen as her lightsaber.

I don't know where I'm going, so I decide to head straight, hoping the unsteady landscape below has deterred them from venturing too far off track. It's pitch black out here, not even the hustle and bustle from Hollywood or its surrounding suburbs can be heard this far out. The thought is daunting, but I persevere.

My shoes aren't equipped for trekking through such impenetrable undergrowth, so I take my time, not interested in plummeting to a painful death. The moon provides just enough light for me to see a small black shelter, most likely an old cage, a dozen or so feet away. I can't hear anything but decide to take a look inside just in case.

There is a rocky slope, overshadowed by tall weeping willows. To get to that shelter, I have to venture along this murky, potholed path. I'm going to kill Belle when I get my hands on her, but the most important thing right now is getting my hands on her.

Blowing my bangs off my face, I psych myself up and take one, then two steps toward this dubious route, which looks like it just may lead to hell. The wind picks up speed; the gentle rustle of leaves has me wondering who else I'm sharing this path with.

It's only a few yards and then I won't be eclipsed by this darkness. I keep telling myself this as my senses are on high alert, searching from left to right, straining my eyes to see in the dark. An unidentifiable sound has me screaming and running faster than a bat out of hell.

I feel a fool when the moon peeks out from behind the cosmos, highlighting what an utter chicken shit I am. "Belle?" I call out, walking apprehensively toward the shelter, which is a run-down enclosure.

All I'm greeted with is a fist full of nothing.

"Belle?" My frightened voice echoes in the silence, alerting me to the fact that I'm out here all alone.

Deciding to take a quick peek inside, I push open the rusted wire gate which hangs limply from one hinge. The weary whine is the soundtrack to the next *Texas Chainsaw Massacre*.

The passageway opens to a concrete cage, which looks like it once was used to house bears. The thought is enough to give me the heebie-jeebies. I walk forward with my hands out in front of me, hoping I feel a head of long blonde hair. The deeper I venture inside, the darker it becomes. Pausing, I take a moment to adjust to the shadows, but nothing's in here.

I trip over a bottle, which rolls along the floor and bounces off the wall. It smells like stale beer and piss. Belle is definitely not in here.

Sighing, I turn the way I came, using the wall as my guide so I don't bump into the solid cement. The surface feels bumpy and aged beneath my fingers, and I wonder what stories it could tell. This place has been closed since the 60's. I'm sure it's seen decades of change.

As I round the corner, my hand still following along the wall, I don't pay attention to my surroundings because if I did, I'd have noticed I'm no longer alone. Stopping dead in my tracks, the blood whooshes through my ears and my heart begins a deafening gallop.

I can sense someone a few feet away, watching me. I don't know how I know, but I can feel their gaze. Every hair on my body stands on end, and my fight or flight instinct takes over. "Who's there?" I call out, faking bravado.

Silence.

I quickly run toward the gate but am jarred to a stop when I knock straight into a brick wall. I bounce backward onto my ass, shaking my head to clear the stupor. I don't remember a wall being there, and I certainly don't remember a wall smelling like sandalwood mixed with a hint of warm cinnamon and vanilla. What I do remember is that I basked in that perfume early today.

"What the fuck are you doing?" I curse, angrily standing and wiping the dirt from my hands.

I can't see him because it's so damn dark, but I know my enemy is standing before me.

I can hear his heavy breathing. I can smell his refined masculinity. There is no denying this is him. But as I'm greeted with nothing but silence, I begin to wonder what happens now that London and I are truly alone.

I've had nightmares about this scenario. No one's here to save me, but even in a room full of people, I've always been alone.

"I knew you were a creep, but this is taking it to a whole new level." I try to shove past him, but he steps in front of me, blocking my path. "You have three seconds to move, otherwise..."

"Otherwise what?" When he finally speaks in that low,

husky tenor, I wish he'd stayed mute, because that inexplicable pull tugs at me once again and I grow soft.

Pulling it together, I step closer so we're chest to chest. I hate this boy with my entire being, so why does his hammering heart excite and anger me all in the same breath? "Otherwise, I'll make good on my promise."

"What promise, Princess?" I can sense the wheels turning in his head, which gives me the perfect opportunity to strike.

Without a second thought, I draw up my knee and connect with his balls in a satisfying crunch. A strangled yelp followed by a string of expletives leave his lips in a garbled mess, which is my cue to push past him and break free.

"That promise!" I call out, running faster than the wind.

Freedom has never felt this good.

The breeze smells sweeter, cooler against my heated flesh as I take off in a dead sprint. I know the moment he gets the wind back in his sails, he'll be chasing me down and ensuring I pay for kneeing him in the groin.

I have no idea where I'm going, but it doesn't matter.

Who would have thought bringing down your enemy would feel so good? A surge of adrenaline kickstarts my heart, and I jump down from a ledge, deciding to steer from the path. My sneakers kick up the fallen leaves and earth, but I continue running, a sense of independence biting at my heels.

I can actually look after myself. Not that I doubted I could, but to bring down London just confirms that I'll be okay in this big, bad world. I may not be privileged like my peers, but I won't let that or *anyone* stand in the way of my dreams.

I push faster and faster, a hysterical bubble of excitement lapping at the surface. I have no idea where I am, but I'll figure it out. I'm Holland Brooks-Ferris, and no one can stop me.

That's the last thought I have until I hear someone hot on my trail. "Stop!"

His voice is like a jumpstart, hurling every part of my body into sensory overload. How did he catch up with me so quickly? A little, irksome voice reminds me that he's not the star quarterback for nothing.

But it'll be a cold day in hell before I stop running from him.

His warning only has me charging forward, jumping over fallen branches and dodging and weaving between trees and massive boulders.

"Holland!" he roars. To hear my name, pass through his lips is beyond foreign to me, as I can't remember the last time he called me by it.

He must be so mad.

The thought drives me faster and farther until everything blurs around me. I keep running, not looking behind, only forward. As I duck past an old enclosure, I see that to the left, about a hundred yards away, a curve seems to lead to a paved path. I decide to head for it, as I have no doubt London will maim me if he catches me out here with no witnesses to note his assault.

The adrenaline surge pulsates through my veins, giving me a new lease on life. As I run toward my escape route, I don't hear him until I *feel* him collide with me, knocking me to the ground. He must have cut through the terrain because he takes me down from the right.

The moment I hit the dirt, I gasp for breath because he's knocked the wind right out of me. He's sprawled out on top of me, his heavy breaths clouding my senses with a hit of pure Sin. His weight is suffocating, but I like it. I like the feel of his sticky body pressed to mine. He is so big, while I can't ever remember feeling this small.

But I shake my head, appalled and disgusted at myself for even thinking such blasphemous thoughts. "Get off me!" I shriek, pounding my small fists against his rock-hard chest.

The strikes are pathetic, laughable in fact, but I can't just lie here and surrender because I hate that a small part of me wants to.

"Sshh!" he hisses, inches from my face, pressing us nose to nose.

His boldness makes me lightheaded because the full moon chooses to come out of hiding, illuminating his brilliance for the first time all night. Looking into his feral eyes, I get lost in the magnetism, completely under his spell.

His long hair flicks over his brow, somehow emphasizing the hardness of his jaw, but the softness of his bowed lips. A bead of perspiration trickles from his hairline, tracing down his angular cheek, before detouring and slipping past his parted mouth. His breath is hot, heavy, fanning my cheeks, and that signature fragrance crashes into me as it's exacerbated tenfold, amalgamated with his masculine, refined scent.

The bead continues its journey, sashaying over his thick stubble before plunging from his chin and landing with a graceful backflip onto my lips. I'm hit in the face with a salty punch, and instinctively, my tongue darts out to lick at the foreign flavor. London's eyes drop to my lips, the surprise clear on his face.

He's a delicacy on my palate, and I hate it.

Enraged at myself for having these constant obscene thoughts, I lash out, ready to end this complete madness once and for all. "Get off, you son of—" My words die in my throat however when he slams his hand over my mouth, gesturing for me to keep quiet by placing his pointer finger to his lips.

I scream beneath his palm, which only comes out as a muffled cry. I squirm under him, but he presses his weight into me, his eyes darting from left to right. I don't feel frightened. Lord knows I should, but I have a gut feeling he's doing this to protect us—to protect me.

All my questions are answered seconds later when the distinguishable flashing of red and blue lights up London's face, and the sound of heavy footsteps charge toward us. London groans and rolls off me, running his fingertips through his snarled hair. Sitting up, he raises his hands in the air, as if he's done this a thousand times before.

It takes my startled brain a moment to register what's going on, but when I hear the words, "Don't move, LAPD!" I know that my freedom has come with a price, one which cost me dearly.

I've never been inside a police car before, and I most definitely haven't been inside a police station, interrogated by a cop who looks like he's watched one too many episodes of *CSI*.

"What were you doing tonight?" he asks me for the tenth time, and my answer is the same it was nine times prior.

"I-I told you, I was looking for my friend." I wipe my sweaty palms onto my jeans, still unable to believe I'm here.

Being hauled to my feet and searched for drug paraphernalia was absolutely not on my list of things to do before I die, but I can check it off. I can also check off being treated like a criminal because I've been charged, yes *charged* with trespassing.

I may as well say goodbye to Stanford now because I'm pretty certain they don't offer scholarships to felons.

Groaning, I place my head into my cupped palms, holding back my tears. I wish I could blame someone, but I can't; this is all on me. If only I had stayed on the path and not veered into an area obviously patrolled by the police. That was why London stopped me. He was trying to protect me. That admission is a lot harder to stomach than I thought it would be.

He could have let me go, allowed me to get caught on my own, but he didn't. He chased after me, and even when the police were yards away, he could have made a break for it, leaving me to take the rap on my own, but he didn't. He stayed.

Why?

They cuffed him after he ran his smart mouth off at them. Memories of him being slammed against the hood, wearing a smug, carefree grin still haunt me. I still don't understand why he didn't run. He had the opportunity to do so, but he sits in the room next door, most likely bored and being his usual wiseass self.

Rubbing my temples, I wonder how long I'll be here. "I want to see my parents."

Sergeant Cooke laughs sarcastically, propping his hand on the back of my seat as he lowers his face to mine. "You're in no position to be making demands, little girl."

Recoiling backward from his coffee-soaked breath, I shake my head. I'm done playing nice. "That's where you're wrong. I'm sixteen. I really should have had an adult present when you questioned me. I know my rights, but I've cooperated because I have nothing to hide. But the fact you're treating me like a criminal has me changing my mind." His rubbery mouth parts, as he obviously was not expecting that response.

I don't like bullies. I especially don't like a bully in uniform. This is one of the many reasons I want to study law. At the moment, I'm up close and personal, but I wish the circumstances didn't involve me sitting in this chair, praying I could erase the past hour of my life.

When the sergeant sees I'm not budging, he sighs and finally gives me back my personal space. The door opens a second later, and I don't think I've ever been so happy to see my parents.

"Sweetie! Are you all right?" my mom exclaims, running into the room and throwing her arms around me.

"I'm fine, Mom. I'm just glad you're here." I snuggle into her, never feeling safer than I do right now.

I can only stay nestled for so long because I know I have to face the music sooner or later. My father's anger is palpable. "What were you doing, Holland? Whatever possessed you to trespass, and with London Sinclair nonetheless!"

"Bobby." My mom releases me, shaking her head lightly. "Not now."

"Dee, I need to know what possessed our daughter to betray our trust this way." The anger I can deal with, but not the disappointment. "Just tonight, she asked we trust her, and this is how she repays us—by getting arrested!"

I lower my eyes, sniffing back my tears. I hate that I've disappointed them this way.

"Is it drugs?"

"*What?*" My eyebrows shoot up into my hairline. "No. How could you even ask me that?" I fold my arms across my chest defensively, angered my father would think that of me.

He paces the room, running a hand down his exhausted face. "Because I'm trying to figure out what was going through your mind." The room falls still, and I run out of fight.

Sergeant Cooke clears his throat before leaving the room. I don't blame him. I wish he'd take me with him.

My parents are right. I did betray their trust tonight, but it wasn't intentional. That doesn't make it any less forgivable, however. "I'm sorry," I whisper, tugging at a loose thread in the hole in my jeans.

"*Sorry*? Do you know what this does to your reputation? What it means for you and Stanford? You've completely ruined your future. Look where you're sitting!" He sweeps his hand around the plain room fitted with a table, a chair, and a two-way mirror.

"I know!" I cry, tears filling my eyes. "I know I messed up my chances at getting a scholarship." The reality of that statement hits home, and a violent sob robs me of breath. I cover my face, ashamed and embarrassed.

"Bobby, we can discuss this at home," Mom says, gently rubbing my shoulder, but I shrug her away because I don't deserve her compassion.

My father is right. One choice, one rash decision, has changed the course of my life forever. I have no idea what to do because never in a million years did I think I'd end up in this predicament.

"Was it London? Did he make you do it?" My mom is attempting to get to the bottom of this, but I can't speak. All I want to do is go home.

As the door opens, I sit upright, blinking back my tears. Sergeant Cooke's poker face is still in place, so when he says, "You're free to go," I stare at him, confused.

"She's free to leave?" my father says, attempting to decode what he means.

The sergeant nods, standing by the open door, hinting we're to disappear.

"What about her charges?" my mom asks, standing behind me, forever my guardian.

"The charges have been dropped."

My mouth hinges open and closed like a stunned goldfish. "W-why?"

The sergeant looks beyond annoyed by the twenty questions, but he humors us anyway. "London Sinclair-Arrington has confessed to forcing you there against your will. He's taken the blame, so he'll be charged, but you're free to go."

It takes me three attempts, but I manage to spit out, "*What*? London did what?"

I know the sergeant's patience is close to snapping, but I don't understand what is going on. "Mr. Sinclair-Arrington has admitted to pinning you down while you attempted to get away. You were held against your will, were you not?"

"I-I…" I'm a blubbering mess, and I doubt a coherent reply

will leave my lips any time soon.

"Were you or were you not held to the ground by London Sinclair-Arrington?" he poses, his eyes narrowing as if he's beginning to doubt London's story.

"Yes, but…"

"Son of a bitch," my father utters with contempt, but I ignore him.

"And did you attempt to escape?"

"Yes…"

"Did he give you that black eye?"

I feel like I'm standing in front of the firing squad. His questions come at me so quickly, my scrambled brain can't process them fast enough.

"Miss Brooks-Ferris, did London give you that black eye?"

"Yes, but…" He's twisting the story, and my head pounds in protest.

"Did you want to press charges?"

"Charges? Against *London*?" I ask, unable to keep up.

He nods, while I gasp, horrified. He's serious. "No. I do not want to press charges. What is the matter with you?" I screech, standing, and spreading my arms out wide.

"I think I should be the one asking you that question, Miss. Now, I have real work to do. I hope I never see you in here again." His dismissal is crystal clear, but the need to defend London's character overcomes me, and I storm forward, ready to give him a piece of my mind.

My father is quick to advance, however, grasping my forearm and stopping me from making a bigger mess than I've already made. "Come on, Holland."

"Dad!" I plead, shrugging from his hold.

I can't allow London to take the fall for this. This isn't his fault, and he never held me against my will. He held me to protect me, and he's protecting me once more.

"Miss," the sergeant's sharp voice snaps me to attention. "If you're so insistent on staying here, maybe I can show you to a cell."

Well, screw you too, buddy.

My mom grabs my blazer from the back of the chair, quickly putting a potentially nasty situation to rest. My parents stand on either side of me, not so gently coaxing me out the door. I stand my ground, however, and glare into the sergeant's eyes.

"What happens to London?"

I don't know why I care, I just do. I can question it during the endless solitary hours I'm sure to face because I know I'll be grounded until I'm twenty-one.

Sergeant Cooke stands arrogantly as if he had a part in nabbing "the bad guy." "He'll be charged. With his prior convictions, he'll probably spend some time in a juvenile detention facility."

A wavering hand covers my mouth. This can't be happening.

A smug smirk tugs at his lips, and I want to slap it from his cheeks. "Don't look so sad. One less thug off the streets makes my job a lot easier."

"London is *not* a thug." It's out before I can stop myself. Yes, he may be an asshole, but he doesn't deserve to do time, especially because of me.

"Let's go, Holland." My parents push me out the door, and I follow, because if I have to look at Sergeant Cooke for one more second, I won't be held accountable for my actions.

The bright fluorescents burn my retinas, but I welcome the pain because I'm an appalling, life-destroying fool. How could I have just stood by and allowed London to take the fall? I was so concerned about what this would do to my future, but thanks to London, tonight never happened.

Stanford is still in sight, but all that is in London's—a rap sheet and a stint in prison.

Oh god, I feel sick to my stomach.

My nausea can take a back seat, however, because a door down the long hallway yanks opens and out emerges London and his parents. My father knows me better than I know myself, because he suddenly tugs me back, but I retaliate and break from his hold.

"London!" I call out, almost falling on my face as I run toward him.

The polished linoleum squeaks under my sneakers, so I know he can hear me, but he doesn't lift his gaze. A navy trucker hat sits low on his head, obscuring most of his face, but the hard press of his jaw reveals he's just as affected as me.

Kayla Sinclair's perfect red painted lips twist into a scowl the moment she sees me charging toward her son. "Ms. Sinclair, please let me explain!" I beseech her to stop and listen, but she turns her regal nose in the air and scoffs.

She's rocking the shit out of her resting bitch face.

"I think you've done enough, young lady. Come on, London." She latches onto his arm, and I'm surprised when he doesn't pull from her vise-like grip. He still won't face me.

"Mr. Arrington, please." I will plead my case to anyone who will listen, but he appears as if he wants to get as far away from this situation as he possibly can.

London's mom never changed her maiden name, but neither did my mom. My mom's reasoning was because she wanted to honor her lineage, while rumor has it that London's parents never married. Whatever the reason, it's not my business. But seeing them together, standing by their quiet son, I think London is the way he is because his parents couldn't give two shits about him.

I never took the time to get to know London because most days, I'd have rather he was living on the other side of the world, but now, I think his behavior was a cry for help. Or maybe… attention.

There is no love between them, and I can't help but compare my parents to London's. They appear beyond annoyed, as if coming down here was a chore and disrupted whatever bullshit thing they were doing, which was obviously more important than helping their son.

Yes, my parents are livid, and I doubt I'll be able to go to the bathroom unsupervised, but I have never questioned their love for me. Can London say the same?

"This isn't London's fault!" I blurt out, desperately beseeching him to look at me. But he doesn't. His downturned gaze never wavers from his scuffed Chucks.

There is no denying Kayla's beauty. Seeing her up close and not from afar, I appreciate just how young she really is—how young both our parents are.

No older than thirty-four, most women her age would be in their prime, dominating life and enjoying their newfound love for being in their thirties. But a heavy cloud of bitterness hangs over her, and that only turns to a thunderous storm when she looks over my shoulder. I know without turning around why that is.

"Your son gave my daughter a black eye," my father spits, placing a steady hand on my upper shoulder.

I sigh. This is war.

Her lips tip up into a crooked smirk. "Well, your daughter got my son arrested, and he'll probably do time thanks to her, so I think they're even."

"Please," Dad scoffs. "I'm sure you'll just bribe your way out of this! That's why he's in this situation to begin with. If you had taught him manners…"

"How dare you!" She launches forward while I shrink back,

afraid she's about to rip out my spleen. "How dare you lecture me on manners and morals."

"Kay, that's enough." My mother's gentle voice reveals her pain, but beneath that is the distinguishable heaviness of her guilt.

She has never forgiven herself for betraying her once best friend, but no one can help who they fall in love with. It wasn't like Ms. Sinclair and my dad were ever a couple, but the way her eyes fall into mere slits, and her lips twist in a disgusted scowl, she seems to think my mom stole something that was rightfully hers.

"Miss High and Mighty, don't you start with me. I have nothing I wish to say to you...ever. You gave up that right when you stabbed me in the back and twisted the knife." Her blue eyes taper on me, hinting I was the final nail in the proverbial coffin. "But every dog has its day."

"It was a lifetime ago. I've said I'm sorry."

But my mother's plea falls on deaf ears. Ms. Sinclair shakes her head violently, a wisp of her golden hair escaping from her low chignon. "It feels like just yesterday to me."

I should not be here, listening to this, because their past has nothing to do with London or me. This tit for tat also won't help London's current predicament. But they seemed to have forgotten this is about him.

"Ralphie, please." My mom implores him to talk some sense into his spouse, but he shakes his head, his jaw fixed.

Looking back and forth between London's parents, there is no denying they look like a power couple straight off the red carpet. Ms. Sinclair is slender, but her curves hint she keeps fit. Her long blonde hair is the color of sunshine, but her striking blue eyes, the same color she bestowed on her son, are the focal point of her genetic makeup. They can lure you in with false promises, but do her wrong, and they can punish and burn just as quickly.

Mr. Arrington is tall, in shape, and radiates wealth. His dark brown hair and gray, penetrating eyes have also helped shape London's refined yet, almost at times, feral look. Those eyes promise you the world, but once you're ensnared, it's nearly impossible to break free.

Just how I feel right now.

London still won't look at me. His gaze is stuck to the floor. I will him to give me a sign he's listening, that he's just as sick and tired of our parents bickering as I am. But he only lowers his cleft chin farther, the peak of his hat shielding him from my probing, desperate stare.

"Keep your daughter away from my son," Ms. Sinclair spits, snaring London's bicep. The touch is one of possession, the warning made only to piss my parents off. "If not, you won't like the consequences."

I still can't shake the feeling that this is all for show.

"That won't be a problem, seeing as your son will be where he belongs," my father retorts. Even I flinch from his harsh words.

He coaxes me to turn around and leave, but I can't. Not until I look into London's eyes and see what he's thinking.

Ms. Sinclair is the first to break apart, tugging on London's forearm forcefully. He could easily push her away as he towers over her small frame, but he complies and follows without a fuss.

My heart threatens to rip free from my chest and spill onto the polished floor. The thought of London turning his back on me without speaking a word twists my insides into a pretzel. Hell, I'd even be happy with a "fuck you." I need to know he's okay because his silence hurts more than his standard abuse.

"Come on, Sweetie," my mother says, guiding me to leave, but the farther away London retreats, the faster my heart begins to beat.

"Holland?" My father's warning is stern, but I'll deal with the repercussions later.

Before I can question my sanity, I take off in a sprint, almost crashing into a police officer as he exits the bathroom. I don't bother apologizing or paying heed to my father's threats of grounding me for life; all I focus on is London's broad back and the way he appears to be carrying the weight of the world on his shoulders.

"London!" my shrill voice alerts everyone to my unexpected madness, but I go with it. "Please, stop!"

I choose to ignore that my pleas are similar to the ones he

made this evening, because if I had listened, none of this would have happened. I pray to whatever god is looking down on me that he listens just this once, and I almost sag in relief when he does.

My sneakers come to a screeching halt when he stops abruptly, and I'm faced with a wall of muscle. Now that he's stopped, and actually acknowledged me, I don't know what to say. But sometimes actions, or a mere look, can amount to a thousand words.

He turns slowly, ignoring his mother's protests that he keep moving. "So help me god, you know what happens if you talk to *her*."

I ignore her ambiguous warning because with his chin still downturned, all I can focus on is the way his broad chest rises and falls with each steadying breath he takes. The sight shoots a zap of electricity straight through me, and a gasp slips past my parted lips.

The sound to most would be hushed and unheard, but not to London. He *finally* lifts his chin, so painfully slow I wring my hands out behind me, awaiting the torturous climax with bated breath. I lick my suddenly dry lips, but when London's stormy eyes meet mine, it's like sensory overload, and my body is ready to rumba.

I take a physical step backward because his presence is nearly suffocating me.

That cocky, arrogant smirk tugs at the seam of his mouth.

He's holding me prisoner with a look alone. Has he always been that tall? And have his arms always been that big?

Have I always been insane?

That question rattles some sense into my hormone-fueled brain, and I clear my throat, my game face slipping into place.

I want to thank him for what he did, but I know he'll just turn his lip up and flip me off. I need to appeal to who London Sinclair really is.

Looking over his shoulders, I know he's nothing like the two phonies standing annoyed and bored behind him. He's Sin. He's never made excuses for his behavior, and this entire time I've known him, he's been nothing but straight up and honest. And that honesty has me suddenly smirking.

I may hate this boy with every morsel of my soul, but like an epiphany, I realize I respect him, and obviously, tonight's proceedings reveal that that respect runs both ways. Who would have thought getting arrested and London going to juvie would have set off this light bulb?

Pulling back my shoulders and tonguing my cheek smugly, I match his stare. I feel confident and brazen. London cocks his head to the side, folding his arms across his chest, indicating the floor is mine.

"Have fun in juvie. Make sure you don't drop the soap."

My words are appalling on all accounts, especially as he's facing jail time because of me, but when a husky laugh spills from his lips and heats me from head to toe, I know he gets it.

His mom, however, looks seconds away from murdering me.

"Maybe I'll come out a changed man," he suggests, arching a perfect dark brow.

"Maybe." I shrug casually. "Or maybe you'll be plotting ways to pay me back." When his confusion is apparent, I step forward, basking in this heady air of confidence. "I won."

A horrified wheeze gets caught in Ms. Sinclair's throat, but I've never seen such passion in London's eyes before. This banter is…getting him off, and the thought has me yearning for more.

"Oh, Princess," he purrs, stepping forward, closing the already impossibly small space between us. Lowering his face inches from mine, his signature fragrance hits me in all the right places and I tingle all over. "This is only the beginning."

Touché.

Unable to stop myself, I stand on tippy-toes and deadpan him. "Bring it."

Both our parents are ordering we leave, but not before London reaches out and runs his fingertip under my left eye. His touch is so unexpected, a hum escapes past the floodgates and my body warms from head to toe.

Licking his upper lip, he nods his approval. "I'd say I was sorry, but you fucking own this. Bye, Princess."

A million thoughts crash into me, and I can't shake the feeling his words are a double-edged sword. I don't have time to ask him, however, because he turns, and just like that, he leaves me wondering what the hell I'm going to do.

"Bye, Sin," I whisper to no one other than myself. I'll never refer to him as anything other than Sin because at this moment...sinning has never felt this good.

3

SIX MONTHS LATER

N o one should be subjected to Christmas carols. They especially shouldn't be subjected to Christmas carols that have been revamped by Mariah Carey.

It's a week before Christmas and I'm getting slammed at work. Kids are off for Christmas break, which means the bored residents of our valley like to hang out at the roller rink to waste time. It's cheap, fun, and most days, we play good music, but today is not one of those days.

I got Belle a job here—not that she needs the money because her family is loaded, but it's been fun working together. She's in charge of wiping down the tables and working behind the snack bar. It's weird being her "boss," seeing as my boss is never here and passes off the responsibilities to me, but it's been a nice distraction, and for the past six months, I've welcomed anything that can take my mind off *him*.

"Sizes three and eleven please. Miss?"

As usual, my mind has wandered to a place I forbid it to go, but it doesn't matter what I'm doing, he always seems to creep back into my head, controlling every waking thought.

"Sorry, Mr. Harrison." I shake the fog from my brain and focus on giving Mr. Harrison and his son, Tom, their skates.

I'm suddenly irritable. I hate that I can't stop thinking about him because I know he hasn't spared one single thought about me. As I'm hunting through the skate rack, I scold myself for even thinking about this—again.

"Happy skating." I slam the skates onto the counter, contradicting my words. Mr. Harrison quickly retrieves them, unable to escape fast enough.

Sighing, I blow my bangs off my face. Once again, Sin has permeated through my safety barrier, and although I hate him for it, I hate myself more.

Reaching for Mr. Harrison and Tom's shoes, I hurl them into the rack. I can't even remember if I charged him for the skates. Today can blow me.

"Whoa, what did those shoes ever do to you?" says a playful voice behind me. Turning over my shoulder, I can't help but smile when I see Lincoln O'Toole leaning against the counter confidently.

I have no idea why, but Lincoln has been hanging around me in public on most days. Since Sin left, he's filled the shoes of high school heartthrob quite easily. I thought that would mean the end of our covert kisses, but it's been quite the opposite.

Rumors we're together run rampant through the school, but I don't even know what we are. We've shared some kisses and some light heavy petting, but that's all, thanks to my parents grounding me until further notice.

"I'm a Chucks girl," I tease, casually running a hand through my hair to make sure I don't look as shitty as I feel.

A smirk tugs at Lincoln's full lips. I'm certain I've heard the swoons of all the girls in a ten-mile radius, but me, I'm still wondering what he wants. He reveals what a second later.

"What time you get off?"

Looking down at my watch, I exhale lightly. "About an hour. Why?"

"Always so suspicious," he muses, leaning forward with both elbows on the counter, oozing confidence and sex appeal.

I purse my lips. "When it comes to you, always."

A husky laugh erupts from his sizable chest. "Well, I'm having a small get-together tonight, and I want you to come."

"Why?" I question, not masking my curiosity.

His lopsided smirk reveals he sees my defiance as a challenge, but I'm genuinely curious to why he wants me there. "Just come," he replies, his hooded eyes showcasing the true nature of why he wants me to attend.

My parents are out for the night. I suppose I could swing by. "Fine," I agree with an exaggerated sigh. Folding my arms across my chest, I arch a brow. "But don't think I'm putting out."

His mouth falls open, and he chuckles deeply. "I wouldn't think of breaking your over the clothes rule." My cheeks heat, and my confidence nosedives. I feel like prey beneath that heated stare.

Thankfully, Belle comes bouncing over, interrupting this suddenly awkward conversation. "What are you two talking about?"

I straighten my shoulders while Lincoln winks, sensing my sudden embarrassment. "Lincoln was just inviting us to a party tonight."

He grins, while Belle squeals in excitement. The mere suggestion of a party always seems to elicit this response from my best friend. "We'll be there," she replies for us. After the zoo incident, we've made a pact never to leave the other's side whenever a gathering is involved, not that I've been to many since then.

Turning around to tidy the massacre of shoes I've managed to create, I tune out, not really listening to what Belle and Lincoln are talking about. He's become the big man on campus, and I've become accustomed to every single girl wanting a piece of him.

I'm hunting for a left Air Jordan sneaker, oblivious to my surroundings, when Belle latches onto my forearm, leaving finger indents in her wake. "What the hell, Belle?" I ask with a chuckle as I peer up and see her face.

I'm certain Brad Pitt has just walked into Paradisco because she looks seconds away from fainting. Her cheeks are rosy and her lips are parted before she snags her bottom one between her teeth. "What is the matter with you? Are you having a seizure?" I tease.

She doesn't reply. She simply places her hands on my shoulders and turns me around. I have no idea what I'm looking for until a mass of people to the far left catches my eye. The excitement is palpable. There are fist bumps, girls fanning away their exhilaration, and people running to join in the commotion.

I can't see who has caused this mayhem because the horde of people surrounding him/her are behaving like this is the second coming of Christ. I stand on tippy-toes, but when Lincoln shakes his head in awe and gasps, "I'll be damned," I get kicked in the guts and stagger backward, gasping for air.

I know without looking who it is.

A million thoughts crash into me, but at the forefront is that he's back—Sin is back.

Belle hunts through her bag under the counter, producing a lip gloss wand. She applies a glossy layer and primps her long blonde hair, while I'm barely able to stand upright without the support of the wall.

I watch with bated breath, anxious for the sea of people to part because my entire body is desperate, yearning to see him again.

It should disgust me that my peers and mere strangers

are hailing him like some hometown hero, but it doesn't. I'm excited he's back, and that fact confirms I need my head read.

"I thought he wasn't out for another three months," Lincoln says, the disbelief and annoyance clear in his tone.

He knows now that Sin's back, his five minutes of fame is over. Judging by the clenching of his strong jaw and flaring nostrils, I think it's safe to presume he's not too happy about that fact. He's furious, in fact.

There is no denying the underlining competitiveness between them that's been present since the first grade. Lincoln has always been Robin to Sin's Batman, but I never thought he cared because anyone standing beside Sin will always be invisible in his shadow. I always felt they were more frenemies than friends.

However, nothing else matters, no one else exists when the crowd finally disperses and I...see...him. Time stops and all I can do is marvel at the man who has invaded my dreams and muscled his way into every single thought.

He looks taller, bigger in fact. His shoulders have always been broad, but everything looks more...defined. The Santa Cruz muscle tank clings to his upper body like it was crafted especially for him. The white emphasizes the golden color of his skin. He's always been tanned, thanks to the Californian sun, but now, everything is rippling and bursting with masculinity. The boy I once knew has been replaced with this rugged, ripped man.

He slaps one of his teammates on the back, drawing attention to his tattooed forearm. He sports intricate, colorful artwork, totally owning the bad boy look. They lead from his left wrist upward and stop at his elbow.

His hair is still that dirty blond color, but it's longer, flicked forward, erasing that quarterback look I remember.

I swallow twice as my cotton mouth threatens to prohibit my breathing.

"Oh...my...god," Belle gushes, appearing just as transfixed as I am. "He looks...wow," she opts for instead, as she's obviously at a loss for words.

In black skater shorts, that tight fitting tank, and scuffed Chucks, he looks like he belongs on a wanted poster, warning all parents to lock up their daughters and secure the locks on their chastity belts.

I place both hands on the wall behind me, bracing myself for what's to come. Helen Tharp, just one of the many Sin Skanks, elbows her way through the crowd and plants a sloppy, indecent kiss straight on his lips.

Sin appears taken aback, but after a few seconds, he returns the kiss half-heartedly. The mob erupts into riotous cheers, with Sin's fellow bros slapping him on the back with pride. I suddenly see red and leave indentions in my palms from my nails. "Good to see some things never change," I spit with a little more heat than I intended.

My words appear to eject a magnetic force field because the

moment they leave my lips, Sin frantically scans the crowd until his gaze lands on me. I expect it to flick to Belle, but it doesn't. When it swings my way, it remains fixed and heated while I squirm under that animated blue stare that holds me prisoner. I suddenly can't breathe.

He breaks the sloppy kiss, lightly brushing a pouting Helen aside, his burning gaze still riveted on me. The blood whooshes through my ears, and my heart punches against my ribcage, frantic to break free. My breathing is embarrassingly loud, and it appears Sin can hear the treachery because that smug trademark smirk tugs at the corner of his bow lips.

I need to pull my shit together and stop this insanity now.

His swagger is all the more confident as he strides toward us. I wish he would look somewhere else because I'm beginning to burn up in places that I should not be—ever, when it comes to London Sinclair.

"Why is he looking at you like you're a big juicy steak?" Belle whispers in my ear, while I play it off.

"Don't be ri-ridiculous." My falter gives away my impending hysteria. I can't tear my eyes away from him, and he doesn't seem to mind, which is contradictory on all terms, considering what has happened these past six months.

"Hey, bro," Lincoln says, lightly punching Sin on the arm. Standing side by side distinguishes the difference between man and boy.

Sin smirks, still holding me captive under that hypnotic

blue stare. "Hey, Linc."

"When did you get out?"

I wish I could move, but I fear my jelly legs won't hold me up.

"This morning," he replies, appearing to want to bypass him and keep walking.

"I thought you had another three months," Lincoln replies, doing a poor job at hiding his sour mood.

"Your dad didn't tell you? I got out on good behavior," Sin replies smartly, while I scoff a little louder than intended.

"My dad?" Lincoln barks, his fingers curling into fists. The football coach is Lincoln's father, which you'd think would work in his favor. But if anything, it's done the opposite. Sin is the star quarterback, and Coach does a poor job hiding the fact he wishes London were his son, not Lincoln.

"Yeah, he's stopped by a couple of times. Keeping me up to date with how the team is doing. Sounds like you're dropping the ball. Good thing I'm back." Lincoln is moments away from combusting into a rage when Sin slaps him on the back smugly.

I snicker once again at Sin's arrogance, but I wish I'd kept my mouth shut because the moment that small breath leaves my lips, the world closes in on me and all that's left is this heavy feeling in the pit of my stomach of…happiness that he's back.

The reason I've been so mad at myself for thinking about him is because…I've missed him, and I hate myself for it. I hate myself because I've guarded a secret, one not even Belle is privy to.

These past six months…I've written to Sin every week, and every week all I've received in return is a big fat nothing. No acknowledgment of my letters, no thanks for sending me the latest edition of *Playboy*, no nothing. All I could think about was him, and he couldn't even reply with a measly thank you.

Thanks to me having a permanent chaperone, I couldn't visit him in juvie, not that I'd want to, because what would I say? 'Thanks for saving my ass?' Because that's what he did. I felt indebted to him, hence me writing the first letter, which eventually turned into one hundred.

At first, I only intended to write him once to thank him for what he did. But the moment I mailed it, I made up some bullshit excuse to write him a second time. I knew what I was doing, but I couldn't stop.

I wrote him about school, updating him on the petty drama that surrounded Harvard-Westlake, but when he didn't reply, I decided to change the pace. I teased him, describing all the fun things I was doing while he was locked up. This of course was all lies, seeing as I was grounded until I was fifty. This banter was how we'd communicated in the past, yet all I got was radio silence.

I baked him cookies, sent him magazines, and I even made him a playlist of all my favorite songs. But week after week, I became more and more deflated, sitting by the mailbox and watching the mailman walk by. I know most of those items probably got confiscated, but still, I know he at least received my letters.

I'm certain my parents thought I'd lost my mind, but they didn't ask, and I didn't tell them why I was so desperate to hear from my archenemy. It made no sense. It still makes no sense, but now that he's here, looking at me like he's missed me as much as I've missed him, I want to slap his cheeks and check myself into an asylum.

These past six months, I've never felt more alone. Sin has been a constant pain in my ass since I was five-years-old, and him being gone has been fucking awful. I felt like he took a piece of me with him. He's wormed his way into my life, and I didn't even realize how much until he left. I guess the saying rings true—absence makes the heart grow fonder.

I almost vomit because I don't want Sin anywhere near my heart.

But that infernal thing continues its deafening staccato when he walks past Lincoln and jumps up onto the counter with a smirk.

I try my best to deadpan him, but I'm suddenly so happy. I'm engulfed in his heady aroma, which both calms and heightens my nerves.

"Miss me, Princess?" he quips as if nothing has changed.

Rolling my eyes, I quash down my elation. "Like a hole in the head." He chuckles, the deep sound striking me down low.

I push off the wall, needing to flee, but he traps me with a look alone. "Aww, c'mon, that's not nice. I missed you."

His declaration makes my heart flutter—the sentimental fool. "Well, that's a load of shit, considering Helen's hooker red lipstick is all over your face. By the way, that isn't your color. Now, if you'll excuse me, I have better things to do. Like not talk to you...ever."

Belle snorts a giggle behind her hand while I high five my confidence. It's short-lived however, when he springs off the counter and blocks my exit. The prospect of being caged by him excites me beyond belief.

I look up at his towering frame, while he openly looks down at mine. The air is charged with a tangible tension and a feral desire to jump his bones. I shake my head, once again appalled at myself.

He doesn't mask his appraisal of my uniform. My pink short shorts and white V-neck tee are modest enough, but I suddenly feel like I'm naked beneath his heated stare.

"Good to see you used your time productively," I snap, making a point to look at his tattooed arm.

I try my best to flaunt disgust, but I've never seen anything more beautiful. The colors are bright, the images animated, and I'm surprised when among the swirling of chaos, I can see the keys of a piano running down the length of his outer forearm. A golden crown sits above.

I want to ask what this means but decide not to, as he'll no doubt mock me for taking an interest in him.

"I'm getting your name right over my heart," he mocks,

pressing his palm against his chest dramatically.

I shove past him, ignoring the way my flesh responds to his. "Hope I give you heartburn then." I need to get away from him because everything is too much. I'm thankful he doesn't follow when I flee.

The blaring disco remixes and flashing lights are giving me a headache. I wish I could leave, but leaving would amount to my surrender and I can't allow Sin to win. I relieve Alice, taking over the serving at the snack bar.

The long line of kids keeps me busy, which is a welcome distraction because I can feel Sin watching my every move. I fumble, give customers the wrong change, and almost fall over my two left feet, but I don't give in to my urge. I want to look at him, to make sure he's really here, but I don't.

"My kid spilled his Coke." Peering up from the till, I see a soccer mom addressing me like I'm her own personal slave. She's decked out in a revealing white pantsuit, which is completely inappropriate for a roller rink.

There are plenty of napkins on the tables, but she's made it quite clear she has no intention of cleaning it up. I suppose I should feel thankful she even told me. She hooks her thumb over her shoulder, widening her eyes, hinting I'm to snap to it.

"Okay, thanks. I'll clean it up in a second."

When she stands at the counter, drumming her French manicured fingernails on the sticky surface, I wonder if there's something else I can do for her. "I need another," she demands, talking to me like I'm some nit-witted imbecile.

My patience is already skating close to the edge, but I suck it up and pour her another cup. She snatches it from me, her gold bracelets jingling from the force. I can only imagine having that much bling because her couture outfit probably exceeds the worth of my entire wardrobe. She saunters off, her red heels stabbing at the weathered linoleum. I hope I never look like her.

At times such as these, I can't wait to blow this town.

Snatching a mop and bucket from the backroom, I ask Alice to man the fort. I have no idea where Belle is, as I'm too afraid to look five feet in front of me. But I ignore it and focus on the task at hand.

The atmosphere is filled with budding excitement, as who doesn't love the holidays? I take a moment to appreciate the carefree laughter of the people skating. I love to skate; it's the reason I applied for a job. But being stuck here most nights after school took the fun out of it. But I remind myself why I'm here.

A couple of kids from my class are making out on one of the tables. This space is small, housing around eight round tables, so I sadly have to push past them to clean up the mess. From the looks of their groping, I'll be cleaning up another mess soon.

"Jesus Christ, get a room," I mutter under my breath, but it goes unheard by the amorous couple.

Everyone is so desperate to lose their virginity. It's all anyone ever talks about. It's been hinted not so discreetly that I'm a lesbian because I'm probably one of the only girls who has

ABSINTHE OF THE HEART

no interest in partaking in locker room talk.

Belle has asked me if I'm ready, and honestly, the answer is no. The thought of any one of those buffoons touching me is enough to make me puke. A little voice inside my head whispers, *"Except for one."* I put that voice out of my head and focus on my puddle of goo.

Reaching the napkin holder off the bright green glittery table, I drop to a squat and sigh. From the looks of this, he dropped more than his Coke. "Disgusting," I mumble under my breath.

Ripping out handfuls of napkins, I toss them onto the sticky puddle of Coke and what looks like a bowl full of Fruit Loops and try not to gag. "Think of Stanford," I chant softly, but I have to stand and take three deep breaths.

As I do, I allow my eyes to wander, and of course they skirt over to Sin. I wish I could stop this insanity, but I'm drawn to him without even trying. He's talking to Lincoln, and whatever they're discussing doesn't look good.

Sin's shoulders are hunched, and I see him crack his neck from side to side. Lincoln raises his hands in surrender, which leaves me all the more curious. I'm about to look away, but Sin peers over his shoulder and pins me with a death stare.

I gulp.

I play it off, putting it down to my very vivid imagination, but when he stalks over, I know shit is about to hit the fan. Lincoln blows me a kiss before turning and leaving. What is going on?

I stand motionless, observing him march my way, but he seems to change his mind at the last second and makes a beeline for the snack bar instead. I watch as he sweet talks Alice, who turns beet red. It's enough to make me sick.

Returning to my colorful hell, I continue to mop up the mess, thankful I had the good sense to grab a pair of gloves and a garbage bag. When the floor is Fruit Loop free, I wring out the mop and begin cleaning it up.

As I'm midstroke, every hair stands on end. I don't have to look up to see why. What does he want now? I continue mopping, ignoring him on purpose. But he slurps on his slushie, watching me. The loud, infuriating slurping continues until I finally cave.

"What?" Peering up, I widen my eyes, hinting if he has a reason to be here, then please share. He shrugs his broad shoulders, giving me nothing as he continues gulping down his drink. "What do you want?"

Now that we're alone, I'm finding it harder to conceal my hurt and confusion.

I don't know what's worse—being picked on or being ignored.

His lips are wrapped snugly around the straw, and the sight has me wondering what those lips would feel like…pressed to mine.

A strangled wheeze gets trapped in my throat. These

thoughts are turning me into a deranged lunatic.

"If you have something to say, just say it, because you're wasting my time."

Sin chuckles, but this time, there is no humor or warmth behind it. The sound sends shivers down my spine.

When he advances, closing the distance between us, I wish I'd just kept my mouth shut. "Your letters never hinted you had a boyfriend." His lips twist into a nasty scowl.

The blood drains from my face, and I feel myself growing faint.

Some small, whimsical part hoped that maybe, just maybe Sin never got my letters. I reasoned that was the only explanation for why he never replied. It spurred me on, it helped me sleep at night, and it made me continue writing.

But now, looking into his fiery eyes, I know I was an idiot for ever wasting one word on this selfish bastard. "You g-got th-them?" I need to make sure. He nods once, ensnaring me with his cold stare. "Why didn't you write me back?"

I'm pathetic, but I need to know. I need to rid him from my system for good.

"Because I had nothing to say," he coolly replies, not a falter to his declaration.

"Yet you read them? Why?" I bite back, gripping the wooden mop handle to stop me from slapping him.

As he raises the drink to his lips, I swat his hand away. I've had enough of his games. My desperation seems to amuse him, and seeing him this indifferent hurts more than I thought it would. Why am I letting him get the better of me? I know why, but I squash it down.

"Answer me!" I demand.

At this moment, no one has ever been more infuriatingly beautiful, and I grapple with the veracity—I don't know if I want to hit or kiss him. He sets the path a second later.

Holding the drink out to the side, he coldly replies, "Because I told you…" He closes the gap between us, attempting to intimidate me, but everything coils within, and I'm fearful of what'll happen when it eventually unfurls. "This is only the beginning."

I want to ask the beginning of what, but I already know.

He pulls away slowly, his face an impenetrable mask. I open my mouth, ready to confess the reason I wrote him, but with one fluid movement, he unsnaps his fingers from the top of the cup, the contents spilling all over my once clean floor.

The sticky blue drink splashes all over my legs and sneakers, but I don't flinch, because this is nothing compared to the inner turmoil I feel. I watch as he walks away, pushing through the curious crowd. Only once he's out the door, do I breathe.

It takes minutes for my racing heart to calm down, and when it does, I'm left standing in a puddle of chaos. I don't know what's worse—Sin caring, or Sin not caring at all.

4

"**A**re you sure you don't mind?" Belle asks, peering over nervously.

Staring out the passenger window, I nod. "For the ten hundredth time, no, Belle, I don't mind." She lets out a sigh of relief until I burst her cushy bubble. "If you want to date a colossal dickhead, then that's your choice."

She groans, running a hand down her face. "We're not dating," she clarifies. "He merely asked if I was going to the party tonight, and I said yes. I probably won't even see him."

"He's pretty hard to miss," I counter, getting lost in the city of lights and glamour. I now, more than ever, wish I could get lost and never be found. "His ego enters ten minutes before he makes an appearance at the door."

Yes, I'm pissed off. I'm pissed off because I'm hurt. Things were so much easier when I didn't care, but the fact is, I do. I'm more than upset Sin didn't have the decency to write me back. But I'm even angrier that I can't stop thinking about it.

Ugh.

I place my forehead to the cool glass, wishing I could tell Belle's driver to turn back around and take me home.

After I cleaned up the contents of Sin's slushie, I held my head high and finished my shift without a word. Everyone saw our altercation, and although it was nothing new, us butting heads, to me this felt different.

His actions were filled with a detached spite, and I can't help but think that whatever Lincoln told him was the reason he went apeshit. I was too focused on the fact that he received my letters to properly digest what he said.

"Your letters never hinted you had a boyfriend."

Obviously, whatever Lincoln said to him had to do with me, and the fact I'm his apparent girlfriend, which is news to me. But even if I were, what business is it to him?

"I'm sorry he was such an ass," Belle apologizes, but she's not the one who should be saying sorry.

"It's fine. Don't worry about it. I'm used to it."

Snapping from my funk, I turn behind me to reach for the mini size bottles of vodka. I don't usually drink, but I need something to take off the edge. Belle claps excitedly when I offer her a bottle. Unscrewing the lid, I don't think twice and toss back my head, the contents trickling down my throat. The burn stings, but I welcome it.

"I know, but I just thought he'd be different," she says, before following suit.

The alcohol gives me an instant buzz, and I inhale a sharp breath through clenched teeth. "Why? 'Cause he went to juvie for me?"

I have told Belle the basics, and she's sworn not to tell a soul. I didn't want everyone knowing my business, and I'm sure Sin feels the same way. Belle nods, screwing up her face when the liquor hits her belly.

Needing another hit, I reach for two more bottles—this time, Scotch. "I'm sure there's a reason why." I've been racking my brain for the past six months, and so far, I've come up with nada. But I don't want to think about this anymore.

That's all I've been doing lately. It's time I let loose.

The rest of the car ride, Belle and I down a dozen bottles between us, so it goes without saying, when we arrive at Lincoln's million-dollar mansion in the Los Feliz Hills, we're trashed. We stumble from the limo, giggling and acting like two schoolgirls. Usually, I would frown at this behavior, but tonight, I'm planning on letting my hair down.

Or up.

I allowed Belle to primp and style me. I needed to change anyway, considering I was sticky and covered in blue syrup. Belle's closet is bigger than my whole room, so it was easy finding something I didn't completely hate.

I opted for a short black dress with a high-neck lace collar. Belle did my makeup and hair. I usually wear my long hair down, but Belle styled it into a high bun. I was surprised that it made my cheekbones look so much more defined and my small nose regal. However, that could be all the makeup she caked on too.

I barely wear any makeup, but tonight, I've broken that rule. Belle applied a dark shadow which made my green eyes pop. She then went to town with foundation, mascara, eyeliner, and to finish it off, she smeared my lips with a dark plum. I kind of feel like Avril Lavigne, but I trust Belle, who said I looked amazing.

As we amble up the ridiculously long driveway, I'm glad I haven't surrendered completely to the dark side. "And you said I couldn't wear my Chucks." Belle giggles, almost falling on her ass in her five-inch red pumps.

Lincoln's house is nice enough, but to me, it looks like every other house in the neighborhood. With its imposing high walls, and endless stories, it reeks of fortune and success. Houses, cars, spouses—in this world, they're all just for show. I would much rather a well-loved, modest home, because if those walls could talk, they'd no doubt have a tale to tell.

As I hear some rap song blaring from inside the house, I know there is no substance behind anything anymore. This superficial world sucks you dry, and it's survival of the fittest. The sooner I wrap my head around it, the better.

No more caring about who, what, and why. I'm here to have fun and forget I ever met someone named London Sinclair.

The moment we enter the white double doors, I see that Lincoln might have exaggerated when he said small get-together. It may be the fact I have beer or whiskey goggles on, but I'd say close to two hundred kids are here.

Belle bounces by my side, shuffling to the music. If this is the radio station we're tuned into for the night, then I need another drink.

"You made it!" Lincoln whispers into my ear, surprising me as he wraps a hand around my waist. This touching in public is new to me, so I jolt. His husky laugh tickles the length of my neck. "Want a drink?"

I don't even hesitate for a second. "Yes, please."

He coaxes me to turn around. When I do, he doesn't mask his approval. "You look fucking hot."

My cheeks heat, and I instantly lower my chin in embarrassment. "Hey." He lifts my chin with his finger before planting an open-mouth kiss on my lips.

The surprises keep on coming it seems, because kissing in public—this is something new. Even though people have speculated about us, we've usually reserved this kind of affection for behind closed doors. It feels so taboo.

Reveling in the uprising, I kiss him back as if my life depends on it.

Wrapping a hand around his nape, I draw him closer,

smooshing our faces until I don't know where my mouth starts and his ends. He kisses me back with so much tongue, I feel like he's panning for gold, but tonight is about forgetting and letting go.

We're pushed and shoved, as we're standing in the middle of the foyer, but that only encourages Lincoln to hold me tighter. His hand slips low, landing on my ass. This is the moment I would usually shy away, but not tonight. I reach around and encourage him to grab me harder. He grunts, thrusting his hips into me, and speaking of hard…

My eyes pop open, as I'm not that drunk. His boner is probing me, and judging by the size of it, he's hot and ready to go. "How about that drink?" I say, pulling away. I may want to forget, but that's not at the expense of forgetting my morals.

"How about we have that drink upstairs?" he counters, licking his plump lips.

"Maybe later," I reply, subtly dancing from his hold.

"Such a cock tease." He smirks before arranging himself in his pants.

He reaches for my hand, and I don't fail to see the unimpressed scowls of every valley girl in the room. It's really a rags-to-riches story, which they obviously don't like one bit. Sadly, someone else will take my place and be the center of their ridicule because that's what they do—they belittle others to make themselves feel better about their shallow, artificial world.

In my horny, drunken haze, I totally forgot about Belle,

which is bad on all counts. The last time I left her unsupervised, I was arrested. Peering around the room, I wonder where she could be. But I find her soon enough. Or maybe, I found *him*.

His presence is like staring into the sun—it's blinding, but it's also too beautiful to look away. He's in the same clothes as earlier, but as our eyes lock and he tilts his head to the side, I realize I'm not.

He's standing on the bottom step of the grand staircase, elevating his position so he can look over his followers like the true king he believes himself to be. The move just makes him look like a bigger jackass, appearing too good to mingle with us commoners.

Belle is by his side, whispering something into his ear. She's nestled against him, pressing her boobs to his flank, but she may as well be touching him with her little toe because he doesn't appear to be listening to a word she has to say.

He's making no secret of checking me out, which arouses and pisses me off all in the same breath. I feel naked under his close scrutiny, but I stand proud, daring him to look away first. But he doesn't. The challenge seems to excite him. He raises his cup in salute before throwing back the contents. His Adam's apple bobs with the force, and a mewl escapes me.

I hate that my inner cheerleader is chanting *RA RA RA!* And I hate that I wish I was snuggled up against him and not Belle. I'm held prisoner by those stormy eyes, but every part of me surrenders, happily submitting everything I am.

He smirks, full disclosure that he knows everything below the belt is tingling. Fuck him.

It'll be a cold day in hell before I allow him to toy with my head a second longer. I have no idea what I feel for him, but tingling and mewling are off-limits. To emphasize my point, I flip him off smugly. I feel slightly better until he winks, spreading a new wave of yearning from head to toe.

"The drinks are outside," Lincoln says, kissing my cheek and steering me away from trouble.

The fresh air is the slap I needed, but it's also a smack to my sudden soberness. I've never seen the appeal of a beer bong, but that soon changes. "Teach me!" I yell a little too spiritedly. Lincoln laughs when I drag him over.

There is no denying my attraction toward him. He's tall, dark, and handsome. He also seems to like me, which is a bonus. Pressing up behind me, he wraps his arms around me and bends low to whisper into my ear. "There are no rules. Just wrap your pretty lips around the hose and chug."

I can't help but cackle at his seedy innuendo. Two can play that game. "I've never done it before; maybe I need some practice." I make my intentions loud and clear when I wiggle my ass into his groin. He groans, the sound liberating my inner vixen.

Just as he goes to grab, I skip out of his hold, blowing a raspberry his way.

The crowd of partygoers chants the infamous, "Chug!

Chug! Chug!" encouraging a bikini clad blonde to swallow until she passes out.

Thankfully, a girl who looks to be a concerned friend gently pries her off the end, making room for yours truly. Lincoln pushes me forward, holding the hose and gesturing for me to fall to my knees. I don't question it because that's what the old me would do. Tonight is about forgetting the past.

Dropping to both knees, I grab the hose, unable to detach myself from the old me completely. I reach for the hem of Lincoln's polo and wipe the end of the hose on it, as I have no idea where that girl's mouth has been.

"Ready?" he asks with a twinkle in his warm, brown eyes.

"Yes!" I scream, fist pumping the air.

"Are you really sure?" he teases, and I laugh.

"Yes. Just do it already!"

"Okay," he warns, unhinging some valve thing. The action sends a thousand gallons of beer down my throat, and I instantly gag, not used to so much fluid running into my mouth. Every part of me is demanding I pull away, but I resist and gulp down every drop.

The wild chants all meld into one, but it's a head rush knowing those chants are for me. I've never been part of the crew, so when strangers call out my name, it's too surreal for words. After what seems like seconds, Lincoln's warm hands gently rest under my underarms to lift me up.

"I want to go again," I slur, the sky kissed night tilting on its axis as I throw my head backward and spread my arms out wide. I'm certain I can fly.

"Maybe later, party girl."

I fall into his arms, giggling. "Party pooper."

The world is spinning, but through the chaos, I see clarity. This is the most fun I've had in...forever.

"Are you okay?" Lincoln asks, brushing a stray piece of hair from my cheeks.

His kindness is so unexpected. I've never had anyone be this nice to me before. "More than okay," I reply, fingering his soft lips.

I'm transfixed by the feel of them, and I know it's because I'm way past drunk. That's confirmed when my stomach churns, and I think I might be sick. "Can I lie down?" I ask, placing a hand over my mouth.

So much for my newfound freedom.

"Of course." Lincoln escorts me through the throngs of people, huddling me into his side because the crowd is making me feel even worse. I snuggle into him, closing my eyes and trusting he won't take advantage of me in my drunken state.

En route to my sanctuary, we suddenly come to a stop. I want to protest, but when a husky voice warms my insides, I sag into Lincoln and everything falls still.

"Princess?"

"I've got her. She's fine," a voice which sounds like Lincoln barks.

"She's not fucking fine. How much did she drink?" The voice sounds like Sin's, but it surely can't be his.

"You take care of your date, and I'll take care of mine."

You can cut the tension with a knife, but after what feels like forever, things quiet down. I hear a door squeak open before we enter a room, which smells amazing. It's fresh, refined, and I instantly feel at home.

"I'm just going to help you lie down, okay?" I nod, my tongue feeling way too heavy for words.

Once my ass hits the mattress, I hum in delight. Lincoln helps me shuffle up the bed so I don't head butt the headboard. The moment my head cushions between the fluffy pillows, my eyes seal shut with no intention of reopening any time soon.

"I'll leave some water and painkillers on the bedside table." All I can do is groan out my thanks.

As the bedside lamp switches on, I blindly reach out. Lincoln grabs my hand. "Sorry for being a lousy date."

The bed depresses beside me. "Sleep it off. You should be feeling a little less lightheaded in an hour or two."

I don't argue and simply snuggle further into the pillows. "Thanks for being so nice to me," I tiredly confess with a yawn.

I wake with a start.

Jolting upright, I groan, cupping my pounding head.

Taking a few seconds to process where I am, I attempt to

catalog the last things I remember. Glancing downward, I see that I'm still clothed, and a sigh of relief leaves me.

The last thing I recall is chugging from a beer bong hose like it was going out of fashion. But I have no idea what happened after that. I'm definitely not at home; the Egyptian cotton beneath me confirms that.

Turning to my left, I see a photograph of Lincoln and his parents sitting on the side table. Near it sits a bottle of water and a pack of Advil. Snippets of Lincoln putting me to bed come back to me.

With a pained groan, I reach for the pills and water and gulp them down. The water feeds my dehydrated body, so I finish the bottle in one swig. Needing to find a bathroom and pronto, I slowly swing my legs to the side and hope the room stops spinning. Holding up my wrist inches from my face, I close one eye and try to focus on the time.

It's early. Not even midnight. I think we got here around ten, so I've only been out for an hour or so.

The room finally stops whirling, so I take three deep breaths and stand. I splay my arms out to the side, hoping to keep my balance. It works.

Wow, I've never been this drunk before. I've been slightly intoxicated, but this is dipping into uncharted waters. Thankful I'm wearing my sneakers, I begin a slow shuffle toward the door. The hallway lights are blinding. I can't help but shield my eyes like a vampire.

The music is still throbbing downstairs, pounding in time with my impending headache. My Chucks scuff on the carpet, but I'm grateful each step seems to clear my head. There are so many doors up here. I have no idea which one the bathroom is. I could always go find Lincoln, but I'm a little ashamed for getting so drunk so quick.

"Do you know where the bathroom is?" I ask a girl I've never seen before. She seems friendly enough and smiles, pointing down the hall.

"Thanks." I continue my journey, thankful the music is muffled down at this end of the house.

The wallpapered walls are void of pictures, so different from our home, which is littered with happy snaps from all stages of my life. Thinking about my parents, I know I'd better sober up and find Belle. My curfew is at one, but seeing as I'm still grounded and snuck out without telling my folks, I want to get home before they discover I'm gone.

With that as my incentive, I decide to try the last door on the left. I'm certain this room belongs to Lincoln's parents, which most definitely would have an en suite, as it's the furthest room away from his. Just as I brace my hand on the handle, I hear a female's voice, which sounds like Belle, coming from the doorway behind me.

I turn over my shoulder to see a door ajar. The dim light spilling out into the corridor reveals that whoever is inside doesn't want to be disturbed. Images of Belle being drunk and taken advantage of crash into me, and I instantly feel like the world's worst friend.

We promised to never leave each other's side, and what do I do? Practically run from it.

Feeling more than guilty, I tiptoe toward the doorway, hoping to make amends for my shitty behavior.

The sliver of the doorway doesn't give me much insight into what's going on inside. I don't want to pry, just in case it's not Belle inside, so I nudge it open just an inch. Peering through the crack, it takes my eyes a moment to adjust to the soft lighting, but when they do, I almost wish I was blind.

There is no mistaking that long blonde hair, nor is there mistaking those five-inch red pumps. I don't understand what I'm seeing because there must be some mistake. My drunken brain must have conjured up this scenario as there is no way my best friend is attempting to seduce…London Sinclair.

I can't help myself. I lean farther forward, no better than a peeping Tom, but I just…I don't believe it. But all doubt is forgotten when Belle reaches for Sin's hand and places it to her backside. The gentle hue of the bedside lamp lights up his tattoos, confirming my worst fears to be true.

My best friend is seconds away from kissing my arch nemesis —I think I'm going to be sick.

I need to turn away right now and go home, but my feet are suddenly cemented to the ground. I'm utterly captivated by the sight of Sin letting down his guard. His eyes are cast downward, watching Belle seduce him just how I'm sure a hundred girls have before. But this is Belle, my best friend.

Why did he have to choose her?

This is disgraceful, but I can question my morals later because the moment she sinks low to her knees and unzips his shorts, I see something I never thought I'd ever see.

Sin is standing at full salute, his sizable cock glistening and catching the light radiating from the Tiffany bedside lamp. I've never seen one in real life before, and never in a million years did I think the first one I'd see would be Sin's.

Belle has lifted the hem of his tank, revealing soft dark curls swathing the base of his cock. Everything about him is so masculine, and his generous shaft is no exception.

A fire begins to burn and my breath leaves me in winded gasps.

Everything about this is so sinfully wrong, but the throb in my center has never felt more right. My body tingles, and I suddenly need a release. Rubbing my thighs together only makes things worse. Every hum of his debauchery is like a sledgehammer pounding away at my resolve.

Sin growls before wrapping her hair around his fist.

I moan at the image, forgetting I hate him, because at this moment, the line between love and hate suddenly blurs. I'm utterly entranced, eagerly awaiting the climax, but my breathless impatience is my undoing.

Sin's eyes unexpectedly tear away from what Belle is about

to do. He focuses on the door. Or more specifically, he focuses on *me*. There is no way he can see me, I reason, but when a cocky smirk tugs at those lips, I know he can feel me as much as I can feel him.

I expect him to scold me or shoo me away, but he does neither. Our eyes remain locked, and he never breaks contact. I'm so turned on; every part of my body is on fire. I feel like I'm going to implode.

Unable to stop myself, I draw my thumb to my bottom lip and glide it along my ripened flesh. It's a poor substitute for what I want, but it feels good nonetheless. Sin growls, watching me as I slip the tip into my mouth. I twirl my tongue around it, imagining it's him I'm tasting.

His eyes widen, and the veins in his neck pop as a smothered growl escapes him. If I didn't know any better, I'd say he was turned on, but that's ridiculous, isn't it?

What the fuck am I doing?

I've just encroached on a private moment, and I suddenly feel sick.

I pull away, almost giving myself whiplash. I take three deep breaths before I turn and take off in a dead sprint. What I just witnessed sobered me right up, and now that I'm semi-coherent, I'm mortified at what I just did.

I push past drunken couples, the walls suddenly closing in on me. I need to get out of here, and I need to get out of here now. I vaguely hear Lincoln call my name, but I don't stop, afraid he'll know what I did if I do.

The foyer is filled with masses of people blocking my exit. Each second trapped inside this prison is tipping me over the edge. Turning on my heel, I make a mad dash for the alfresco doors. I bypass classmates, too riled up to apologize for breaking up their make-out sessions or interrupting their D and M's.

The moment the crisp air hits my heated cheeks, a moment of clarity collides with me—I need to get the fuck away from here.

I have no idea where I'm going, but I continue running, the soft grass cushioning my heavy footsteps as I race toward the hills. I've completely blown whatever progress I've made with the "cool kids" but I couldn't care less. If being one of them transforms me into a perverted slime bag, then I'll take solidarity any day.

The darkened night passes me by in a blur. The farther I run, the more I escape my demons and what I just did.

How am I supposed to face Belle? I'll never be able to look at her the same way again. Not to mention the fact Sin caught me watching him…and he knows I liked what I saw.

The muscles in my legs protest as the incline of the terrain gets steeper and steeper, but the pain is my new best friend. I persevere, almost slipping down the rocky field many times, but I eventually manage to get to the top. The landscape is flatter, but as I peer out over the edge, I take two steps back. I can see why they call it Los Feliz Hills.

Taking a moment to catch my breath, I stand beneath a towering sycamore tree and get lost in the world in front of me. The twinkling of lights over the horizon has me wondering if the millions of faceless people out there feel as vulnerable as I do.

Images of what I witnessed slash across my vision, the excitement of seeing Sin that way thrumming through my body.

Tonight was a night of many firsts. I got ridiculously drunk, I somehow managed to be a part of the "beautiful people" for five minutes, but the icing on the cake was that I saw Sin's... dick.

Wow. Dick and Sin are two words I never thought I'd use in the same sentence unless it was attached to head or wad. But what I'm more surprised about is the fact I had multiple chances to turn and look away...but I didn't.

I lower my face into my palms and wish I could hide away forever.

"You shouldn't be up here. You could hurt yourself."

That deep voice sends a sharp shiver through me, and I hate myself for it.

With that as my driving force, I put on my big girl panties and stop hiding in the dark. "Why do you care?" I cry, uncovering my face with force.

He's standing a few feet away, the high moon illuminating his good looks and this inappropriate attraction I feel for him.

"I don't," he replies with an unruffled shrug, his hands dug deep into his pockets.

Those words are my tipping point, and I explode. Marching over, I don't care that I'll probably fall to my death, but I shove at his chest with both hands. "Fuck you! I hate you!" I scream, shoving at him over and over again.

He stands rigid, his face unmoving, and his apathy enrages me even more. "You're a selfish asshole, and I was a fucking idiot to think you cared!" My tiny fists pound against him, hating him, but hating myself more for getting this worked up. I don't even know why I'm so mad.

Tears leak from my eyes, but they're tears filled with anger and betrayal. "Stop it, you're hurting yourself," he demands, but fuck him, he doesn't have the right to tell me what to do.

"No!" I bellow. As I attempt to strike him again, his hands snap around my wrists. His hold is punishing, but it only stokes my inner banshee. "Let me go!"

I fight with him, but it's fruitless. He's entertained me long enough. "Why are you so angry?"

We move in a deadlock, as he's not releasing me an inch. "You really need to ask me that?" I scoff, glaring at him something wicked.

His puckered lips lift into that cocky smirk, and the sight is my undoing. I let years of anger and confusion burst out of me, uncaring that it'll cross this imaginary line of hatred we've drawn over the years. "I'm angry with you because you're a self-centered, egotistical asshole who has made my life hell! You've picked on me and called me names; you've gone out of your way to torment me, and after a while, I got used to it. I got used to hating you with every inch of my being. But then..." I take a deep breath, the truth bubbling so close to the surface, I'm afraid it'll burn me if I don't force it out. "But then you go and do some fucked-up thing and act all chivalrous..."

The star-filled sky sets his blue irises on fire. He watches me closely, his jaw tight. "And..." he coaxes, the tightening of his fingers around my wrist is akin to manacles clenching around my heart.

"And then I write, figuring I owe you a thank you, but then that thank you doesn't seem like enough, and before I know it, I can't stop writing you because I fucking missed you!"

It's out before I can stop myself. Those vile, indecent words are my vulnerability handed to him on a silver platter. I'm a mixed bag of emotions. I would rather cut out my tongue than continue, but I'm suddenly possessed and I can't stop.

"How fucked up is that? I miss the person I hate the most in this world. What the hell is the matter with me?"

"You don't hate me," he states, his voice low, heavy with unspoken words.

"Yes, I do!" I rebuke, shaking my head angrily. "I hate you, but I hate myself more. I hate that after everything you've done to me, I can't stop thinking about you! I hate that I care what you're thinking." I need to stop—now. But I can't.

Beneath the stars and the moon and the sky, I will bare my

soul to this boy because I'm afraid it'll eat me up inside. With tears streaming down my face, I sob, "And I hate that my best friend was down on her knees before you because I wanted it to be me!"

I don't have time to process what I just said because Sin is on me before I can move. I'm engulfed in his scent, his pull, and nothing has ever felt more aligned than it does right now. His warm lips smash brutally against mine, robbing me of breath and sound. I want to fight him, but I can't. My traitorous, needy lips have had their first taste, and every part of me is hooked.

I don't move a muscle, too afraid of what'll happen if I do. His mouth is pressed against mine, his hot breath sparring with my winded exhalations. My eyes are wide open, searching his poignant baby blues. I'm desperate for him to tell me what he's doing...I'm desperate for him to make the first move because I'm too afraid if I start, I'll never stop.

"Princess, nothing happened with Belle," he whispers against my lips. I can't hide my surprise.

"But I saw..." Although I've just given myself away, I don't care. I need him to soothe this heartache I feel.

"If you stuck around, you would have seen me tuck myself back into my shorts and offer Belle a ride home. I don't...I don't want her."

We are toeing a very dangerous line.

"Then who do you want?" I whisper, my lips still pressed to his.

But no further words are spoken because he finally closes the distance between us and shatters the past sixteen years of my life.

He kisses me with such ferocity, I stagger back a step, but one hand wraps around my middle while the other presses gently to my cheek. Our mouths work in sync, tasting and teasing for the very first time. His lips are smooth, sinful, and utterly addictive. He angles my head, moaning into my mouth when I surrender, avid to be his.

His large hand cups my face, his fingertips circling my blistering skin while he slips in his tongue. I gasp, the feel of him stroking me so intimately strikes a delicious resonance between my legs. The flick of his tongue has me imagining he's working that magic somewhere else, and I'm instantly turned on. The heavy press of his scruff abrades my skin, but it's a sweet tingle of pleasure and pain.

He hums when I match him stroke for stroke, standing on tippy-toes to engulf him whole. His fingers squeeze my waist, but I suddenly wish nothing was between us. I want to feel every part of him imprinted on my body, and when something deliciously hard strikes me in just the right way, I latch onto the longer wisps of his hair and pull.

We're frantic, tearing and pawing at each other, our mouths never missing a beat. This kiss is frenzied and messy, but it's everything I've been craving. He bites my bottom lip before sucking it into the warm cavern of his mouth.

Every part of me is crackling, and kissing is suddenly not enough. The hard-on pressing into me displays just the same. I tug at his soft hair and fist his tank, kissing him like I'm ready to devour him whole.

He seems to like my aggression, which really is no surprise considering who...he...is.

I get doused with a bucket of icy cold wake the fuck up! What the hell am I doing? I'm kissing London Sinclair, and I like it—a lot—which is funny, considering I hate, or should hate, his guts.

I pull away with such force I stagger backward, gasping for breath. It takes me three seconds to realize what I've done—what I can never undo.

Sin appears just as stunned as I am, his chest rising and falling with a staggered tempo. His lips are plump, his hair wild, but most of all, his eyes are eating me where I stand.

"Oh my god. What have I done?" I scrub frantically at my lips, hoping to wipe away the sins of my past, but nothing will ever rid me of his taste because like a junkie, I need another fix.

"That will never happen again!" I exclaim more to myself than him as I rub the back of my hand over my lips hysterically.

He's standing still, that perfect poker face in play. I want him to corroborate my story, confirm we had a lapse in sanity because what happened was pure madness. But he doesn't. He doesn't say anything at all.

"Stay away from me."

"Princess…" He takes a step forward, but I use my arm as a barricade to keep him away.

"No, don't. That was a mistake." The waning moon dips low, masking my lies. But I can't do this with him. What kind of self-respect would I have for myself if I allowed that to happen again? He's been my abuser, my tormentor, not to mention his mom is a downright bitch who takes great pleasure in seeing my family hurt. But most importantly, my best friend was just on her knees before him. Even though he said nothing happened, this still needs to stop.

Nothing about this equation will add up…the only thing this equates to is tears.

"Say that, and you can't take it back." He's seething, but underneath that, I can sense he's wounded. I've never seen him vulnerable before, and my heart aches and flutters at the same time.

Pulling back my shoulders, I stand tall. I don't allow that to cloud my judgment. Sin and I are fighters, not *lovers*. And nothing will ever change that. Nothing. "I don't want to take it back. I never will. *You're* a mistake." The lie lodges deeply in my throat, but I shake my head. I need to get out of here.

"I never took you for a liar, Princess. That was what I liked most about you. But now, there's nothing left to like." He folds his arms, his face blank.

Tears instantly sting my eyes, his admission cutting me deep. But it's what I should want. It's the only way to rid myself of this addiction. "Good. For once, we see eye to eye. Goodbye, London."

We're locked in a stalemate, and a small part of me hopes this isn't really the end. But that small part gets crushed, absolutely obliterated when his mask slips into place and London is gone for good.

I've never liked goodbyes. I especially don't like goodbyes that change your life forever.

"Goodbye, Holland."

5

2006

"**S**weetie, are you sure you don't want to go to prom?"

Even the word is stupid.

Peering up from my Law 101 textbook, I shake my head. "Yes, Mom, I'm sure. It's a stupid rite of passage for girls to get drunk and make excuses for forgetting their virtues and underwear." My dad splutters up his coffee.

I smile, going back to my study, which makes sense. Me going to prom—that doesn't.

I know why she's so insistent that I go. She never went to hers, thanks to me. But not once has she ever made me feel guilty for that fact. She just doesn't want me missing out, but I'd rather chop off an arm than go.

I'm three weeks away from turning eighteen. Most girls would be planning their big day, but I'm planning on staying in my pj's and watching *Dexter* all day. Lincoln has insisted we go out, but he knows how I feel about…people. Well, two people in particular.

Who would have thought my best friend and my best enemy would hook up and live happily ever after? That's a slight exaggeration, but after "the incident" between Sin and I, he's gone out of his way to torture me in unfathomable ways—he pretends I don't exist.

I would give anything for a spark of acknowledgment, a "Hey, Princess, out of your training bra already?" but I get nada. He walks by me like I'm a shadow, one he can't see. And to make matters worse, he's now "dating" Belle.

I use the term lightly because someone like Sin doesn't date, but Belle is living in denial, thinking she's the woman to change someone who is set to be an asshole forever.

We're still best friends, but things have changed between us. I hate myself for kissing the guy she's been crushing on, and it's kind of hard double dating, seeing as Lincoln hates Sin, and Sin hates everyone. Belle has suggested we try to be civil, as she and Lincoln are two peas in a pod, but unless there are several continents between us, that's not happening in this millennium.

So I sit in silence, suffering, hoping that one day he remembers my name.

"You'll be late for school," Mom says, passing me an apple, which looks like a pea in comparison to the massive brown paper bag she slides along the kitchen counter.

Peering down at the arsenal, I arch a brow and poke at it with my finger. It doesn't budge an inch. "How much is in there?"

She wrings her hands nervously; it's a discussion we've had before. "Honey, you're so skinny."

"I'll eat after exams." But truth be told, everything has lost its taste since *that* night.

I don't like to separate my life into BS and AS—before Sin, after Sin—but that's how I feel. I've lost a sense of who I was. Who I've been for the past seventeen years, and I hate it. I hate that I need him to remember who I was. To remember what it felt like to be alive.

Pushing away such depressing thoughts, I humor her and snap the apple from the counter, taking a bite.

What will I do without her when I go to Stanford? The thought, while sad, is also so exciting in the same breath. I got accepted into my dream school and on a scholarship, too.

I'll be out of here in three months' time, and although I will miss my parents like crazy, I need to spread my wings and fly. Lincoln is certain he'll get into Berkeley, which means he won't be too far away from me.

Lincoln and I are sort of dating. It's still so hard to wrap my head around it. I will never be one of the "mean girls," which suits me just fine, but I'm merely tolerated now, as opposed to being treated like a social pariah. It sucks that to get to this kind of "status," I had to date a jock. The rules of high school have always remained a mystery to me, and I'll be happy to say goodbye.

Goodbye.

That word is still a sore point for me. In fact, I've become part French and opted for *au revoir* nowadays as *that word* does not exist in my vocabulary any longer.

Thoughts threatening to tip to the dark side, I gulp down my juice and reach for my lunch. "I'll see you guys later. Have a good day."

Mom kisses me on the head, still treating me like a child. "You too. If you change your mind about prom…" I hold up my hands in protest, but she pushes a fifty into them in response. "Then here. If you don't, get yourself something nice to wear anyway."

"Mom, I don't need this." I attempt to give it back, but it's a losing battle. Belle's horn sounds from outside, hinting we're late.

She would usually come inside and have coffee with my folks, but today, we're not late for class; we're late for Belle's regimented schedule to get her organized for prom.

"We'll discuss this later." My parents laugh lightly as I put the fifty in my back pocket and run out the door.

Belle's Mercedes idles near the curb, her petite frame barely visible over the steering wheel. Her huge sunglasses eat up her heart-shaped face, but her red pout could take out an eye. I run across the front lawn and open the door, about to make a smartass remark about prom, but when I see her pale skin and that she's in sweats, instead of sequins, I know something is wrong.

"Are you okay? You look like shit." I place my hand on the doorframe and peer inside, not game to enter without a bubble suit and a spray can of Lysol.

She chuckles, but it gets stuck in her throat. Clearing it, she shakes her head. "Gee, some best friend you are. You're supposed to tell me how beautiful I look and that I'm hours away from being prom queen."

I move my lips from side to side, holding back my smirk. "The fact you're wearing two different colored shoes would probably contradict that claim."

Belle shrieks, her head snapping down to look at her pink Chuck versus her yellow Nike. Groaning, she runs a hand over her face, drawing down her lips. "Oh my god. Today can go to hell."

Jumping in the car, I turn in my seat to look at her. "What's the matter?"

Belle is one of the only people I know who doesn't get sick. It's just not in her DNA to catch a cold or even have a headache. So it goes without saying I'm concerned.

She sighs and reaches for a bottle of water from her bag. "I think I ate a bad burrito. I feel so bloated." To emphasize her point, she snaps the elastic waist of her sweats. "See, even my stretchy pants are tight."

I don't mean to laugh, but Belle is anything but fat. She's got a dancer body thanks to all the ballet classes her mom made her take when she was a kid. However, no matter how many times I tell her this, she doesn't believe it. Thanks to her mom saying she could lose five pounds every chance she gets, Belle's insecurity about her looks worsens every day.

"I'm not going tonight. My dress probably won't even fit."

I jerk backward in surprise. "You definitely aren't feeling well." I reach across the middle console and playfully feel her forehead. She shrugs from my hold, smiling half-heartedly.

We pull into peak-hour traffic, both groaning at the gridlock ahead. Belle taps her fingers against the wheel, rapping in time to a song on the radio. She seems edgy, and I wonder what's wrong.

"Spit it out," I bark, raising a suspicious eyebrow.

She turns slowly, her mouth parted like she's not sure if she should say what's on her mind. "It's fine," she finally says, which means it's totally not.

"Belle," I press. For the past couple of weeks, she's been off and hasn't been herself. I've asked her if everything was all right. All I got back was a mere shrug and her getting lost in whatever place her mind wanders to.

She sighs heavily, her shoulders drooping in defeat. "I know you don't want to discuss him…"

I sit up taller in my seat, my curiosity piqued. "You're my best friend; you can tell me anything." I'm hungry for any small shred of information she wants to share. I should feel pathetic, but I don't.

Her straight white teeth tug at her bottom lip, but she finally spills the beans. "I think Sin is losing interest in me."

My insides do a double back flip, but I quickly quash down the urge to break into song. "Why do you think that?"

She shrugs in defeat. "It's just a feeling I have. He hardly seems excited to take me to prom. And we don't talk anymore. I think he's going to dump me."

When her lower lip trembles and she sniffs intermittently, I feel like the world's worst friend for not being as upset as I should. I hate that she's hurting, and I would take away her pain if I could, but a small part of me is…happy.

And the award for the biggest bitch goes to…

I can deal with my personal judgment later because all that matters right now is Belle.

Reaching across the console, I gently stroke her hand. "Have you talked to him about it?"

"That's the problem, he won't talk. He's shut off…from everything. I'm used to him not being a big talker, but I thought he liked me." A single tear traces down her porcelain cheek, but she quickly wipes it away with the back of her hand.

My heart breaks for her. Although we have one another, I know she's craving a partner to fill the gaping void of belonging to someone mind, body, and soul.

"I see you and Lincoln together and wish I had that with

Sin." I furl my lips together tightly, afraid of what I'll say if I don't.

Lincoln is nice, but that's all he is. He doesn't give me butterflies, or that tiny flutter you read about in every Jane Austen novel. With him, I feel safe. There are no complications, no altercations, no nothing, and a small part of me is so bored that sometimes, I want to pick a fight on purpose.

Something must be seriously wrong with me.

Focusing on Belle, however, I reply, "Lincoln and I have our issues, too. It's not all hearts and roses." Which is true. I blame my study on the fact I don't want to stay over or see him every day. I blame my job, needing to wash my hair every second day, walking the dog—any excuse I can muster to why we haven't had sex yet.

Every time we get close, I just…I freak out. All I can think about is kissing beneath a sycamore tree under a starlit sky.

"I know that, but at least he likes you. I don't even know if Sin likes me," Belle says, breaking my train of thought.

All Belle wants is to be loved. I blame her constant search for approval on her parents.

Sighing, I try my best to console her. "How can he not like you, Belle? You're beautiful, funny, not to mention you're totally thumbing your nose at him for talking to me when I'm sure he'd rather you find a new best friend. I bet that just eats him up inside." His annoyance has me smiling like a deranged circus clown.

However, when she remains quiet, I feel like I've just swallowed lead. "Right?"

She toys with the gold ring on her pointer, as if stalling for words. "Not really. He doesn't really say anything about you. It's like you don't exist."

And there it is...the truth. It hurts more than humanly possible. Every part of me deflates like a punctured balloon. I want to scream, cry, but most of all, I want him to call me princess just one more time.

"Are you...upset?" The pause reveals Belle's surprise, and also her regret that she said anything.

Needing to get my head in the game, I pull back my shoulders with a scoff. "Please, upset? I couldn't be happier. You do remember I hated his guts, right?"

The slipup is small, but it doesn't go unnoticed by Belle. "Hated?" she questions, turning to look at me. Her eyes may be covered, but I can feel her watching me, watching for any wrong move.

My fingers tremble as I tug at the frayed hole in my jeans. "Yes, hated, because just like Sin, I've forgotten he exists too."

If only that were the truth. My life would be so much easier if it were.

My excuse seems to appease her when she turns her eyes back to the road. "So you're sure you're not coming tonight?"

"One hundred percent," I counter without pause. She seems somewhat relieved, and I suddenly wonder why.

We travel the rest of the way in silence, but the silence speaks volumes and fills in the blanks.

"This is really good work, Holland."

After my shitty morning, it's nice to get this news, especially news which cements me getting the fuck out of Dodge. The red A+ on my lit paper is one step closer to Stanford, and Mrs. Anthony, my English teacher, is the one I need to thank.

Mrs. Anthony is everything you'd expect a sixty-plus-year-old English teacher to look like. I don't think I've ever seen her with a hair out of place or looking less than refined. She was always eager to share her wisdom with her pupils, but sadly, her expertise wasn't sought out by many.

"I'm going to miss you. You've been one of my favorite students," she whispers from behind her wrinkly hand.

I smile, honored she thinks so highly of me, because once upon a time, she was a rock star in the literary world. She penned three novels, all international bestsellers, but now, she teaches twelfth grade English to jaded, uninterested students.

Mrs. Anthony wrote a glowing letter of recommendation to Stanford on my behalf, and I have no doubt her praise helped me get in. I'll miss her dearly. She's one of the few happy memories I'll take away with me.

"You know," she says, gathering her books into a neat pile on her desk. "You could always do the rest of your work via correspondence. Use the spare time to get ready for Stanford."

I pause from placing the paper into my backpack, both eyebrows raised in question. "I can do that?"

Peering down her nose over the rim of her silver framed glasses, she nods. "Yes. You don't need any extra credit. All you need to do is sit the exams. With that scholarship under your belt, you just have to make sure your grades don't drop."

All of this is news to me, but it's fantastic. "It's definitely something to think about. Thank you, Mrs. Anthony. I'm really going to miss your classes."

She appears genuinely touched by my admission. "Just don't forget about me."

"Not a chance." I wave goodbye, squashing down my tears, because it's people like Mrs. Anthony who have made my time at Harvard-Westlake bearable.

Stepping out into the hall, I pause in the doorway, holding my books to my chest as I take in the bustling corridors and study the faces of people I've known for more than half my life. I wish I could say we're a mixed bunch, but we're not. With age hasn't come wisdom. But when we all leave here, we'll be fresh meat, and the hierarchy will shift. My peers will no longer be king or queen, and a small part of me can't wait to watch them fall from their thrones.

A small titter has me wondering just where Belle and I will be once high school ends. She hasn't been too worried about where she'll end up because her dad knows every board member on the school facility at Berkeley. Regardless of her grades, she'll get in. It must be nice to know people in high places.

The laughter continues, and when I see Belle and Lincoln, heads locked in chatter, I smile, thankful they get along so well. To onlookers, it may appear like they're more than just friends, but I know better. I know she's head over heels for Sin.

I watch with interest as she whispers behind her hand, which has Lincoln leaning against the lockers, smirking. Belle has always been flirty by nature, and even when she caresses his bicep, not a lick of jealousy arises. I ignore why that is and instead focus on the fact that I trust her. I trust them both.

However, I don't trust myself whenever *he* enters a room, like right now. I don't know whether I want to slap or hug him, but London Sinclair has elicited that response from me for as long as I can remember.

He looks his usual aloof self and doesn't raise an eyebrow when he sees Belle yank away from Lincoln, guiltily brushing away invisible lint from his football jersey. I'm too far away to listen in, but when Belle's mouth suddenly hits the ground and Lincoln clenches his fist, I know the topic of conversation is most likely me.

I cling to my books, the walls closing in on me as I watch a few heated words being exchanged between both boys before Belle turns a sickly green. Her eyes snap my way, as I've caught her attention. She bites her lip, giving away her remorse. The action seems to give away my location to Sin, because with slow, calculated precision, he turns over his shoulder. Our eyes lock for a mere second, but it's the best second, I've experienced in many months.

I've forgotten what it felt like to be pinned by those stormy baby blues, but what I haven't forgotten is the pull I still feel to him. Every part of me gets zapped with a million volts of electricity, panting for more. But I get doused with a reality check when he drills a hole straight through me, before focusing on a spot just above my head.

We connected for a fraction of time, but that measly moment has left me jacked up and hungry for so much more. Lincoln snickers, which has Sin grinning his lopsided smirk, before continuing on his way as cool as a cucumber.

Belle gnaws at her lip, eyes peeled to her mismatched sneakers, unable to look at me. That instantly sets off alarm bells. Excusing myself, I push through the crowd. Lincoln spins, only just aware of my presence.

I don't give him a chance to speak. "What did he want?"

He sighs, fisting his light brown hair. "Babe, don't worry about it."

I stubbornly shake my head. He should know me better by now. "Tell me."

"You know that whatever he has to say is not—"

I cut him off, uninterested in his chivalry. "Lincoln, just tell me. I'm a big girl, and I don't need you to protect me."

I'm expecting more of a fight from him, so I stand completely mute when he reveals, "He said that I was to make sure...you didn't come to prom because he wasn't interested in fighting over what's his."

When I think I can speak without gasping for air, I exclaim, "What the fuck is that supposed to mean?" There is so much venom behind my words, Belle takes a physical step back.

"I guess prom is a big deal to him. He wants to hold title to every high school tradition there is and doesn't want to share his limelight with us." When I scrunch up my nose, so lost in translation he may as well be speaking in Chinese, he spells it out. "Everyone knows it's a dead heat between us for prom king and queen."

I shake my head. There must be some mistake. I couldn't give a rat's ass about prom. Sin doesn't care for such trivial bullshit either, but when I look at Belle, I know that she does. His comment is not only directed at the inconsequential title, it's directed at Belle as well. In his eyes, Belle is his, and her losing something which she dearly wants is cause enough to pick a fight.

No wonder she can't look at me.

They can shove their tiara where the sun don't shine. I want to believe that Sin feels the same way, but I obviously don't know him at all.

I'm certain the entire corridor can hear my teeth grinding. I'm a woman scorned, and I want my revenge...and I want it now.

"Holland, no."

Lincoln's pleas fall on deaf ears as he knows better than to stop me. I tear down the hallway, bowling down anyone stupid enough to stand in my way. My peers part like the Red Sea because what is about to go down is of biblical proportions.

I know where he'll be, and even though it's off-limits to any female with a brain, I push open both locker room doors and hunt down my prey. It's everything I'd expect a boys' locker room to look like, and usually, on any given day, I would turn redder than a tomato with so much flesh on display, but my bashfulness can take a back seat.

The air is plumed with a light mist from the showers, but I could walk into here blind and still find him. My asshole compass finds my north. He's topless, standing in front of his locker.

I don't even think twice about my actions as I march toward Sin, ignoring the catcalls from his teammates. He turns to see what the commotion is, but it's too late. I shove at his chest with both hands and he stumbles back into his locker, completely caught off guard.

"Who do you think you are?" I spit.

It takes him a moment to register that I am actually in here, about to wage a war, but when he does, he attempts to turn. I latch onto his bicep, ignoring the volt of a billion currents which courses through my veins.

His heavy, erratic breathing forces the hair from my cheeks, but he doesn't speak. We're caught in a stalemate, and I hate it. In the past, his insults have hurt, but ignoring me…that hurts more.

I can't stand the silent treatment a second longer. "What right do you have to tell me where I can or cannot be? You've ignored me for months, and now you think you can call the shots? Screw you, you arrogant, self-important asshole!"

Just as I attempt to shove him again, he snatches both biceps and spins me so quickly, the world blurs around me in a kaleidoscope of color. He slams my back against the wall, pressing his very naked torso to my heaving chest to subdue me. I try to fight him, but a small part of me yields unreservedly.

We're caught between two sets of lockers, shielded from prying eyes. It should scare me that I'm bound and his potential prisoner, but I finally feel…*something* after feeling dead inside for so long.

I'm unable to control my flouncing breaths because being this close to him is literally leaving me gasping. His blistering skin burns right through the thin cotton of my t-shirt, and the thought of being so close to him has an ardent whimper slipping past my parted lips.

I muzzle it however, because I want answers, and I want them now.

I lift my eyes, armed to exchange blows, but my plans are ambushed when he feverishly raises both my arms and locks my wrists in his huge palm. I'm suspended, trapped, with nowhere to go, as I'm pinned to the wall by this seething, beautiful boy.

I'm shaking in anger, but I'm also bursting with anticipation. Now that he has me, I'm yearning to uncover what he plans to do.

"For someone who said I was to stay away from them, you sure as shit can't seem to stay away," he states, shaking his head with poise.

They may not be ideal first words, but they're better than no words at all.

I want to snap back with something sarcastic, but I'm currently drowning in his musky, vanilla smell.

"I don't like being called a mistake," he poses, going straight in for the kill.

He remembers.

I thought he'd forgotten me, but this entire time, it appears our last exchange was never far from his mind. I want to fight him, but I can't. He's right. I did tell him to stay away, but he's so wrong about everything else.

"And I especially don't like liars." The anger explodes from him, and then spreads like wildfire through my veins.

I could argue, but what would be the point?

This is the most he's spoken to me in forever, and I'll do anything to keep him talking.

"Why don't you want me there tonight?"

He tightens his hold on me, a bittersweet sting. "You're a

clever girl; you'll figure it out yourself."

"Figure what out?"

With a languid speed, he lowers his face to mine, searching every plane. It's been so long since we've been this close; I can't consume him quick enough. My memory has done a poor job remembering him because it's sensory overload and I don't know what to appreciate first.

The fullness of his pink lips lures me back to the moment they were pressed to mine. He wets his bottom lip, and I suppress a moan when I remember that tongue dominating my mouth with a ferocious appetite, intent on devouring me whole.

My mind races a million miles a minute, but I take a moment to bask in the fact his thundering heart is thrashing wildly against mine. My eyes dip, impatiently taking in every stripped inch of him, but a gasp becomes imprisoned within when he sinks forward. Our bodies are pressed so close; I don't even know where mine starts and his ends.

I am so turned on, my flesh is igniting. My cheeks are a rosy red, and my center is suddenly throbbing. I'm horrified because I'm certain he can read my desire.

"Figure out that things aren't always what they seem."

I'd almost forgotten we were speaking because my body was doing the talking for me.

My arms are still suspended above my head, secured in his hand, while the other slips to my waist and finds the flesh where my t-shirt meets my jean shorts. He runs his finger along the waistband and smirks when I bite my lip to impede the whimper.

"Like that, Princess?"

This time, my hum of approval breaks past the floodgates because he just called me princess. "Why do you care what I l-like?" I pose, hoping to fake confidence, but the stutter in my question gives me away.

In an indirect way, I've just confessed that I do like it—a lot, but I'm suddenly so sick of pretenses. Lincoln has never stirred these deep-seated feelings in me.

I feel sick to my stomach because a wave of realization drags me under and I gasp for breath. I want Sin—I want him with every shred of my body, and while I'm horror-struck by that fact, I can't ignore it a second longer.

I'm in love—in love with my enemy—and I don't know how to make it stop.

I don't know when the line was crossed, or if there ever was a line, but the thought of letting him go punches a hole straight through my chest. Tears sting my eyes. He's able to hurt me because I've never wanted anything more than I do him.

I turn my cheek, embarrassed. When did this happen? How could I have been so stupid? For my entire life, it's been drummed into my head that the boy standing before me is nothing but trouble, and his surname alone is a reminder of what his family did to mine. That should have been enough of a deterrent, but all it's done has made me want him more.

"I don't care," he whispers, leaning in close, his warm breath bathing my neck. "But I like seeing you, *feeling* you…" To accentuate his point, he glides his fingertip over the top button of my shorts. "Squirm." And squirm I do.

But I can't help but think he's lying.

I bite the inside of my cheek to stop from asking him something I know I'll regret.

My flesh sparks alight when he dips low and glides his nose along the column of my neck, inhaling my perfume. "Oh, Princess…" His breath continues to tickle my heated skin. "If you want it, all you have to do is ask." I go weak at the knees, and stars flash before my eyes. I don't even know what he means by it because I want it all.

"What the fuck? Get off her!" Lincoln's voice smashes through my hormone-fueled fog, and I sag forward, thankful Sin is holding me up because I would have crumpled without him.

Sin turns over his shoulder, an amused grin pulling at his lips. "Your knight in shining armor has arrived," he says, tongue in cheek. He breaks our connection, and I instantly miss his warmth.

"I-I don't need any saving. I can save myself," I whisper, impressed I managed to spit that out without choking.

His attention snaps back to me, both eyebrows raised. "I know, Princess." He knows? This is news to me. "I've always known that. But does he?"

We both focus on Lincoln, who comes charging over, fists clenched, nostrils flared in rage. His Hulk Hogan impersonation reinforces Sin's train of thoughts. Lincoln doesn't know me at all, but to be fair, it's because I've never let him in. I've never wanted to.

"Have fun with Commando Ken," he mocks, walking backward and completely ignoring Lincoln's abuse.

I want to say so many things, but most of all, I don't want him to go.

"Are you okay?" Lincoln says, rushing over and holding me out at arm's length.

I know I should be thankful, but his concern is entirely unnecessary. "I'm fine," I reply with more bite than intended. When he tries to touch my cheek, I shrug from his hold.

"Whoa, I'm not the enemy here. He is." He hooks his thumb toward Sin, who is slipping into his jersey, uncaring. "That motherfucker. I'll kill him." Sin whistles a tune happily, the sound mocking and provoking.

Just as Lincoln lunges forward, I latch onto his bicep. "Stop it. I'm fine. I don't need you jumping to my defense. I can look after myself."

"It didn't look that way five seconds ago."

"I had it under control," I counter stubbornly.

This gallant act pisses me off because it just corroborates what Sin said—Lincoln doesn't know me at all.

"Whatever, Holland, you're shaken up. We can discuss it

later."

The more he speaks, the madder I become, and the more amused Sin becomes. "She's a big girl, Linc. Probably has bigger balls than you do."

"You're a real asshole, you know that?" Lincoln spits, the veins in his neck popping.

"Thanks for the reminder," Sin replies with a grin, slamming his locker shut. He's getting off on this. He knows I'm about to tell Lincoln to close his mouth for good.

I need to end this before it gets out of hand. "If you're done comparing who has the biggest dick, I have homework to do."

Lincoln's mouth falls open while Sin bursts into laughter. "There's no competition there, Princess."

"Fuck you, man." Lincoln shakes his head, angered that I've shot him down.

"You're not my type," Sin replies, adding fuel to the fire.

"What's going on here? Break it up!" Coach's booming voice shatters the spectacle, reminding me I probably should be leaving now.

"Sorry, Coach. I was just leaving," I apologize, but Coach turns his annoyance toward his son.

"You know better, Lincoln. Jesus Christ!" His face turns a beet red.

"Coach!" Lincoln protests but is swiftly cut off.

"You can sit this one out."

"What the hell? What about the game this weekend?"

Coach's discipline is a little extreme, but I know better than to intervene.

"You can sit that one out too." The locker room falls silent.

I feel awful because this is kind of my fault. Lincoln glares at me before shooting Sin a glower dripping with pure venom. Sin merely smirks smartly.

Lincoln storms out of the room while his father pats Sin on the back. He doesn't seem concerned he just embarrassed and penalized his child. "Ready, son?"

"Always," he replies, looking at me smugly. That's my cue to leave.

I push past the boys, shielding my peripheral vision with cupped palms and only focusing ahead. Now that I'm not shaking with rage, I realize my outburst has drawn the attention of the entire football team, some of whom I will never look at the same way ever again.

"Come visit us again," a few of them tease, only adding to my embarrassment.

"Not on your life. I've seen what's on for show, and it ain't nothing to write home about." I attempt to stage confidence, but squeak when one of the boys emerges from the shower without a towel.

Sin's highly amused chuckles are hot on my heels as I run out the door.

6

toss my math textbook to the floor and fall onto my back, groaning. Today made me a useless mess. I left school early and came home with the intention of forgetting whatever epiphany I thought I had. But so far, all I can think of is the way I felt in Sin's arms.

As I peer around my modest bedroom from the floor and take in the family pictures on my dresser, I continue asking myself where my loyalty is. My parents have never taught me hate, but I know they would be furious with me if I told them how I feel.

My eyes land on a tattered copy of *Romeo and Juliet* on my small desk. I now understand Juliet's woes.

What's in a name? that which we call a rose
By any other name would smell as sweet.

But this isn't a Shakespearean play, nor is Sin a Romeo in disguise. It's a full-blown tragedy, and I'm a fool for even entertaining such a notion.

Sighing, I fold my arms over my stomach and look up at my glow in the dark star-filled ceiling. I wish these stars would guide the way, light up my path, and tell me which way to go. But none shine brighter than the others. They all twinkle with the same potential to change my life forever.

"Sweetie, can I come in?" My mom knocks softly, checking on me for the tenth time in the past hour.

Sitting upright, I tighten my lopsided ponytail and reach for the textbook I had tossed aside in haste. "Sure."

The door opens a second later, and I pretend I'm too lost in mathematical equations to hear her enter. "I brought you some juice."

"Thank you. You can just put it over there." I point at the three untouched glasses on the bedside dresser. She's hovering, and even though I appreciate it, I just want to be left alone.

"Are you sure you'll be okay? Your father and I can cancel our reservation. We booked this night away months ago when we thought you'd be at prom."

My parents are staying at a fancy hotel downtown. It's not something they do often, and I refuse to allow my bad mood to affect their night too. "Mom, go." I meet her worried eyes and instantly get hit with the guilt bat. "I want you to go and have an awesome time."

She wrings her hands together, her dilemma apparent. "I'll just cancel. We can stay home and watch *Pretty in Pink*. Who needs prom?"

When she makes a beeline for the landline, I shoot up and gently grab her slender shoulders. "Go," I repeat with a smile. "You look too beautiful to stay indoors. And besides, I have a paper to finish." This is a lie, but she believes me.

"Oh, Sweetie, I feel horrible." Her tender eyes soften.

"Mom, seriously, I'm fine. Please don't cry; you'll look like a racoon otherwise." She laughs, and I'm thankful the mood shifts. "You look really pretty."

She shyly brushes at the skirt of her red dress and smiles. "You don't think it's too much?" Tilting my head to the side, I tap my chin in contemplation. She looks seconds away from running out the door to change.

"You look stunning, but…" I raise my finger.

"But?" She pales, smoothing a hand over her curled hair and nervously tugging at her small diamond earrings.

Dashing over to my wardrobe, I crouch down and hunt through the half empty shelves. When I find what I'm looking for, I offer them to her, and she smiles. "But you need these."

She fingers the gold strappy heels, biting her lip. "I couldn't." But I can see that she could.

"Of course, you can. Belle gave them to me because they pinch her feet. I'm pretty sure she wore them for five minutes." I pat the bed, indicating she's to kick off her grandma flats and show off those killer legs. She finally gives in, not that I needed to twist her arm.

As she crosses her leg to slip on the five-inch heels, I decide to ask her a hypothetical question before it eats me up inside. "Belle is going to prom with Sin. London," I correct quickly.

She works the buckle while looking up at me. "I thought she might. Aren't they dating?"

It's been a general rule we don't speak about the Sinclair's and Belle knows better than to mention Sin to my parents.

"I don't know if you'd call it dating. Belle doesn't think he's interested in her anymore."

"That doesn't surprise me. That boy doesn't exactly have the best role models."

I nod, watching her fingers work the clasp, unable to face her. "I know, but…"

She pauses mid loop. "But what?"

I swallow past the lump in my throat and meet her questioning stare. "But do you really think he's that bad?"

My question has bowled her over. She appears visibly stunned and opens and closes her mouth twice before answering. "Holland…is there something going on between you two?"

"*What?*" I shake my head firmly, my ponytail whipping from the force. "No, god, no, I just…" I tug at the silver locket around my neck as she exhales in relief. "I mean, he went to prison for me. He can't be that bad."

She takes a minute to find her words. "No, he's worse." Standing once she's buckled her shoes, she places a hand on my cheek. "Just stay away from him, okay? Nothing but trouble follows him. You've got a big heart, and I know you want to see the good in everyone, but London doesn't deserve a second of your time. After everything he's done to you over the years…" She takes a deep breath, her cheeks flushed. "Just promise me you'll stay away from him."

I've never seen her so adamant before. She hasn't really given me a reason to stay away, but I don't argue. Her resolve is clear, and I know nothing will change her mind.

"Okay. I promise."

"Good girl." She kisses me on the forehead, my answer appeasing her concerns.

I am no better off than I was five seconds ago, but I was stupid to think that my feelings toward Sin would be reciprocated. Just because I've had a lapse in judgment doesn't mean my mom will too.

"Now if you need us, you call. I've left the number on the kitchen counter along with twenty dollars just in case you feel like pizza." She smiles, her beautiful face lighting up.

"Thanks. Have a nice night."

"You too, Sweetie." She kisses my forehead once again, lovingly brushing the hair from my temple. "My little girl is all grown up." Her nostalgia is clear, and for some reason, it brings tears to my eyes.

I'm sure she never pictured her life turning out the way it did. The easy way would have been having an abortion, but having me shows her strength and the fact she never turned her back on me. I plan on doing the same.

"Make sure you're home before one," I tease in a low voice, doing a poor imitation of my father. She laughs, hugging me one last time, before sauntering out of my room like a runway model in those shoes.

When the front door closes and the car starts with a sputter, I walk over to the window and watch my parents through the lace curtains. In a way, this is their belated prom. I can live vicariously through them.

As the car reverses down the driveway, the headlights growing smaller and smaller, I peer up into the clear night sky and focus on the arch of stars. When I was younger, I used to sit by this window and wish upon every star as far as the eye could see. But as I've gotten older, I've come to realize that wishes come true with hard work and determination. There is no magical potion that one can take to miraculously transform into someone other than themselves. If we want something… we have to go out and get it.

Well, that rule of thumb applies to most things…but some, we have to forget and move on.

That curtain of sadness swathes me once again, but I push it aside because I've made a promise to my mom. London Sinclair is off-limits, and no matter what I think I feel, that rule can never, ever be broken.

Giving up on the notion of studying, I decide to take a bath and make it an early night. The twenty my parents left still rests on the kitchen counter since the thought of eating twists my stomach into knots.

I'm lounging on my sofa watching a Disney marathon because the magical worlds of make-believe help me switch off. It's now a little past eleven, and prom is no doubt in full swing.

Lincoln hasn't attempted to call me after today; not that I blame him, considering I treated him like he was the enemy. I know he meant well, but Sin is right—I can take care of myself. After all these years, he should know because he's the reason I'm no damsel in distress.

I suppose that's the reason I love *Beauty and the Beast* so much. As the credits roll, I decide to call it a night. I haven't snapped out of my funk, so I'm hoping some much-needed sleep will help iron out the creases, and I'll feel a little more like myself tomorrow.

I turn off the lights and make my way down the narrow hallway to the bathroom. We don't have the luxury of having two bathrooms, but after a while, you learn to deal. Belle is still horrified I have to share with my dad, but there are more pressing issues in the world, like if she and Sin are booked into The Beverly Hills Hotel like the rest of my classmates.

Belle's champagne-colored dress is stunning, and after a few twirls, she decided that regardless of the fact she felt like a beached whale, she was going to wear it. I helped her get ready, but after an hour, I bailed because the thought of Sin helping her out of it at the end of the night made me nauseous.

She still seemed a little off color when I left, but I guess the status of her and Sin's relationship was playing in her mind. We avoided what happened this afternoon because I didn't want to ruin her night with my woes.

I'm brushing my teeth, lost in a completely different dimension, when a thunderous pounding thumps at what sounds like my front door. I pause to listen, hoping it's just a car backfiring. I wait, breathing out a sigh of relief when it's silent, but that breath is taken in vain because it sounds once again, only louder this time.

There is no way in *hell* I'm opening that door.

I make a dive for the light and switch it off, so my home is cloaked in darkness. I don't bother rinsing out my mouth. Creeping out into the hall, I stare down the passage, the front door a few yards away. Maybe whoever it was had the wrong house and is gone.

My heavy breathing fills the corridor, my knees knocking together in anxiety. Yes, we don't live in the best part of town, but I've never had a random try to bash down my door in the middle of the night.

Crossing my fingers behind my back, I don't dare move a

muscle, too afraid the movement will alert the knocker that someone is home. Just when I think they're gone, the banging sounds once again, but the raps are louder and a lot more frantic this time. I slap my hands over my mouth to mute my yelps.

Before long, the knocking is one continuous song, getting more and more intense as each second passes. I need to stop standing around like an idiot and do something because I doubt an intruder would knock, alerting the occupants of their arrival.

Maybe someone is in trouble.

That has me tiptoeing toward the door, the worn-out carpet muting my steps. I have no idea what I plan to do because by the time the police arrive in this neighborhood, I'll be bound and gagged, and smuggled over the Mexican border.

Reaching for the baseball bat which conveniently sits in the umbrella holder by the door, I unlock the handle as quiet as a mouse but leave the chain in place. Just as I'm about to demand who's there, a winded plea changes the course of everything.

"Open...the door. It's me...Princess." The blood whooshes through my ears, and my stomach drops thirteen floors.

I fumble with the chain with butter fingers because there is no way he is standing outside my door. But as I yank it open, baseball bat still in hand, I see that he is.

Holy fucking shit.

He looks a little different from when I saw him last. He's in a tux, but that's not what I'm referring to. The fact he's slathered in blood and looks as if he's gone five rounds with Mike Tyson is my major concern.

"Sin? Wh-what happened?" I cover my mouth, horrified.

His bloodied hands are gripping his side, and when he staggers forward, he hisses in pain. "Can I come in?" He doesn't wait for my answer, but instead half collapses into me. I drop the bat and instantly catch him, afraid he'll face plant on the floor.

When he sags against me, I almost lose balance because he's so damn heavy. "Can you walk?" He nods, biting his swollen lip to stop from grunting out in pain.

We commence a slow stagger inside, him barely making it two feet before placing his hand on the wall to catch his breath. I'm trying my best to keep him upright, but he's wobbling and so unsteady on his feet, I'm scared we won't make it to the kitchen in time.

My bedroom is closer, so I lead the way, never letting him go as I wrap my arm around his waist, coaxing he lean against me for support. He stumbles like he's drunk, but I know the swelling in his right eye is probably the reason he can't walk straight.

I'm running on pure adrenaline because on a normal day, there is no way I could half carry him down the hallway and into my room. The moment we enter, I steer him toward my bed, where he collapses and I fall with him. Thankfully, the mattress breaks our fall. I scramble out from under him, flinching when he groans in pain.

Standing at the foot of the bed, I bite my nails, not sure what I'm supposed to do. "Should I call an ambulance?"

He manages to roll onto his back but shakes his head with force. His red-stained hair sticks to his brow. "No. I'm fine. I just need…to catch my breath."

That's an exaggeration, to say the least. "What happened?" I ask again, standing statue still.

"I ran into a…door," he pants, clutching his side as he attempts to sit up. I dash forward to help him, unbelieving he's making jokes right now.

After three attempts, he's sitting upright, but his face is a hot mess. He swipes at his busted lip with the back of his hand, coming away with a smear of red.

"I'll be right back." I don't wait for him to answer and dash down the hall to the bathroom.

Our measly cabinets hold little to no first-aid supplies, but I grab what I can and quickly make my way back to my room. He's slouched in the same position I left him in, which worries me. Maybe he has a concussion?

"I wish you'd let me call someone."

"No," he barks, shaking his head stubbornly.

Not interested in arguing, I tie back my hair and have no idea where to start. "Can I clean your face? Your war paint is s-scaring me."

I'm scared not because of the blood, but rather, because he's hurt. Who did this to him?

He looks up at me, the blueness of his irises now merged with droplets of angry red. "Sorry. I shouldn't have come." When he attempts to stand, I stop him. He tilts his chin to look at my hand pressed to his shoulder. Finally, he nods.

Reaching for the bag of cotton pads and antiseptic wash, I dab a few pads with the strong smelling liquid and pull a pained face. "This is going to hurt."

Dropping the rest of the supplies by my side, I kneel before him and hesitantly reach up to brush the matted hair from his brow. He hastily yanks away, appearing like I'm crossing some personal boundary, but I gently grip his chin and look into his eyes. "Stop being such a crybaby and let me help you."

Insulting him has the desired effect, and he stops fighting me.

I could approach this with baby steps, but why start now? With that as my motto, I press the soaked gauze to his eye without any warm-up. "Holy motherfucker. Fuck!"

I pull back, afraid I'll lose a finger. "Sorry. I thought it'd be like a Band-Aid. Do it quick," I explain, while he continues cursing like a sailor.

"How about a little warning next time," he barks without any bite.

"I did offer to call an ambulance, but you refused." I shrug, scrunching up my nose. This is the only way I can get through this. If I don't laugh, I'll cry.

"Oh, you're so enjoying this," he says, shaking his head with a hammered smirk.

"Just a little bit," I confess, showing him just how much by using my thumb and pointer as a ruler.

He blows out a deep breath and nods. "Fine, I'm at your mercy."

"That's a nice change," I mumble under my breath as I reach for another cotton pad. I apply a small amount and attempt to dab at his eyebrow, but then pull away, giving him warning that I'm near.

"Just do it," he instructs, rolling his eyes.

"Wow, someone grew a pair." I press the gauze to his eye and gently wipe at the gunk. When it comes away a bloody mess, I reach for two more.

We're quiet as I tend to him, both appearing to be lost for words. Not in a million years did I ever imagine myself nursing Sin back to health, considering most times I imagined I was the one who inflicted these sorts of wounds. "So are you going to tell me what happened?"

"No," he replies without pause but hisses when I dab a little too forcibly at the cut above his right eye.

"You can't just show up on my doorstep in the middle of the night looking like shit and not expect me to ask any questions."

"You should see the other guy," he mocks, attempting to whistle, but it comes out a deflated shrill.

"Did this happen at prom?"

His jaw clenches, answering the question for me.

The fact he's covered in blood and dirt and missing a jacket and tie hints I missed out on a night of fun. "Where's Belle?" He yanks his face away, but this time, it's not because I've tended to him too roughly. "I-is she okay?"

My heart begins to race.

When he senses my concern, he nods. "She's fine." But he's not telling me something. I've come to know him as well as he's come to know me. I take a moment to compose myself, but I can't stop the tremble to my hands.

His eye is as clean as I can get it, so I decide to wipe away the blood coating his lips. But the thought of touching them and being this close to him suddenly highlights what a big, fat liar I am. I promised my mom I would stay away from him, yet here he is, in my bedroom. I need some air.

"I-I'll just get you some water and maybe some ice for your ribs?" I ask pointedly, looking at where he still clutches his side.

"Thanks." He watches me closely, waiting for a sign to give away my thoughts. But I've mastered the perfect poker face thanks to him.

The air is filled with an uncomfortable vibe, so I pass him the gauze and antiseptic wash. He accepts, but surprises me when he gently overlaps my fingers with his. Peering down at our connection, I cringe when the light shines down on his bloodied knuckles.

"I'll be back in a minute."

I don't wait for his response, but instead, I practically run from my room on the cusp of a nervous breakdown. When I reach the kitchen, I brace my hands on the counter and bend low and take three steadying breaths.

I have no idea what's going on, but something inside me says I'm somehow involved. I really should call Belle or Lincoln, but I'd rather hear it from Sin. He's the only one who doesn't sugarcoat anything because he knows I can deal.

Inhaling and exhaling, I feel remotely better. I open the freezer and reach for a bag of peas. I grab a bottle of water and make my way back to my room. Sin is still seated on the edge of my bed, but his face looks somewhat better now that it's not caked in dried blood. However, in its place are the underlying bruises beginning to form. He's going to be sore in the morning.

"Which do you want first?" I ask, juggling the peas and water. He points at the bottle of water.

As I casually walk toward him, I notice his eyes do a quick sweep down my body. I have no idea why until I too look down and see my unicorn sleep shorts and white lace tank staring back at me. In my panic, I completely forgot a little thing called a bra.

My arms instantly fly up to cover my very exposed chest, but that only draws attention to my pinkening flesh. He smirks, but beckons for the water, his thirst taking precedence over my sheer mortification.

I pass it to him with one arm still draped around me.

He unscrews the lid and throws it back, chugging it down thirstily. I wonder how he got here. He's in no state to drive. But the most pressing question of all is why did he come here? I stand in the middle of the room, biting my thumbnail, attempting to decipher this baffling riddle.

"Peas?" he simply says, extending his hand. His voice shatters the twenty questions bouncing around my head, and I toss him the bag.

His shirt is already untucked, so he lifts the hem slightly and places the peas to his ribs. He hisses, closing his eyes for a second, but reopens them moments later.

"I'll split in a few. Sorry I ruined your night." My cream comforter catches his eye because it resembles a piece of bloody abstract art. "Shit, and your quilt. I'll have it dry cleaned."

"It's fine. Don't worry about it."

The uncomfortable silence pervades the room once again, a mist we're both bound to choke on if we don't stop dancing around the subject at hand. "What happened?" I press once again, hoping he sheds some light this time.

Sighing, he runs a hand through his hair, the mussed strands standing up in protest. It's apparent he's weighing what to say next. "Promise me something?" I nod shakily.

My heart sounds to a deafening cadence when he clutches the end of the bed and slowly stands. He looks like he's been in the wars, but I can't help but compare him to a warrior, fighting until his last breath. "Listen to what Belle has to say."

I cock my head to the side, rivaling Scooby-Doo. What the hell is that supposed to mean?

"I know that doesn't make sense to you, but it will." I stand frozen, waiting for more, but that's it. The final act. "Thanks for the water. Send me the bill."

As he hobbles forward, a silent dismissal that this conversation is done, my body acts before my brain can catch up. "What the hell? You can't say that and then just leave." I latch onto his forearm, my fingertips digging into his skin.

"Just trust me, Princess."

"Trust you?" I can't help the sarcastic snigger which escapes me. "Why on earth would I do that?"

"Because it's not my story to tell." His reply punches me in the stomach, and I let him go.

A darkening sense of foreboding blankets me, and I know my original thought was right—whatever happened, happened because of me.

"I didn't mean to make you cry." I didn't even know I was until he's towering over me wiping away my tears with his thumbs.

"I'm not crying." I sniff, rebuking his claims.

Vulnerable and scared, I lean into his touch and allow this untainted moment of sincerity between us. The tremble of his caress has me lifting my eyes, curious to why he's quivering. But what I see takes my breath away.

Sin's layers are stripped back, and he's standing before me

naked and utterly exposed. "London?" I gasp, not understanding what I'm seeing.

That uncertainty lingers when he continues touching me long after my tears are gone. With two fingers, he traces the apple of my cheeks, and then continues along the slope of my nose, but when he outlines the curl of my mouth, everything becomes crystal clear.

His focus is on my lips, which he fondles with delicious strokes. His fingers swallow up the surface, overlapping from left to right as he paints over my top and bottom lip over and over again.

I stand perfectly still. Too afraid to move. Too afraid to breathe.

He continues his journey, fixated on my pouty bottom lip, which he tugs between his thumb and pointer. I can't help the low, rasping whimper. "You're so…infuriately beautiful."

I almost topple over because his admission is foreign. But he doesn't allow me to recover.

"I have never met anyone who I…love and hate…in the same breath as I do you."

"You…what?" I don't pause for dramatic effect. I pause because I'm about to faint.

"You're the cause of my chaos, but when I'm with you… nothing has felt more real."

My head is reeling, my body combusts, but suddenly, everything aligns, and through chaos, London and I find clarity.

He feels it too. We're meant to hate one another, be feuding enemies for all time—but how can you hate something that you love most in this world? Something that is a part of you, as you are of yourself.

"Tell me this is a bad idea," he declares, the low tenor warming me from head to toe.

"This is a bad idea," I state with no ammunition.

He meets my eyes, and I fucking explode. I dissolve, I liquefy; every part of me turns to mush. None of this makes any sense. London Sinclair is the literal bad boy my parents warned me about growing up, but seventeen years of life lessons get thrown out the window because I've never wanted anyone more than I want him.

He rewards me with a lopsided smirk, but this time, that cocky smile is laced with wanting and belonging.

I don't know who dives for whom first, but when our lips connect, the world disappears and no one but us exists. I cry into his mouth, unable to control the inner turmoil eating away at my soul. I should push him away, but I'd rather tear out my fingernails and cut off my hands before I even think about doing that.

His tongue slides into my mouth, commanding mine to surrender and succumb to him completely. I yield, wrapping both arms around his nape and drawing his face down to mine. We kiss like ravenous beasts, biting and clawing at one another until I can no longer breathe. I know I should be gentle, but I can't.

He threads his fingers through my hair, my hair tie long gone as he suddenly jerks my head backward and exposes the length of my neck. I close my eyes and tip my head farther back when he lowers his lips and bites over my pulse.

Nothing has ever felt more sinful, but when his lips descend my neck, suckling and licking along the way, I know this is just a taste of what's to come. I squeeze my eyes shut, panting so goddamn loud, I'm certain my neighbors can hear.

"You smell so fucking good," he hums against my throat, tightening his hold around my waist.

His tongue circles over the dip between my collarbones before leading up to my pulse once again. He bites and sucks, no doubt leaving a hickey the size of Texas, but I'll wear that sucker with pride.

He continues kissing my jaw, biting my chin before smashing our lips together once more. I devour him like he's my last meal and trap his bottom lip in mine. He pulls away, hissing, and I see I've drawn blood. I'm a complete sadist, because the sight pleases me beyond words.

I reach for him, fisting the lapels of his shirt to reconnect our lips, but he pulls away, teasing with a grin. I huff in frustration, but that leads to a gasp when the hand around my waist slithers to the front of my shorts.

He watches me closely, never breaking eye contact as he rubs in a small circle with two fingers over my most treasured part. I cry out, slumping forward, resting my forehead against his shoulder as he quickens the speed and delves in deeper.

I can't believe how good this feels, and he's not even touching me in the flesh. As he finds my ripened center, he pinches lightly, making me see stars. "Oh fuck," I grunt, biting his shoulder, needing something to give.

"Like that, Princess?" he hums when I melt around his hand, demanding more. I'm so turned on, every part of my body is tingling, and I'm afraid I'll explode.

"More," I manage to push out past my wheezing.

He doesn't need further instructions and plunges his hand into my shorts, breaking past any last standing reservations. I scream when he slides two fingers along my slick entrance.

My arousal coats his fingertips, which has a rumble of approval splitting the room. "Holy fuck. You want to come already?" I whimper my response, desperate for this burning to end. "Not yet. I promised you…this is only the beginning."

Oh god…

I don't have time to process what that means because he slowly works a finger into me, obliterating all other thoughts. My needy body clenches around him, milking him and pleading for more…more…more.

The intrusion is painful because this is the first time anyone has touched me this way, but the sting is bittersweet. I want him to stop, but the need for him to continue overrides any pain. I spread my legs, shyly demanding I want more, and more I get.

He inserts another finger into me, coiling and stretching until I can no longer stand it a second longer. "Please…" I beg, hating how weak I sound.

"Please what?" he smugly poses because he knows what I want.

When I seal my lips shut, he submerges deeper, his thumb flicking over my ripened bud. "London, please, oh god." I squirm, attempting to scamper away, but he's holding me in the literal palm of his hand with no intention of ever letting go.

Just when I think I'm about to die, he yanks his hand out from my shorts, my body shrieking in protest. "Wh—" My question dies in my throat when he wraps his hands under my ass and lifts me. I instinctively loop my legs around his waist and hold on tight when he walks us toward the bed.

I know what he's doing, and I know I should tell him to stop, but I can't.

He lowers me onto the mattress but doesn't fall with me. I shuffle up the bed, resting against the pillows, waiting anxiously for what comes next. He sits on his heels, watching me, savoring every inch.

He points to my tank. "Take it off."

"W-what?" I stutter, a blush spreading over me.

"Take it off…please," he repeats with a slow, sexy grin.

I'm beyond bashful as no one has ever seen me naked before. But when his fingers begin working the small buttons of his shirt, I know it's tit for tat. We're on equal playing fields, and what's good for the goose is good for the gander.

I watch in utmost interest as with each button flicking open, the smooth expanse of his chest becomes more and more real. I'm utterly hypnotized when he unfastens the last button and slips the shirt off his shoulders. It falls to the floor.

He's still aching from his injuries, that much is clear, but it appears another ache has taken precedence.

"Your turn," he commands, still sitting back on his heels, watching me.

Up until now, I was completely spellbound by what he was doing to my body that I didn't notice what was going on with his. My attention slopes to his groin. I gulp because an impressive bulge is tenting the front of his pants.

I know if I want the show to continue, I need to shed some clothes.

Slowly rising, I sit before him, biting my lip in fear. But when I look into those stormy eyes, I know this was meant to be. It was always going to be him.

Letting go of my reservations, I grip the edge of my tank and draw it over my head slowly. The moment I'm bare, I bashfully wrap an arm around me, covering my breasts. I don't know where to look.

I can feel him scouring over every single scrap of flesh. "Look at me, Princess." His command is laced with a tenderness I've not heard before. Lifting my eyes, I meet his. "Let me see you."

My long hair falls around my shoulders and will hopefully provide some sheet of modesty. My heart is about to explode from its confines, but I slowly uncover myself, baring everything I am.

The moment I'm exposed, something changes in Sin. He almost always has an air of indifference surrounding him, but now, all I see is pure adoration. My nipples pebble as I feel like a worshipped goddess. Being bare hasn't made me feel vulnerable. It's made me feel powerful. I suddenly let go of all misgivings and just lose myself in a moment I will never experience again.

"Your turn," I whisper, gesturing with my chin to his pants.

My voice seems to break whatever spell he's under, and he raises his eyes from where they're devouring my breasts. He licks his bowed lip with a nod.

With deft fingers, he unfastens his belt and then unsnaps the top button of his pants. He doesn't unthread his belt. Why does that make him look all the more hotter?

Now that I'm not suspended in shock, I skim down his body, not believing he is real. His chiseled muscles and rock-hard abs give Michelangelo's *David* a run for his money. His body is carved from pure granite.

He's virtually hairless, apart from a dark scruff which paints his belly button and then leads down...down. His V muscles are defined—years as a quarterback have fared him well. He lowers his zipper and each inch reveals more of the soft curls nestled below.

He never breaks eye contact as he hooks his fingers through the waistband of his pants and lowers them down his thighs.

I blink.

London Sinclair is kneeling before me...naked.

He's not wearing any boxer shorts, so I can see him—hard, hot, and huge. The sight has me rubbing my legs together.

I don't know what I expected to feel when I saw my first cock up close and personal, but I suddenly think I'm running a fever because my god...he's epic.

He shifts off the bed to disrobe completely and stands by the foot, totally bare.

Everything tingles. I'm certain the tips of my ears are also turned on. I can't tear my eyes away from him. "You're fucking incredible."

A coy smirk tugs at his lips. "Thank you, but I pale in comparison to you. I'm so not worthy, but I want you...so bad."

"I thought you hated me," I whisper, his confession leaving me winded.

"I never hated you, Princess." He stalks forward, placing one knee on the mattress, followed by the other. He commences an unhurried prowl toward me, his injuries appearing to be long forgotten. I instantly surrender.

The moment my head hits the pillow, he sits on his heels by my feet. He takes his time exploring me, his sight landing at the junction of my thighs. "I hated myself for feeling what I felt... what I feel for you."

He crawls up my body, placing both hands on either side of my head, but keeps his full weight off me. "My whole life, my mom told me you were off-limits, that I could have any girl but you…" He lowers his lips, kissing my jaw and along my neck. "But I never wanted any of them. All I ever wanted…was you."

My eyes roll into the back of my head as he bites over my pulse before licking his way down. He kisses the tops of my breasts, languidly switching between the two. When he dips between their valley and traces the inner crease with his tongue, my hips rocket off the mattress, the feeling too incredible for words.

He chuckles against me, the warmth of his breath setting me alight. With one hand, he cups my left breast, while he glides over to the right and takes my nipple into his hot mouth. The moment he sucks with a sharp tug, I'm unable to hold back and cry out in frantic demand. He tweaks my nipple between his fingers and fondles my breast in his large palm. All the while, his lips and mouth continue to torment its partner, circling his tongue around my areola.

I have never felt something so powerful before. Lincoln has never stirred these feelings in me. I suppose he's never touched me so intimately, but a little voice inside me whispers that no one could ever make me feel this way—no one.

A burn eats at my center, and I scissor my legs, hoping to douse the flames before I explode. "I've never met anyone I wanted to strangle or…savor…" He sucks my entire breast into his mouth, then lets it go with a pop. "As much as I do you."

By this stage, I will do anything he wants just as long as he puts me out of my misery. "Stop talking already and please… get me off."

Not exactly poetic, but I know he'll appreciate the candor.

He hums against my flesh, inhaling deeply and grunting out his approval. "Such a princess," he hums, giving way to why he uses that pet name for me.

With his mouth nipping and teasing my breast, he walks a hand between us and rubs over my aching flesh. I gasp, squeezing my eyes shut. When I buck my hips, he chuckles before finally giving me what I want. He thrusts his hand into my shorts and works two fingers inside me.

He begins pumping in and out quickly, the friction setting off a chain reaction of need, want, and an untamed longing to become one. I cry out and writhe under his hold, but he never stops, and I don't want him to. Before long, I'm humming with a pulsating energy, and if I don't release, I'll explode.

He's skating around where I want him to be on purpose, flicking over my clit but not paying the attention I so desperately need. "Please, please…get me off," I cry out, frustrated and on the verge of tears.

"Oh, Princess, I plan to…" My head snaps up, and I watch with heated horror as he releases my breast before crawling down my body. He comes to a stop between my legs. Looking up at me, he hooks his fingers into the waistband of my shorts before sliding them down my legs. I lift my ass so he's able to take them off with ease.

This is the moment I should close my legs because Sin is inches from my center, but any qualms have long been forgotten, and I open my legs in welcome. He takes a moment to appreciate my nakedness, the blue of his eyes eaten up with wanton pools of desire.

He leans up on one elbow, tracing his fingertip along my quivering stomach and circling my belly button. "You are a fucking vision. I've jacked off to you countless times, but my imagination could never compare to the real thing."

I wheeze, his admission turning my skin pinker. "Have you thought about me when you've touched yourself? Touched this—" he hums low "—pussy?" For emphasis, he cups me in one hand, and I lift my hips and moan.

I know he's waiting for an answer, and will torture me until I reply. "Yes," I confess, because it's the truth. "You're the only person who can make me c-come."

He grunts, tonguing his upper lip in pride. "And they call me a bad boy. You, Princess, are one bad, bad girl. Maybe that's why I like you so much. You're unapologetic…just like me."

I don't see the point in arguing. Even if I wanted to, I couldn't, because when he lowers his head and buries his face between my splayed legs, he takes my breath away. Every molecule in my body throbs uncontrollably, and I think I'm on the verge of dying when he lifts my left leg over his shoulder and begins licking and tonguing between my wet folds.

His hand skims up my body to cup my breast while he continues to eat me with a ravenous need. I thread my fingers through his soft hair, needing something to hold, as I'm afraid I'll float away. He doesn't stop and continues to lick and suckle me, delving his tongue as deep as he can reach inside me. His scruff is scratchy against my untouched flesh, but I grind down harder.

I scream out, my back bowing as he flicks his tongue over my clit, spreading me wide with two fingers. "Oh...god," I bellow, grinding on his face, chasing my release. He hums against me, which just adds to the sensation.

When he sucks my swollen bud, I rocket off the bed, shattering. "Fuck," he groans against me, tunneling deeper. "You taste amazing." He clenches his fingers around my thigh, opening me up wider.

I want a release, but I don't want that to happen around his tongue. I want to feel him...all of him...inside me. "Sin—" I gasp, pulling at his hair, hinting I want more.

He pulls away, peering up at me, my arousal coating his lips. "Are you sure?" I nod without missing a beat.

He kisses over my entrance one last time, before briskly lifting himself off the bed and hunting through his pants to find his wallet. The moment he finds the gold packet and rips it open, things start to get real.

I'm about to lose my virginity to the one boy I promised to

stay away from. But as I watch him slip on the condom, I know this belongs to him—it always has. He's the first boy who made me feel anything, and he's the only person who understands how much I hate loving him, and myself.

He's standing at the foot of the bed, erect and so ruggedly beautiful. I lean up on both elbows, unable to take my eyes off him. "Please." I don't know what else to say because that one simple word amounts to so much.

He runs a hand through his dirty blond hair, as if weighing up the seriousness of what we're about to do. "You're sure?" he questions again. "Because I don't want to be a mistake."

I lower my eyes, ashamed I ever referred to him in that way. "I'm sure. I'm the one who made the mistake of not telling you how much I wanted you sooner." His chest rises and falls, and he closes his eyes in sweet victory.

Settling onto the bed, I wait for him. My heavy breathing gives away my sheer terror, but that fear is replaced with an excitement for what we're about to do. The mattress dips with his weight, and I gulp when his lips kiss a trail from my ankle up toward my sex. He continues to kiss me, working his way up my stomach and taking a detour to my breasts.

My eyes are sealed shut because I'm lost in the feel of him. He's gentle but rough all in the same breath. It's perfect.

"Open your eyes," he lightly commands, and I comply. I get lost in those blue depths and doubt I'll ever be found.

He bites his lip before lowering his mouth to mine. We kiss, but unlike before, this union is laced with a sweet longing—it's my most favorite kiss of all.

I interlock my arms around his nape while he reaches down between us, dipping two fingers inside me to ensure I'm ready. I am. I lose myself in the feel of his mouth, tongue, smell... but when he pauses, as if grounding himself before he inhales deeply and pushes into me, nothing else exists but this.

I moan around his tongue when he nudges into me, but he suddenly freezes, his eyes frantically searching mine. "What the fuck, Holland?" he hisses when he feels my wall of virtue impeding his progress. "I thought you and Li—" He leaves the sentence unfinished, but I know what he's asking.

Slapping my hand over his mouth, I shake my head. "Don't say his name. It's just us. It always has been." I'm afraid he'll stop, my virginity somehow making him change his mind.

"Are you sure you want this?" He's wrestling with his morals, but I put any doubt to rest.

"...I want you," I whisper, raising my hips and arching into him. He grunts, his eyes slipping to half mast, and I know I've won.

He sinks into me, breaking down the walls between us. "Oh." I moan, never feeling fuller.

"Are you okay?" He once again stills, allowing my body to accept him.

"Yes, just go slow." I cringe because he stretches me wide, my body blaring in protest.

He kisses the tip of my nose and smiles. "Anything you want, Princess."

He begins to move, inching in and out, gauging how it feels by watching me closely. It hurts, it hurts a great deal, and I'm short of breath when he pushes into me all the way to the hilt. "I'll stop." He attempts to pull out, but I latch onto him and clench my muscles below.

"No. Don't you dare." He smirks, and the sight loosens me up.

I reach up to merge our lips, and he kisses me with a languid, desirous speed. Closing my eyes, I focus on the pleasure and not the pain, and slowly begin to meet him thrust for thrust. He sinks in so deep, I think he's tunneling through me, but it's exactly what I want, because I feel us becoming one.

He hums into my mouth, driving into me faster, but the friction no longer hurts because it hurts...so good. I attempt to match his speed, but I can't. I'm paralyzed, engulfed at this moment, but he seems happy to control just how he wants me to move.

I'm pretty certain I'm lying like a starfish, but Sin's grunts and tender kisses reveal he's receiving as much pleasure as he is giving. I hook my leg around his waist to deepen the angle, but then cry out, not expecting it to feel that good.

"You okay?" he pants, searching my face for any signs of discomfort.

"Yes, just don't stop," I breathlessly reply, clenching onto him.

"I wouldn't dream of it."

He begins to drive into me, faster and harder, and although it hurts, the pain is interlaced with pure ecstasy and pleasure. My body devours him, savoring the way his bow lips are slightly parted, his mussed hair flicks forward over his brow, and the way he works into me like he was crafted especially for me.

We fit…perfectly.

I tilt my head back, and he licks the pillar of my neck, biting and sucking. That, combined with him pushing and pulling, is driving me over the threshold. My release begins building and burning, and I cry, tears stinging my eyes.

"Once this is over, promise me…" I pant, fastening my arms around his nape, never wanting to let go. "Promise me this changes us."

At this moment, I am London's and he is mine. I know what that means, but I'll deal with the aftermath tomorrow. With London by my side, I can handle anything.

"Princess…" he purrs against my neck, "this changes everything. You belong to me. You always have."

The possession is exactly what I need to hear. "And you belong to me?" I sound needy and scared, but I need to know.

He bores into me faster…harder…deeper…but I take everything he gives, my body moving up the mattress from the force. He unexpectedly sits up and drags me up with him, slamming me onto his lap. The angle feels so different, but it feels so good.

With eyes locked, he nods. "Always."

It's exactly what I need to hear, and I begin springing against him, bouncing when he latches low onto my waist to encourage me to move. "You feel this?" He drives in so deep, I see stars.

"Yes," I cry, wrapping my arms around him and riding him fast.

"No one will ever make you feel this way. No one. You and I will always be unfinished business. All these years, everything... it's all for you."

I'm too far gone to even interpret what that means. My release races closer and closer to the finish line.

"Are you close?" I nod, biting my lip. "You first." He won't come until I do. "Come on, Princess. Let go. I want to see you."

My heart is galloping, my body is sticky and spent, but when I look into Sin's eyes and see the boy I've loved from the moment I met him, everything crashes into me and I explode with a thunderous howl. I milk him, biting his shoulder as I slump forward, everything detonating before me.

"Fucking beautiful," he hums. With two quick pumps, he shudders with a low, husky growl.

We fall back onto the bed, his body pressed to mine. Our hearts are kicking against one another, displaying that what we felt was larger than life. He's still rooted deep inside but doesn't attempt to shift off me. He brushes the matted hair from my brow and kisses my lips.

We stay like this, never moving, but on the inside...I've never felt more alive.

7

I wake the next morning from the most vivid dream. I dreamed I had sex with Sin, and I liked it—a lot.

The standard feelings of repulsion don't pervade every limb, so I crack open an eye, wondering why. The answer lies on the pillow beside me.

Shooting upright, I brush the matted hair from my face, scanning the room as my sleep-clogged brain plays catch-up. There is no one in here but me; however, the scribbled note left behind reveals that wasn't the case last night.

Erotic visions of naked flesh, tangled limbs, and holy shit…I lost my virginity, and I lost it to London Sinclair.

Lifting the twisted sheet from my torso, I see that I'm very naked. My muscles protest the moment I move, but the sting is a reminder of the delicious things Sin did to my body. But where is he?

A sense of dread fills me to the brim, and I glance at the note, hoping to god this isn't a Dear John letter.

Without further ado, I reach for it.

Meet me tonight after work.

I won.

L xx

I stare at his note, not really knowing what it means. I've received letters from Sin in the past, but they've been more like ransom notes. But this, this signoff is something new.

I don't know what to make of any of this, but now that the harsh light of day is streaming in through my window, things have never been clearer. Yes, I betrayed my family, my sort-of boyfriend, and my best friend, but would I take back what I did?

No.

I can't remember a time when things have ever felt more aligned, like everything was where it should be. Things aren't going to be easy, but Sin is worth fighting for. My parents are probably going to disown me at first, not to mention Lincoln will dump my cheating ass and Belle will probably never speak to me again, but I can't lie to myself any longer.

Happiness comes with a price.

Guilt eats away at me, reminding me that maybe I'm more like my mother than I thought. Didn't she do the same thing to Sin's mom as I have just done to Belle?

But I refuse to believe this is a case of history repeating itself, because we're different. We're meant to be.

Groaning, I kick off the sheets and stand, desperate to escape the teenage cliché I've just turned into. I hope this giddy feeling is temporary because I'd hate to turn into a lovestruck fool. Collecting my clothes for work, I peer over at my phone on the dresser and wonder if I should call Sin just to say hi.

So much for not turning into a cliché, I reprimand in my head.

Needing a shower, because every time I move, his scent punches me in the face, I peek my head around the doorjamb to ensure my parents aren't home. The coast is clear, but just in case, I tiptoe down the hall and lock the bathroom door behind me.

Taking a deep breath, I turn on the faucet to hot as my protesting muscles are looking forward to soaking away this sting between my legs. The bathroom fills with mist quickly, and usually, I wouldn't be such a water hog, but I need the time to figure out what I'm going to do.

Lathering up the vanilla scented soap, I wash away the traces of my treachery. Too bad I can't wash away the permanent damage it's done to my soul. I don't regret what we did; I just regret that our actions have hurt so many people.

I'm not expecting Sin and me to be wearing his and her matching t-shirts in public or expressing our undying love, but I do hope last night meant as much to him as it did to me. His note is typical Sin—ambiguous and hard to read, but the fact he left a note at all and didn't just sneak out has got to mean something, right?

In times such as these, most seventeen-year-old girls could ask their mother or best friend for advice, but seeing as both will hate me for what I've done, I'm on my own. As I wash over my neck, I feel a tenderness matching the one between my legs. I recall Sin biting and suckling me like I was his favorite dessert.

I instantly turn the faucet to cold because if I continue this trip down memory lane, I'll be one hot and bothered girl. Peering down my body, I see a faint bruise, the distinct impression of fingerprints on my inner thigh. I remember how they got there, and how Sin's mouth brought me to the pinnacle of wanting to die.

This needs to stop now.

Turning off the faucet quickly, I reach for a towel and dry off. Thanks to the fact my shower turned into a sauna, I wipe down the mirror, leaving a slash in its wake. Peering at my haggard appearance, I find a splash of purple catching my eyes. Inching closing, I jump backward, my hand flying up to cover my neck.

I have a hickey the size of Europe.

A small part of me is hula dancing with pride while the other kicks her in the shins and groans.

How am I supposed to cover this? There isn't enough makeup in the world to cover my whoredom. This is like waving a red flag in front of an angry bull. There is no way I can hide this from my parents. Too bad I didn't realize Sin chomping on my neck like a starved vampire was a bad idea *last night*.

Lifting my chin and pulling at the skin around my neck to examine just how bad the damage is only confirms I need to be a scarf wearer for the next three to five days. I slip into my work clothes, groaning when the low V-neck seems to highlight my night of depravity.

I open the bathroom door quietly, thankful the coast is still clear as I make a mad dash to my bedroom. Peering around my meager possessions, I have no idea how I'm going to get away with this because I don't own a scarf.

A sleeveless turtleneck top is balled up into the corner of the room. It must be Belle's. That'll have to do for now. I can go to the mall after work to invest in some scarves and indecently heavy foundation.

A light knock on the front door interrupts my plan of attack, and I pause mid step, wondering who it could be. My parents wouldn't knock, seeing as they live here, and it's way too early for Belle to be awake after prom. My stomach drops as I know I can't avoid her forever.

Lincoln hates this part of town, so he wouldn't just turn up unannounced. A light flutter bounces in my belly because religious devotees know better than to preach about whatever their beliefs are in this neighborhood, so that only leaves one person...

I almost fall over my bare feet as I run down the hallway, only composing myself when I stop inches from the front door. My wet hair hangs limply around my face, and I have on no makeup, but I don't care.

The need to see Sin overrides any small smidge of vanity I may have. I must look into those baby blues to confirm last night actually happened and it wasn't my mind messing with me. I'll deal with the awkwardness and morning-after talk later because right now, I just want to see him.

Without a second thought, I jerk open the door, but the bright sunlight must be playing tricks on me because there is no way Lincoln is standing on my porch, looking worse for wear. My heart begins an incline as I shield my eyes from the morning sun and attempt to dissect what I'm seeing.

"Can I come in?" he asks after a second of me gawking at him like he's grown a second head.

"Wh-what happened? To your face?" I raise a trembling finger, but he doesn't need to answer. I know what, or *who*.

"I'll explain inside." He looks over my shoulder, a silent charade he wants to enter, but my brain can't seem to digest what's happening fast enough.

Lincoln is in sweats and a baggy t-shirt—his usual gear— but his busted-up face is anything but normal. His chin is covered with a dark scruff, which also indicates something is off because he's usually always clean shaven. He looks like hell.

"Holland?" His pointed command snaps me from my

stupor, and I shuffle to the side, allowing him to enter. He brushes past me, not greeting me with his customary kiss hello, but I suppose nothing is normal anymore.

I stand in the doorway, peering out into my exhaust fumed street, so tempted to run, my feet itch. Mrs. Edelstein hobbles past with her Rottweiler, giving me a small wave. I almost beg she take me with her because although her dog would bite my leg off the moment I stepped within three feet of her, his bite would be a mere scratch compared to Lincoln's, who is seconds away from biting my head clean off.

But I wasn't raised a quitter, and it's time I paid my dues.

I appreciate the morning sun for a minute longer because I know tomorrow's sunrise won't be as bright. Everything has changed, and I have no one to blame but myself.

Unable to escape the inevitable, I close the door and press my forehead to the woodgrain. What the fuck have I done?

"He was here, wasn't here?" Lincoln's question is obsolete because he knows the answer.

"Yes." I don't see the point in lying to him.

He inhales sharply, the sound kicking me where it hurts, hurts because of what Sin and I did. "That *motherfucker*."

Wishing I could click my heels three times and end up anywhere but here, I take a deep breath and slowly turn around. I take a moment to compose myself before I lift my eyes and look at Lincoln standing in the middle of the hallway, his shoulders drooped.

His black and blue appearance does leave me disconcerted, but I know he gave as good as he got. "What happened?" My voice is a mere whisper, but I'm afraid it's all I can muster.

Lincoln's lips twist into a nasty scowl. "Have you spoken to Belle?"

His question has me suddenly remembering my promise. *"Listen to what Belle has to say."* That's what Sin asked of me, but she's not here. Lincoln is, and I know he has the answers I so desperately seek.

"No, I haven't. What's going on?" I hate how weak I sound.

Lincoln turns his head, shaking it with a sinister grin. "What happened is that Sin has once again played you for a fool."

"What?" I gasp, unbelieving. "That's not...how?"

Lincoln appears too calm, but I know this is only the calm before the storm. "Last night, Belle—" The moment he pauses, I know this is the beginning of the end. "Belle came onto me. She kissed me. I, of course, pushed her away, but that's not what Sin saw. Before I had a chance to defend myself, he was tackling me to the ground and beating the shit out of me for touching what was *his*." His emphasis makes me sick to my stomach.

"No." Tears sting my eyes, but I furiously brush them away.

"It's true, Holland. Didn't he make it clear Belle belonged to him, like some piece of property, when he said you were not to come to prom?"

"He said that I was to make sure...you didn't come to prom

because he wasn't interested in fighting over what's his." Lincoln's words bash loudly against my skull, and I press the heel of my hand to my brow.

I'm going to be sick.

"Once he was done kicking my ass, he warned me he was going to make me pay, hit me where it hurts." I thrust my palm out, begging him to stop. "I didn't know how...until, well..." His focus drops to my neck, the evidence written as clear as day.

"Please stop." But he doesn't give me a reprieve because I don't deserve one. I brought this clusterfuck onto myself, and now, I have to deal with the repercussions.

Lincoln fists his snarled hair, leaving his fingers threaded atop his head. "He's taken everything from me. *Everything.* Quarterback, girls, my dad even likes him better than me...but not in a thousand years did I ever think he'd win...you."

A single tear traces down my cheek, but my heart drowns. I'm disgusting. I don't even recognize the person I am anymore. I'm standing here in my own skin, but never have I felt more detached from myself than I do right now.

"Sin doesn't like to lose...you should know that," he spits, appalled. "And he has won the biggest prize of all—" he spreads his arms out wide "—you." I don't know how he knows we had sex. Maybe I look different, maybe my sins are seared into my flesh.

A sob slips past my lips, but I cover my mouth, afraid I'll never stop if I start.

I think back to last night, and all the touches, kisses, stolen words we shared; it all felt so real, like he loved me as much as I loved him, but if what Lincoln says is true, then he meant none of it. I was just a pawn in his sick, twisted game, but haven't I always been?

My stubbornness overrides my fears, refusing to believe this as truth. There wasn't a hint of maliciousness to his actions; he cherished and worshipped me. He made me feel like I was the center of his universe and that things had really changed.

"You don't believe me, do you?" Lincoln asks with a sarcastic scoff.

"I-I…I don't know what to believe," I confess, not knowing anything anymore.

He doesn't hide his hurt but pulls back his broad shoulders and digs into his pocket, producing his cell. "Call her. Call Belle and ask her yourself."

I recoil backward, as the phone may as well be a loaded gun. Yes, I could call Belle and ask her if what Lincoln says is true, but the moment I hear her voice, it will fortify the fact that what I did to her was so much worse. I slept with her sort-of boyfriend, her sort-of boyfriend who played me, but the worst thing is, I played straight into his hands.

His smile, his fragrance, his body pressed into mine smashes into me, and I suddenly feel faint. I slap my hand against the wall, afraid I'll crumple without the support. My actions have destined me to forever be alone.

Shakily extending out my palm, I furl my fingers, needing to find out once and for all. Lincoln places the cell into it, and the fact he avoids touching me adds salt to the wounds. I'm an untouchable, and I may as well sew a permanent scarlet A into my clothes.

He's got her number up on the screen, so all I have to do is press call. One simple touch can end something that should have never started. But one simple touch was what started all this.

My fingers fumble, but after three attempts, I press the button and hold my breath. I've never been more nervous than I am now, but when I hear Belle's voice, everything disappears and all that's left is this.

"Oh, thank god, Lincoln. I've tried calling you like five hundred times. Where have you been?"

When my eyes lock with his, he pulls in his lips, as if knowing what comes next.

"Lincoln?" Belle's desperation is palpable through the phone line.

I can't stay mute forever, although, I wish I could. "It's me, Belle."

"Holland?" Her surprise has me sniffing back tears.

"Yes, it's me."

"Oh." She clears her throat.

This is so awkward, and not once do I remember us ever at a loss for words. Our friendship was easy, but now, it'll never be the same.

"Why do you have Lincoln's phone?"

"He's here," I explain, barely holding it together. Lincoln folds his arms across his chest, waiting for me to put this to bed.

"Oh," she repeats.

The silence speaks volumes, and I need to know. No matter how hard it'll be to hear, it will allow me to accept the responsibility that this is all my fault. "Belle…" I swallow, blinking back my tears. "Did you kiss…Lincoln?" The boy in question frowns.

Silence.

The phone leaves an indent in my ear, but I keep it held tight, the pain a welcome sting. "Belle?"

"…Yes."

One simple word has the ability to change the course of one's life so dramatically. I never thought a word which usually is associated with happiness and acceptance has forever been ruined for me for good.

"Is that the reason they fought?" Lincoln nods, but I need to hear it from her.

I don't need to clarify who the "they" is because she knows. It always comes down to him.

She sniffs, but I can still hear her tears. "Yes…I'm s-so s-sorry, Holland." She bursts into uncontrollable sobs.

I stand mute, numb. I want to console her and tell her it's okay because what I did to her is so, *so* much worse, but all I can think about is Sin. The reason he wanted me to listen to Belle is because he knew I'd believe her. He knew how much more it would hurt hearing it from her.

He made sure that by accepting the truth, I'd piece it all together. I'd realize that he slept with me to get back at Lincoln, and maybe Belle, too. I don't even know what's real anymore.

"Holland, please fo-forgive m-me," she pleads with hysterical tears. But I can't listen to this because I'm the one who should be saying sorry. I'm the one who should be on my knees, begging for forgiveness for what I did.

But images of Sin sinking into me and remembering how much I loved it, how much I love *him* assault my brain, and I gag. I'm going to throw up.

Dropping the phone on the carpet, I take off in a dead sprint and make it to the bathroom just in time. I heave up the contents of my stomach into the toilet, tears spilling from my eyes as I attempt to purge up the wickedness within.

It's not enough, however, and I force myself to expel more and more. I'm sobbing, thumping my hand against the wall, wishing I could dig myself from the trouble I'm in.

Oh god, what have I done?

I fell for the oldest trick in the book—bad boy turned good. I thought I changed him. That by giving up my virginity, we'd ride off into the sunset and live happily ever after. But I should know by now that HEAs are not in my future. They never are for people like me.

I was just a game to Sin, and finally, it's come to an end. This is payback for taking away his toys.

He's won. His note now makes perfect sense.

I thought he meant he won me, but now I know he's talking about winning a whole different ball game. He won because he *played* me.

"Holland?" I groan, burying my head in the bowl. "It's okay. I forgive you."

But I don't want his forgiveness because I'll never forgive myself. "Go away. I just want to be left alone." My voice bounces off the porcelain, but I know Lincoln heard me loud and clear.

"How am I the bad guy? You're the one who fucked your best friend's boyfriend!"

I close my eyes, the emptiness and loneliness pervading my soul. He's right. I can't hate him for skywriting what everyone will know to be true. Looks like the apple doesn't fall far from the tree. It's in my DNA to hurt and destroy.

"Please…go." I'm barely holding it together, but I try not to break down in front of him. My head wedged down a toilet to hide my shame is the tipping point of losing face for good.

"Fine, but just remember who your enemy is. Goodbye, Holland." If only I'd heeded that warning last night, none of this would be happening. The front door slams shut, jarring a jolt straight through me. I feel it all the way to my toes.

I don't know how long I stay sobbing into the toilet, my pained cries heavy with ache and regret. I need to call Belle and tell her that *I'm* the one who is sorry. I'm the one who should be apologizing until I've lost my voice for good.

How could I have been so stupid? This entire time I thought I was different—and I suppose I am. I'm *worse* than any one of those girls who threw their morals to the wind because I knew what he was like; I knew because I am a selfish, lying, cheating asshole as well. It appears the saying rings true: *birds of a feather flock together.* Or in my case, birds of a feather flock together and crap all over the people I love.

How does one come back from this? They don't. All they can do is live and learn.

Peering down at my watch, I see that it's almost crazy o'clock.

So much for living and learning, because if I learned my lesson, I wouldn't be standing outside the back of work, waiting…waiting for Sin to tell me there is some mistake.

I called in sick, another first for me, but there was no way I could face people. I was too afraid they'd see what I'd done. I couldn't stay home, seeing as my parents would smell a rat, so I wrapped up my soiled sheets and threw them and my future into the dumpster in the alleyway behind my home.

With nowhere to go, I roamed the streets, hoping the farther I walked, the farther I'd venture away from the mess I've made. The crème of the crop was out in force, and I shared the streets with the pimps, drug dealers, and gang members who looked no older than ten. I was propositioned for sex more times than I could count. I simply shrugged it off, not biting back as I usually would because they could probably smell the whore on me.

I passed endless phones, but each time I inserted a quarter, dialing Belle, I hung up before she had a chance to answer. After a while, I ran out of money and excuses, and all that was left was this guilt eating a hole right through me.

I walked the streets of Los Angeles in a daze until I ended up at work and sat behind the rink, waiting...waiting...I didn't know what I was waiting for until I remembered Sin's letter. He asked me to meet him, and a small part of me believes that he will. But as day became night, the clarity of what happens next was shadowed by my shame.

I'm sitting on the back step, head cradled in my palms. He will come, I assure myself, but that hope fades with each stroke of the clock. As each second ticks by, I sniff back my tears and attempt to compose myself as best I can.

When footsteps sound lightly against the uneven pavement, I turn so quickly my ponytail whips me in the face. I'm unblinking, too afraid I'll miss a second if I move. He came. He's here to tell me the truth.

"Holland?" That voice deflates my last shred of hope.

Standing feet away is not Sin, but Thomas, my work colleague. He doesn't hide his surprise to find me skulking behind work seeing as I'm supposed to be sick. "Is everything all right?"

His fingers clutch around the top of the black garbage bag he's holding, most likely ready to wield it as a weapon if I launch forward and demand he feed me his brains.

Pulling it together, I nod. "I'm fine. I just…" But I don't bother. I've run out of excuses. "What time is it?"

There must be something wrong with my watch. It reads 10:08 p.m. Shaking it, I hold it up to my ear to ensure it's still ticking. It is.

Thomas pulls out his cell, the screen lighting up his face. His confusion is clear. "It's just after ten. How long you been out here?"

"I don't know," I vaguely reply, those impossible tears threatening to break past the floodgates once again. If I shed any more, I'm sure to dehydrate.

Thomas is a few years older than I am and has always been nice enough. "I'm just going to lock up and then I'll take you home, okay?" He's talking slowly, approaching me like he would a cornered, rabid animal.

I nod, but the thought of going home…I can't go back there ever again. The thought of sleeping in my bed, the same bed I shared with him, evokes visions of me setting my room on fire. I need to douse the flames, otherwise I'll never rest again.

"Can I borrow twenty dollars? I'll pay you back, promise." I'm begging, but I need to do this before I chicken out.

Thomas doesn't argue and reaches into his pocket to retrieve his wallet. The green catches the full moon, a beacon of what I must do. "Thank you." I leap forward and snatch it from his fingers. He yelps and jumps back, dropping the garbage with a plop to the ground.

I suppose I look as bad as I feel.

Turning quickly, I take off as fast as my feet can take me, waving madly at a cab idling by the curb. The passenger hasn't even exited, but I jump into the front seat, bouncing nervously. The lady throws the driver a twenty and grabs her bag in haste.

When I rattle off where I need to be, the driver looks down his nose, wondering why someone like me would need to be going to the most lavish zip code in LA. I'm dressed in my work gear, so he probably presumes I'm fulfilling some perverted millionaire's schoolgirl dreams.

"Go!" I command, tapping the dash with force.

He thankfully puts the car into gear and pulls into traffic with a sharp turn. We're greeted with an orchestra of horns, but the noise is welcome, as it drowns out the clatter within.

The entire ride, I wonder what'll happen when I see him. I'm beyond outraged, taking no greater satisfaction than smacking that smug smile from his lips, but beneath that rage, I feel betrayed and hurt. London has torn out my heart, and I don't know if it'll ever heal.

The Hollywood sign catches my eye, and I think about all the times I looked upon it, wondering if I'll ever find my dreams. I can't remember a time when I've felt this lost. No matter what happened, I used to have hope, but now...I just feel so empty inside.

I betrayed, but I was betrayed in return. Maybe two wrongs do make a right?

Pressing my head against the glass, I block it all out and allow this moment of silence, knowing it'll be the only one I have for a while.

"Miss? We're here." I jar awake, rubbing my weary eyes.

It was just a dream...a bad, bad dream, but when I see the towering white palace before me, I know my nightmare has only just begun.

"Thanks," I mumble, passing the driver the money before opening the door. I take a moment to gather my bearings and hope I stop trembling sometime soon.

The lights are on. Someone is home.

My feet hit the pavement, but the ground has never felt shakier than it does right now. I don't want to prolong this, and no matter how scared I am, I persevere, climbing the winding driveway leading to my doom.

I attempt to smooth out the wrinkles in my clothes and brush out the snarls in my hair, but it's pointless. I will never iron out the damage done to my soul. The doorbell vibrates low, a groan which sets the already somber mood.

My fingernails are already down to the wick, but I bite my thumb anyway, needing something to do before I throw up.

Once the door opens however, nothing can keep the nausea at bay. The pillar of perfection stands before me, while I look like I robbed the needy and stole his clothes.

"H-h…" I clear my throat twice. "Hi, Ms. Sinclair. Is London home?"

Her lip curls in repulsion or amusement, I can't tell, but either way, I know how this will end. "No, he is not, and even if he were, why on earth would I allow you into my home? Did your mother put you up to this?" She peers over my shoulder, standing on tippy-toes, as if hoping to catch a glimpse of my mom hiding in her roses.

"What?" Shaking my head, I get back in the game. "No, she didn't. Do you know when he'll be back?"

She cocks her head to the side, as if for the first time seeing through my desperation. "No idea. He's probably off with some new squeeze. They come and go so quickly, I can't keep up." Tears sting my eyes. I know what she's doing, yet I can't stop. She examines her French manicured nails, uninterested. "Do you think you're special?"

"Excuse me?" I question, not understanding where she's going with this.

Lifting her steel blue eyes, she pins me to the spot I stand. She examines the brand on my neck, the brand her son put there to mark me as his…his conquest. "You're just one in a long line of many, a warm body for the night, and if I know my son, he *slummed* it with you to remind you…you're a Brooks," she spits in disgust, "and he's a Sinclair. Don't you ever forget it."

I bite the inside of my cheek until I taste blood, as I refuse to allow this unfeeling woman to see my tears. "I'll never forget because I'm proud of who I am. We may not have all of this—" I sweep my hand toward her riches "—but what we do have is what you'll never have, because the person you want the most...doesn't want you."

She recoils, her mask of perfection crumbling. She brushes back her hair, but the waver to her fingers betrays her. My words have had the desired effect. "You're just like your mother," she snarls, turning up her nose when she continues scowling at my neck.

Her distaste only spurs me on further. Stepping forward, I lean my arm against the doorjamb, ignoring all personal boundaries. "I may be exactly like my mom, but I'd rather that, than be someone like you." Her intake of breath has me fist pumping with pride. "London was doomed the day you settled for second best." Her mouth pops open, her eyes falling wide. "Goodbye, Ms. Sinclair. Thank you for showing me that no matter what riches you possess, it doesn't make you a better person."

I turn on my heel, but stop, holding my head high. "Oh, and by the way...I don't think I'm special...I *know* I am. I'm Holland Brooks-Ferris...and I'm fucking fabulous." I tighten my lopsided ponytail, never feeling more affluent and important than I do right now.

I don't bother waiting for a response because no matter what she says, she can't tear me down. I may be a liar and a cheater, but I accept that, and I'll attempt to make amends for it as long as I live. Living means making mistakes, but being human means learning from them and growing. Failure is the only way to begin again, only wiser the second time around. And I don't plan on making the same mistakes twice.

The door slams shut behind me, a silent victory, but I've learned that no one wins in life—it's an uphill battle, and all you can do is try your best.

Peering up into the star-filled sky, the heavens which I've looked up at with nothing but contempt, I suddenly realize that it's always looked down at me with nothing but promise. I take a deep breath, the first one I've taken since this mess began. I don't know what the future holds, but life's journey starts with one single step, and I can't wait to take mine.

A movement from the corner of my eye catches my attention, and I raise my chin, focused on the window on the top floor. I know whose room it is, and I know he's most likely watching me from inside. I should care, should bash down that door and demand he see me, explain what the hell is going on, but I won't.

At this moment, on this day, I let go of who I was and concentrate on who I will become. After tonight, I will never see this home, this neighborhood, this boy ever again, because this is my past and I'm only intent on my future.

The curtain across the bay window draws to a close, just how the final call closes on my heart. As I walk down the driveway, I see Belle's car parked off to the side. I have no doubt London has told her everything. I know she'll never forgive me, but I don't expect her to, because I'll never forgive myself.

I continue walking with my head held high, the tears I once shed now replaced with a smile. Live and learn, that's my new motto, and what I've learned is that London Sinclair may have taken my dignity away from me once…but he'll never do it again.

Fool me once…shame on you. Fool me twice…not on your fucking life.

8

PRESENT TIME

"No, Julio, tell that asshole that unless he has an offer that's even remotely appealing, then he's wasting my time."

Flipping down the visor of our rental BMW, I cringe when I see a disgusting mark the size of Texas smeared across the mirror. Snapping it up, I reach into my Prada black leather handbag for my compact and hand sanitizer instead.

Julio, the asshole attorney representing the deadbeat dad who decided he wants to claim responsibility for his seven-year-old daughter *now* that she's the hottest child star in Tinseltown, has five seconds to say something productive before he's greeted with the line going dead.

"Holland, stop being such a hard ass. It's a good offer," he pleads in his whiny voice, as he knows what my response will be.

I touch up my plum lipstick in the mirror, fingering the corners of my mouth with no hurry to my step. When I'm satisfied with my appearance, I snap the compact shut, snapping much like my last tether of patience. "A good offer would be that sad sack of shit going back to whatever hole he crawled from and stop trying to sponge off his daughter. Goodbye, Julio. Don't waste my time again."

As I toss my Blackberry into my bag, I can feel his eyes watching me with humor. He loves seeing me riled up, and now is no exception. "What?" I ask without a hint of bite as I turn in my seat to look at my fiancé.

"Nothing," he replies, shaking his head with a smile, eyes focused on the road. He knows better than to argue with me. It's my job to argue, so he knows he doesn't stand a chance.

"Okay, I'll let you off the hook, but only because you bought me this extraordinary..." I place my left hand out in front of me, the rock on my finger rivaling the bright Los Angeles summer sun. "Completely over the top ring."

"I'll take it back then," he counters, his full lips twitching.

"Don't you dare!" I admonish, shielding my hand against my chest in protection. Yes, I'm totally resembling Gollum, but I'm still getting used to the fact that in just three weeks, I'll be Mrs. Lincoln O'Toole.

His husky laugh fills the car, reminding me of all the countless laughs we've shared over the past few years. Our road has been rocky, to say the least, but we made it work because everything happens for a reason.

"You nervous about going back home?" I know what he's really asking, but I refuse to entertain that memory ever again.

"Home is our apartment on the Upper East Side. We're merely going back to the place we grew up because your parents would never miss a party and my mom doesn't like to fly."

Lincoln smirks, the sight reminding me so much of the boy I met in high school. But so much has changed since then. *I've* changed. Sometimes, I barely recognize myself as the penniless outsider I once was. I brush my fingers through my hair, passing over the diamond hair clip which sits in my low chignon. It and my white Chanel pantsuit are just some of the many things that remind me I'm no longer the pathetic little lost girl I once was.

The moment the Hollywood sign comes into view, I feel a bittersweet reminiscence swirl within, and I'm transported back to the last time I saw it.

After I said goodbye to a boy who changed my life forever, I went home and told my parents everything. It goes without saying that I broke my mother's heart and my father was intent on committing first degree murder. But after endless hours of lectures and tears, I convinced my parents to let me move to Florida with my aunt Cora and finish my studies there. I couldn't stay in that home a second longer. Every inch of my room reminded me of him and reminded me of what I did.

Mrs. Anthony's suggestion became a reality because early the next morning, I was on a flight bound for Florida with no intention of coming back until I had to. My parents didn't want me to go, but the time away to digest what I had done would do us all some good. I've never seen my parents so upset, but more so, they were just disappointed and felt betrayed.

I understood and gave them their space.

Another person who was affected by my astronomical fuckup was Belle. I tried calling her a week after I moved, chickening out countless times, but she never picked up, and after a while, her phone was disconnected. I took that as her silent *fuck you, leave me the hell alone*, so I did.

Looking back now, I know I got off easy, because I never spoke or heard from Belle or...*him* ever again. I could have sent her a letter, hell, I could have turned up on her doorstep with a thousand bouquets of flowers begging for forgiveness, but I didn't.

Yes, I was hurt that she kissed my sort-of boyfriend, but that's not the reason I stayed away. It was easy for me to escape what *I* did, which was so much worse, if I never spoke to her ever again. Not my finest moment, but you live and learn—that motto is still one I march to every day.

So I focused on my studies and aced all my tests. It was the only way I knew how to move on. Once that welcome pack arrived in the mail announcing my official acceptance into Stanford, nothing I did ever went away, but things became easier.

Stanford was nothing like I expected it to be—it was better.

No one knew who I was. No one knew what I did. There was no stigma associated with my name. We were all fresh faces, desperate to find a new identity and escape the ghosts of our pasts.

And escape I did.

I found myself in college in ways I never thought I could. I excelled and thrived in all my classes, the freedom of living on campus unleashing a new, confident me. I made friends with girls who actually wanted to be my friend and not whisper about my secondhand clothes behind my back. Thankfully, it was all the craze to wear recycled clothes in college. I was a hipster before it was cool.

I worked part time at the local Starbucks, where I got to know a lot of my peers. For two years, things were the best they were my entire life. The burden and guilt I felt for what I did never left my side, but day after day, it wasn't as blinding as the day prior, until one night when I went to a party on campus and saw Lincoln.

He was the only person who knew the real me because the bubbly, witty Holland Brooks-Ferris my friends knew would never cheat on their best friend and casual boyfriend with a boy who was nothing but trouble. Feelings I'd tried so hard to keep at bay lashed at the surface, threatening to dredge up old memories I never wanted to relive. I thought that I finally had a chance at living a normal life without having to look over my shoulder, but when I locked eyes with Lincoln, I knew I'd never rid myself of the guilt.

He went out of his way to ignore me at first, which suited me just fine, but when I almost burned him with a scalding pot of Earl Grey, my boss insisted coffee was on us for the next month. No college kid could refuse free coffee, so even though he ignored me every morning, I got used to seeing him again.

It turned out he went to Stanford instead of Berkley, so I would be seeing a lot of him.

But the boy I once knew had transformed into a man. His hair was cut short, emphasizing the warmth of his deep brown eyes. Unlike when we were in high school, he had a permanent five o'clock shadow, which just added to his rugged look. He was still big, and he still played football, but I guess we just both grew into who we were supposed to be.

One morning when I was cleaning the tables, he came over and actually spoke to me. It may just have been him informing me that someone had spilled their coffee by the front door, but those words and that spilled coffee changed our lives forever.

We began talking, baby steps at first, but after a while, the pull which we felt, the one which originally drew us together, sparked brightly, and we became friends. Friends then turned into lovers, then turned into boyfriend and girlfriend, then turned into affianced.

It wasn't easy sailing, and early on, we learned that for us to survive we had to discuss what happened once and for all, and then leave it to the breeze. Lincoln mentioned them once, and once only. He told me he didn't speak to either after what happened, but Hollywood being Hollywood and the inability to keep a secret, he heard it through the grapevine that Belle and London were together.

Saying his name aloud or even thinking it is like my Voldemort, so I decided then and there to save myself the pain and forget the sins of my past for good. I accepted that I was a revenge fuck for what Belle and Lincoln did to him. Collateral damage, I suppose you could say. He used me for his personal gain, but instead of crying myself to sleep at night ever again…I lived and learned.

His mother's comment also paved the truth. I would always be a Brooks-Ferris, and he, well, he would always be an asshole.

In a moment of weakness, however, after speaking to Lincoln about Belle, I called my mom and asked if she had ever come around asking for me. My mom told me what I already knew, but I needed to hear it from her to move on for good.

Belle didn't call, write, she didn't visit; it was like she and I didn't exist, and although I would never forget her, I've forgotten the me I was when I was with her because I grew up.

But regardless, not a day went by that I didn't think of her and what I did. The long hours I put in at work and school, the sleep-deprived days and nights were all punishment for the sins I'd committed. It was always at the back of my mind, and I'd hoped that maybe one day I would no longer look at my reflection with disappointment, guilt, and regret for what I did.

That day is still not in sight.

Lincoln and I never spoke of them ever again, and because of that we started our new life together. Two years into our relationship, we moved in together. It was a tiny one-bedroom apartment above a laundromat, but it was ours. Even though Lincoln could buy the whole block, we decided we were going to build our lives together and spend only what we saved.

We studied hard, we worked until we passed out on our laptops, but by the end of our time at Stanford, I graduated top of my class with a double masters in law while Lincoln graduated with an MBA. He was going to take over the business world and be the youngest—not to mention richest—CEO Los Angeles had seen in years.

But the thought of staying in California wasn't what I wanted; it wasn't where I wanted to practice law. There was only one place I wanted to be, and that was New York City.

We moved right after graduation and both found jobs we loved. We bought a home in Brooklyn, much to the disgust of Lincoln's mom, but we were different people now. New York brought out a side to us that Los Angeles had kept under lock and key.

Something is truly magical about living in New York. The hustle and bustle keep a constant thrum of excitement pumping through your veins. There is never a dull moment, but opposed to the star-kissed drama the Los Angeles life offers, living in New York makes you feel alive. You step off that subway and everything has its own pulse. The vivacious energy jumpstarts your engine and you're ready to tackle whatever is thrown your way. Someone once told me you move to LA to make movies, and you live in New York to make money, and money we made.

We loved Brooklyn, and we made it our home. But we moved to the Upper East Side about a year ago when I was made partner at one of the biggest law firms in Manhattan. I represent the underdogs because I know what it feels like to be at the bottom of the food chain.

I was doing okay for myself, but a promotion gave my bank balance way too many zeros.

My parents refused until they were black and blue, but they finally allowed me to buy them a home in Beverly Hills. They were back at their old stomping ground, but they never forgot their roots. They may be welcomed back into the land of the rich and famous, but they won't be having a happy reunion any time soon.

Life couldn't get any better—I had the dream job, perfect home, but most of all, I had Lincoln dropping to one knee in our favorite Chinese restaurant asking me to marry him. I choked on my pork bun, but once it was dislodged and I realized he was serious, my amazing life was complete.

I called my parents, who couldn't be happier. They loved Lincoln. He was everything every parent wanted for their only daughter.

Not seeing the point in having a long engagement, we

decided to get married right away. If it were up to us, we'd be riding the 6 a.m. subway to city hall, but my mom begged me not to take this rite of passage away from her and asked if we'd consider getting married back home.

Alas, that's what has us driving along the I-10 in this rental, pepped up on pre-wedding cheer.

My life is somewhat picture perfect; I have everything I could ever want, but nothing is ever perfect—I should know that by now. My handbag sits innocently by my five-inch pumps, but what's inside is anything but innocent. It's been a thorn in my side for the past six months, and honestly, it was part of the reason I agreed to come back to LA. I need five minutes alone because lately, I've been looking over my shoulder once again.

"Babe, are you all right?" Lincoln keeps one hand on the wheel while he reaches the other over to still my bouncing knee.

I jerk at the contact, lost in the past. "I'm fine. I just…I don't like coming back here." Enough said.

"Pre-wedding jitters?" he asks, tongue in cheek, but I know a small part of him wonders if it's true. We have jumped into the deep end without a life vest, but love isn't supposed to make sense, right?

Although I haven't seen Londemort for ten years, three months, and fourteen days—not that I'm counting—coming back here feels like it was only yesterday, only yesterday he broke my heart and hung it out to dry.

Edging forward, I keep my cheek pressed to the chair; I

look at Lincoln and shake my head once, putting his doubt and mine to rest. "No. I want to marry you. If I had my way, I'd already be your wife." He rewards me with a small smile, but his clenching of the wheel reveals something else is on his mind. "But seeing as my parents are set on watching me walk down the aisle in white on my father's arm, we're stuck here for the next three weeks. But it'll be kind of nice."

He peers over with a frown, not following. I clarify, creeping closer. "We get to spend the next three weeks together. I can't remember the last time we did that." What with the grueling hours both our jobs demand of us, it's a miracle if we're in the same room at the same time sometimes.

It's been so long since we've been intimate—there just never is any time. However, a voice deep down, a voice which rears its ugly head time and time again, says these are just excuses in disguise.

We ride the rest of the car trip in silence, the low hum of the talk radio background noise for us both.

Everything looks so foreign, yet it looks exactly the same. The plume of smog still clouds my vision, and the gridlock of crazy Californian drivers still has me cringing and covering my eyes, but as the Hollywood sign grows bigger and taller, I know that some things do change.

The moment we turn off the highway and navigate through the chaotic streets of Beverly Hills, the gravity of what we're doing, that we're actually back here hits home, and I'm suddenly clawing at my seat belt, as it's cutting off my air supply.

I need to breathe.

So what if I bump into people I once knew? I'm a grown woman now. I'm twenty-eight, almost twenty-nine years old. I'm one of New York's finest lawyers. I have a fiancé who adores me. I need to remind myself of that fact when houses, mansions, freaking fortresses come into view because I suddenly feel like the awkward outsider I once was.

Taking three deep breaths draws attention to my mini meltdown, but Lincoln simply squeezes my knee. He knows not to smother me. I'm a big girl, and he's learned the hard way that I can take care of myself.

The notorious palm trees line the streets' edges like regimented soldiers, standing tall and guarding the elite who call this neighborhood their home. Seeing these houses through different eyes has me appreciating the wealth that this part of L.A. is known for, but I still think the towering white mansions and expensive Euro trash cars are superficially lavish and emit a sense of desperation of wanting to fit in and belong.

That's the difference between the architecture and lifestyle of New York and L.A. New York is engrossed in history and beauty, New Yorkers too preoccupied in their own state of affairs to care what others are doing, while L.A.'s mentality is anything you can do, I can do better.

It's funny driving through these streets as an adult. Even though I could afford to live here now, my apartment on the

Upper East Side feels more like home than this city ever did. It just confirms I'm where I'm supposed to be.

"It's just up here on the right," Lincoln says as he turns down a narrow, hilly street.

I've never seen my parents' house in the flesh before. It looked amazing online, and Lincoln's realtor friend assured us it was everything the listing said it was. I know what house it is before Lincoln points it out because although it may be the smallest and least extravagant of the lot, it's the most beautiful and well-loved of the bunch.

The French villa-inspired home sits on a hill, shadowed by two mansions on either side of the modest home. Lincoln stops at the gold gates and whistles. "I heard Jackie Chan lives there," he says, pointing at the glass dome to the left.

"I hope he doesn't make a habit of practicing his martial arts in the nude," I reply, making Lincoln chuckle. He drives up to the intercom and presses the button.

We wait, and wait, but to no avail. I know they're home, so I have no doubt my technology illiterate parents are still attempting to work out what each button does. Yes, my father grew up in such wealth and my mother had a taste for a short while, but that was a lifetime ago, and things have changed dramatically since then.

Unsnapping my seat belt, I slide across the middle console and lean my arm out the driver's window to press the intercom. "Hello, it's your only daughter."

"Holland?" my mother's frazzled voice squeaks out from the intercom speaker.

I can't help but smile. It's so good to hear her voice. "Yes, Mom, it's me. Do you have another daughter I don't know about?"

She playfully scoffs lightly. "Bobby, Holland is here. How do I—" The line goes dead, and I cover my face, laughing.

"Mom, you have to keep holding the button to speak. I can't hear you."

"At this rate, we should be married by Christmas," Lincoln says, looking at his Rolex. I ignore his sharpness. Something is suddenly bugging him, and I can't help but wonder what.

"Holland, how do we open the gate?" My father's serious tone has me remembering how I once broke his heart. But I focus on the task at hand.

"There should be a button near the intercom."

"What does it say?"

"I don't know…open sesame, maybe." He laughs deeply, and it's good to be home. Well, home away from home.

Moments later, the gates swing open with a groan. "Did that work?"

"Yes, Dad. What did you do these past few months? Turn your visitors away?" I ask, jokingly.

"We haven't had anyone visit, so it's the first time we've used this intercom thing."

His reply turns the mood, and I slide back inside the car,

sitting in my seat. Lincoln clears his throat, sensing the change in my disposition. This is so typical of this city—so judgmental and shallow. Even though my parents' zip code has changed, it doesn't change the fact my mom's surname will always be Brooks. Although my father is a Ferris, it's guilt by association. And the Ferris name has had its fair share of scandal over the years.

My grandfather's fall from grace, and my mother's apparent cheap ways and having a child at sixteen will never be forgotten or forgiven. She was seen as a gold digger, coming from nothing and working her way to the top, but what they all seem to forget is that both my parents experienced highs and lows, yet their love for one another never faded.

And that's quite a milestone for living in a place such as L.A.

"If it makes you feel more comfortable, we could rent a room close to your old home."

I turn with a measured pace, narrowing my eyes. I understand why he would suggest that, seeing as I did make some happy memories in the "hood," but being anywhere near my old neighborhood will just bring back old memories hours of therapy helped me forget. "I'm sorry, I didn't mean—"

But I cut him off. "It's fine. I know what you meant." The car fills with an uncomfortable silence and feelings of being that awkward seventeen-year-old return.

We haven't even been here an hour and I already want to

leave. The City of Angels can go to hell.

Lincoln pulls the car up, parking it near a rounded courtyard where the centerpiece is a cherub fountain sitting in a tiled mosaic circle. Water falls from the vase the angel holds, and although it's truly beautiful, it saddens me that I'm probably the first one to see its elegance.

On cue, I break out in a rash and begin scratching under my chin.

"Babe, you need to relax. We came here to get away and already you're breaking out in hives." Lincoln kills the engine and turns to look at me. "We can always leave. It was your idea to come here."

Nothing but concern reflects in his gentle eyes, but it never leaves, especially since…thoughts are quickly and thankfully detoured when my parents step out onto their white marbled terrace, waving happily.

Just seeing them puts my woes on the backburner, and I unsnap my belt. "Sweetie!" Mom bounces on the spot with my father behind her, a hand placed lovingly on her shoulder.

They look great. Both in their mid-40's, life has been kind to them, as they're still as youthful and vibrant as I remember them. I saw them about nine months ago, or maybe it's been longer. Sometimes, my life is like a time warp, and five minutes may actually be five months. But that's how I like to live—if I slow down, my mind tends to wander.

"Ready?" I smile, turning to look at Lincoln, who nods.

"Let the crazy begin."

I step from the car, hating that a voice I buried years ago states that the crazy never ended—I was just running away from the inevitable.

My heels click on the pavement as I quicken my step to meet my parents. I didn't realize how much I missed them. No matter your age, your parents have the ability to make you feel like a child again. If only I could forget the responsibilities that come with being an adult. "Miss me?"

My mom runs down the steps and hugs me so tightly, I almost lose my balance, but as far as reunions go, it's the best one I've had in forever. "Oh, Sweetie, we missed—" *sniff* "—you."

"Hey, no tears," I whisper in her ear, rubbing her back. If she starts, I'm afraid she'll set off a chain reaction which won't stop.

"I know, I know, but they're the happy kind," she replies, squeezing me tighter.

"I missed you too." For a mere second, I let down my guard and am vulnerable to the only person who won't judge me. For so long, I've erected my walls ten feet high because my job, my life doesn't allow weakness. But in my mother's arms, I can let go.

"I hope there's some room in there for me," my father teases, which sets off my mother's happy tears.

She lets go, but my dad takes her place, and they both

embrace me in a human sandwich, which has me laughing.

"It's so good to have you home," Dad says, pulling me out at arm's length to look at me. "You look just like your mother. My two beautiful girls." His comment has my mom bursting into tears once again.

"C'mon, show me around this beautiful house of yours," I say, needing to change the subject as I wipe the tears from the corner of my eyes.

"How was the flight?" Dad asks, offering to take a suitcase from Lincoln, who gratefully accepts, as I may have overpacked a smidge. I know there are another two suitcases in the trunk.

Mom loops her arm through mine, leading me up the stairs. "The place is beautiful, Holland. Thank you so much. Your father and I—"

But I intercept, as I don't want her thinking that way. She doesn't owe me anything. I wanted to do this for them because they've done so much for me. "Sshh, none of that. Now show me where my room is."

As we step into the grand foyer, I stop, needing to take a moment to absorb its opulence. "Wow, the pictures did not do this place justice."

Turning in a circle, I raise my eyes and appreciate the arched window which sits high above the front door, allowing bursts of sunlight to light up the polished limestone flooring. Dual staircases lead to the second floor, each step decorated with Tiffany glass.

Once I'm done gawking at the decorative gold touches on the walls and ceilings, Mom leads me off to the right, where the formal living room is an elaborate setting flaunting inlaid hardwood flooring, a fireplace, and intricate ceiling moldings. A crystal chandelier is suspended from the soaring ceiling, setting off the magnificence. White leather couches and a huge glass coffee table complement the room nicely.

"Wait until you see the kitchen," she says, guiding me past the family room, which has a gorgeous Persian rug nestled on the white carpeting.

I whistle and my stomach growls the moment we step into the gourmet kitchen. The breakfast area is set in a sunny alcove and includes double glass doors which open to the green grounds. Granite counters and plenty of work and storage space make me think of our old kitchen. My mom loves to cook, and she made the most of the tiny, outdated space we had, but this room is her palace and tears sting my eyes.

She deserves this. They both do.

I follow in silence, afraid I'll burst into tears if I speak, because a wave of nostalgia rolls over me. Although I knew this place was beautiful, actually stepping inside has me appreciating just how far we've come. When I was a teenager, I could only dream of living in a house like this, not that I wanted to. But now, my parents are where they deserve to be.

We walk the grand staircase and I marvel at the stained glass steps. "I've never seen anything like it," I comment, the back of each riser set with a small pane of glass. The huge bay windows along the far wall spurt streams of sunrays, lighting up the staircase like a literal stairway to heaven.

The upper level has five heavy wooden doorways leading off the long carpeted hallway. Abstract pieces of art, courtesy of my mom, no doubt, adorn the pristine white walls. "This is your room," Mom says, opening the last door on the left.

She smiles as I step past her in awe. The monster bed draped in gold and black linens has me wondering if that mattress feels as soft as it looks. I toss my handbag onto it and watch as it sinks into the cushy bliss.

The eggshell white bedroom includes a sitting area, a vast walk-in closet, and a marble en suite featuring a claw tub. The plush carpet feels like clouds beneath my heels as I peek my head around the doorjamb. A double sink vanity and frameless glass shower finish off the sleek, modern design.

"Do you like it?" Mom asks from behind me.

With eyes still glued to that tub, I nod slowly. "Like it? It makes my apartment look like a sardine can. It's beautiful." Turning around to face her, I gently caress her shoulder. "You're finally home."

"It doesn't matter where we live; wherever you and your father are will always be my home." And this is one of the many reasons why I love this woman to death. "Let me look at you," she says, changing the subject, placing me out at arm's length.

Her hazel eyes begin at my head and work their way down.

My long brown hair is twisted into an elaborate chignon, just how I usually wear it. My makeup is light, but that's no different to when I was young. I barely wear any eyeshadow, opting for a dark mascara and kohl to emphasize my green eyes instead. My foundation is only a light dusting to cover my freckles and sunspots, thanks to growing up under the California sun. My lips are always covered with a bold lipstick or gloss, but on weekends, my trusty ChapStick is my go-to essential.

She takes in my white pantsuit, which has a sweeping V-neck and sleeveless top leading into flowy pants with pockets. I've tied the sash around my waist into a low bow, giving the outfit a more casual feel.

She smiles when she sees the black heels. "I never thought I'd see the day my little girl wore high heels." It warms my heart that she still refers to me this way. "Wow, you look so… different. So grown up."

After I left for Florida, my relationship with my parents was strained. It took months, but they finally wrapped their heads around what I did. But still, our relationship was never the same, which made moving to New York all the more easier. It's taken years for us to get back to the way things were, but I can still see the disappointment in my mother's eyes when she lets her guard down. She will never understand why I slept with the enemy, and neither can I.

Shaking my head and pushing down feelings which have been long buried, I smile. "I can't exactly show up to work in sweats now, can I?"

She presses her linked hands over her chest in pride. "We're so proud of you, Holland. You're changing the world...but we always knew you would."

There's nothing like hearing those words from someone whose opinion you value most in this world.

"Thanks, Mom."

The sparkle from my diamond catches the sun, scattering tiny rainbows all over the room. "Oh, it's beautiful. Show me." I have no idea what she's talking about until she points to my left hand.

"It's going to take some getting used to," I confess, showing her my ring.

She examines it, nodding her approval as she takes my hand. "And you're happy?"

It's the first time she's asked me, and I can't help but wonder why. "Yes. Very. I love Lincoln. He's a good man." I have no idea why I suddenly feel the need to defend his honor to my mom. She knows what kind of a man he is.

"Yes, he is. Maybe you'll stop working so hard and give me some grandbabies." She accents her suggestion with a wink. I can't help but laugh.

"Yes, maybe." That even sounded unconvincing to my ears.

Lincoln and I are on two totally different planets when it comes to kids. I want them and he, he seems to want to avoid the topic like the plague. Whenever I've brought the subject up in the past, he's used our careers as an excuse not to try. Yes, my job is important to me, but so is having a family to share that success with. However, it's one fight I'm bound to lose, which is a first for me, and I don't like it; I don't like it one bit.

"Are you looking after yourself? You look so skinny. Are you eating? Proper food, I mean. Not these vegan, werewolf diet things I read about online."

I purse my lips from side to side, biting back my smile. "Yes, I promise I'm eating my meat and three vegetables."

She waves off my cheek playfully. "Good. We worry about you. That Rossi case was all over the internet. You helped NYPD put away a very dangerous man. Fancy him using his thirteen-year-old daughter to sell drugs..." Her voice blends into the background because suddenly, my ears are filled with nothing but white noise.

Alberto Rossi was New York's most notorious mafia boss, and I helped put him away for a very long time. For years, he ran the streets of New York, dealing drugs and instilling the fear of god in anyone who crossed his path.

His band of lowlife thugs terrorized, blackmailed, and killed for over a decade. New Yorkers didn't feel safe because of Alberto and his crew, but thanks to a yearlong operation, NYPD finally brought Alberto down.

He did the most despicable thing a parent could do to their child—he used his daughter as a pawn, not caring that having a thirteen-year-old running the streets, peddling his drugs, meant she was put in harm's way time and time again.

NYPD got wind of his dealings, and a sting operation was organized. Theresa was responsible for a shipment of heroin worth a cool thirty-seven mil. Alberto wasn't even man enough to oversee the deal, knowing if it went belly up, they'd kill her and not connect the dots because she was his illegitimate love child. He had a cover for everything, and even though everyone knew ninety-eight percent of New York's drugs were supplied by Alberto Rossi, no one was game enough to take him on.

However, the police were two steps ahead and arrested Alberto at his holiday home in Aspen, armed with all the evidence they needed. Theresa's mom was some poor woman Alberto promised the world to, but in reality, all he wanted was to build a small army with Rossi blood. Natalie tried for years to get her daughter back, but no one would touch her—no one but me.

When my firm got wind of the high-profile case, I offered to represent Natalie pro bono. Not only did I want to put this scumbag away for life and throw away the key, but I also wanted Theresa reunited with her mom, who she hadn't seen for years.

When I first met both, they were such scared little mice, afraid of the big bad wolf that had allies everywhere. They were put into protective care, but the pressure got to Theresa and she eventually refused to testify against her dad.

I worked for months with her, gaining her trust, and finally, after nine months, we were ready to go to trial.

After a grueling ten weeks, the jury came back with a guilty verdict. I had helped put away New York's most dangerous criminal, and in turn, in the mafia's eyes, I became public enemy number one.

The win was what prompted me to become partner and earned me the respect and notoriety among my peers. It was a media frenzy, offers from all different news sources begging for the inside scoop, but I wasn't interested in any of it.

At the end of the day, I was just doing my job. I reunited a mother and daughter and helped clean up the streets of a city I'd grown to love. But sadly, not everyone was happy with my patriotism because six months ago, the game changed and the hunter became the hunted.

"Holland, are you all right? You're as white as a ghost." I'm not even aware of my trip down memory lane until I feel my mother's warm palm press to my brow.

"I'm fine. Just tired from the flight. I might go lie down for a bit."

She doesn't look convinced, her pink lips pulling into a thin line. "I'll make you some tea."

There's no point arguing. "Thanks, tea sounds good."

Her concern for me is visible. It must be mother's intuition because I think I've mastered the perfect poker face, but she doesn't look convinced. "I'll be back soon." She leans forward and kisses me on the forehead, her homely scent of citrus and wildflowers embracing me tightly. When she closes the door behind her, I take a moment to steady my breathing.

Slumping onto the end of the mattress, I cradle my head in my palms. I promised myself I wouldn't think about it, but Alberto Rossi is never far from my mind. Sighing, I reach for my bag and unzip the zipper, a complete glutton for punishment.

What's inside is what you'd expect to find in most female's handbags—wallet, keys, phone, but I put money on the fact that I'm the only one who carries around this yellow envelope like some sick serial killer needing to keep his trophies close to relive his crimes.

My manicured fingers tremble as I slip my nail under the seal to open the door to my nightmares. The moment the small pieces of paper see the light of day, I'm transported back in time to when I received my first one.

I'd just come back from my daily run around Central Park. How I loved the summertime in New York. The air pulsated with energy and radiated with endless possibilities. It made you appreciate being alive.

I waved hello to Gary, the front desk manager, while collecting my mail. That day was no different than any other, but when I unfolded that crisp white piece of paper, everything changed and has never been the same since.

You're a whore...and you're going to pay.

I had to read it twice, disbelieving that the words I'd just read were actually written in red ink before me. But they were. No matter how much I wanted them to go away, I knew this was only the beginning.

The notes arrived sporadically, the sender, of course, unknown. Sometimes it was radio silence for days, sometimes even weeks, but whenever I thought they'd stopped, I'd receive another with a message even crueler than the one before. It was always written in the same handwriting. Always in that deep red ink.

The theme was pretty much the same. The words "whore" and "pay" were repeat offenders, and when I'd finally had enough and went to the police, they confirmed what I feared to be true. The letters were most likely coming from Rossi headquarters as payback for what I did to their boss.

I played it off, but the police told me not to be careless and that from now, I was to watch my back. And watch my back I did. I felt like a prisoner once again, constantly looking over my shoulder and wondering when the next assault was to come.

Now, I'm escaping New York to be held in yet another prison. I don't know what's worse—the danger that lurks out there, or the danger that festers within.

"You brought them?" Snapping my head up guiltily, I bite my lip, completely busted.

The strain has not only impacted me, but Lincoln as well. He has been short, snappy, and impatient—traits which I never knew existed in him until six months ago. Our lives have become even more stressful, and because of this, our relationship has suffered. This is one of the reasons I agreed to marry him with such haste. I know marriage is not a Band-Aid, but I'll try anything to go back to the way things were. Am I ready? I suppose we'll soon find out.

Quickly stuffing the note inside the envelope, I shove it into my bag. "Of course, I did. They're evidence, Lincoln. In case you've forgotten, I'm a lawyer; collecting evidence is kind of what I do." I hide behind my humor, not wanting to worry him further.

"Ha, very funny," he says, stepping into the room. He takes a moment to look around, clearly impressed. I exhale, thankful he's happy to let the matter rest.

His cell is curled into his palm, so I ask, "Who'd you call?" He cocks a brow, and I point at his hand.

"Oh." He shakes his head, as if to clear it. "A couple of old friends wanted to see if I was free for a beer."

"Who?" I question, crossing my legs and leaning back on my hands.

Lincoln runs a hand through his short hair, giving away his sins. "Just Chook and Boof. Remember them?"

My lip curls involuntarily. "Yes, sadly I do. Jesus, good news travels fast in this place." I can't keep the sarcasm from my tone.

"Want to come?"

I scoff, sitting up and shaking my head with conviction. "No thanks. I wasn't even nice to them when I was supposed to be, so I have a feeling things may get a little uncomfortable if I tag along."

He laughs, accustomed to my honesty. "Okay, fair enough. I won't be long."

I watch as he unzips his suitcase and changes into a Yankees t-shirt. He is so handsome. I can't help but crawl toward him on my hands and knees. Gripping the collar of his shirt, I draw him down inches from my lips. "Are you sure you have to go out? There is a claw tub." I open my mouth in excitement, before singsonging brashly, "You could wash my back."

I want this staleness between us to clear. It's been lingering over our heads for months, and I thought coming here would help clear the air. But he still seems detached, distracted.

He places his hands over mine and squeezes lightly. "I sort of promised I'd go. Maybe later?"

"You certainly know how to make a girl feel loved." I let him go and fall onto the mattress with a huff. I'm pretty sure I just heard our sex life fizzle out for good. I've never been good at this flirting thing, and it's times such as these that I don't know why I bother.

"I'll be two hours tops. Unless…" His pause has me rising and leaning up on an elbow.

"Unless what?"

He points at my handbag. "Unless you want me to stay."

His chivalrous offer has me rolling my eyes because I don't want him to know just how freaked out I truly am about my Dear John or, in my case, Dear Whore letters. "Please. Have you seen this place? It's like a fortress. I'll just take a bath and relax."

"Okay, babe." He bends down and gives my lips a peck. I'm saddened it didn't take much convincing. "And besides, I'm pretty sure you're safe with all those self-defense classes you've been taking."

He's right, but his aloofness to this situation does piss me off. Even in New York, he was so certain nothing was going to happen, assuring me that it'll be all right. I don't know if he's living in denial, or if he doesn't realize the seriousness of having a Rossi target on our backs.

However, I don't want to nag, so I nod with a staged smile. "Have fun. Say hi to all your ex-girlfriends."

He freezes, obviously not seeing the funny side to my comment. "See you soon. Love you."

"I love you too," I reply, giving him a small wave.

He's out the door, a skip to his step. It appears Lincoln has missed LA more than he let on. I, on the other hand, am thinking of all the activities I can plan indoors, because I don't intend on leaving the grounds for the next three weeks.

With that thought in mind, I spring off the bed and hunt through my suitcase for my toiletries and my tattered copy of *Emma* by Jane Austen. Kicking off my shoes, I peer over at my handbag, which sits innocently on the bed. R&R starts in three, two, one, so I reach for it and stow it away in the bedside dresser drawer.

L.A. has already given me a headache, and the scary thing is…I know there is so much more to come.

9

"If I eat one more bite—" I place my hands on my bloated belly and slouch in my chair "—you'll be rolling me down the aisle." My parents laugh lightly, but I'm only half joking.

After soaking in the tub until my fingers resembled tiny prunes, I decided to dress and explore the grounds. My mom finally got her rose garden because she now lives on approximately five hundred square feet of perfectly manicured grounds complete with rose and vegetable gardens, and of course the picturesque Beverly Hills palm trees.

The in-ground pool isn't too shabby, either.

I was ready to put in my dinner request because I had a hankering for my mom's enchiladas, but she surprised me when she revealed she'd made dinner reservations at some gourmet burger place on Sunset Boulevard. I couldn't refuse, seeing as that part of L.A. was one of my favorites, and a burger sounded too good to pass up.

I tried calling Lincoln, but it went to voicemail, so it looked like it was just us three.

Sitting in the back of my parents' Mercedes and taking in the sights which were my backdrop for so long was a little disconcerting. No matter that years had passed since I'd been here; it still felt like yesterday.

Buildings have been erected where others were torn down, making room for the latest high-rise or five-star hotel. That's one of the many things I loved about New York. With no room to build out, they build up, adding to the existing architecture while keeping the historical feel. It's a concrete jungle, and it's easy to lose oneself in the madness.

"Speaking of aisles…have you decided on a dress yet?"

The thought of discussing this with my mom and dad suddenly has me reaching for a ketchup-covered French fry.

Lincoln and I both decided on a small wedding with just family and a few friends. My parents offered to host the ceremony in their home, and after seeing the gardens, I couldn't think of a more perfect place.

But that's as far as I've gotten.

I haven't even thought about catering, or decorations, or even a guest list. So when my mom mentions the word "dress," I, of course, break out in hives. "I was just going to wear something I already had," I reply, discreetly scratching under my ear.

But my mother looks as if I've just told her I've opted to go naked instead. "Holland, no, this is your wedding day. It's a day you'll always remember. I know you have lovely clothes, but you have to get a dress."

Swirling my leftover fries in the puddle of ketchup and mustard, I avoid answering her for as long as I can. I have no idea why this is making me so uncomfortable. The thought of trying on dress after dress with endless buttons, tight-fitting bodices, and enough tulle to make me look like a meringue sets off my allergies and everywhere begins to itch.

"Maybe we could go shopping tomorrow? And pick up some supplies too?"

Beads of sweat begin to gather on the small of my back, and I'm suddenly blistering in my seat. Reaching for a stack of napkins, I use them as a makeshift fan. "Is it hot in here?" I in no way address my mother's question, which has both my parents looking at one another in worry.

"You do want to marry Lincoln, don't you?" It's now my father's turn for the third degree.

"Yes, of course, I do," I reply with a little more heat than I intended. What the hell is the matter with me? "We can definitely go wedding dress shopping." I swallow past the lump in my throat.

"Sweetie—" my mom reaches across the retro-style booth

and grips both my hands "—if you're having cold feet, you can always postpone. This has come about awfully soon and no one would blame you if you needed more time…"

The fact she leaves her sentence suspended in midair has me wondering what exactly she intended to say. But there is no way I need more time to do anything. I love Lincoln, and I want to marry him. Yes, it's sudden, but this is what I want. This is what we need.

Yet you can't stomach the thought of trying on a dress. Why? a small, bothersome voice says, playing devil's advocate. That voice can go to hell.

"I need to use the bathroom." I shoot upright, sending the plates and silverware on the countertop about five feet into the air.

"Holland…"

"I'm fine, Mom." Tell that to the rash spreading up my neck like an out of control wildfire.

I don't wait around for her reply. Instead, I push past the diners and practically run to the restrooms at the back of the restaurant. The moment I scamper inside, I take three deep breaths, afraid I'm on the cusp of passing out.

Thankfully, no one is in here to witness my meltdown because I have no idea what's wrong and how long this freak-out will last.

Once my breaths have returned to a semi-normal pace, I amble over to the basins and turn the silver faucet to cold. My flesh is still burning up, so the cool water feels heavenly against my heated skin as I bend low and splash it onto my face.

Bracing both hands against the white marble counter, I peer at my reflection in the mirror. I cringe when my mirror image reveals I look as crappy as I feel. "Pull it together," I whisper to myself.

I haven't felt this anxious since...

My hands begin to shake as I smooth out the already straightened wisps of hair brushed back into my chignon. I've changed into a black pencil skirt and a white silk camisole, but I suddenly feel like a stranger in my own skin.

The seventeen-year-old Holland Brooks-Ferris would be shaking her head at me and scoffing—I've sold out, she'd say. I've turned into something I used to hate. My designer clothes are because of work, I reason with her, but in response, she flips me off.

I suddenly remember the soccer mom who demanded I clean up her child's mess when I worked at Paradisco. At the time, I thought I'd never turn into someone like her. And I haven't—or have I?

Sighing, I shakily hunt through my bag and try my best to reapply the makeup I scrubbed off. Mid lipstick stroke, a voice shrieks to my left, transporting me back in time.

"Holland? Holland Brooks-Ferris?"

With my lipstick still in hand, I turn slowly and focus on the pretty girl beside me. It takes me a moment to remember her face, but when I do, I'm suddenly sixteen again.

I recap the lipstick, afraid I'll detour from my lips and make a mess otherwise. "Oh my god, Chloe Helm?"

She nods excitedly, her sea green eyes lighting up with glee. "Yes, it's me. Holy shit! Look at you. I hardly recognized you."

You and me both, that niggling voice whisper-yells in my ear.

Ignoring it, I smile, happy to see my high school friend. "I could say the same thing. You look incredible, Chloe." Chloe was a little chubby in high school, not that it mattered to me, but now, she looks like a freaking supermodel.

She brushes a hand down her red summer dress with pride. "Thanks. It's amazing what being happy can do. Speaking of..." Her gaze drops to my hand which rests limply by my side. "You're engaged?"

"Oh, yes, I am," I reply, snapping from my daze.

"Show me!" she squeals, making grabby fingers. I offer her my hand. She examines my ring, whistling. "Who's the lucky guy?"

"Lincoln O'Toole," I reveal, not thinking it's a big deal until her jaw drops to the ground.

"Oh my god!"

I recoil backward, a little overwhelmed by her excitement. If this much excitement was articulated in New York, we'd be questioning if the government laced the air with happy gas. "Yes, we're getting married in three weeks." I have no idea why I just told her that, but I suppose it's normal behavior for a bride-to-be, right?

The seventeen-year-old me shrugs.

"What are you doing right now?"

"I…um, nothing really." Not my most eloquent moment.

She clutches my bicep, her Tiffany bracelets jingling. "Come get a drink with me. I'd love to catch up. It's been so long." My hesitation may as well be written across the California sky. "Please. One drink." For emphasis, she interlaces her fingers, on the cusp of begging.

How can I say no? "Okay, just one drink."

She claps, jigging on the spot. "I've missed you so much. One of my favorite memories is the night we ventured into the woods, looking for Belle…"

The memory slams into me, leaving me grinning uncomfortably because I think I'm seconds from throwing up. "Yeah, we were stupid kids," I say, hoping I sound casual and aloof. "I just have to let my parents know we're going out. I'll meet you out there?" Chloe nods, her plump pink lips tipping into an energized grin.

The moment I step from the bathroom, I take yet another breath to liberate my lungs. It seems to be all I'm doing these days. Even though I'm hit with a waft of burger and fries, it helps calm the nerves. The diner is hip and retro, everything you'd expect from an establishment located on the strip. It's bustling with locals and tourists alike, all in good spirits, ready to tackle whatever the weekend throws their way.

A thought occurs to me. I've never actually been out bar hopping in L.A. I left for Florida when I was seventeen, and even when I went to Stanford, the nightlife on campus kept me more than entertained. But deep down, the thought of venturing back out into the wilderness was far scarier than I cared to admit. I was happy to leave the old Holland Brooks-Ferris behind and focus on reinventing myself, which I thought I did, until I came back here and realized the ghosts of my past wouldn't leave well enough alone.

Chloe only had to say Belle's name, and it was enough to transport me back in time. I remember his smell, I can taste his touch, but more than anything, my heart remembers how easy it was to love him, even when it shouldn't have.

My mom stares at me from across the room. Her concern and fear are palpable from here. Does she wish things were different? Is she wondering what her life would have been like if I were never born?

Tears sting my eyes because a small part me knows how much easier things would have been if she'd just done what almost anyone her age would have done. She gave me life and all I seem to do is ruin hers.

Pulling back my shoulders, I stage a smile, hoping the sadness doesn't show behind my eyes. I have no idea what's wrong with me, but it needs to stop, and it needs to stop now. "You guys wouldn't mind if I went out for a drink with a friend?"

My mom pales while my dad sits tall in his seat, his fists clenched. "Who?" And just like that, I'm seventeen again, reliving the worse night of my life.

They've forgiven me for my sins once before, but I don't think they'll be so understanding a second time around. But they won't have to. Whatever temporary insanity plagues me is no longer. I've come here to marry the man of my dreams and forget a small sliver of my heart still belongs to someone else.

"Chloe Helm. We went to school together. I won't be long."

My parents' disposition instantly changes, their relief clear. "Of course, Sweetie. Go, have fun. Do you want to use the car?" My dad raises the keys.

"No, no, it's fine. I'll grab a cab. I'll see you soon." Bending down, I kiss my mom's cheek. "Oh, and tomorrow sounds great. I'll make a list of places we can visit. There's a store in Bel Air I wouldn't mind checking out. Lots of white and puffy tulle."

Mom's eyes swell, and she nods happily. "Sounds wonderful. I can't wait. Chloe can come along too. We can make a day of it."

I know what she's doing. She thinks this change of heart has got to do with seeing an old friend and reminiscing. Not wanting to disappoint her further, I nod. "Sure, I'll ask her."

Chloe emerges from the bathroom, searching through the throngs of people. I give her a small wave, my parents following my line of sight. Their shoulders relax when they see I'm telling the truth. No one is to blame for planting that seed of doubt but me.

"Hello!" Chloe has always been sociable, and it seems even in adulthood, she can make friends easily.

"Hello, Chloe. It's so lovely to see you again. How are your parents?"

"My mom is great, thanks. She's opened a boutique in Beverly Hills. As for my dad, he's onto marriage number five, with someone twenty years his junior, so I'd say he's tired and probably broke."

I snort beside her, quickly covering my mouth to mute my outburst. Chloe was always full of spunk. Looks like some things never change.

"Holland and I will be going dress shopping tomorrow. Please feel free to come along."

Chloe spins, eyes wide. "Wedding dress shopping?"

I nod, needing a pep in my step. "We sure are!" I rein it in, however, because that's pep jacked up on Red Bull.

"Oh my god, you must come down to mom's boutique then. I should have mentioned the store she opened was a bridal boutique." Whatever gods are looking down at me are laughing rowdily at my expense.

"Yay," I reply with little to no oomph, but Chloe doesn't seem to notice or care.

"It's settled then. Girls' day out!"

Both my mom and Chloe clap in excitement, while I discreetly check my glands as I'm running a fever and am certain I've caught Ebola.

"Have fun, you two." I can't remember the last time I saw my mom so happy, but I suppose we have missed out on a lot of the girly stuff growing up. This will be good for her, and I guess I do need a dress. Two birds, one stone...

"See you guys later." I wave goodbye to my parents, pleased Mom looks so joyful at the prospect of spending the entire day shopping.

Chloe loops her arm through mine, chatting a hundred miles a minute, while I allow her to guide me because I have no idea where we're going.

As Chloe details her job as a dental hygienist and the importance of flossing, my mind wanders to my mom. We haven't really had a chance to do all the mother-daughter things most families do because I've lived so far away from her for years.

Stanford was over six hours away from where we used to live. We visited one another, but my mother never smothered me. She let me spread my wings and fly. I don't regret my decision because my early twenties were some of the best times of my life. I lived, learned, and I loved. But now, I realize, I've missed so much.

I don't remember seeing the fine lines around her eyes when she laughs. I wasn't there when she won a trip to Disneyland but decided to give it to the Donaldsons, our old neighbors who had a son with cerebral palsy. I've grown, but I feel like that growth came at a price. I knew coming back here wasn't going to be easy, but I'm certain I've gotten an ulcer, and it's not even been twenty-four hours yet.

"I'm so sorry. I'm boring you, aren't I?"

"Yes. What? Hang on, no?" I reply in a rushed breath. I was barely listening to Chloe, once again lost in my head.

Our arms are still thankfully linked because if I was left to fend for myself, I'd have knocked over a dozen or so pedestrians in my stupor. "I am just so happy you're here. You just vanished. The school was rampant with rumors."

I gulp but keep my cool. "I bet. It wouldn't be Harvard-Westlake otherwise."

Our heels click against the pavement, the bright glow from billboards and neon lights lighting up our path. "Where did you go?"

This question was unavoidable, and I knew she'd ask me sooner or later. I figure I best answer it now and clear the air. "I went to Florida to stay with my aunt." She nods. "I needed to get out of L.A. The air was toxic, and I mean that in every literal sense there is."

Chloe's warm eyes soften. She knows exactly what I mean. She may not know the reason, but at one time or another, we've all wanted to get lost and never be found.

Just as she opens her mouth, my cell chimes loudly, saving me from her twenty questions. Hunting through my bag, I'm thankful for the derailment.

It's Lincoln. "Hey."

"Hey babeee," he slurs, hinting he's completely shitfaced—so much for a quick catch-up.

"Where are you?" My tone isn't accusing, just curious.

My question is answered seconds later when a riotous roar blares through the phone. I yank it away from my ear, the holler still echoing loudly. "Just some sports bar. We're watching the game."

"Okay, so you'll be staying a while."

"Um, yeah. The boys are all here—"

I cut him off. "It's fine. You don't have to explain anything to me. Have fun."

"Thanks, babe. I'll make it up to you tomorrow." The thunderous background chatter reminds me of all the football games I was forced to sit through.

"Linc—c'mon, next round is on you!" says some cheapskate buffoon.

Chloe smoothly steers me toward a darkened doorway as I attempt to keep walking straight. The gigantic bouncer extends his palm, a silent demand for 'show me your ID.' As I rummage through my bag, I cradle the phone between my ear and shoulder. "Tomorrow I'm going dress—"

A deafening, "Touchdown!" followed by men hollering and hooting encroaches on my news.

"Okay, babe, have fun, bye."

My mouth moves in wordless animation because I'm midsentence. The phone is still pressed to my ear, but the line is dead. Well, this is new.

"Miss?" the annoyed bouncer snaps, jutting out his palm. Disgruntled patrons behind me announce their annoyance because I'm holding up the line. "Your ID." He rolls his eyes, as the need to speak is obviously not part of his job description.

I quickly compose myself and find my license. Handing it to him, the Hulk Hogan wannabe, handlebar moustache and all, snatches it from my fingers. "I figured. I didn't think you were asking for a clue, although, you could probably use one, seeing as it's California law that you can't carry a concealed weapon. I hope you have a permit, otherwise your boss is going to be pissed." His hand shoots out to touch his badly concealed piece at the small of his back.

I grin smugly, jutting my own hand out, demanding my ID back. He flicks it over to me, the corded veins in his neck threatening to pop. He doesn't even bother looking over Chloe's and moves to the side, allowing us entry.

Chloe snorts while I brush past him, grinning smugly. He touches his earpiece, mouthing something into his microphone, eyeballing the hell out of me. I wave my finger in response. "You go, girl," Chloe shouts into my ear to be heard over "Bad Romance" by Lady Gaga.

The song seems fitting as this bar is unlike anything I've ever seen before. Too caught up in my phone call, I paid no attention to where Chloe was leading me, but now that I'm inside, this place has my undivided attention.

This luxurious lounge-meets-nightclub-meets-bar is sexy, grungy, and regal all at the same time. Red booths and plush tables are scattered around the darkened room, giving the venue an intimate feel. Gold and black velvet walls look plush and majestic, but to the left, a brick wall has one wondering if they've stepped into a different room.

In the center of the dance floor is a podium with red velvet carpet. Sitting dead center is a shiny stripper pole.

My eyes can't take in the sights fast enough. The mixed bunch of patrons waiting by the bar, bopping to the music, come in all different shapes and sizes. Hipsters, valley girls, scene kids, and yuppies all play nice together, which is a first. It could be the copious amounts of alcohol flowing freely, however, because that bar is the biggest I've ever seen.

Its mirrored countertop could add to the illusion, but the brick wall behind the bar has shelf upon shelf stocked full with every bottle of booze imaginable. The shelves are lit by bright fluorescent blues and pinks, the outlandish colors mingling with the enormous crystal chandelier hanging low above the bar staff's heads as they work the floor with ease.

They're all gorgeous, young, and scantily dressed—I bet their tips are off the scale.

"What is this place?" I cup my hand and shout into Chloe's ear. The place is packed. The energy pulsating through the air.

"Absinthe of the Heart," she replies, but she may as well have spoken to me in Swahili.

"Huh?" I scrunch up my nose, turning to look at her. She laughs and shakes her head. In response, she yanks me by the elbow and leads me to the bar. I don't protest as I'm still reeling in the potency of this place.

Granted, I haven't been a big party animal, but this place is pretty incredible. With the right balance of sex and sass, this has to be one of the hottest places in L.A. The line moves quickly thanks to the practiced bartenders who flip, shake, and pour their drinks with skill.

One girl in particular catches my eye because she's just one of those women who have an air of confidence about her. Her two sizes too small white Metallica tank met with unfortunate circumstances because it's coarsely ripped and sits just below her breasts, which look like flotation devices. Her midriff is completely exposed, showcasing a dangly belly button ring and some kind of floral tattoo leading up her side.

Her hair is jet black and convenes like a mane around her pointed face. Her makeup is heavy-handed, and her glossy, collagen-infused lips look like a flapping hot dog bun as she talks to the patron who is not so discreetly checking out her ass cheeks, which spill from her barely there black shorts.

I suddenly feel overdressed.

Chloe bops to the music, thriving on the energetic vibe. When it's our turn to order, Chloe smirks. "What's your poison?"

Scanning the wall, I tap my chin, suddenly feeling daring.

"Dirty martini."

Chloe expresses her delight at my choice of drink by bouncing on the spot. Those killer pumps don't seem to hinder her bopping. "I'll have the same!" she yells, leaning over the counter so the bartender can hear her. Thankfully, the woman behind the bar is a little more dressed than her co-worker to her left.

As I scan the room for a table, a sudden blanket of uneasiness drapes over me. I physically shake my head to clear the fog because I have no idea what has come over me. It's hot in here, as it's packed to capacity, but this warmth comes from deep within.

Chloe passes me my drink. I lunge for it like an addict seeking out her next fix and throw it back in one gulp. She cocks an eyebrow and purses her lips. "Another, thanks!" she shouts at the bartender, waving off her change.

I steal the glass from her hand and knock back her martini too. "And two tequilas!"

Offering the empty glass, I pull an apologetic face. "Sorry. I have no idea why I just did that."

She giggles, looping her hand around my shoulder and drawing me in close. "It's okay. This place has that effect on people."

"No kidding," I mumble, the vodka going straight to my head and killing at least a dozen brain cells.

A shift crackles in the air, and I swipe at the back of my neck, which is dotted with perspiration. I can't shake this feeling of... momentous change of epic proportions. My stomach clenches into a tightened knot of dismay, but the undertone is stronger— it's desire.

What on god's green earth would cause me to burn up like I'm knocking on the gates of hell?

The music changes, the lights dim, and the alcohol goes straight to my head. I clutch the bar for support, afraid I'm about to face plant and not ever get back up. Chloe's concerned voice sounds in the background, but my attention is suddenly riveted on the doorway as I turn to stake it out over my shoulder.

"Animals" by Maroon 5 suddenly blares over the speakers, setting the stage for what's to come. I can't stand still, so I spin and crane my neck to peer over the bouncing heads of people busting a move on the dance floor, but they part like the Red Sea, because what or *who* just walked through the door is of biblical proportions.

The room begins spinning and the walls close in on me. I... can't...fucking...breathe.

The lyric of being eaten alive is my spirit animal because I'm certain a fire is about to consume me whole. The flames lick at my epicenter, and my heart explodes from the confines of my chest.

Every moment before this suddenly pales in comparison, because all I can focus on is the man who steals every breath I take and replaces it with nothing but constant craving. I don't even know what I'm thirsting after, because every part of me is desperate to flee, but I can't move.

Just how I remember, he turns every head in the room, his confidence almost suffocating, but his magnetic pull is intoxicating, and like addicts, we're all hooked.

Snug blue jeans sit low on his hips, the denim at both knees ripped. An ashy gray Harley Davidson t-shirt, which complements his black biker boots, showcases his upper body bulk, as it's tight and clings to him like a second skin. Tattoos run down the length of both taut arms, the colorful ink coming to life under the bright fluorescents. His shoulder width goes on for days, hinting that beneath that shirt lies a well-defined, muscular landmine.

Swallowing past the lump in my throat, I lift my gaze and sag against the bar because that face, *his* face…I'd almost forgotten it had the ability to render me speechless. Although it's changed slightly since I last saw it, covered in a dark, heavy scruff and matured with years of wisdom and experience, when I look into those eyes, those stormy blue eyes of promise and punishment, I know that beneath those layers is the man I love to hate…or hate to love…the line suddenly blurs.

His hair is shorter on the sides, the longer strands at the top flicked and styled into whatever way the dirty blond strands fall. He still carries that air of arrogance on his shoulders and stirs the longing which I thought long dead.

As if some rock star just walked through the door, everyone

mills around the entrance, waiting for their turn to talk to the hometown hero. He nods and smirks, that lopsided grin kicking me in the solar plexus and replaying a moving picture of every single time he smiled at me.

When he runs his long fingers through his mussed hair, another punch leaves me winded, and I recall the way those fingers felt on me...inside me.

Sweet baby Jesus...I need to leave...like now.

Sadly, he's standing in front of my salvation, so I turn around so quickly, I topple to the left. Thankfully, Chloe is there, and I lean against her, hoping my mini meltdown goes unnoticed. My body is a traitorous whore because memories of what he did to me and how he ruined my life float to the surface, and that is the only thing I should be remembering.

"Holland, are you all right?" Chloe backs up, probably terrified my crazy is contagious. I nod, too afraid to speak. Reaching for the tequila, I toss it back, not bothering with the garnishing. "Want to sit?"

Yes, I want to sit...on the moon because I can't stay in here with him...with London Sinclair...a second longer. Even thinking his name has me feeling like I've just committed the ultimate sin.

She doesn't wait for me to reply; instead, she loops her arm through mine and leads me through the crowd. I instantly sink low, wishing I could slide along the floor and slither out the door. How the fuck am I going to escape undetected?

The throngs of people don't help with my sudden claustrophobia, and I spread my arms out, needing space. I have no doubt Chloe thinks I've gone completely nuts, but this is my something like normal because the fact I'm not rocking in a corner is a miracle in itself.

We find a booth near the back of the room. I dive into it, sinking low. Chloe has two beers, and both are calling my name, but I remember my manners and graciously accept one.

"So tell me everything," she says, propping her foot underneath her knee, poised and ready for the juicy details.

The distraction might be nice, but I'm on high alert, peering around as if we're stranded on a capsized boat surrounded by hungry sharks. "There isn't much to tell. I graduated, went to Stanford, and found myself. During my journey, Lincoln and I crossed paths. We've been together for about five years." Or has it been six? I suddenly can't remember. "We live in New York. I'm an attorney, and Lincoln works on Wall Street." I know I'm talking a million miles a minute, but I'm afraid if I stop, I'll have to face the fact that I'm sitting in the same room as London.

"Wow, you guys have lived quite a life." We have? "I still live in Beverly Hills with my mom," she reveals, as if that pales in comparison to my life.

"Home is where the heart is, Chloe," I tenderly state. I'm not here to pass judgment. We've both had enough of that over the course of our lives.

Her face softens, and I can see her guard shift. We aren't in high school anymore, and I never want her to feel like she has to be anyone but herself.

"When did you guys get engaged?"

Raising the Budweiser to my lips, I take a quick swig before replying. "Not long ago. That's why we're back. Our families want the big traditional wedding." I can't keep the sarcasm from my voice.

She nods with a laugh. "My mom would be the same. I haven't met Mr. Right just yet, but when I do, I have no doubt the queen and her kinsman will be invited."

Chloe's humor takes my mind off the dilemma at hand, but when "Marry Me" by Bruno Mars comes on, Chloe shoots up, lunging for my arm. "I love this song! Come dance with me."

I shake my head hastily, as there is no way I'm moving from this spot—ever. This song choice is also adding to the nerves. She blows a raspberry and sashays off on her own, not bothered that she's dancing among strangers.

The moment she's sandwiched between two guys, I let out the breath I've been holding and liberate my lungs. Sadly, my heart doesn't have the same reprieve because it fucking aches. I pensively rub over it.

Feeling a little braver, I sit up taller and scan the room. I know he's in here. I can feel him. Every fiber of my body is pulsating, unable to keep up with the chaos which is rattling me to the very core. Everyone is in party mode, the drinks and conversations flowing freely. It's jam-packed, so I can't see him, but when the music fades and is replaced with The Killers "Mr. Brightside," nothing has been clearer.

Somehow, the sea of people parts, leaving behind a path which leads to sin. London is casually slouched back against the bar, both elbows behind him. He doesn't seem to care he's propped in the middle of swarms of patrons, taking up vital space, because all he seems to care about is me.

I bite the inside of my cheek and grip the leather beneath me because I'm seconds from sliding into a messy heap with no chance of recovering anytime soon. I haven't felt this way in so very long.

The lyrics drum in time with my heart because they ring true. It started with a kiss, but that kiss set the wheels in motion for an abysmal trainwreck, one which feels like it's picking up speed once again.

I want to break eye contact because that slow, cocky smirk tugging at his bow lips reveals he knows...he knows he still affects me in ways he shouldn't, but I can't look away. I appreciate the way his muscular, commanding presence is akin to a lion stalking its prey.

I'm pinned by that stormy gaze, but I deadpan him, as I'll be damned if I back down and be the lesser man. I won't allow him to make me feel like that ever again.

This could continue for days, because neither of us appears intent on breaking eye contact, but I refuse to look away. I'm not the seventeen-year-old little girl he once took advantage of.

I've dealt with bigger, badder bastards than him, and I would rather cut off my own arm than let him win—again.

I sit up, turning around completely so we're staring at one another face on. He makes no secret that he's appreciating the full frontal view, and a small part of me high fives my ego because I know I look good, but so does he.

He's completely rugged and wayward, but his badass look isn't staged—he is the epitome of what every bad boy strives to become when they grow up. He always has been. I lick my suddenly dry lips, and London follows the movement with a smirk.

The air is charged with an undeniable pull and so is every part of my body. The rational part of me is screaming to get up and go, and forget I ever met this man, but the part I've kept under lock and key for ten years demands vengeance and believes it's time to settle the score.

Throwing back the remainder of my beer, I slide across the booth and straighten out my skirt with no real hurry to my step. London never wavers from me, watching with interest as I stand, my chest rising and falling, the adrenaline punching a hole straight through me.

Taking a deep breath, I walk toward him, my pace measured, my head held high. He shifts to stand taller but still doesn't move an inch. He draws a glass to his lips, his Adam's apple bopping as the brown liquid slides down his throat. I keep stalking toward him because the hunter has just become the prey.

People somehow move when they see me coming, probably sensing World War Three is seconds from erupting and they don't want to be anywhere near me when it does. I gently push past a couple, who look up at me and then back at London. They instantly huddle off to the side, ready for the smackdown from hell.

The moment I'm a few steps away, his familiar fragrance of warm cinnamon and trouble whacks straight into me, cementing me to the spot. I have waited so very long for this moment. I've dreamed of it often. But our reunion would never be a happy one.

London Sinclair didn't just break my heart; he fucking set it on fire and threw the ashes to the wind. I loved him, and in return, he danced on my grave.

The music blaring around me and the throbbing memories animate me, and I take one step, then two, until we're inches apart. My heels give me some leverage, but he still towers over me. Looking up at him, I quash down the urge to caress his face to ensure he's real.

He's changed so much, yet he's still the same.

I examine every curve of his face, marveling at the vastness of his blue eyes. He allows me to visually molest him, standing coolly, not caring that we're in everyone's way.

I want to say so many things, but where do I start?

But London and I, we were never good with words. And

now is no exception.

Reaching for the glass which sits loosely in his fingers, I pay no attention to the absolute yearning I feel when my thumb brushes over his. Drawing the glass to my lips, I toss back the bitter contents, the burn welcomed because I need the pain to remind me that this man will only be able to offer me that.

He watches my every move, that fucking smile still tugging at his lips. I wonder just how many times he smiled when thinking about what he did. He won...well, I hope it was worth it.

With a slow, calculated speed, I lean forward, purposely pressing my body into his as I place the empty glass on the bar behind him. A small victory for me when he hisses low.

But I intend on finally taking back what's mine.

He opens his mouth, no doubt ready to say some smartass remark or rub salt in the still raw wounds, but I'm done. I'm done with him, and I'm done with this constant need to seek him out in a crowd.

This is goodbye for good.

Years of anger explode from me, and before I can question myself and the repercussions of my actions, I raise my hand and slap that smug smile from his face. The whack can be heard above the rock music, but the sting in my hand is worth it because it can never compare to the pain he's caused me.

His head snaps back as he cups his reddening cheek, but when he meets my eyes, nostrils flared, breaths heavy, he nods once.

We're even…

My hand trembles by my side and tears threaten to break through the floodgates soon, but with my dignity in tow, I turn and leave, and this time, it's for good.

10

"Oh, Sweetie, is your hand okay?" I don't even realize I'm cradling it until my mom asks me for the third time today.

We're on our way to Sienna's, Chloe's mom's bridal boutique, but it goes without saying that shopping is the furthest thing from my mind. My heart is still lodged in my throat after last night, and I doubt it'll dislodge anytime soon.

After I escaped Absinthe of the Heart, which now takes on a whole different meaning, I caught a cab back to my parents' and was secretly thankful Lincoln decided to stay with his friends. I went to bed, hoping I'd pass out, but I didn't. I stared up at the ceiling for hours, wondering what happens now.

I've finally given London a piece of my mind—so why do I feel so empty inside? Could it be because last night was the first time I've felt…alive…in so long? The irony of that statement is not lost on me.

Lincoln and I have never had a raging sex life, but I understand the basis of a good, solid relationship isn't the physical part but rather the emotional. He understands me and respects that I'm not interested in swinging from the rafters and calling him Big Daddy.

At first, I felt like he was resentful that London stole something from him which didn't belong to anyone but me, but then I realized I was just paranoid because not everyone felt how I did. In the beginning, sex between us was awkward, to say the least, because the only other person I could compare it to was someone I wished to forget.

Sex with Lincoln is… nice. I don't have the toe-curling big O's, but I learned quickly enough you can't have it all. We are in a stable, loving partnership, and I'll happily sacrifice the wild monkey sex and butterflies for what we have. I had a taste of that, and all it left me with was heartburn.

I remind myself of that fact when a flutter of butterflies takes flight even thinking London's name.

"I'm fine," I reply, looping my arm through Mom's. I need to forget about last night because I can finally put the matter to rest. "I haven't even thought about what kind of dress I want to wear." My mom squeezes my arm, letting out a small, excited squeak.

When we round the corner and are confronted with a swirly

pink neon sign, I know that this dilemma is soon to be put to rest, because this store is every bride's dream...on steroids.

The bell above the door chimes jovially as we enter. Looking around Sienna's, my cheeks puff out with my trapped breath. There is so much white—the floors, walls, the hundreds of dresses suspended from hangers around the room. A small red podium dead center with white leather couches arched around it. This is obviously where one is to parade the bridal catwalk for her friends.

"Oh, this is amazing," Mom exclaims, still clinging to my side.

"It's something," I mumble under my breath but lack her enthusiasm as I scan around the room and absorb how much... white and frilly lace is on display.

"Holland!" Chloe's vibrant voice snaps me from my stupor, and I turn to face her.

I totally bailed on her last night without an explanation. When I arrived back at my parents' house, I sent her a quick text, using the migraine from hell excuse. As far as excuses go, it was lamer than lame, as I'm certain she saw my altercation with London.

I literally shake my head, needing to expel him from my thoughts—especially when in here. "Hey, Chloe. This place is incredible."

Chloe looks gorgeous in a peacock-colored dress, the splash of green highlighted in the otherwise stark room. "Just wait until you see the new summer line of dresses my mom just got in."

Both my mom and Chloe appear as if they've just won the bridal lottery while I subtly scratch at the heat rash budding under my chin.

A striking lady splits apart a red velvet curtain at the back of the store, carrying three silky dresses draped over her forearm. With her chocolate-colored hair, tender light green eyes, and welcoming smile, there is no doubt this is Chloe's mom.

Her heart-shaped face lights up. "Holland, let me look at you. How you've grown." She rushes over and holds me at arm's length, tilting her head from side to side while examining me from head to toe.

I don't really remember her, seeing as I've catalogued my life in two boxes— before and after L.A. The before I've tried my hardest to forget.

"Thank you so much for giving me first pick of your new line. Chloe told me you've put something aside for me." Lowering my eyes, I see the elaborate dresses look like they're my size.

Shaking her head as if snapping from reminiscing about the good ol' days, she smiles. "Yes, these are for you." She raises her forearm, the crystal beads on the first dress catching the sunlight streaming in from the front windows.

My mom steps forward, giving Sienna a small hug. "Hello, Sienna. I'm Delores, Holland's mom. We met once when the girls were in school together." I can tell by the waver in Mom's voice she's embarrassed she didn't attend more school functions or make more of an effort with Chloe's mom. But she was busy working fourteen-hour shifts to put food on the table and to keep me in school.

Sienna waves her off, brushing away her concerns. "Yes, I remember. You were the only parent I could stand. And your daughter wasn't a spoiled little brat."

My mother tugs at her pearl earring, hiding behind a tilted smile. "I feel the same way." And just like that, we all seem to bond, a band of misfits who never fit in.

"Come, sit, I can't wait to show you these dresses." Sienna's heels tap along the polished floors, leading the way to the bridal arena.

I gulp.

Mom and Chloe happily bounce behind her, while I lag behind, running a hand down my face, my cheeks inflated with my strangled breaths. I suddenly feel like I'm walking a death march, and the wedding dress Siena unveils is my executioner.

She unzips the clear carry bag, the ivory-colored dress catching every ray of light in the room. The neckline swoops into a sweetheart style, Swarovski crystal beads embedded into the plush silk. As she holds it up high, excited by its grand reveal, I steady my breathing.

"Oh, it's beautiful," Mom says, a hand cupped to her mouth. Chloe nods in harmony, clapping. Everyone seems excited, whispering at the dress's beauty, while I'm moments away from running out the door. All three turn my way, realizing I haven't said a word.

I suddenly feel like I've swallowed lead.

"You hate it?" Sienna says, the disappointment clear in her tone.

My mom tilts her head to the side, examining me closely. If she looks close enough, I know she'll uncover my inner turmoil—a turmoil which should not be there.

Clearing the lump from my throat, I shake my head firmly. "I love it, Sienna. I love them all, I'm just…overwhelmed, that's all." Making grabby hands, I quash down my nerves and smile. "I'll get over that soon enough, because my god, is that Vera Wang's new summer line?"

Sienna beams, impressed I know my fashion. "Good eye. It most certainly is. You must try it on." As she offers it to me, I focus on nothing but the task at hand, because nothing else matters. I'm marrying the man of my dreams in this Vera Wang dress, and nothing, not even the second coming of Christ, will stand in my way.

Happily reaching for it, I ignore how it feels like I'm carrying the Grand Canyon on my shoulders and march toward the fitting rooms, a woman on a mission. I yank the curtain closed, shakily hanging the dress from a gold hook. The walls are mirrored, which is ideal for any blushing bride, but to me, it only emphasizes my mini breakdown tenfold. I literally have nowhere to hide because behind every turn is a mirror reflecting my freak-out.

"Do you want me to help you get into the dress?" Sienna offers from just outside the curtain.

"No, no, it's okay. Thank you. I won't be a minute." I stare at my reflection, telling myself to woman the fuck up and stop being such a drama queen.

With that as my driving force, I kick off my heels and slip out of my dress. Standing in front of this many mirrors is daunting, to say the least. I run a hand over my slender hip and across to my concaved stomach. I've lost about two pounds since this ordeal started. Looking at my reflection, I cock my head to the side, suddenly not recognizing the woman staring back at me.

To the outside world, I appear like I've got my shit together, and on most days, I do. But coming back here has rattled my cage, and no matter how hard I pretend that I'm okay, things only seem to be getting worse.

Exhaling in frustration, I reach for the dress, hoping once I step into it, I'll return to the old me. A week ago, everything was clear cut, and I knew where I was headed. But one minute— sixty fucking seconds—was enough to undo the past ten years.

Damn him, but most importantly, damn me for still giving a shit.

As I shimmy the dress up my legs, I suck in a deep breath because the mermaid-inspired gown squeezes me tight. Each tug suddenly feels like the flames of hell licking at my heated flesh. I hold the bodice to my chest as I need help fastening the ten billion buttons on the back, but the thought of even doing up one measly button has my already heightened skin breaking out into a rash.

I scratch at my chin and then work my way down to the column on my neck. Each stroke seems to set off another wave, and I suddenly feel like I've rolled in a vat of poison ivy. Parts of my body I didn't even know were capable of being itchy begin to prickle, and before long, I'm scrubbing my body with one hand.

A hotness burns up from the balls of my feet to the crest of my head, and I'm certain I'm running a fever. My vision blurs, and to stop myself from face planting, I reach out to lean against the wall.

What is the matter with me?

"I'm coming in," sings Chloe.

"Chloe…" My voice is barely audible, so I don't blame her when she talks over me and happily goes to work on tightening the confines of my doom.

"This dress was made for you!" she exclaims, her deft fingers working quickly to button me up. Each tie sends me closer and closer to an edge I didn't even know was there. "You look so beautiful. This color is absolutely stunning, and the style—wow. It's sexy, but in a church-approved kind of way." She giggles while I'm seconds away from passing out.

"I think you could get away with wearing smaller heels. You don't want sore feet on your big day." She pulls at the material at my waist, a pained gasp escaping me as I try desperately to breathe. "Anything you want altered, let my mom know. I do think everything fits perfectly, though. I mean, jeepers, your boobs look ah-mazing. Lincoln won't know what hit him."

At once, Chloe's chipper words all morph into one giant hum and the walls begin to close in on me. I need to focus on one thing because so many thoughts are using my brain as a roller coaster, and I'm afraid if I don't rein it in, I'm going to faint.

"Almost done," she affirms, the pinching of my skin confirming her words.

The gentlest sounds suddenly feel like a sledgehammer amped up to a billion watts, and I cover my ears, squeezing my eyes shut. I vaguely make out Chloe asking if I'm okay, but I'm not.

"Take it off," I whimper, hoping I said the words aloud and not in my head. When there is silence, I plead, "Please, take it off."

"Holland?"

The itch which consumes my body rapidly turns into an inferno, and I claw at the dress, it seeming to be the cause of the unexpected firestorm.

"What's the matter?"

With my eyes still sealed shut, I feel my flesh blistering and burning, the dress melting onto my skin, forever uniting us as one. I violently scratch at the neckline, attempting to rip it from my body, but the buttons are done up tight.

"Get it off!" I shriek, shaking my head from side to side, a crazed lunatic as I rub at my chest, which is red hot and raw. My heart thrashes wildly within, the blood whooshing through my veins. It takes every ounce of self-control not to scream.

"Oh, my god! It's okay. Calm down, Holland. I'll take it off. Just calm down." I can sense the urgency of her words and actions as she works with haste to help me undress, but it's not fast enough. With every second I'm in this garment, the itchier, hotter, and more anxious I become.

I attempt to breathe as I learned in yoga. I go to my happy place. But nothing helps because each attempt is ruined by a blueness which drags me under and ruins me, just how it did all those years ago.

"I'm almost done." Each button which flicks open is like the unwinding of the manacle siphoning off my air supply, but when Chloe pauses and says, "Oh no, shit, you're stuck," I can't take it a second longer. With adrenaline coursing through my veins and running on nothing but fight and flight, I inherit the strength of Hercules and tear the dress from my body. Beads bounce off the mirrors and scatter onto the carpeted floor.

The moment I'm stripped bare I can finally breathe again.

Pressing a hand to my racing heart, I calm my breathing and beg the world to stop spinning. It does.

Now that it's not tipped on its axis and I can think clearly once again, I slowly peel open my eyes, gasping when I see the mess I've made. The once beautiful dress now sits in a saddened heap by my feet, the floor littered with confetti beads. A gaping rip down the side allowed me to escape, but my getaway came with a price.

I don't even know what to say, so I decide not to say anything at all. With whatever small shred of dignity I have left, I bend and reach for my dress. The tremble of my fingers betrays my overwrought state. "I'll pay for the dress." I can't meet Chloe's eyes, as I'm afraid of what I'll see reflected in the depths.

"Don't worry about that. What happened?" There is no anger, only concern. Her kindness only makes me feel worse.

Once I'm dressed, I feel a touch better, but nothing can excuse the fact I had a very public meltdown in a situation most would be pegging down to one of the best days of their lives. Yes, I will always remember today, just not the way most brides-to-be would.

I don't have the balls to tell her. I'm ashamed I have let someone who doesn't deserve a second thought get the better of me once again.

"It's London, isn't it?" The moment she says his name, it makes all this real. If someone else says it, it'll mean that I'm not the only one who sees it. "I saw you guys last night. Holy shit, Holland, the chemistry between you two…it was explosive."

Jerking my head upward, I finally meet her eyes. "Explosive?

Yeah, like an atomic bomb mess."

But she shakes her head firmly. "No, more like a hot kinda mess."

Cradling my face in my palms, I groan. "I hate him, and he hates me." I wish saying those words aloud were believable, but they only confirm the truth.

"I'm pretty sure you two have always had a more love-hate relationship. And I use the term hate loosely. I can't believe after all these years you guys are still so into one another."

Her comment has me almost giving myself whiplash as I shake my head from side to side. "I'm not into him. I hate him. I always have." Chloe arches a disbelieving brow, which only has me defending my claims further. "I love Lincoln. I'm *ma-marrying* Lincoln." The word catches in my throat, and I thump my chest to dislodge it.

The more I talk, however, the less Chloe seems to believe me. She folds her arms over her chest and smirks. "Who are you trying to convince? Me? Or yourself?"

My mouth parts, amped and ready for a comeback, but I don't have one. I could argue with her until I'm blue in the face, but the twisted sad heap at my feet says enough.

"I have no doubt you love Lincoln, but something's different about you."

Peering down, I wonder if she's seeing the crazy radiating from me as well. "Different?"

She nods. "Yes, you look…alive."

And there's that word again. Ironically, because that's the last word I should ever associate with London Sinclair.

"I need to go. I can't be in here. Can you distract my mom? I just need…a minute to think."

She nods, her eyes twinkling at the prospect of being my evil wingman. "There's a back door. I'll take care of it. Make a run for it when the coast is clear."

I nod, slowly feeling better at the likelihood of getting out of here and away from my greatest fears. "Thank you, Chloe. I owe you."

But she surprises me when she shakes her head. "No, you don't. You owe this to yourself. Work out if it's cold feet or maybe it's something else." There's no need for her to elaborate on the "something else." She sympathetically rubs my forearm, then slips out of the changing room.

It may be in vain, but I pick up the dress and try my best to hang it from the hook. It's a sad mess, and there is no way it's salvageable. I'll just add it to the long list of things London has broken.

"Is everything all right in there? I heard yelling." Pinching the bridge of my nose, I wonder when this shitstorm will end.

"Yes, fine. Your daughter is just being a bridezilla and wants some jewelry and shoes before she makes her grand reveal."

"Oh, of course. That's my fault," Sienna says, clearly flustered she forgot this small detail. "Let me see how the dress fits so I know what kind of necklace would work."

"No!" Chloe's shrill voice can be heard two blocks over, and I'm certain I'm done for. But she bounces back like a pro. "Mom, didn't you hear what I just said? You can't see her until everything is perfect. Show us where everything is and then we can choose a few different options for her. I'm sure Ms. Brooks would love to choose a few things, right?"

Silence.

My mom wasn't born yesterday. She knows something is fishy, but she entertains Chloe anyway, and for that, I love her. "Sure. Sounds wonderful. Come, Sienna, show us what you think will work."

Exhaling steadily, I part the curtain an inch so I'm able to see just what is going on. Chloe is manning the fort, standing behind my mom and hers, pushing them toward the front of the store. She turns over her shoulder and waves her hand frantically, which is my cue to get the hell out of here.

With heels in hand, I tiptoe quieter than a mouse, my eyes never wavering from my mom. Just when I think I'm home free, Sienna suddenly stops and goes to turn. "I'm so silly. I have a beautiful Mikimoto necklace and bracelet which I think will go wonderfully with that dress. It's just in the back. Let me grab it."

I pause like a deer in headlights as I literally have nowhere to hide. This is it—time to confess to my mom that her only daughter is losing her mind.

"No, stop!" Chloe tackles her mom and locks her arms around her back, hugging her in an awkward back to front embrace. Sienna freezes and shakes her head at her daughter's insanity. "Have I told you how much I love you?" Chloe is an evil genius, and she buys me the time I need to disappear behind the back curtain and out the door. Once the breeze hits my heated cheeks, I instantly feel better.

Placing my palms on my knees, I bend at the waist and take three steadying breaths. The air may be a little on the polluted side, but it feels good to breathe.

I have no idea what the hell just happened. Yes, I've been on edge, but that was something else. My thoughts have me remembering Chloe's comment. Standing upright, I know I need to bail because Chloe can only evade our moms for so long.

Slipping into my heels, I amble down the alleyway as quickly as I can and make a right, headed where exactly, I don't know. The sidewalk is busy, bustling with locals and tourists alike. Most are window shopping as the goods on display without price tags are a sure sign that everything in this neighborhood is overpriced.

I continue walking, my head filled with a million and one thoughts.

After last night, I hoped I could put this insanity to rest, that having the final say would somehow miraculously erase this festering within. But it hasn't. It was petty and naïve to think that it would. The problem is, I don't know what to do.

I love Lincoln, I truly do, but he's not the first person I

thought of when I went to sleep last night or when I awoke this morning. Everything is so messed up.

I continue walking with no real direction, but the lack of purpose is a nice change. We never should have come back here. LA has never brought me anything but pain.

In New York, I was on the go 24/7. I didn't have time to worry about the ghosts of my past. A small, bothersome voice whispers that maybe the reason for my busy lifestyle was to escape the truth I was too afraid to face. Groaning, I slip on my sunglasses, wishing I could view the world with a rose-tinted filter.

As I notice fellow pedestrians' style and looks change, I know I've ventured down here without a second thought. I'm intrinsically drawn here, which just adds to the shit pile. Sunset Boulevard is filled with trendy, jaded people, too strung out on sex and drugs and rock and roll to spare a second look at someone like me.

My heart begins an intermittent beat the closer I get, but I persevere. Not many bars are open at this time of the day, so a false sense of security wraps around me when I stop and peer upward at the non-blinking sign.

Absinthe of the Heart.

I can't help but think that whoever owns this bar has probably experienced the highs and lows that come with loving with all your heart. The only cure for a broken one seems to be written in big letters above me.

My phone chimes, a welcome distraction from this clusterfuck of a day. My enormous Coach handbag looked amazing in the store with its separate compartments and eight different pockets, but now it only adds to the confusion. I hunt through each pocket, cursing the one before it because I have no idea where my phone is.

With a huff, I yank open both handles and dig around the middle compartment. When I see the screen light up with Lincoln's name, I sigh in relief. With one handle hanging limply from my hand, I reach for it, but never get to take the call.

When I realize what has happened, it's too late, because the whoosh of air which rustles past me matches the air which gets snatched violently from my lungs when I fall onto my ass. It takes me a second, but when I brush the hair from my brow, I see that someone has just rudely bumped into me, but if that isn't enough, he's taken off with my bag.

It wasn't an accident—that asshole just stole my handbag.

Such a rookie mistake, but I can scold myself later, because now I have to put my self-defense classes to good use. Ignoring the shooting pain radiating down my leg, I jump up and give chase, because I sure as hell won't get mugged in LA. I've survived the mean streets of New York, so this is just insulting.

Methodical spin classes have shaped my calves and given me the stamina I need to hunt down this bastard and make him pay. When he turns down an alleyway parallel to the bar, I push my muscles harder as I will not let him slip away. That theory is all good and well, but when I round the corner, intent on payback of biblical proportions, I don't take into consideration that running into this blind is probably not the smartest thing to do. Waiting on the other side are two other men, one of which has no problem beating up on girls.

The wind gets knocked from my sails the second time today as this chump has watched far too much UFC and clotheslines me with his meaty forearm. I don't stand a chance and fall to the ground like a sack of potatoes. To add insult, I twist my ankle, thanks to my Jimmy Choos. I attempt to crawl forward, but I'm not moving an inch. The three men don't look back as they jump into a black SUV and race off into the sunset.

"Come back here, you assholes!" I scream, pounding on the cement, which only adds to the pain engulfing me from head to toe. The taillights grow smaller and smaller, announcing my defeat.

Every inch of my body throbs, but I drag myself to the side and lean up against the wall to catch my breath. I can't believe this. I should be horrified, but I'm pissed off—pissed off that I let my guard down so easily. It appears that's the common theme for this place.

Groaning, I slump my head back against the bricks and close my eyes. I have no idea what to do, and I can't move. I don't have my wallet or phone, so it looks like I have to wait it out until a good Samaritan walks by.

It's early, and I'm not exactly sitting in prime real estate, either. Speaking of which. Peering down, I cringe when I see I'm sitting in an unidentifiable liquid which smells like piss and sauerkraut.

"Fucking great," I mumble to myself but screech and attempt to move to the side when an animal which could be a cat or a gigantic rat slinks by, smelling my toes.

Lunging forward, I scramble for my discarded shoe, which sits just beyond reach, taunting me. I tongue the corner of my mouth in concentration, bobbing forward, hoping that by some miracle I can reach my heel and use it as a weapon until someone can save my sorry ass. Five minutes later, I'm still only wearing one shoe.

The rat-cross-cat isn't deterred by my curses and rummages through the trash cans beside me.

This has got to be the worst day of my life. Nothing worse can possibly happen, says me, who wishes she kept her mouth shut.

Every girl wants to hear a door opening when she's sitting in filth, unarmed, and completely at this mutant creature's mercy. But when I look to the left, I raise my eyes to the heavens and curse whatever god I can.

My heart wishes it was drowning in absinthe because it's the only way I can deal with the next thirty seconds. His motorcycle boots stop mid step, and I can feel his gaze combing over every inch of my flesh. How I'm wishing I'd rendered myself unconscious.

When his steps get closer and closer, I attempt to test the theory; out of sight, out of mind. I focus on anything other than that warm cinnamon smell, and that deep husky voice which should be illegal in every country in the world.

"Holland? What the fuck are you doing?"

I ask myself that daily, and so far, I have no idea what.

11

"What do you think I'm doing? I'm not here for Taco Tuesday." My words may seem big and brave, but inside, I'm trembling like a leaf. London is here, in the flesh, in broad daylight, and I'm shoeless, covered in brown goo.

He breathes slowly and steadily through his nose and exhales in a long-winded spiel. Good to see I still have the ability to get under his skin.

Kudos to me, but when I move, my victory is short-lived. "Ow!" I cradle my ankle, cringing in unbearable pain.

London finally clues onto my situation and drops the two garbage bags he's holding. He rushes to my aid and crouches by my feet. "What happened?"

His concern for my well-being throws me for a loop because

in the past, he'd usually be the cause of my pain. But pulling back my shoulders, I steady my pulse and look him dead in the eye. I instantly get lost in those depths, and a charge of a gazillion volts of electricity kickstarts my heart.

Last night, I didn't really have a chance to soak him up, but now, under the bright sun, it's all I can do. His dirty blond hair is kicked high to the heavens, the longer strands styled into a faux hawk; his blue eyes appear clearer, more intense if that is even possible, but the dark beard he has may be the reason the contrast is so apparent.

His lips are still sinful, constantly marred with that cocky, lopsided grin. However, a small scar traced above the left side of his upper lip is a new addition, making him appear all the more depraved.

He's always been big, but now it seems like he's grown into that vastness. He's muscled, taut in all the right places, and his impressive arms are showcased in the tight white t-shirt he's wearing. Once I'm able to swallow past the lump in my throat, I admire the colorful artwork inked on both arms. The swirls of color burst from his bronzed skin, and among the beautiful chaos, I can make out the elegant script of one single word, which sits dead center on his right forearm.

Defy.

An archway of stars surrounds the simple yet powerful command, leaving me with more questions than answers, but that's nothing new. Neither is the fact I'm burning up inside.

As if the heavens are reminding me of where I am, the sunlight catches my five-carat diamond, blinding me into submission. "Can you just call me a cab?"

I need to get the hell away from here because his signature fragrance brings back so many memories, memories which feel like they were only made yesterday.

I should have known he'd completely ignore me, however, and do the total opposite. He cups my ankle and squeezes gently. I try not to flinch. "It's not broken," he reveals, running his thumb over the sensitive flesh. My skin instantly breaks out into tiny goose bumps, and I curse every single one.

"I didn't realize you were a doctor," I snap, jarring out of his grip and shifting away from him. "Call me a taxi and I'll do both of us a favor." Our eyes lock, neither of us backing down.

He's the one to finally cave. "You didn't say the magic word," he mocks, standing to full height, brushing down his ripped jeans coolly.

"Fuck and you?" I quip, rolling my eyes. I've always felt dwarfed in his presence, but now, I feel beyond minuscule, especially since he has no intention of fulfilling my request.

When he goes to turn, unappreciative of my sarcasm, a sheet of panic drapes over me for two reasons. The first is, if he leaves, I'll be at the mercy of the elements, and I'm pretty certain I just saw a family of rat's scurry by, and the second, which overshadows any need before it, is I don't want him to go.

"No, wait!" I demand a little louder than intended. I exhale when he pauses, but his back is still turned. "You can't leave me out here."

He raises his broad shoulders, slipping his hands into his pockets. "I'm not your butler. Call a cab yourself. Last I checked, your ankle was sprained. The rest of your body works just fine, especially your mouth."

"I would, but seeing as I was just mugged, that might be a little difficult," I bite back, angered that I'm once again allowing him to get under my skin.

My words are like fire beneath him because he turns so quickly, I recoil, stunned by the savage look he bestows upon me. "*What*? Why didn't you say anything?"

"Me sitting in an alleyway, shoeless, was kind of a dead giveaway." He shakes his head, jaw clenched. Good to see some things don't change.

His cheeks puff out as he blows out an exasperated breath, but that's where my victory ends because before I know what's going on, he charges over, bends down, and scoops me up into arms. "Put me down!" I exclaim, attempting to kick and scream, but he chuckles, my request appearing to humor him. "You barbarian!"

In response, he cradles me closer with an arm wrapped under my knees while the other is fastened tightly around my shoulders. My head is spinning because my face is inches from his, and his warm breath sends a chill straight through me, but I quash it down, as it has no business being here.

He pays no attention to my demands as he carries me like a helpless baby down the alley and shoulders open the back door he came from. I have no choice but to surrender.

He ventures down a long hallway with faded band and gimmicky stickers plastered all over the black walls. There is no doubting he knows his way around, which has me wondering why?

"Did you break in here?" I question, ignoring the way his heart beats soundly against me. He scoffs but doesn't answer my question. He instead boosts me up higher, which has me yelping as I'm afraid he'll drop me on my ass.

We pass the restrooms before he takes a left and comes to an archway, opening up to a place which is all too familiar because I was here…last night.

"Do you work here?" I ask, snapping my head from left to right, taking in my surroundings to ensure I'm not seeing things. The all too familiar red leather couches and well-stocked, lengthy bar points to the fact I'm not.

London has gone silent on me, which I would usually celebrate, but if he doesn't work here and has broken in, then I need to get out of here now. "I can't be in here if we're trespassing. I'll lose my job."

"Oh, that's right, you're some hotshot lawyer, living it up in the Big Apple now, aren't you? Shouldn't surprise me that you get paid to argue with everyone and bust people's balls on a daily basis."

My mouth falls open, not because I'm insulted, but because I'm utterly speechless. I don't have time to question how he knows what I do to earn a buck because my ass is slammed onto the bar. He smirks when I glare at him something wicked.

Before I get a chance to scold him, he presses his chest to mine and slowly reaches behind me. We're caught in a deadlock. I'm barely breathing while he licks his bowed upper lip, unaffected. I shuffle backward, uncaring that I'll probably fall off the edge because that alternative is far better than burying my nose into the length of his neck. He smells so good. I just want to take a bite.

But up goes my guard as I refuse to succumb to this insanity a second longer. "This is a new low, even for you. Manhandling a defenseless, injured woman."

He has the gall to laugh. "You? Defenseless? That is one word I would never associate with you, Princess." When that momentous nickname slips past his lips, we both freeze, him gingerly meeting my eyes.

A thousand emotions are reflected deep within those shadowy depths, transporting us both back to being seventeen. And just like that, my walls crumble. He clears his throat while I avert my eyes, focusing on a lone beer bottle cap on the floor.

There are bottles clinking and some sort of rustling happening behind me, but I don't dare turn around to see what the commotion is. When he finally pulls away, I take a breath, but it's in vain because he drops to his knees before me.

I have no idea what he's doing until he lifts my injured ankle and presses a dishcloth filled with ice to the swollen flesh. The relief is instant, so I don't fight it. I watch as he tends to me, on his knees, as it's a sight I never thought I'd see. I envisioned London on his knees, begging for forgiveness more times than I care to admit, but this is different.

Something is selfless, almost repentant about his actions, and I can't take pleasure in seeing him this way. I may be a bitch, but I'm not a fucking bitch.

"Here." He breaks the silence when he offers me his cell from his back pocket. My brain short-circuits. Not only is he tending to my wounds, but he's now giving me a lifeline to get the hell out of here. But now that it's within reach, I don't want it as desperately as I thought I did.

Regardless, I accept the offering. The screen lights up with a picture of an adorable black Labrador. I don't know why, but it throws me.

This is a part of London's life, and I begin to wonder what else he holds close to his heart.

Over the past ten years, I exorcised London from every crevice of my mind and body, never allowing myself to slip back into the past. But being here now, I can't help but be curious, especially because he looks different...he looks happy.

Is that happiness due to the bouncing Lab on his phone? Or could it be he has someone special back home? A girlfriend? Maybe a wife? I don't realize I'm curling my fingers into claws until the screen lights up once again under the force.

Shaking my head, I unlock his cell, ready to call Lincoln, but stop mid dial. What am I supposed to tell him? There is no acceptable explanation for my actions today. If Lincoln knew what I did, I'm sure he wouldn't be in such a hurry to come to my rescue.

"So you didn't answer my question," I say, placing the phone beside me on the bar.

London peers up, glancing at the unused cell, but returns his attention to my sprain. "Which one?"

"Do you work here?" I repeat, a glutton for punishment it appears.

He moves the makeshift ice pack to the other side of my ankle before replying. "You could say that."

I think he's going to elaborate, but of course, I'm left waiting. "What sort of answer is that?"

"An honest one." Tact has never been my strong suit, but even I surprise myself when I scoff with sheer contempt. He pauses, while I regret nothing.

I'm certain a fight is about to erupt but am surprised when he ignores my insolence. "This is my bar. I own it," he adds when I cock my head to the side in disbelief.

I have no idea why his admission shocks me. It could be due to the fact I never really gave much thought to the adult London Sinclair, the one nursing me back to health, even though I'm insulting him every chance I get. All I focused on was how the seventeen-year-old Sin broke my heart and forever changed me. Maybe I should move on? Get over it and accept it as character building.

But when I look into those blue eyes, I know I'll never forget. I'll never be able to get over it because the betrayal is just as raw as it was ten years ago.

Sniffing back my tears, I reach for the cell. "I have to go."

London doesn't hide his surprise, but he nods casually, before standing. He was never one for small talk, and I'm glad that hasn't changed.

Lincoln answers on the third ring. "Hello?"

I hate calling him on this number, but I have no intention of telling him just whose cell this is. "Hey, it's me. Can you come pick me up?"

"Holland? What happened to your phone?"

I can feel London's eyes dissecting my every move, watching for my nerves to betray me. But they don't. "I'll explain when you come get me." I rattle off an address about two blocks from here. London tongues his cheek, shaking his head with an incredulous smirk. I don't wait for Lincoln to reply.

London rounds the bar, his fist clenched tight around the dishcloth in his left hand. Turning slightly, I flinch when he pitches the soaked rag into the sink behind him. "And you think I'm dishonest," he has the gall to say, referring to when I questioned his honor.

But me evading my fiancé is the far lesser evil than what

London did. I'm done playing nice.

Even though my ankle is still throbbing, I jump down from the bar, masking my pain as I hobble toward the door.

"So that's it?" His words stop me dead in my tracks.

Closing my eyes for the briefest of moments, I steady my galloping heart. "What were you expecting? For us to grab a beer? Catch up on old times?" My comment is nothing short of sarcastic, but I have no idea what he thought would happen.

"Run away then...just like you always do."

Spinning so quickly I almost fall flat on my ass, I rush forward, running on nothing but pure adrenaline. "How dare you." His back is still turned, but the curve of his rising shoulders alerts me to the fact he's heard me loud and clear.

I limp around the bar, latching onto his bicep, demanding he look at me. It's akin to turning a boulder, but he finally budges when I make clear I'm not letting go. He resembles an angry bull—nostrils flared and wide-eyed—and I'm pretty certain I'm the red flag because he charges forward, pinning me to the far wall.

Our heavy, anger-soaked breaths mingle as one, and before long, I'm not sure where mine ends and his starts. He's about a foot taller, but I stand my ground, refusing to back down. "I'm not the one who ran away...you did. I may have left, but I never ran away." My entire body is trembling, years of anger bubbling close to explosion. "Well, I hope it was worth it."

"It was," he bites back, evading my personal space with zero qualms.

I push him backward, unable to have him this close. "Well, it's good to see my memory hasn't failed me."

He arches a brow, confused by my statement. I clear up any confusion a second later. "I was right all along. You *are* a mistake." He hisses, pulling backward as if burned.

"Say that, and you can't take it back."

We're suddenly transported to that fateful night under the stars. If only I knew then what I know now, I would have told the teenage me to run—run far away and not look back. I can't undo the past, but I can dictate my future. "I should thank you because if it wasn't for you, I'd be stuck in this hellhole in a dead-end job I hate. Maybe I'd be your competition on the Boulevard, manager of some shitty bar too."

My comment hits him where it hurts.

"But your uncanny ability to be an astronomical asshole forced me to fend for myself and grow the fuck up. I made something of myself. Little Holland Brooks-Ferris is not so little and defenseless anymore. So thank you for making me a better person."

He applauds me, patronizing me further. "I never once thought you were defenseless. You were the bravest person I knew." I recoil, offended he refers to my bravery in the past tense. He reveals why a moment later.

Stepping forward, I'm caged in a London prison, but I don't move a muscle. "But now—" the air whooshes from my lungs when he presses his chest to mine "—that rock on your finger just confirms that yes, you grew up, but who did you grow into? The girl I once knew wouldn't be caught dead with that weight around her neck. She was spirited, wild, and she was free. But you come here, thinking you're different than the girls you grew to hate, but Holland…" He gently cups my throat, arching my neck backward. "You're exactly like them. Maybe even worse," he mock whispers, tightening his grip.

I swallow against his palm, his aggression exciting and pissing me off in the same breath.

"These fancy clothes hide the real you, but I see beneath the layers, Princess…I always have."

"Let me go," I whimper, bowing farther backward when he cups my jaw in one hand.

"You can leave at any time. No one is stopping you. But you always seem to end up on my doorstep, don't you?" Tears sting my eyes, but I blink them back.

Is he confirming what I always thought to be true? Did he see me that night I turned up at his house, desperate for him to tell me it'll be okay?

"Never again," I vow, shaking my head once. "You may have taken the one thing I can never get back, but you live and learn, and I've learned that you, London Sinclair, are my past." Holding up my hand, I flash my ring with pride. "And Lincoln is my future."

It's like an atomic bomb implodes between us, and he

strokes my neck deliriously slow. It's a fine line between pleasure and pain, but I snap my head to the right, breaking his hold.

"You're marrying *that* asshole?" He inhales sharply, his eyes narrowing into slits. "You do realize his surname is O'*Toole*, right? But I suppose it's fitting." His childish jab does a poor job of concealing his anger.

"Looks like the better man won," I counter with a shrug, challenging him when I purse my lips.

He takes the bait. "It was never a competition, Princess," he snarls, jaw clenched. "Good luck to you. You'll need it." His dig is a silent dismissal, but neither of us moves an inch.

The air is crackling with embers of raw electricity, ready to electrocute us both, but leaving now feels like I'm being cheated somehow. This is the showdown I've been craving for years, but why do I feel so empty inside?

Did I want him to fight me? Tell me that marrying Lincoln is a mistake? Such a notion is beyond absurd, but why are my feet still glued to the floor?

"I don't need it," I refute, my wavering voice contradicting my claim.

"You don't know what you need." His lightning quick response catches me off guard, but I bounce back, done with this conversation.

A hair's breadth away, I declare, "That may have been true once upon a time, but not anymore. I have everything I want… everything I need. In three weeks, I will be out of here and back to my perfect life in New York with my perfect husband. Where will you be? Stuck here, running this shithole and hosing down the hallways after happy hour ends. Good to see you've made something of yourself. Your parents must be so proud."

This is the moment I should break out into a victory dance and celebrate the fact that I've managed to get under London's skin, but I don't. I've never felt more ashamed of myself than I do right now.

I'm waiting for a smartass response, a jab to completely undermine mine, but all I'm greeted with is silence...and the grinding of London's jaw. "You think just because you come here in expensive clothes, bragging about your perfect life that you're somehow better than I am? Happier than I am?" He shakes his head, laughing with malevolence. "You know nothing, Princess. Go back to where you belong...because you sure as hell don't belong here anymore."

I deserve everything he just said because he's right. What is the matter with me? I used to hate the girls who thought their shit didn't stink, but I'm no better than them. I'm worse.

This place isn't a shithole, and the name has now left me even more curious because I know who the owner is.

Just as I'm about to apologize for being an utter bitch, a sultry voice sounds to the left. "Hey, boss, everything all right?"

Out comes the claws when I see the busty barmaid from last night. She's in short shorts, the pockets hanging from the frayed edges which are cut quite high. A pair of well-loved cowboy boots sit prettily on her small feet, offsetting the plaid shirt she's wearing, tied at the waist, Daisy Duke style. Her long hair sits in a high ponytail, showcasing her plump lips and striking green eyes.

An immediate sense of possession fills the small space between us, and I have no doubt if she could mark her territory, she'd be cocking her leg the moment she entered the room.

"Everything is peachy, darlin'."

"She lost?" she asks, not even having the common decency to look at me.

London folds his arms across his broad chest. "She was just leaving." I leave half crescent moons in my palms as it takes every ounce of willpower not to slap the insolence from her plastic primped face.

"I know the way out." I push past him, squashing down my offense because it has no right being there.

"Don't let the door hit you on the way out."

Her voice is like nails clawing down a blackboard. Without missing a beat, I counter, "I'm pretty sure Donald Duck wants his lips back, so how about you do everyone a favor and shut the hell up?"

Once upon a time, London would have appreciated my spunk, but not now, as I'm quite certain I've just insulted his blow-up doll. I hobble out the door, shoeless, but with my head held high.

As I limp down the street, ignoring the blatant stares of

passersby, I attempt to decipher what exactly I'm feeling. Today was the perfect opportunity to ask London what happened all those years ago, but instead, I led with my pigheadedness and am no closer to getting over this once and for all.

The look on his face, his words, everything will haunt me for the rest of my life. No matter how together I thought my life was, London Sinclair has always had the ability to make me feel like I'm sixteen-years-old.

A horn tooting snaps me from my misery, but when I see Lincoln's face near smooshed to the windshield, I slip into a deeper despair. I should stop walking, but I don't. What am I supposed to say?

"Hey, Holland, it's me." Our rented BMW crawls along the sidewalk, matching my idling pace. "Babe?"

Raising my eyes to the heavens, I ask the universe for strength and finally come to a stop. Turning over my shoulder, my heart crumbles when I see Lincoln half leaning over the passenger seat, looking out the window, concerned. His eyes dart back and forth between me and the traffic. "Get in," he says, confused why I wouldn't do so on my own accord.

I'm sick of the smog and the ache in my chest, so I comply.

The moment I settle into the seat, I instantly feel like I'm going to cry, but I don't. "Thanks for picking me up."

He waits for me to elaborate. When I lean my head back against the headrest and close my eyes, he realizes that's all I wish to say for now.

"Where are your shoes?" It seems to be the most trivial of questions.

Replying lethargically, as it's all I can muster for now, "In the alley."

"Oh?" he answers. "Well…isn't it lucky you brought ten pairs."

All I can do is laugh because it's either that or burst into uncontrollable tears.

My fingers resemble prunes, but I have no intention of getting out of this tub anytime soon.

After we arrived back at my parents' house, I trudged upstairs, desperate to wash off the filth—both physically and metaphorically. I know I need to get over this. It happened over ten years ago. So much has happened since then, since *him*, but I just can't.

London was my first love, and as much as I hate it, I think he'll forever be scorched into my soul.

I can't lie to Lincoln; it's not fair. I have to tell him what happened today. I'm just trying to figure out how. I know he's just outside the door, waiting for me to explain what the hell is going on. I can't hide in here forever, no matter how tempting that thought may be.

With a heavy sigh, I raise my weary body and reach for a towel. Drying off, I don't bother dressing because if I don't do this now, I will chicken out and hate myself even more than I do right now. Opening the door with force, I storm forward. Lincoln launches off the bed, surprised by my sudden entrance.

"I freaked out today while trying on a wedding dress. I got mugged. And I saw London," I blurt out in one long breath. When I'm done with my purge, I inhale deeply, hoping to fill my lungs with the strength to go on. Lincoln takes a literal step backward, running his fingers through his snarled hair.

Now that it's out, I realize I probably should have led with something a little subtler, but I can't take it back. All I can do is wait and hope he shows mercy.

I tighten the towel around me, my raspy breaths the only sound filling the otherwise still room.

Lincoln is pissed. He confirms how much when he begins to pace the room like a caged tiger. With hands interlaced behind his nape, he mumbles gibberish under his breath. I decide to get out of the firing line and plonk onto the foot of the bed, watching him walk backward and forward, afraid he'll wear a hole in the carpet.

I open my mouth, but close it soon after when he finally stops and spins to face me. "You saw *him?*"

My insides drop. "It was an accident. I bumped into Chloe Helm yesterday when I was out for dinner. We got to talking, and I agreed to have a drink with her. We ended up at some bar, and as it turns out, it's London's bar." I bite my lip, toying with the short hem of the towel, too afraid to meet Lincoln's eyes.

"That doesn't explain why you were there today." His tone is accusing, and although he has every right to be pissed, he seems to have overlooked the fact that a bunch of other things happened today as well.

"Just in case you didn't hear me, I got mugged. So thanks for the concern." I have no right to be snappy, but if the tables were turned, I would have pushed down my jealousy and first of all asked if he were okay.

"Don't you turn this back around on me, Holland! I'm not the one who ended up at my ex's front door. We haven't even been here for forty-eight hours, and he's already managed to worm his way back into your life!"

Shooting up from the mattress, I hobble over to where he stands. "Are you even listening to me? That was not what happened. I had a complete meltdown at the bridal store and—"

"And what? To help deal with your cold feet you decided to go see your ex-boyfriend? That makes me feel a whole lot better."

"Stop it," I demand, latching onto his bicep but am surprised when he yanks out of my grip violently. "He was never my boyfriend. Lincoln—"

"No," he interrupts, shaking his head. "I can't believe you went to see him. Did you kiss him?" He levels me with a cold stare—one I have not seen before.

I pull back, horrified, but more so, utterly offended. "*What*? Of course not. How can you even ask that of me?"

"Oh, I don't know. History repeating itself maybe?" He begins pacing once again while I watch. The truth has done the complete opposite of setting me free.

"I thought we were past this. I've told you a million times I was sorry. I was a dumb kid. I made a mistake. You can't hold it against me for the rest of my life." I know what I did was wrong, and he'll always hold a grudge, but I would never do that to him again. I've learned my lesson. Yet the fact I ended up at London's bar begs to differ. However, I swallow past that niggling voice and focus on my fiancé. "Would you stop moving and talk to me!" I plead.

"I don't even know what to say," he reveals, which hurts.

Lincoln and I have fought in the past, but something is different this time. London has always been a touchy subject for him, as their rivalry has obviously survived the decades, but this is ridiculous.

Raising my hands in surrender, I approach him as I would a cornered animal. "I love *you*. I'm marrying *you*. No one else matters but *you*. You know this." A small piece of my heart rises in protest, rattling its confines, but I quash it down because I can never see London again.

He does nothing but destroy.

"Lincoln?" I'm not used to losing an argument, but I know this is one I have to back down from. He meets my eyes, nothing but pain and betrayal rising to the surface. Does he not trust me?

The thought turns my stomach because not once did I question his whereabouts last night. Lincoln was a complete player in high school, including playing me in the beginning, but the past is in the past, and I thought we had moved on. Obviously, I was wrong.

Turning, I make my way over to the walk-in closet to hunt for something to wear. Rows of designer threads hang from the cushioned hangers, but for some unknown reason, I reach for a pair of torn jeans and a ratty t-shirt I forgot I had. Once I change into them, I realize this tee was one I owned when I was sixteen. Mom must have brought it with them when they moved.

Fingering the soft material, I remember wearing this Greenpeace t-shirt to death. It was one of the better pieces of clothing I owned, but looking at it now, I recall just how poor we really were. No wonder the popular girls looked down their nose jobs at me. They saw me as nothing but white trash. Tears sting my eyes, not because the memory cuts me deep but rather, the adult me would think the same thing if she saw me all those years ago.

"You come here, thinking you're different from the girls you grew to hate, but Holland…you're exactly like them. Maybe even worse." London's words pierce fiercely at my temple, and I fist both my eyes in rage.

I've made something of myself, so screw him. But at the expense of what? I barely see my parents, using my busy lifestyle as an excuse. There was a time when my parents were my world, but now, I know they look at me like I'm a mere stranger.

I live with my fiancé, but I may as well live alone. And now, the thought of stepping within a hundred yards of a wedding store has me breaking out in hives. What is the matter with me? I knew what I wanted. I had a life plan. Life was simple back in New York, but now, that life seems like an eternity ago.

Slipping into my Chucks, I suddenly have the urge to get out of here to clear my head. Lincoln still won't look at me, which is fine, because it appears we both need time. His navy blazer is draped over the back of the chair, so without a second thought, I hunt through the pockets to find the car keys. But when my fingers pass over a sharp, crisp edge, I know I've got more than I bargained for.

"Holland, no!" But it's too late.

With a lump in my throat, I slowly pull the envelope from Lincoln's pocket. The date stamp reveals this was sent yesterday, and it was sent to my parents' address. They know I'm here.

"What the hell?" I whisper, shaking my head, blinking back my tears. "They know where my parents live? They know I'm here?" A complete glutton for punishment, I flip open the seal and reach for the folded piece of paper.

It floats to the floor when I read what's inscribed in the all too familiar red ink.

It's only a matter of time...slut.

Only a matter of time for what?

"Why didn't you tell me?" I cry, a hand cupped over my lips.

"To protect you," Lincoln replies, tipping his head back in frustration.

He knows what my response will be even before I say it. "I don't need you to protect me. I need you to tell me the truth. I can't believe you had the nerve to grill me, while all along, you were guarding your own little secret. At least I had the balls to tell you."

"Nothing is going to happen to you. I promise." But he can't promise that, especially now.

"I wish I could believe that, but the fact you hid this from me shows me otherwise. You know the threats are getting more personal, more serious. I need to go to the police."

"No!" he nearly yells, which has me raising an eyebrow.

"No? Why not?"

He sighs, suddenly appearing beyond shamefaced, which has me wondering why. It only takes me a second to figure out why.

"You're unbelievable," I spit, shaking my head. "You're worried about what a scandal like this would do to your precious reputation, aren't you?" He doesn't need to reply because his guilty conscience almost blinds me with the truth.

I've never felt more betrayed than I do right now.

I don't even bother waiting around for him to explain because his silence speaks volumes. Slamming the door shut behind me, I haul down the stairs, ignoring the pain in my ankle. I'm thankful my parents are nowhere to be found. I need to be alone.

A small part of me hopes Lincoln will come chasing after me, apologizing for being an asshole, but he doesn't. The engine starts with a splutter, and the moment I put the car into gear, I take off like the devil is on my heels. I have no idea where I'm headed, but the farther I drive, the better I feel.

I'm thankful I still know these streets like the back of my hand because I'm driving on auto-pilot. My mind is a million miles away. How did they, whoever they are, know where I was? My parents' address is not made public for this exact reason, but I should have known there is no hiding from the Italian mafia.

This has just stepped up a notch. I know I'll have to contact the investigating detectives who worked on the Rossi case because they did warn me that something like this may happen. I, of course, led with my hard head, but now that my parents have been dragged into this, I have no other choice but to report it. I can't let anything happen to them on account of me being a stubborn ass. They've protected me my entire life, and now it's my turn to do the same.

Clenching the steering wheel, I suddenly realize that the streets have become less crowded, and the streetlights are not shining as brightly as before. I know where I'm headed, but the question is why.

I need to pull a U-turn and go back to where I belong, but being here in the one place that, regardless of how poor I was, makes me finally appreciate that I never once felt unsafe or unloved. I may not have had everything I have now, but there was a naïve beauty to the simplicity. I never worried about being one of the cool kids or wearing the latest trends because all that stuff didn't matter. It still doesn't.

All I wanted in life was to be happy, and for the most part, I was.

My parents and I made our house a home, and I miss that. My apartment in New York may tick all the right boxes, but it's missing one essential element—love.

The four walls around us may have been slanted and the off-yellow paint faded with age, but if those marred walls could talk, they'd tell a tale of laughter and love and a family who made something out of nothing.

My vision is blurred, thanks to the tears streaming down my cheeks, but the moment I take a sharp, crooked left, I could navigate down this road with my eyes closed. I roll down the window, the familiar smells taking me back to when I was ten. I remember riding my secondhand bike up and down this potholed street, singing Michael Jackson at the top of my lungs. When I fell over a crater, Mrs. Tully and her fifteen cats came to the rescue, stitching me back up so my mom wouldn't know.

Mr. Ito, our neighbor five doors down, bought a dozen eggs from the corner store every week, but he was unmarried and had no need for so many, so every Tuesday when there was a knock on the door, I knew it was him, splitting his loot in exchange for a cup of coffee and a chat about the good ole days.

At the time, I saw this neighborhood as a mark of my social standing to the outside world, but now I see this community as a band of people who stuck by each other when the world turned their backs on us, banishing us for not fitting into their perfect little lives. But now that I'm a part of it, I see that it's the imperfections that make life beautiful.

Wiping away my tears, I pull the car up in front of house number five hundred and forty-nine. The outside still looks exactly the same way it did when I closed that rusted iron gate over ten years ago. The bottle green exterior complemented with pale yellow trimmings gives this home a tender touch. It depicts to the outside world that regardless of the zip code, home is where the heart is, and my heart, well, a piece of it, was lost within those walls the moment I left for Florida a changed woman.

I tried so hard to forget my roots because remembering them was remembering *him*, but in the process, I forgot me. I never once was embarrassed about who I was growing up, but now, can I say the same?

Turning off the engine, I unsnap my belt and exit the car. Standing here under the full moon brings back so many memories, and I suddenly feel like a teenager, a small child once again. I walk toward my old house, careful of the uneven sidewalk which still hasn't been fixed. Once I'm a few feet away, I stop, never feeling more at home than I do right now. It looks so much smaller than I remember, but back then, the world was my oyster.

There is a single light glowing from the front window—our living room. There are no signs to indicate who resides inside. Regardless, I hope they're as happy as I once was. The familiar sounds catching on the warm summer breeze transports me back to when they lulled me to sleep at night.

You have to embrace the noise to appreciate the silence, and at this moment, I have both. With eyes closed, I lift my face to the heavens and bask in the freedom of having absolutely nowhere to be. Lost in my own private oasis, I almost tune out the world around me, but when I hear a squawk, my senses prick in remembrance because there is no way I would ever forget that sound.

My eyes pop open, almost unbelieving, but the bright orange fluff ball rubbing up against my legs confirms that Mrs. Tully's most favorite pet still lives. Dropping to a squat, I rub him under the chin, and just like years ago, he purrs like a lawnmower.

"Hey, Ninja. How you doing, buddy?" In response, he purrs louder and headbutts my hand.

Peering up ahead, Mrs. Tully's porch light flickers dimly. I know that she's home, and regardless of the late hour, she'd be overjoyed to see me. She may be the crazy cat lady, and I'll end up leaving her home covered in cat hair, but I don't care. I have fond memories of her rescuing every stray cat in the neighborhood, her kindness on full display when although she could barely feed herself, she never turned her back on a stray.

With that decided, I give Ninja one final pat before proceeding to stand. However, when a branch snaps behind me, eliciting the hair at the back of my neck to stand on end, I freeze on the spot. I'm mid crouch, too afraid to move.

My choppy breaths leave me in small bursts because something ominous is lurking beyond the shadows. A sheen of sweat coats my entire body, and when Ninja's ears fall back flat against his head and he lets out a low growl, I know he senses the threat too. He hisses before taking off in the opposite direction, his little legs almost unable to keep up.

That now leaves me alone with whoever is skulking behind me.

Counting to three, I stand tall and turn slowly. The entire time I'm attempting to convince myself that I'm overreacting, but when I see a hooded figure standing a few yards away, I know that this person isn't just a passerby—they're here for me. It's a game of cat and mouse because I have no doubt if I make a move, he will hunt me down.

His head is downturned, a hood covering his features. His hands are dug deep into his pockets. There is nothing distinguishable about this person. The only small clue I have is a red dragon embroidered on the upper left corner of the hoodie. The clue is pointless, however, as I have no idea what it means.

He's waiting for me to make the first move. I want to call out, ask him what he's doing, but I've never been more frightened in all my life.

Call it women's intuition, but I know this is the person who has been tormenting me for the past six months. He's finally grown a pair and come out into the light. But now that he's here, I can't help but wonder what happens next.

A swell of adrenaline spills from me. I managed to stay safe growing up in this neighborhood, so I'll be damned if that changes now. He's methodically watching my every move, so I know my window to make a break for it leaves no room for error.

There are ten steps separating me from freedom. My assailant could catch me in eight. But regardless of the odds, I have to make a move, and I have to move now. Taking one final deep breath, I lock eyes with this bastard.

Fisting the keys in my pocket, I gently finger the one I need, my gaze never wavering from his. I've thought of this scenario often, but now that my attacker is feet away, all I want to do is flee.

One…

Two…

Three…

My feet kick out from under me as I make a mad dash

for the car. I can hear his heavy footsteps beat wildly on the ground, but I continue running, using the remote to unlock the door. Ten steps suddenly feel like ten million, but when I'm within reach, I yank open the door and throw myself into the driver's seat, locking the doors.

My heart is beating so wildly, I can hear the rhythm pound piercingly against my eardrums. It's almost a distraction, but I pull it together and shove the key in the ignition. The car splutters to life and I slam it into drive. The parking brake is still on, stalling me, a total amateur move, one which will cost me dearly.

I'm waiting for the darkened shape to appear at my window, shattering it and snatching me once and for all, but none of the above happens because nothing happens at all. I frantically search my mirrors, hunting for where he went, but it appears he disappeared into the shadows just as quietly as he appeared.

I jerk my head from left to right, turning over my shoulders to search for his location, but he's nowhere to be seen.

I should be relieved, but I'm not. I know this is only the beginning.

With a trembling hand, I release the parking brake and glide into the night. The entire drive back, I keep checking my mirrors to ensure I'm not being followed. I'm not. A wishful part reasons that maybe my exhausted mind was playing tricks on me, conjuring up something that wasn't really there. But I can still taste the fear, and the constant chill I can't kick reveals that he was real, and it's only a matter of time before he comes out of the shadows for good.

12

There is no greater smell than coffee. There especially is no better smell when you've had about an hour's sleep, too afraid to close your eyes in case the bogeyman is ready to finish what he started.

After last night, my body seems to be in a state of hyper awareness, and I don't see that changing anytime soon. I came back to my parents', thankful that Lincoln was sound asleep. The bottle of whiskey tucked under his arm was probably the reason he was passed out by eleven p.m. This town has changed us both.

Back in New York, we rarely fought, but I suppose that was because we barely saw one another. The fact we can't seem to see eye to eye has nothing to do with Los Angeles and everything to do with the fact that being here has unleashed old feelings and exposed hidden insecurities.

I know a small part of Lincoln will never forgive me for sleeping with London. He can play it off, pretend it doesn't matter, but his reaction yesterday was all the confirmation I need. He still feels threatened by him, and he has every right to be angry with me for seeing him. I still don't know why I ended up there, but it's a mystery which will remain unsolved because if I want this marriage to last, then I have to let London go.

I have to let go of the anger and betrayal and get on with my life.

"Babe?" Cracking open an eye, I see Lincoln sheepishly sitting by the side of the bed. He comes in peace. "I brought you coffee."

Slowing rising, I reach for the porcelain cup before leaning backward against the headboard. I inhale the liquid gold, needing a moment to collect my thoughts. I know I owe Lincoln some kind of an apology. He had every right to be angry with me. Even though I don't appreciate him pointing the finger, I understand why he did.

Just as I open my mouth, ready to pay my dues, Lincoln beats me to the punch. "I'm so sorry for acting like a complete jerk. This wedding stuff, work, just everything…it's all getting to me. Forgive me?" I know exactly what he means. These past six months have been tough on us both. "I know getting married so quickly seems insane, but I don't want to wait."

His confession is exactly what I needed to hear. We've

both been under so much stress; it seems we both needed to remember why he proposed to me in the first place. All my doubts and fears drift away for now.

"I'll only forgive you if you forgive me. I'm sorry for… everything too." The pause is because I know better than to mention London's name.

Lincoln sighs in relief and shuffles closer. "I overreacted. I just—"

I stop him. "I know." There is no need for him to explain.

"I thought getting married would solve everything." He fists his hair, while my heart suddenly drops. Solve what exactly?

"You don't want to get married?"

"What?" he asks, horrified. "Of course, I do. Do you?"

He waits patiently, and I hate that I need a second to reply. "Yes, I do."

His relief is clear. "I didn't tell you about the letter because I didn't want you to worry. It was stupid, but you've been under so much stress, and I didn't want to upset you."

"I understand, but from now on, we have to be completely honest with one another about everything, okay?"

He nods, staring me deep in the eyes. "I promise."

A weight instantly lifts from my shoulders, but I still want to address the big, pink elephant in the room. Cradling the cup, I get lost in the impending truth. "When we get back to New York, I want to report everything that's happened."

"Of course, babe, anything you want." This is a conversation we should have had months ago. Things would have been so much easier if we had.

Taking a deep breath, I confess, "I think I'm being followed."

"What? By whom?" His eyes widen to the size of saucers.

"I don't know. Last night, I went to visit my old neighborhood. Stupid, I know. But when I turned around, someone was definitely behind me, watching me."

"Did you see who?" he asks, his fists clenched by his sides.

"No, they had on a hood. I couldn't see their face, but I just know it was him. The person who has been tormenting me these past six months."

I have never seen Lincoln this mad before. "From now on, you don't leave my side."

I can't help but smile, touched by the sentiment. "That's hardly necessary. I'll just be more careful from now on and not wander into strange neighborhoods at night." It was meant to be a joke, but Lincoln doesn't seem amused in the slightest. "I want you to trust me."

"I do." Lincoln's response is heavy with misgivings.

"I like to think that you do, but I know when it comes to some things...certain people, you don't." Lifting my gaze, I'm not sure what I'll see.

"Okay." Not exactly poetic, but it's music to my ears.

"Okay?" I question, raising a brow. "Wow, that was easy. Case closed."

He grins, leaning forward. "Nothing is easy with you. But

I wouldn't have it any other way." I still can't kick the feeling he's hiding something, but that's probably just my suspicious nature.

His honesty touches me, and I suddenly reprimand myself for ever doubting my commitment to him. I may have freaked out when it came to the wedding stuff, but that doesn't mean I don't want to marry him. Every bride has a bout of cold feet, but it's time I stopped and accepted my fate.

After an afternoon of catching up on emails and sleep, Lincoln told me his parents had invited us to go out for dinner. My future in-laws have always been semi-civil toward me, but deep down, I know they still hate the fact that their only son was marrying a Brooks-Ferris.

Sylvia and Harold won't appreciate my pushiness, but I invited my parents too, because eventually, we all have to get along. Lincoln is up ahead talking to my dad while my mother and I lag behind.

We haven't really spoken since my runaway bride stint. I know she's giving me time to approach her myself. I do owe her an explanation, but I don't know where to start. "Sorry about yesterday."

My mother would make a terrible lawyer. She has the worst poker face. "Sweetie, there's no need to apologize, but I am worried."

I gulp. "Why?"

No matter one's age, our parents have the uncanny ability to make us feel like a child again. "You're not ready to get married." She holds up her finger when I attempt to object. My courtroom prowess won't cut it with my mom. "You may think you are, but you're not. I know you better than you know yourself. You're a part of me."

Hearing someone else confirm my worst fears doesn't clear the fog. Lincoln's heartfelt confession repeats loudly in my ears. What is the matter with me? "For argument's sake, let's just say you're right. What should I do?"

She loops her arm through mine, leaning into my side. "You need to uncover the reason. I know you love Lincoln, but you need to marry him for the right reasons."

"So love isn't the right reason?" I counter, suddenly so confused.

"Love is the *only* right reason," she objects without a second thought.

"I do love him," I stress, lowering my voice and peering up ahead to ensure Lincoln can't hear our conversation.

"Well, in that case, marrying him shouldn't leave you in a cold sweat and seeking out people from the past." I trip over my heels, almost falling flat on my face.

I don't know how she knows, but she knows. There isn't a trace of disappointment or anger in her tone, merely concern for my happiness.

"Coming back here was a mistake." I sound like a spoiled child.

"Why?" When I'm silent, mulling over the many reasons, she offers, "A place shouldn't affect your feelings for someone. Your love for that person should be universal, wherever you go."

Game. Set. Match.

Sighing, I suddenly feel a weight settle deep within my gut. She's right. But the question is, what am I going to do about it?

All thoughts are put on the backburner, however, when we approach Belle Bocca, an upmarket Italian restaurant in the back streets of Bel Air. I come to a complete stop.

"Have you got something against Italian all of a sudden?" Lincoln teases, turning over his shoulder to see what the holdup is.

But I can't even muster a laugh as the name of this place draws out even more skeletons from my closet. I have tried my absolute hardest not to think of Belle, but seeing her name spelled out before me makes it almost impossible to ignore.

If this is a sign, then I want to know exactly what it's supposed to mean. My mom gently guides me toward the entrance, knowing all too well why the sudden standstill.

We're greeted at the door by a waiter wearing the finest silk suit. Taking a quick glance around, I see that this place exudes wealth, not that that surprises me, seeing as Lincoln's parents chose the location. Harold stands when he sees us, giving us a small wave.

The moment we make our way over to the long table, Sylvia turns over her shoulder and gives my mom a onceover. She clearly doesn't like what she sees as she turns up her pink stained lips and reaches for the red wine. My mom shifts beside me, nervously smoothing out her beautiful blue dress. She looks incredible, and I'll be damned if anyone tells her otherwise.

"Lincoln." Sylvia makes grabby hands at her son, who bends down to kiss her cheek. Regardless of the fact she can be downright superficial and judgmental at times, Lincoln loves her just the same. As for his dad, he's constantly seeking his approval, both on and off the field.

"Hi, Mom. Dad." After kissing her cheek, he shakes his father's hand firmly.

The O'Tooles live so far outside the real world, they've forgotten their manners it appears, as they completely ignore my parents and focus on me.

"Darling, you look just ravishing," Sylvia says, standing and offering me an air kiss on both cheeks.

"Thank you. So do you," I reply, giving her a small smile.

"Oh, thank you. It's the latest trend in Paris at the moment." She brushes over her unsightly frock. "Isn't this material just to die for?"

I bite my tongue and don't point out that a small bear probably *did* die, donating his fur for her 'latest trend.'

Sylvia has always had a good eye for fashion, and usually, I would humor her, but now, her blatant disrespect toward my parents has me nodding once. "You remember my parents." It's a low blow, but I can't deal with pretenses after the past few days.

Harold clears his throat and adjusts his spotted bow tie. "Yes, of course. Nice to see you again." He shakes my father's hand and smiles politely at my mom. I'm moments away from turning around and leaving, but refrain when my mom shows the table who's the bigger person and greets Sylvia with a gentle hug. We all take our seats, the mood set to uncomfortable immediately.

I reach for the menu, ignoring the small talk passing back and forth between Lincoln and his parents. This isn't anything new, but my reaction to them is. "The lasagna sounds amazing." My mom nods, smacking her lips in concurrence, but Sylvia's face twists into horror.

"Two weeks out from the wedding you simply cannot eat all those carbs. How about a salad?"

I jerk my head so far to the right to look at her, I'm certain I've just pulled a muscle in my neck. Just as I'm about to tell her what I think of her suggestion, Lincoln reaches for my curled fist beneath the table and squeezes lightly. He's silently begging I don't make a scene.

Swallowing down the urge to confute, I simply reach for the bottle of wine and drown my sorrows in the 1981 Merlot.

"So how's work?" Harold asks my dad, who peers at him from across the table.

"It's great, very busy. How about you?"

Bless my dad, but Harold hasn't worked a hard day in his life. Yes, he owns one of the biggest technology companies in the USA, but he has many minions doing the dirty work for him. And he coached high school football only because he wanted to live out the heydays that passed him by.

Sylvia's take on hard work is having to park her own car when the valet is full.

"Business is going well." I down my glass of wine, watching this ship sink further and further by the second.

The waiter takes our orders. I ensure mine can be heard loud and clear. "I'll have the lasagna. Extra parmesan, please." I hand him the menu, ignoring the scowl Sylvia throws my way.

Another bonus of living over two hundred miles away is not being subjected to family dinners. Children and parents are two things Lincoln and I don't see eye to eye on. I'm in no way ready for kids now, but down the line, I can see myself being a mom. As for Lincoln, it would appear a lobotomy would be far more appealing. I can only hope his opinion changes soon.

"Have you decided on a dress?" Sylvia asks, sipping from her goblet. The mere mention has me shuffling uncomfortably in my seat.

"Not yet." She takes a hint from my clipped response, and the awkwardness gets jacked up to maximum volume.

Usually, the dim lights and comforting atmosphere would be soothing after the lunacy of the past few days, but tonight, it grates on my nerves. The cellist who sits in the corner of the room is providing background noise by playing a Bach piece, but the supposedly melodic tune sounds like someone is running their long fingernails down a chalkboard.

"What's the matter? Are you okay?" Lincoln asks, softly running his fingers down the back of my neck.

I know he's only trying to make me feel better, but his touch makes me feel worse. "I'm fine." I subtly shrug from his hold.

I reach for the bottle, but Lincoln beats me to it. He fills my crystal goblet with wine, but I reach forward, tipping the base, implying to fill it right up. His mother glares at me while I sarcastically raise my glass.

"Cheers." I smirk and gulp it down in one big, unladylike mouthful.

She tries to hide her disapproval, but the tugging at her high necklace is a dead giveaway her Chanel panties are in a twist.

"Babe, maybe you should wait until we eat?" he whispers as I refill my empty glass. His request falls on deaf ears, however, as I fill it to the brim.

"So have you seen Dr. Lombardi's new receptionist?" Harold changes the subject, trying to clear the tension in the air.

Sylvia nods. She loves nothing more than a good gossip. "Oh dear god, yes. Has he gone blind in his old age? She looks like a giant elephant behind that desk."

I sag in relief, thankful they've found someone else to focus on besides me. Looks like I'm in the clear…for now.

The rest of the evening drags on and on, and after appetizers, I feel like I'm on the verge of having yet another breakdown.

Dinner smelled delicious, but sadly, I could only stomach two bites. The tension at the table can be cut with a knife. It appears our parents can't seem to agree on anything; the difference between both, however, is that my parents know when to let it go. The same can't be said for the O'Tooles.

"I do wish you'd allow the wedding to take place at our house. It makes sense," argues Sylvia, not needing to spell out the reason.

Their home is bigger, and in their eyes, nicer and more suitable than my parents', but the choice is mine, and I've decided that if I'm forced to walk down an aisle, it will be at my parents' house.

"Thank you for your extremely generous offer, but the arrangements have already been made." This is an all-out lie, but she doesn't know that.

Lincoln however, does. "What arrangements? You don't even have a dress. If your parents wouldn't mind, maybe we could move location." He looks at his dad, as if seeking approval for speaking up. His dad merely continues hacking into his steak, which appears to be far more appealing than his son.

The sadness emanating from my mom whacks me in the

stomach, and I suck in a small breath. "They may not mind, but I do."

Lincoln's surprise is evident, but it'll be a cold day in hell before I give in. My parents would be heartbroken and devastated, and I refuse to do that to them again.

Sylvia leans forward, turning on the charm. "Delores, you wouldn't reconsider? With both you and Bobby working such long hours, let us take the pressure off. We'll pay for everything. You wouldn't have to do a thing." The napkin in my lap resembles papier-mâché as I scrunch it into a small ball.

I can see my mother conceding because she doesn't want to make a scene. She's accustomed to giving in, being frowned upon most of her life.

I glare at Lincoln, visually berating him for not standing up to his presumptuous mother. Last I checked, this was our wedding, not hers, and she has no right to dictate just where she thinks it should take place. But Lincoln simply leans back in his seat, silent. Does he agree with her? Does he too think my parents aren't worthy?

Just as I open my mouth, my dad, my forever hero, swoops in and levels her with those dogged eyes—the ones I see staring back at me every time I look into a mirror.

"Thank you for the offer, Sylvia, but we don't need anybody to pay our way. The wedding will be taking place at our home. It's what my daughter wants. If Lincoln objects, then I most certainly would be happy to discuss alternative arrangements with him, but if not, then I don't see the point in harping on this further."

I bite my lip, afraid I'll burst into a hallelujah if not.

Sylvia has just heard a word I'm sure she doesn't hear too often—no—and to add insult to injury, it was spoken by someone she sees as nothing more than a nuisance. My mom looks across the table at my dad, nothing but love and appreciation glowing from every pore. He has her back—he always has. I thought Lincoln had mine, but apparently, I thought wrong.

Lincoln doesn't curb his annoyance that my father told his precious mother in a roundabout way to shut the hell up, but if he decided to voice that infuriation out loud, then there may not be a wedding to argue about after all. After today, I thought we'd made peace and everything was back on track.

The table grows quiet, all attention on the looks of love darting between my parents. Their affection should make me want to throw up, but it doesn't. I'm envious that after so many years, their love is still so unbending.

As Lincoln tosses back his beer, clearly exasperated, I can't help but wonder if push came to shove, would Lincoln pick me over his mom? I would never ask this of him, but I can't help but speculate. I know my parents have a special kind of love, but it's impossible not to compare it to mine and Lincoln's. What kind of love are we?

"Holland Brooks-Ferris? Oh my god, is that you?" In a town

where I was overlooked by so many, it now seems like everyone knows my name. Peering upward, a tacky blonde rests by our table. She's hanging off the arm of someone who could be her great grandfather.

My mind catalogues through all the faces I tried so hard to forget, but it remembers this one as Helen Tharp—one of the Sin Skanks. She's still the queen of skanks. I'm surprised they let her in here with half a dress.

"It's me, Helen Tharp," she clarifies when I continue staring at her, unsure what she expects me to say.

"Hi," I reply, giving her a small wave. I'm hoping she accepts the gesture as a goodbye kiss. She doesn't.

"It's so great to see you. And you too, Lincoln. Where have you guys been?" Her gaze swings to Lincoln, who methodically arranges his silverware. He's anxious. Why?

When no one speaks, I decide the quicker I get this over with, the quicker she leaves. "New York. We live there now."

"Together?" she asks, swiping her finger between us.

"Yes, together." I don't check my irritation at her tone.

Lincoln looks as interested in this conversation as watching paint dry. Another reason to slap him upside the head. What is the matter with him tonight? I know he's still hung up on his dad playing favorites with everyone except him in high school. Maybe him being here and the past few days is scratching at old wounds. But regardless, his behavior tonight is unacceptable.

Helen smooths out her gold outfit and primps her blond

mane. "Wow, how things have changed since high school."

"Yes, we all grew up. Some more than others," I add, making a point to look at her fake, sizable chest.

She purses her lips, the Helen I once knew rearing her ugly head. "Speaking of which, do you still speak to Belle?"

My fumbling fingers knock my glass of red over, causing a big puddle of Merlot to stain the white tablecloth. A waiter is by our table in a second, cleaning my mess as Sylvia apologizes profusely for my clumsiness. I would be apologizing, but my mouth feels like it's been stuck together with glue.

Belle's name is like a grenade, and everyone at the table is ready for the shrapnel to wound them deeply. My parents shift, Lincoln finally shows interest, and Sylvia and Harold are paling by the second. "No, we lost touch after school."

Helen folds her arms, drumming her long fingernails against her arms. "Oh, so you don't know."

I gulp, while Lincoln's jaw clenches. "Know what?"

She looks as if all her Christmases have come at once, being the one to reveal this grand secret. "Know that Belle had a—"

"Enough!"

I actually jump in my seat, startled by Lincoln's fist striking down on the tabletop with brute force. The anger trickles off him in deep-seated waves, and I actually fear for Helen's safety. The waiter quickly dashes off, clearing himself from what most certainly will be a brawl.

His hulking body is seconds away from combusting.

"You've said enough, Helen, now leave," he demands between clenched teeth. Both fists are pressed to the table, hinting he's barely holding it together. I can't believe how angry he is. I thought I'd seen him mad before, but this is something else.

Helen takes a step backward. It's apparent she's surprised by his rage. "I said *leave*. No one wants you here. Go back to the corner you came from."

My mouth hinges open. I actually am speechless. The grandfather figure at her side seems confused by the commotion.

Helen's eyes water, but she holds back her tears. "I suppose I was wrong. Some things never change." She spins on her heel, leaving me with so many questions, but currently my mouth has forgotten how to function.

I watch with wide eyes as my father digs out his wallet and throws a couple of hundred dollar bills on the table. "That should cover our share. If we owe anymore, send us the bill." He gestures to my mother and me that it's time to go. I can't sit here another second because I'm afraid I'll suffocate if I do.

Placing my napkin on the table, I go to stand but am jarred back into my seat when Lincoln tugs on my arm. "You're not leaving with them, are you?"

The world is on crazy drugs; that's the only plausible explanation. Yanking out of his grip, I feel the tips of my ears burn in rage. "With *them*? If you're referring to my parents, then yes, I am."

He snickers, shaking his head. "Let her go, son," Sylvia

has the gall to say, looking down her noses at us. I know what she's going to say even before she says it, but actually hearing it doesn't soften the blow. "She's a Brooks-Ferris. Nothing will ever change that. This is what you're marrying into. Welcome to your future."

You can hear a pin drop as the disturbance has caused most diners to look our way. These people love nothing better than a scandal, and what better scandal than this. I was stupid to think I was ever in their league because finally, I've come to realize that I'm not—I never will be.

I'm better. And so are my parents.

"After tonight, I wouldn't be so sure." I'm shaking in utter fury as I stand. This is the moment Lincoln needs to jump up and fight for what he wants—fight for me—but he doesn't. He simply stares straight ahead, his jaw moving from side to side.

"I can't believe you're just going to sit there and not say anything."

"I think you've said enough," he bites back, still not having the common decency to look at me. Tears sting my eyes, and I choke on the bitter taste of betrayal.

"C'mon, Sweetie." My mom gently loops her arm around my shoulder, her comforting fragrance cocooning me when I need it the most.

"So that's it?" I press, unable to let it go. "The only thing that got you riled up tonight was the mere mention of Belle. What about the fact your mom slandered me and my parents? That didn't offend you in the slightest?"

Sylvia scowls while Harold sighs, accustomed to this sort of drama. It's just another Friday night for them.

"Lincoln?"

When he meets my eyes, I wish he didn't. There is nothing there. "Just go, Holland."

I blink once, his dismissal angering me more than hurting. "With pleasure. I'd say this was fun, but I'd be lying. Let's never do this again." Pulling back my shoulders, I smirk a million-dollar smile, never prouder. "And by the way, yes, we're Brooks, and we're Ferris's, and we're fucking proud of it." Sylvia covers her gaping mouth while Lincoln places his head into his palms. Only then do I leave, with no intention of ever coming back.

My mother has never looked more delighted, and my father struts smugly, his head held high. We will never fit in, but that's okay because we've found our tribe.

The air feels wonderful as it slaps at my heated cheeks. I take a moment to calm my raging nerves. Bending at the waist, I place my hands on my knees and take ten deep breaths. I feel somewhat better, but the urge to kill has yet to subside.

"Are you okay, Sweetie?"

I can't believe my mom is asking me that, but I suppose that's what family does—they care more about their loved ones than they do themselves. "I'm fine. I'm just sorry about the way Lincoln and his parents spoke to you. It was unacceptable."

A small part of me hopes my parents jump to Lincoln's

defense, but they don't. "I'll pull the car around." My father kisses me on the forehead before tightly hugging my mom. They share a silent exchange—its meaning one only they're privy to. We watch after him, his figure getting smaller and smaller, symbolizing how I'm feeling inside.

Rubbing my temple, I attempt to decipher what in God's name just happened. How did we end up here? Were Lincoln and I doomed from the beginning? Are our differences winning out in the end?

The past few years weren't for nothing, but the man I saw tonight was not the man I fell in love with. The man I thought I knew would fight for what's right. He would fight for us, but he didn't. He rolled over, all because of the ghosts of our past? If so, he isn't the man I believed him to be. I suddenly feel as if I've been sleeping with a stranger.

Something doesn't add up, it hasn't for a long time, and I know the answer lies with one person, well, two.

"Mom..." I have to go.

"I know," she says, even before I've finished what I started. Turning to look at me, she brushes the hair from my cheek. "Just remember...we all make mistakes."

I have no idea what she means, but I suddenly feel nostalgic.

If only I had spoken to my mom in the past, told her about my feelings, then maybe, just maybe things would have turned out differently for us all. But that's the thing about hindsight; it doesn't make a lick of difference when you're always destined to be on the same path.

I hail a cab and am thankful the street is littered with a sea of yellow. I can only hope that relief continues when I venture down the boulevard on the quest to find out the truth once and for all.

13

It's hard to believe I've only been here a few days, as it feels like I never left. I never anticipated my life could alter so dramatically in the blink of an eye. I also never foresaw that I'd be stepping into this bar ever again.

I don't bother with pretenses, and after being patted down by my new favorite security guard, I make a beeline straight for the bar. The place is crowded, packed full, but seeing as I don't want to order a drink, I walk over to the end of the counter and hail a young bartender. The mohawked server doesn't see me, but sadly, London's squeeze does.

Her eyes narrow into slits when we lock gazes, but I stand tall and wave her over. If she decides to ignore me, I have no reservations pulling her down this long aisle by her hair. She tosses the dishcloth she's holding onto the bar and whispers into mohawk's ear.

He looks me up and down and snickers, but nods.

She saunters over in no real hurry, obviously knowing I'm here because I need something from her. She owes me no favors, and I'm sure she'll ensure I know it. "What do you want?"

It's so loud in here, I have to scream to be heard. "I need to see London. Is he here?" I don't see the point in sugarcoating it.

She tongues her cheek and shakes her head. "You've got some nerve coming here. Just in case you didn't know, Sin is my man."

If she's looking for a fight, then she has another thing coming. "My condolences," I bite back, annoyed. "My name is Holland, and I…"

I linger midsentence because her reaction derails me from my thoughts. She looks as if I've just solved some longstanding mystery. "*You're* Holland?"

"Um, yes," I reply, unsure if this is a trick question.

Her entire demeanor goes from bitch to scolding lover in a nanosecond. She marches forward and jabs her finger in my chest. "Get out. Now."

"*Excuse me.*" I swat away her hand because she has three seconds to remove herself from my personal space before I snap her finger. "Get your hands off me. I don't know where they've been."

"If you don't leave, so help me god…" She tries to intimidate me by thrusting her fake boobs into my chest. I do not appreciate the sentiment in the slightest.

"What are you going to do? Suffocate me to death?" I push back twice as hard, getting into her face, refusing to back down. It's survival of the strongest, and I eat little girls like this for breakfast.

Just as I'm about to resort to hair pulling, a strong hand grips my upper arm and spins me around. It takes the wind from my sails, but when I see London standing before me, a little intrigued, but a lot pissed off, I'm rendered incapacitated.

"Why are you here?"

Regaining my composure, I yank from his hold and match his heated glower. "What happened to Belle?" The room drops to subzero temperatures.

London is the only person I know who will tell me the truth. I could have gone to her parents, but they never cared about their daughter, and I don't see that changing over the years.

"Did you hear me?" I press when he stands before me, weighing up what to say.

This is not exactly the response I was hoping for. I'd hope he'd tell me Belle was living the high life with the man of her dreams. But his troubled expression reveals I'd hope wrong.

"Why is she here? Throw her out now."

"Sandy, enough!" London growls, running a hand through his snarled hair. Even I recoil from the wrath behind his words.

Tears prick her eyes, but she bravely blinks them back.

"After all this time, I finally get to meet the third wheel."

Her comment winds me. What the hell is that supposed to mean?

Just as I'm about to ask her, London latches onto my arm once again and drags me away from Sandy, who allows the tears to break past the floodgates. A small part of me feels sorry for her because I know what it's like to be held under London's spell.

But I have other things to deal with, like London dragging me through the crowd like some underage troublemaker. I could attempt to break free, but I'm hoping wherever he takes me has the answers I desperately seek.

I'm surprised when we walk through the door together and my ass doesn't hit the pavement. "Is she causing trouble again?" asks the security guard.

I roll my eyes at him while London tightens his grip around my bicep. "She's always causing trouble, Manny. That'll never change."

I don't appreciate being hauled away like some criminal, but when we continue walking, headed toward the parking garage, I seal my lips and wonder what happens now. London escorts me to a monstrous black Chevy pickup, where he opens the passenger door.

"Get in," he commands when I stand still. Breaking from his hold, I scrunch up my nose, far from impressed with his demands. When I open my mouth, prepared to give him an

ABSINTHE OF THE HEART

earful, he steps forward, caging me in his burn. "You can either get in of your own accord, or I can help you."

There will be no helping on his behalf. "You wouldn't dare," I contest, but yelp when he bends at the knees to pick me up, intent on throwing me over his shoulder.

I dance out of the firing line, hands raised in surrender. "Okay, fine."

Without much of a choice, I climb up the step and boost myself into the truck. I'm in six-inch heels, but I don't let that deter me. Once I'm settled, I make a point to reach for the seat belt and buckle myself in. Satisfied, he slams the door shut, the reality of what I'm doing sinking in.

I watch as he rounds the hood, clearly frustrated. I secretly exhale in relief when he opens the door and gets in beside me. The motor comes to life with a roar, a reflection of how we both feel. Neither of us says a word when London puts the car into drive and sails into traffic.

Now that I'm semi-rational, the consequences of my actions hit home. Lincoln is probably never going to talk to me again, but that was a probability even before I decided to walk into the bar. I have no idea what is next for us. I saw a side of him I didn't like—it made me feel like I was only ever worth covert kisses.

Turning to peer out the window, I watch as my life flashes me by. So much has changed, but could it be some things haven't changed at all? I refuse to believe Lincoln is someone other than I believe him to be. The past few years cannot have been for nothing.

The rest of the ride pans out in silence, but the unspoken is enough to fill in the stillness.

Before long, the salty smell of sand and surf permeates the air. Snapping from my thoughts, I see we're in Santa Monica. I've always loved this neighborhood. Still a touch of bohemia lingers. London takes a left and drives up a long driveway, coming to a stop at a keypad. He punches in some numbers before the boom gates open, granting us entry.

I'm still deathly quiet as he parks the truck beneath an apartment complex and kills the engine. Scoping out my surroundings, I shrug. "Why are we here?"

"Because I live here." There is no further explanation.

When he jumps from the truck, I figure that's my cue to do the same. I unsnap my belt, a bundle of nerves. I don't let it show as I very ungracefully dismount from the beast, almost re-twisting my ankle. I straighten out my dress, however, head held high.

London's lips twitch, but that's where the humor ends. He reaches for a set of keys from his pocket and enters the stairwell. Again, I'm presuming I'm to follow.

As each floor passes, a weight settles heavier in my stomach. I have no idea what I'm walking into, but just like always, I trust London. When we finally reach the fifth floor, London opens the stairwell door, holding it ajar for me.

I brush past him, instantly engulfed in his warm scent.

"Which way?" I ask, the huskiness to my tone betraying my nerves. London points to the left.

I make my way down the very sophisticated looking, glassed hallway, but it doesn't stink of arrogance or wealth. I have no doubt this place with ocean views straight to the west and all the way up the Malibu coastline would cost a small fortune, but something is almost homey about it.

It's quiet, something that doesn't happen often in this town, but the serenity helps clear my head. Just like the rolling waves beyond me, a sense of calm surrounds me and sweeps away the anxiety.

When we stop at door five fifteen, I take a deep breath. I have no idea what's just beyond this door, but I'm ready to find out. It whines open like the hinges on my heart when I step inside this beautiful home.

I don't know what I expected his residence to look like, but this is something else.

The first thing that hits me is how bright and buoyant it is. The open kitchen, living, and dining areas are surrounded by floor-to-ceiling glass, giving me a three-sixty view of the breathtaking scenes. Peering upward, a white staircase and pleated railing reveal the elegance continues on the second floor.

"Do you want a drink?" London asks, disturbing me from my gawking.

"Sure. Thanks." I continue gazing around, taking in the sights, liking what I see.

A painting on the far wall in the living area catches my eye, so I walk toward it, wanting to take a closer look. When I see what it actually depicts, I stop dead in my tracks, barely breathing. It's spectacular, the centerpiece a sycamore tree resting innocently beneath a star-filled sky. I've seen this before, not on paper but in my head. I've relived this moment too many times to count because it kicked off a chain reaction which changed my life forever.

"Here." I jolt, lost in memories. London passes me a beer.

This seems so civil; I'm waiting for the catch. Is someone going to jump out of the closet and shake things up further than they already are?

"I promise I didn't spit in it." I recoil backward because is he making jokes now? As he tosses back his beer, I sense he's as nervous as I am. This can't be good.

Needing the courage, I take a long sip, cringing at the bitterness, but the moment the bite hits the back of my throat, I relish in the taste. I have no idea how this is going to end. He knows why I came to him, but I still don't know why I'm here.

"London, what's going on? As much as I hate to admit it, you're the only person who will tell me the truth." The desperation is clear, but I'll beg if I have to.

"What happened tonight?"

A sarcastic snicker escapes me. "I have no clue. Lincoln just transformed from loving fiancé to gigantic jerk in a heartbeat."

London shakes his head, the anger rising. "He's always been a jerk. That's never changed."

"Well, that's a little harsh, don't you think, considering last I checked you weren't exactly in line for sainthood."

"I never claimed to be. You knew what I was, who I am, yet here you are," he offers, tipping his beer in salute before he downs the entire bottle.

His smugness irks me. I place the beer on the glass coffee table before I'm enticed to use it as a weapon. "I'm here because you owe me answers."

"And you owe me an explanation as to why the fuck you would ever consider marrying that asshole," he snaps, his breath leaving him in winded exhalations.

I take a physical step backward before I slap him. "Because I love him," I weakly reply, but London sees straight through me.

"You do not."

"Don't you dare tell me who I do or do not love. I'm not sixteen anymore."

His gaze scalds my flesh as he studies me from top to bottom. "I can see that. But even then, I never told you who you should or shouldn't love."

My lips clamp shut. Where is he going with this?

He takes one step forward. I take two back. But my retreat only seems to spur him on. "Why are you here?"

"I told you…" I swallow, suddenly feeling like prey.

"You're here for answers." He fills in the blanks but seems unconvinced. We continue our slow dance around the living area, me retreating, he advancing. "Why don't you ask your perfect fiancé?"

His antagonism is not helping, and I suddenly regret coming to him for help. "Just forget about it. I should have known nothing would have changed between us."

I turn to make a mad dash for the door, but London reads me like a book. He steps to the left, blocking my exit. "Move out of the way," I demand, but he doesn't budge.

"You're right; nothing has changed between us." I have no idea how to interpret his comment because it can be read in so many different ways.

His arrogance is my undoing, and I charge forward, ready to lay all my cards on the table once and for all. "In case you've forgotten, you're the one who left me!" I jab my thumb so hard into my chest, it's bound to leave a bruise. "You're the one who ruined me, and now, now, I think…I think I'm broken," I confess to not only London, but also myself. What other explanation is there? "You broke me."

I hate how weak I sound. I hate myself even more so when tears leak from the corner of my eyes.

"Princess…"

But I don't want his sympathy. All I ever wanted was his love. "No, don't." I retreat when he attempts to console me. "I don't want you to feel sorry for me. I just want t-to k-know the tr-truth."

"Please don't cry. I can't stand to see you cry."

"Why? My tears never seemed to bother you in the past! If I remember correctly, each tear was a notch on your victory belt." Big, fat ugly tears cascade down my cheeks, but I don't bother wiping them away as more will only take their place.

He closes his eyes, pained. "That's not true."

I can't stand this a second longer. With wrath as my driving force, I storm forward, pressing us front to front. "Then why did you do it? Why would you play me like that? I never thought you hated me that much!"

He hisses, turning his cheek, my words slapping him harshly.

"Tell me the truth, please, just this once. Please." A god-awful sob escapes me, and I know it's the first of many to come. "I can't do this anymore. If you feel anything, *anything* at all for me, please just tell me the truth."

This conversation is ten years in the making. It was inevitable it would come to this.

London's shoulders slump, and he finally, after all these years, he finally surrenders...to me. "I wasn't the one to move away without a word! You knew where I was, but you just vanished. You disconnected your phone; how was I supposed to call you to make sure you were all right?"

"You c-called me?" The stutter highlights my utter surprise.

"Of course, I did! It was like you disappeared, but after a while, I knew you didn't want to be found." He bites his upper lip, sucking the scar deep into his mouth.

"You could have tried harder," I whimper, unbelieving what he just revealed.

"I did try! Ask your dad how hard I tried."

"My dad?" The room begins spinning. "What has he got to do with this?"

When London chews over his scar once again, lost in the past, I remember my mom's ambiguous warning. *"We all make mistakes."*

I had no idea what she meant, but now, I think I do. "My father gave you that, didn't he?" He raises those soulful orbs, but he doesn't need to reply. The answer is reflected deep within. "Oh god." I hug my arms around my middle, needing a minute to collect my thoughts.

"For obvious reasons, I couldn't ask your parents, but after a while, I just couldn't stand it. I knew I was committing suicide by knocking at your front door, but I had to know where you were."

I blink past my tears, clinging to this small snippet of information, hopeful it'll lead to more.

"I begged your parents to tell me where you'd gone, but your dad had every right to throw me off that porch and beat the living shit out of me. I hurt you, and I deserved everything I got. After everything I put you through, it was long overdue."

I cover my gaping mouth, shaking my head in disbelief.

"Once he was done, your mom told me that you were happy, and that if I felt anything for you, I'd leave you alone. I'd let you live your life and not interfere because you deserved a chance to be happy."

I bite the inside of my cheek to stop my breakdown. It sounds like something she'd say. But little did she know, London *was* my happy.

"What she meant was that you could never be happy with me. And she was right. What kind of future could we have?" He exhales heavily, interlacing his hands behind his nape.

"So everything you said to me…the night we made love, was that all bullshit? Just to get in my pants? To teach me a lesson?"

London is throwing me breadcrumbs, but I'm still no closer to finding out the truth.

He advances forward, catching me completely off guard when he cups both my cheeks. He searches my eyes, my face, the look accelerating my heartbeat to an unhealthy rhythm. "It wasn't just sex to me…it was everything."

I burst into a strangled sob. He felt it too. After all these years, I lived with such regret, but now a small piece of my soul is remedied. "So you didn't use me as some pawn to get back at Lincoln and Belle?"

"*What*?" He shakes his head; incredulous I would even ask that of him. "Of course not. Why would you ever think that?"

"Because that's what Lincoln told me." London's breaths begin to mount. "And that's what you confirmed."

His hands slip from my face, the confusion as bright as day. "I confirmed? How?"

Sniffing back my tears, I confess, "I came to see you the day after, when you stood me up at work. Your mom was her usual charming self, but before I left, I saw Belle's car…and then I saw you looking out your window. You let me go."

The memory is just as raw as it was when I lived it.

I have no idea what London is thinking. He looks to be on the verge of destroying something or slipping into a comatose state. "I never saw you."

"Don't," I whisper, unable to stomach anymore lies.

"It's the truth. Do you think I would have let you leave after that night?" he poses, appearing disgusted I would ever think that of him.

"I don't know. Why would Lincoln lie? Why did Belle confess to kissing him? Why didn't you meet me? Tell me, London. What else am I supposed to believe?" My pleas are honest and heartfelt.

But the most damning piece of evidence is one that still torments me. "And your note." I shake my head, distraught. "You said…you won. Won a game I never wanted to play."

London fists both hands through his hair before he begins pacing the room. I watch as he grows more annoyed, incensed. "I can't believe this. Is that why you left?"

I nod slowly, my lower lip quivering. "That, and what I did. I'm a horrible person. I'm a coward. I ran away because I wasn't woman enough to face my sins." There, I said it. I've run away for so long, but eventually, our demons all catch up to us. "This guilt has eaten a hole straight through me, and each day I live with this regret, I'm losing sight of who I am."

"What a fucking mess," he mumbles, interlacing his hands on the top of his head.

His tattoo of the piano keys, coupled with a crown, the one which caught my eye all those years ago, does the same once again. The vibrant colors jump out at me, and I don't know why. London stops pacing, eyeing me closely. When he realizes what I'm staring at, he sighs.

"Do you believe me?"

That's the million-dollar question.

"I don't know. I don't know anything anymore." My eyes feel like sandpaper as I rub at them, wishing my vision would clear. "Why were you so adamant for me not to come to prom? You stated loud and clear that you weren't interested in fighting over what was *yours*." The memory has bile rising up my throat. "Were you afraid I'd steal Belle's limelight?"

"That is the most absurd thing you've ever said." He deadpans me.

"Did you or did you not say Lincoln was to make sure I didn't come to prom because you weren't interested in fighting over what was yours?"

"Yes, but it's not what you think." I wait, frantic for him to explain. He averts his gaze, running a hand down his face. "Everything I've done…I've done for you."

A small whimper slips past my lips. He's said this to me once before. When he was inside me, when nothing else mattered but us, he declared, *"All these years, everything…it's all for you."*

But what does that mean?

"You really think I could give two fucks about prom? C'mon, Princess. Think about how ridiculous that sounds."

Thinking about it now, I suppose he's right. But back then, all this made perfect sense. Now, it's all a bloodied massacre. "I know, but Lin—"

He raises his hand in warning. "If you say his name one more time, I won't be held accountable for my actions when I find that lying son of a bitch and kill him." I promptly seal my lips shut.

I'm too afraid to move. So when London walks over and reaches for my hand, I submit and allow him to take charge, as I don't even know what I want anymore.

My hand fits perfectly in his, the warmth thawing out the permanent chill in my bones. He silently leads me through his home, marching up the carpeted stairs. I wish I could appreciate the elegance of his home, but all I can focus on is not having a nervous breakdown.

He never lets go of my hand, and the charge is still as evident as it was from the first moment we touched. We enter his bedroom, still not a word exchanged. He leads me over to the bed, gesturing for me to sit down. I don't argue because I'm not sure how long my legs will keep me upright.

He stands in front of me as if weighing up how to do what he wants to do next. "Fuck it," he mumbles before walking over to this closet. I watch with interest as he reaches to the top shelf and slides a shoebox toward him.

The way he handles the box with such great care, I can only speculate that inside is something he truly values. With the mystery locked in both hands, he unhurriedly paces toward me. I have no idea the significance of what's inside until he offers it to me.

Biting my lip, I hesitate, gazing at the offering as if it's a loaded gun. I have no idea what's inside, but a small part of me knows that once I lift the lid, it'll be like opening Pandora's box. I shift my attention from the box to London, hoping he'll give something away.

He doesn't.

Reaching for it with a tremble, I run my fingertips over the lid, the faded cardboard giving away its age. London has held this keepsake for quite some time. With one final deep breath, I gently open the box and peer inside.

At first, I have no idea what I'm looking at until I reach for a yellowed envelope and turn it over. When I see who it is addressed to, a whoosh of air escapes me. I don't understand what I'm seeing. The seal is not affixed, so I lift the pointed edge and slide out what's inside.

The pieces of paper are aged, just like the envelope, but what's written in the messy, left-handed script will be forever young.

Princess,

I've lost count how many times I've written to you. With each letter, I'm always hopeful I'll grow a pair and finally send one. But how can I? How am I supposed to tell you this without everything turning to shit?

I'm trapped—as much as a prisoner within myself as I am behind these bars.

I want so badly to tell you that I miss you. I miss you so fucking much.

Reading over the letter twice, I finally lift my eyes and meet London's. "W-what is this?" I question because I need him to confirm what I think to be true. But the truth is so farfetched, there is no way it can be correct.

Lifting the letter, I turn it around so he can see *his* handwriting on the letter he wrote to *me*. And the abundant number of envelopes sitting beneath this one reveals he wrote many more.

"You know what it is," he replies, jutting his chin out to the box in my lap.

"It looks like letters you wrote to me while you were in juvie, but that's crazy, right?" When he remains silent, his stance unyielding, I know it's not so crazy after all. "Why didn't you send them? I thought you didn't care. Those entire six months, I waited for one single letter, one single word to tell me you were okay."

I don't understand any of this.

The tone of this letter is heartfelt, and it's almost the most beautiful thing I've ever read.

"How could I? Our story was always going to be a tragedy. But those letters, I could finally tell you how I felt. And even though I never sent them, they made what I felt for you real."

Tears pool and I let them fall, unashamed.

"You were the only thing that made me feel alive inside. And after feeling dead for so long, the feeling became an addiction. The more I pushed you, the harder you fought. I had never met anyone like you, and all I ever wanted…was you."

He tongues his upper lip, the movement stirring a sudden longing within.

"But us being together, our surnames made it completely impossible. We've suffered because of the sins of our parents' past. Every night, I wished I bore a different name because if I did, things between us could have been so different."

I'm barely breathing, too afraid to move.

My glance flicks down to his tattoo, and the word *defy* suddenly takes on a whole different meaning. "What does your tattoo mean?" I point my quivering finger.

London runs his hand over the ink and smiles. "I defy you,

stars."

"William Shakespeare?" I recognize the passage instantly as he's my favorite poet, a fact London knows.

"Yes."

"Why?"

Taking one step forward, then another, he comes to a stop when he's a mere hair's breadth away. "...My only love sprung from my only hate."

Time stands still.

A kaleidoscope of emotion wavers within, but the one single phenomenon that leads the pack is the only emotion that matters—love.

London follows my complete disbelief, and in response, he raises his forearm, turning it so the piano keys and crown come into view. "You have always been the beat of my heart."

I cover my mouth, shaking my head sluggishly. "You got that for me?"

His bowed lips tip into a graceful smile. "Of course, I did. You were my everything, Princess."

My mind stumbles and falls, unable to keep up. "B-but why were you so m-mean to me? And what happened at prom?" This night set off a chain reaction of events which forever changed me.

London sighs, before sitting beside me. He knows not to smother me. He's always known me better than I've known myself. He glances off into the distance, his smoldering eyes far,

far away. He finally divulges what happened. "I saw Lincoln…I saw him kiss Belle. I had my suspicions something was going on between them for a little while."

His admission kicks me low, and I wrap my arms around my middle. "*Lincoln* kissed Belle? He told me she kissed him." I should feel utterly betrayed, but funnily enough, I'm not.

"He's said a lot of things, most of which have been bullshit."

Trying to piece everything together, I press. "So that's why you got into a fight? You were jealous? That's why you didn't want me to come to prom. You warned Lincoln you'd fight for what was yours. Belle."

The words feel like acid bubbling from my throat, but it's the truth. I just need him to confirm it so I can finally move on. But what he does next shatters the past ten years.

With the slowest of movements, he brushes the fallen tears from my cheek with his thumb. "No. I got into a fight because of you. I couldn't care less about me because…" His pause sends a trickle of goose bumps across my flesh. Taking a breath, he turns so he's facing me, surrendering. "All I ever cared about was you."

"You got into a fight because you were defending *me*?" He nods once. This is too much.

"Yes, I didn't want you to come to prom because I couldn't stomach watching you and that *asshole* together. It was my arm you should have been on, not his, and I knew—" he inhales, steadying himself "—I knew that I'd fight him for you once and for all."

"Why was Belle so shocked in the hallway that day?" I remember her face when London said what I now know he said.

"Because I told her that sooner or later all her sneaking around would come back to bite her in the ass."

"Sneaking around?" London nods.

I can't process this fast enough. "Did Lincoln know what you were insinuating by that comment? About me not coming to prom?"

"Yes."

That one single word can amount to a thousand. "Why?" Another word which can alter a person's life forever.

London lowers his eyes. It's apparent what he wants to say next is eating him up inside. Leveling me with nothing but honesty, he confesses, "Lincoln chased after you because he knew how much I wanted you. You were the only thing he could have...that I couldn't. I'm sorry, Princess, but it's the god's honest truth."

"No," I cry in barely a whisper, the stab of betrayal slashing at the same wound over and over again.

"I've never lied to you." He's right. He's the only person who has been brutally honest with me because he knew I could handle it.

I think of when Lincoln and I first hooked up. Our kisses were in secret, as if he were embarrassed by me. But I have no doubt he rubbed his victory in London's face time and time again. Even when we made our "relationship" public, it only really heated up when London returned.

Oh god, I've been such a fool.

"Why, London, why didn't you tell me this?" I don't mean to be angry, but I just can't understand why he'd put us both through this torture.

He reveals why a moment later. "Because of your mom."

"My *mom*?" My heart is seconds away from exploding from my chest.

"My mom knew I had feelings for you, and she saw it as the ultimate betrayal. In her eyes, your mom had taken everything away from her. She despised you because you should have been hers. And she hated me because I was a reminder of everything she'd never have."

My heart breaks for him.

"She wanted me to hate you, but I just...it was like hating myself. She knew her only son was—" He stops, his confession not an easy one to make. "Was in love with her enemy's only daughter, and that just fueled her hatred tenfold."

The shock of hearing him confess something which was so unfathomable an hour ago has me gasping for air. "You l-loved me?"

"Always," is his simple, yet tear-jerking reply.

This entire time...London loved me...and I loved him, too.

I don't get a chance to express how I feel because London continues, needing this purge to finally rid the secret within.

"She warned me to stay away from you; otherwise, she'd drag your family name further through the dirt."

"How?" I whisper, my hoarse voice almost given up.

He swallows, shaking his head in anger. "By spreading rumors that she and your dad were having an affair. She knew everyone would believe her, and she'd ensure she ruined your family's reputation forever."

I close my eyes, unable to stomach this a second longer. Her ambiguous remarks now make perfect sense.

"I knew what that would do to you, what that would do to your scholarship. And what that would do to your mom. So the meaner I treated you...the safer you were from her. To make sure you were protected, I had to make you hate me. I just...I wanted to die every time I saw you and Linc together. But I had no other choice. But the night of prom, I fucked up. I couldn't stay away any longer."

Everything is spinning out of control. "But your note. You said you won."

"...I won *you*, Princess."

If I've ever heard anything sweeter, then I don't remember what. "Why didn't you meet me then? What happened?"

Brushing the back of his fingers along the apple of my cheek, he smiles, but it's bittersweet. "That's not my story to tell." He's said this once before, which kickstarted this entire clusterfuck of events.

Another word of warning comes to mind. "*Listen to what*

Belle has to say." I didn't know it then, but now I do.

"This all has to do with Belle, doesn't it?"

"…Yes."

Whatever secret Belle is guarding will shatter everything I thought I knew.

"Why has Lincoln lied to me for so long? Why did he lie about kissing Belle? Why did he lie about you? About us?" I add, wishing our history wasn't crowned with a ring of lies.

"To protect himself."

"From what?" I throw my hands up in exasperation.

"From you. If the truth ever came out, he knew you'd destroy him. And I think it was his way to ensure that…"

"That what?" I have no idea what to think. Nothing is what it seems.

"That you'd stop wanting me…maybe…" He arches a brow, appearing hopeful I'd corroborate his claims. "He knew you'd never speak to me again if he turned it all back on me. It was his final fuck you to me. *He'd* won.

"You know how much he hated me. I was the apparent cause of everything going wrong in his life, and he'd do anything to take away the only thing I…loved."

My cheeks redden for so many different reasons. "How could he do this? He's ruined…everything."

"He didn't care. You *were* a pawn, just not for me."

I think back to London and Lincoln's relationship and how the anger blinded Lincoln at times. There always was a rivalry between them, but I just didn't realize how deep it ran. I also know Harold's favoritism toward London upset him profoundly.

This entire thing was about getting back at London, and I *was* collateral damage, just not his.

"We've been together for years! We're getting married in two weeks! Has he lied about his feelings the entire time?" I'm on the cusp of a meltdown, not knowing what's real anymore.

London turns his cheek, shaking his head, wounded. I realize this is the first time I've mentioned how long we've been together. "No, he hasn't. I have no doubt he fell in love with you. How could he not? He grew up. We all did."

"That doesn't excuse what he did. He should have told me the truth."

"Yes, he should have, but would it have made a difference so long after the fact?"

Thinking about his question, I know the answer is no. I settled because I couldn't have the man I wanted. The person I've wanted all along. Lincoln was familiar; he also didn't have the ability to break my heart because I would never love anyone the way I loved—*love*—London.

"You destroyed me," I whisper, eyes peeled to the floor. "All the times you hurt me, though, you were doing it for me. I just wish I had known."

We've wasted so many years, so many possibilities, and now, we will never know. One simple lie has changed the course I was on. I can't help but think, what if...

With hesitation, he reaches for my hand. The touch takes on a whole different meaning because it's the first one we've shared where the truth has finally been set free. "After what happened with your parents, I knew your mom was right. I would just drag you down, and the farther away you were, the safer you and your family were.

"When I saw you on the news, after you won that case, I finally felt like I did something good. You looked happy. You'd made something of yourself, and that's all I ever wanted for you, Princess. I can never offer you the life you have."

I purse my lips, not fully understanding why. Surely, he's still not worried his mom will tarnish my family name. We're not kids anymore. "Why not?"

He runs his thumb over my knuckles, deep in thought. "My life is…complicated," he settles on after debating what to say.

A horrifying thought occurs. "Is it Sandy?" She was clearly staking her claim on London back at the bar. "Are you guys…a thing?" I swallow past the lump lodged in my throat.

He shakes his head without thought. "No, we're not anything."

Relieved, I address his declaration. "Mine isn't exactly a walk in the park," I reply, not sure what I even mean. "I'm supposed to get married in two weeks, but after everything, I can't…" I can see London's guilt, but I shake my head, interlacing our hands. It's the first time I've reached out, and his surprise shows. "Even if this never happened, I wouldn't have married him. How can I, when…"

Every inch of my body is telling me to do this, to finally be honest with myself and strip bare. I was hiding, too afraid to breathe, but looking into these blue eyes, I've at long last remembered how to live again.

Shifting closer, I bask in his warm cinnamon perfume and never want to stray far from it ever again. "How can I…when I'm still in love with you?"

A weight is lifted from me and I feel a hundred pounds lighter. Who knew the cure was sitting in front of me all along?

When London remains quiet, his jaw clenching and unclenching, I suddenly regret jumping into the deep end. I probably should have led in with something a little less forthright. He squeezes my fingers before standing, running both hands through his hair. I have no idea what he's thinking.

I try my best to recollect my thoughts. Lincoln's hatred toward London was what spurred him on to show an interest in me. Even after I left for Florida, he never made an effort to contact me. But why would he? He'd won.

London is right, however. We all grew up, and call me naïve, but I know Lincoln's feelings for me are now real. Being together for years with nothing for him to gain proves to me that he does love me, but if he loved me enough, he'd have told me the truth.

I still have no idea where Belle is and what part she plays in all this. The pieces of this puzzle are finally coming together, but

I'm missing the vital piece.

So many people had a say in my life. And the one person I've seen as the enemy was the only person who let me be free. I need to touch London, need to tell him again that I love him, but he's pacing, appearing someplace else.

I'll give him all the time he needs because he's done the same for me.

When I think I can stand, I walk over to the iPod docking station and scroll through the selection of music. London's tastes are very similar to mine, so when I find a song which allows me to escape for even a fraction of time, I let the music take over.

The moment the music starts, I close my eyes and let go.

The song choice seems perfect for how I'm feeling, for how I've felt for so long. As long as London stands by me, I think I'll finally be okay. The melodic tune transports me to another world, the lyrics striking a chord because I can relate to every single one. I won't be afraid…

Swaying to the music, I forget about tomorrow and the day after and just focus on today…focus on the now. So when a warmth presses against my back, I reflect on the way every inch of my body bursts alive, desperate for so much more.

My heart is nigh on exploding, but I embrace the feeling because I've forgotten what it feels like to be in love. London's sweet breath is tepid as it ripples down the column of my neck, but I continue rocking. Tears slip down my cheeks as I can't remember the last time I've felt this free.

Memories of every moment leading to now flicker before me, and I can't help but smile. It's only taken me ten long years, but finally, I'm home.

London wraps an arm around my middle, closing the distance between us as he molds us into one. A sigh escapes me, and I arch backward, needing to feel every inch of his body pressed to mine. We rock to the music, both lost in our own private oasis.

We fit perfectly, our bodies in sync as if we've always danced to the same beat. Tears continue falling. London nudges his face over my shoulder, nuzzling into my wet cheek. "Why are you crying?" he whispers.

"Because I'm happy," I reply in a tone matching his. He tightens his hold on me, adding another arm. I'm enclosed in his entire being, and I never want to leave.

Leaning my head to the side, I'm exposing myself, hoping he soothes this fire burning me up inside. He does. His lips press against my neck, kissing softly over my feverish pulse. A soft moan escapes me, as I never remember feeling this good.

He drags that luscious mouth up and down, feasting on my heated flesh, consuming me until I'm whimpering, growing weak at the knees. If he doesn't turn me around, I'm positive I'll explode. He reads my need and huskily chuckles, the sound striking low. I almost buckle with the intense force.

With one arm still enclosed around my middle, the other

slides up the center of my torso, coming to rest between my breasts. He splays out his fingers and presses his hand to my heart. The gesture is filled with nothing but love.

"I don't know what happens now." His misgivings remind me of his earlier comment, but I don't care.

"I don't either…but I'm excited to find out."

He's quiet, but the tension is thrumming through him. Is he nervous? Does he think once tonight is over with, things won't change?

Everything has changed for me, and although I shouldn't, I do.

Fastening my fingers over his wrist, I gently remove his hand from my chest and turn around submissively. Our eyes lock, and I get lost, never wanting to be found. Peering down for a long moment, I have no uncertainties when I slip Lincoln's ring from my finger. I place it on the dresser, committed to giving it back to him when the sun rises. My finger instantly feels lighter. I never should have worn it in the first place.

London's mouth parts, but he's done enough talking. I just want to feel.

Hooking my thumbs beneath the thin straps of the dress I wear, I slide them down my shoulders and allow the garment to glide down my body and pool on the ground. I'm standing before London in my black lace underwear and heels.

My nipples pearl when his Adam's apple bobs, his undivided attention on my barely covered breasts. The pillowed tops spill from my strapless bra, rising and falling vehemently as I gulp in mouthfuls of air.

He makes no secret that he's examining every scrap of flesh, tonguing his upper lip as his eyes blaze. Every inch of my body is popping. Unable to take the heat, I rub my legs together, desperate to appease the burn.

London hisses through clenched teeth, rubbing the back of his neck. If he doesn't make a move, then I'm bound to explode.

I point at his shirt. "Take it off."

He smirks, my words the exact ones he said to me when we found ourselves in this same position all those years ago.

"Take it off...please," I repeat, remembering the slow, sexy grin he bestowed on me because he's rewarding me with it once again.

He's complete perfection standing before me in all black, the recipe for a sublime disaster. And although I appreciate the way his t-shirt hugs him in all the right places, showcasing his brute masculinity, I know that once I see him in the flesh, all barriers between us lowered, I undoubtedly will never want him clothed ever again.

I'm tempted to disrobe him myself, but when he reaches overhead, tugging at the back of his collar and lifting the garment, I freeze, not wanting to miss a thing. The shirt rides up higher and higher, revealing inch after inch of glorious, bronzed, muscled flesh. My fingers itch, tempted to trace every hardened bump on his abs, but when I see a flourishing tree tattooed on his flank, I want to get down and worship him on my knees.

I don't know where to start because every part of him is truly epic, but when the shirt falls to the floor by his feet, I zero in on a tattoo over his heart. A gasp escapes me. Just when I think he can't shock me further, he goes and does something like this.

"Like it?" he asks, rubbing over the ink, his permanent badge of honor.

"L-like it? London, I…" But I don't even know what to say because this is just something else.

"I told you," he states, his palm flat on his chest.

"I know, but I thought you were joking." With eyes wide, I step forward and place my palm over his. "This is…just…oh my god," I settle on, unable to vocalize how I feel seeing my name tattooed on his chest over his heart.

Sandy's comment now makes sense. I guess I have been the proverbial third wheel. Even though I don't have London's name tattooed over my heart, his memory and my love for him never faded from mine.

Gently asking permission, he allows me to lift his hand and stare in awe at this work of art. It may only be my name, written in a cursive script, but it's the most beautiful tattoo I have ever seen. Acting on pure instinct, I swoop my hair to one side and lower my lips to our everlasting union.

"It's beautiful. Thank you."

His skin is warm and has my taste buds salivating in hunger. Now that I've had a sample, I want more…more…more. Kissing over his heart, I saunter over to his left pec, boldly tonguing his nipple. I'm rewarded with a sharp hiss, spurring me on.

I can't help myself and work my way down, my hands tracing his sides as I kiss every inch of flesh. His skin prickles beneath my lips, a low moan slipping from him as I outline each ridge of his washboard abs with my tongue. Just as I work his buckle, desperate to taste everything and more, he scoops his hands around me and lifts me up.

I'm moments away from protesting, but when he fists one hand in the hair at my nape, and the other low on my waist, all speech escapes me, because my body is the conduit. He guides my head to the right, before leaning forward and running the tip of his nose along the column of my neck. He inhales and groans low.

Every part of me trembles, desperate to crawl inside him and never emerge. "Please," I beg, indicative of the first time I had a taste. My pleas are unheeded, and he continues his torture, turning my passion into delicious pain.

He suckles over my rampant pulse, taking his sweet time. "I'm…"

"You're what?" I coax, tipping my head backward and opening myself up to him completely.

He kisses and sucks at my ripened flesh, intent on leaving me a writhing mess well after dawn. "I'm still in…love…with you, too," he confesses against my throat. "I never stopped. Game over. You won, Princess." His admission is my final undoing, and the walls I've erected around my heart crumble down around me.

I can't stand to be separated from him a moment longer, so I cup his cheeks into my palms and draw his face to mine. He is truly extraordinary, and he's all mine. "We both won."

I don't have time to utter another word because London smashes his mouth to mine, putting an end to a drought which has drained me dry for ten years. We kiss like starved animals, pawing and clawing at the other, needing to unite as one.

He hauls me forward, pressing us breast to breast, our lips never breaking apart. He takes my bottom lip into his mouth, sucking and running his tongue along the seam. I groan around him, the feeling comparable to total bliss.

My tongue meets his as he deliriously licks his way inside. He tastes me, samples the goods, slow and sluggish, as we have so many years to make up for. We collide with languid, learning strokes, reacquainting ourselves with this all-consuming, penetrating feeling of being connected mind, body, and soul.

Each taster has both of us wanting more, a glutton for this decadence to never end. I feel him growing hard against me, shooting a shockwave of pleasure all the way to my toes. I cry out in ecstasy when he rubs me in just the right way.

I writhe in agony as the simmering fire within me sweeps out of control. Still locked in a frenzied union, I work my hand between us and unbuckle his belt. As I unsnap his button and yank down his zipper, my heart threatens to explode from its confines because I have no shame dipping my hand down the front of his jeans and palming his hot, swollen shaft.

He grunts in the back of his throat, the sound echoing between my legs.

He's not wearing any boxers, so I'm working him in the flesh, which is exactly what I need, what I crave. I work my hand up and down, the feel of his hardened flesh almost too much. Our kisses become more frenzied, but I have no intention of stopping any time soon.

My nipples are pebbled and aching for his touch. He reads my desperation because he tears his mouth from mine, only to replace his kisses all over my aching breasts. He bites the tops of them, growling in frustration when the lace shelters what we both want.

He unsnaps the front clasp of my bra, ripping the garment from my body and hungrily sucking my left nipple into his burning mouth. I cry out but don't let him distract me from the mission at hand. I continue working his shaft from the root to the tip. He grows harder, longer, if that's even possible, but the image of him driving into me, punishing me over and over again has me growing so incredibly wet, I feel it pool between my legs.

He circles my areola, then suckles my nipple one last time. It pops from his mouth, and before I can question what happens next, he sinks to both knees before me, his face level with the junction of my thighs. He inhales deeply, and I redden, as I'm certain he can smell my arousal. Peering up at me, he smirks, licking his swollen, red lips.

I tremble, awaiting his next move.

When he runs his finger along the band of my underwear, I'm certain he leaves a trail of fire in its wake. My stomach ripples, so turned on, I can't contain the quiver consuming me whole. He fists the front of the lace, and with one sharp, unapologetic tug, he tears them clean from my body.

I yelp, but that soon turns into a low-seated moan when he buries his face into my bare center and laps at my needy flesh in one long, languorous move. He squeezes the tops of my thighs, gently spreading them farther apart. I cry out, knotting my fingers through his hair, needing to anchor myself before I explode. My hips ripple and roll when he presses the flat of his tongue against my swollen clitoris. He sinks his tongue into me, penetrating me as deep as he can go.

My arousal coats him. I can feel it, a slick varnish on his face as it acts as the perfect lubrication. I'm slippery and ripe, and when he twirls his tongue in a way that should be illegal, I scream in utter delight.

"I want you everywhere. All over me. I can't get enough of you," he hums against my flesh, his words adding to the incline I'm presently mounting.

He plunges deeper and deeper, his tongue and mouth

never missing a beat. To add to the delicious torture, he reaches a hand behind me and palms a cheek. He's now holding me prisoner, both back and front, but being held hostage has never felt this good.

The sting of his tongue as he sucks over my inflamed bud is too much, and my eyes roll to the back of my head. He grunts when I pump my hips forward, riding his face without a lick of shame. Just when I think he can't torture me further, he dips lower and runs his tongue from bottom to top.

I whimper, but it gets caught in my throat when he slaps my ass—hard—and finally gives into my not so subtle demands. He consumes me with a fierce need, sucking and lapping at my clit, knowing I'm riding close to the edge. The tickle of his beard adds a whole different dimension to being devoured this way.

My fingernails dig into his scalp, but he seems to like my aggression because he tunnels in deeper and deeper, not showing an ounce of mercy. He flicks his tongue in just the right way, and when he squeezes my ass in both hands, forcing me to ride his face, I come like I've never done so before.

My orgasm overtakes me, and it's the most amazing feeling in the world.

Aftershocks rock my body, and I don't think I'll come down any time soon. But London doesn't allow me a moment of reprieve. He stands, taking me into his arms, and advances toward the bed. He tosses me onto the mattress. I like that he acts with aggression.

This is us.

We don't make excuses for what we want because we want it all.

His pants hit the floor, and I lean up on my elbows, not missing a second of seeing him standing before me completely nude. He is glorious—hard and ready in all the right places. He opens a drawer on the dresser, the unmistakable sound of foil crinkling. Feeling completely wanton, I shake my head.

"No more walls between us. I want all of you."

"Be careful what you wish for, Princess…" With my desire slathered all over his face and lips, he couldn't look sexier as I confirm I want all of him, now and forever.

"I've already got everything I've ever wished for. You." A lopsided smile tugs at his lips, and he nods once. He crawls onto the foot of the bed while I tumble backward, settling onto the pillows.

His hulking body shadows mine when he presses us nose to nose. I shift my legs to accommodate his size, and he nestles between them. I'm ready and waiting—I want him so badly I can scarcely breathe.

Reaching up, I run my fingers over his cheek, through his beard, coaxing him by the back of his neck to kiss me. It doesn't take much swaying. He kisses me, but this time, the passion is simmering. We're lost in the laziness of our hunger, the sluggishness a heady aphrodisiac.

As our tongues spar, ready to wage a war where we both

win, London slips his hand between us. Everywhere he touches sends ripples of pleasure straight to my toes. However, when he circles my clit with the pad of his thumb, everything shifts, and the focal point is my needy center.

I'm still slick and delicate, so when London inserts a finger into me, I bow off the mattress, the feeling amplified tenfold. "Such a greedy little thing," he hums against my lips.

"I am when it comes to you," I gasp, spreading my legs farther. He works his way in slowly, testing and stretching, preparing me for what's to come.

"More," I plead, fumbling and guiding him to fill me to the brim. He adds another finger, all the while massaging my center with skill. A sheen of sweat coats my body, adding to the velvety slide as he rocks against me, his fingers never missing a beat.

The knot begins to build low once again, and as good as this feels, I'm ready and needy and the only thing that will suffice is him burying himself deep within me. I've been a selfish lover. It's now my turn to give.

"My turn," I state, gently coaxing him to a standstill. I kiss his lips before rolling us over so I'm straddling him.

He looks up at me with nothing but love, a vision that will forever be singed onto my soul. With my name staring back at me, I raise my hips and grip his hot shaft, stroking him up and down. A profound breath escapes him as he arches his neck into the pillow. His hot weight has every part of my body slavering, and unable to wait for a second longer, I guide him into me.

We both hiss when I rub his tip along my entrance, coating him with my arousal. Inch by inch, I lower myself onto him, biting my lip because the stretch is almost to the pinnacle of pain. But that ache rapidly fades and is replaced with complete euphoria.

London places his hands low on my hips, his gaze flicking downward to see where we are connected. When I'm halfway down, he stops me from progressing, suspending me on his cock. I attempt to shift, needing so much more, but he holds on tight. "This is everything. It changes everything. I love you. Promise me…never run from me again."

I place my palm over his thundering heart, over my name, and seal our fates forever. "I promise."

Satisfied, he loosens his hold, but just when I think he's handed over the reins, he slams my hips onto him, impaling me to the hilt. My body undulates, as I've never felt this full.

"Then I'm yours." His offering sends me into overdrive because it's what I've wanted to hear for so many years.

Raising his hands in surrender, he silently gives me permission to take what I want, and all I want…all I've ever wanted was him.

Placing both palms flat on his chest, I begin rocking my hips. Slow and steady at first, as he's so incredibly big, but when I see him tonguing his upper lip, a look of utter possession slathered on his cheeks, I buck faster and harder, needing to unite as one.

He groans, watching the way my breasts sway as I ride him like a stallion. "Faster," he orders between small, erotic breaths. Each stroke hits me in just the right way, but I quash down my need to come because I want to feel him explode around me first.

I bounce on his lap, the feeling of him re-entering me countless times taking my breath away. Stars flash behind my eyes, but I continue to dominate him, powerless to stop because this feels so good. Slapping one hand behind me and resting it on his knee, I grind on his shaft, the friction hitting my clit every single time.

"Fuck," he hisses, gripping one hand on my waist to help with the measured momentum. A wildfire begins to burn at the tips of my ears and work its way down.

His abs ripple and roll, the sycamore tree on his flank coming alive as his breathless rumbles fill the air. I take him in, admiring every inch—his besotted face, his glorious body, but most of all, my name imprisoned over his heart.

The love I feel for him will rule me, dictate me from this moment forward, and the thought of belonging to him irrevocably has tears pricking my eyes. My mind takes a back seat, and I rule with my body and heart. I devour him, bouncing and bucking until the familiar burn takes over, and I chase my release, unable to stop. I shatter around him, milking him, certain I've bled him dry.

He is still hard, indicting this has only just begun. "Ready?"

"For what?" I'm almost afraid to ask.

He answers what a second later when he lifts me from his lap, and spins me around, only to slam me back down when I'm facing the far wall. My head is spinning, but I don't have time to recollect my thoughts because he gently pushes between my shoulder blades so I fall onto all fours. He fills me once again.

"That," he whispers into my ear as he drapes his body over mine, biting the side of my neck. "I was just warming up." Rising, he pulls out of me, only to sink into me over and over again.

My breasts swing below my bowed body, my nipples scraping the blankets, adding to the stimulation overdrive. He rocks into me from behind, his hands controlling the angle of my hips because he knows all the right moves to make me feel like I'm dying inside.

He pumps into me so vigorously it brings tears to my eyes, but I take everything he gives me, an instant addict to this feeling of unrestrained hunger. He grunts and hisses, increasing his brutal strokes until I can no longer take it and collapse onto my stomach.

He hums with the sight of my ass high in the air, but he never misses a beat as he owns my body, drawing me closer to the threshold once again. "Welcome home, Princess." I'm unable to vocalize a response because he's robbed me of breath.

This is the first time I'm glad to be back…back home where I belong.

London twirls his hips and strikes me hard—the money shot—and I scream in utter delight. His rumbles resonate all the way through me, and I feel him pulling back, about ready to join me. But I clamp my muscles around him. "Bring it home," I shamelessly demand, and he growls, unable to refuse my command as he spills his seed into me.

The tremors hum through our bodies for minutes after we've both had an orgasm that has left us sticky, breathless, and spent. When we finally untangle our limbs and settle beneath the covers, London kisses my lips and promises me the world.

"You are my home. Always and forever."

His vow has me closing my eyes and falling into a deep, happy slumber because now I know...we are always and forever.

14

I have been bitten, spanked, tortured, and worshipped within an inch of my life, and I have loved every minute of it. Just when I'd collapse in utter exhaustion, London would bundle me into his arms and torment me once again. After orgasm number five, I lost count and just surrendered, but we both did.

There was an underlying gentleness and a sense of fulfillment every time we touched because we both knew this was finally our time. Now that the sun has risen and the dawn has peeked over the storm clouds, I can see clearly for the first time in a long time.

I have no regrets about what I did. I know I should, but I don't. It's difficult to feel remorse when the foundation of your relationship was based on a lie. Lincoln lied to me, and although it was a lifetime ago, I will never understand why he did what he did.

He dragged me into his sick plot of revenge, a scheme I never wanted a part of. Things could have turned out so differently for me, but now, the stars have aligned, and I have found my true north. But a weight settles in my belly, a foreboding premonition of things to come. Things won't be easy, but they never are with London and me.

The view from the balcony is awe inspiring. I can almost taste the magic in the air. I've been out here for countless minutes, pondering on what happens now. I know we face a lot of hurdles, but we will tackle them together. I can only hope love does prevail all.

A small part of me was angry with my mom for what she did to London's mother, but I now understand that she never had a choice. Love is messy, inconvenient, and at times, heartbreaking, but when you find it, you'll do anything to hold it because you're at its complete mercy. Love ruins you, but when you find the one you're meant to be with, you'll move heaven and hell for that one single moment in time.

"Hey." Just like right now.

My skin prickles and memories of what he did to me flood my senses. "Hey."

London wraps his arms around my middle, embracing me to his chest. "You sleep okay?"

I can't help but chuckle. "The hour I managed to squeeze in between your groping, it was great."

He makes no apologies as he rubs his morning hard-on against my back. "Making up for lost time."

His comment brings home the fact we have so much to discuss. Our lives are so different; we live in different states. But we've taken the first step, and like most journeys— that's the hardest one to take.

London senses my grave train of thoughts and kisses the side of my cheek. "I'll make us some coffee. Meet me downstairs?" I nod, thankful he gives me the space I need.

When I hear him rustling around for something to wear, I can't help but turn around and watch him slip into a pair of ripped jeans. They sit low on his narrow hips, emphasizing his wicked V muscle, which I lapped at more times than I can count.

My cheeks redden to the color of the ripest tomato. Who knew watching a man dress could be as sexy as watching him undress? London's lips are red and succulent, and his hair is styled into a mussed faux hawk. The tattoo across his heart still takes my breath away. My god, he is so incredibly gorgeous, and I need to stop staring before I throw him down onto that bed.

He smirks, well aware of the effect he has on me, but doesn't linger. He shoots a wink my way, before turning and leaving me to wipe the drool from my chin.

Once my heartrate returns to a semi-normal pace, I decide to go downstairs because eventually, we have to discuss what this all means. I'm completely naked and know that having "the talk" in the nude may derail us from figuring out what to do. The thought is daunting because the road ahead won't be smooth sailing.

London's bedroom is a mess. There are clothes and other objects strewn around the place. An abstract piece of art lies haphazardly where it fell onto the floor when London slammed me against the wall and had me seeing stars.

I give up on looking for my dress and instead decide to wear something of London's. The thought of being swathed in his smell is far more appealing anyway. The dresser which served us well last night sits innocently feet away. If only these walls could talk.

Walking toward it, I open the first two drawers, but only find underwear, socks, and t-shirts. The breeze skimming off the ocean is a little nippy, so I elect to wear a hoodie instead. When I open drawer number three, I'm in luck, but as I push a few garments aside, I get a little more than I bargained for.

I stand speechless, unmoving, because what I'm seeing can't be true. I don't understand; there must be some mistake. But with trembling fingers, I reach for the evidence, the California sun confirming what I thought could never be true.

Not again, please, no, not again.

But the proof is staring me in the face. There is no denying it. How could I have been so stupid...again?

So many emotions coil within, but my survival instinct overrides any other. I'm a scorned woman on a mission as I reach for a blue sweater and slip it on. Taking three deep breaths, I tuck the evidence of his treachery under my arm and commence my walk of shame.

A small voice inside me is screaming, demanding I rethink this decision because there is no way this is true. There is no way he could do this to me. But I force it down because this is far easier than having to figure out how we can make this work.

He is a Sinclair…and I will always be a Brooks.

A staircase has never looked so daunting because I know once I reach the bottom, I doubt I'll ever be able to get back up. But I persevere because this scenario is one I've lived through before. My breaths leave me in winded gasps, and I'm on the cusp of passing out, but once my feet descend the last step, I pull back my shoulders and soldier on.

London is in the kitchen, back turned, hands braced on the counter as he waits for the coffee to brew. He's none the wiser what I'm about to do.

Peering down at the proof in my palm, I persuade myself to speak before history repeats itself. "I'm really disappointed in your creativity. I expected more." I bite the inside of my cheek to stop the tears. They can wait until after I leave because once they start, I doubt they'll ever stop.

London turns over his shoulder, arching a brow. "I didn't hear you complaining last night." I scoff, appalled I fell for his bullshit once again.

When I deadpan him, not at all amused, his cocky grin

fades. "What's wrong?" His eyes drift to what I'm holding, but as usual, he has the perfect poker face.

Taking a step forward, I hide behind my bravado because I'm not interested in a longwinded affair. "What is this?"

London turns, folding his arms across his chest, obscuring the tattoo, and for that, I'm glad. "It's a sweater," he replies, pursing his lips, confused.

"Is it yours?"

"Yes, it's mine. So what?" My heart shatters into a million pieces and this time, nothing will be all right ever again.

Clutching the black hoodie, I peer at the red dragon on the upper left corner. I wish I'd never seen it, I wish I'd never seen *him,* because ignorance is truly bliss. This entire time, the enemy was right under my nose, and last night, I slept with the enemy and I liked it. I liked it a lot.

The letters, they never came from the Rossi crew. They didn't care for the likes of me. My assailant was closer to home.

Home.

Last night's admission rings loudly in my ears, cementing the fact that I'm a fucking idiot. "How could you? Do you hate me that much?"

London Sinclair should be an actor because right now, his innocent act could win him an Emmy. "Are you high? What are you talking about?"

"Stop it!" I yell, angered he would make jokes. "I know it was you. Your ruse is up. This entire time, I know it was you sending me those letters."

There, I said it. I have all the proof I need. I'm holding the proverbial smoking gun.

The night I saw the hooded figure standing outside my old home, stalking me, I knew that he was the one who had been tormenting me these past six months. I just never thought that person would be the man I love.

London is my stalker. He said he knew I worked in New York and was a lawyer because he followed my case on the news, but it wasn't big news here. My parents only knew so much because they read about it online. Has London been stalking me for longer than these letters? How else would he know? Oh, god, this makes sense. I wish it didn't, but it all adds up.

The letters, although short, always had a personal feel. They spoke of retribution but never really specified why. Could it be me up and disappearing without a trace angered him because in a way, it meant that I had won? It seems petty, but he has hurt me for less.

London never liked to lose, and it seems some things never change, like him being a sadistic, vindictive bastard.

"What letters?" he demands, stalking forward. But I retreat so far backward, he stops midstride. "Princess? Please explain to me what is going on."

I shake my head, refusing to fall victim to him again. "I can't believe I fell for your bullshit again. There is something seriously wrong with me! Just tell me why!" I beg, interlacing my fingers, on the cusp of breaking down.

"I don't know what to tell you because I have no fucking clue what you're talking about!" he shouts, running a hand through his hair.

"I saw you, the other night, wearing this!" I exclaim, hurling the sweater into his face. He catches it, jaw clenched. "I have been receiving letters for the past six months. The gist of them is always the same. 'You're going to pay, whore. Watch your back, slut. Blah, blah, blah.' The point is, I went to my old house the other night and I saw someone wearing that hoodie." I jab my finger at it. "I had no idea who the sender was, who my stalker was. I thought it was retaliation for doing my job, but how did they know where my parents lived? Where I used to live? They didn't, because the only person who knew that was you!"

I'm so angry, I'm shaking with rage.

"It wasn't me," he firmly states, his lies infuriating me further.

"Then how did you know I worked in New York? How did you know I was a lawyer? It's not like we've got any friends in common who would innocently mention it in passing. I must say, I'm disappointed in your choice of phrasing although I should be happy you actually took the time to send these letters!" Unable to stop myself, I storm forward and slap his cheek.

I'm expecting him to fight me, to defend his honor, but he

doesn't. He stands with his head bowed, his palm cradled to his reddening cheek. I should run from this house and beg Lincoln for forgiveness. Beg he forgive me for ever believing London, but I can't. My feet remained glued to the floor.

"So you have absolutely nothing to say?"

He snickers, his anger palpable. "It doesn't seem to make a difference what I say because you don't trust me. I have told you the truth, yet you don't believe me. After everything, how can you still doubt me?"

And that's the cliffhanger. I know why. And that reason makes me a coward.

He is not intimidated by me in the slightest and stalks forward, lowering his face to mine. "You're just afraid of everything I make you feel because I push you, and you're scared of being hurt. Of losing control. I have always told you the truth. I'm not like Lincoln. I won't stand by and watch you become everything you hate. I will tell you when you're being an irrational pain in the ass, like right now, but guess what, that's what love is! You will sacrifice everything for that person because without them, YOU DON'T EXIST!"

But I stand my ground and push down my tears.

"I'm sorry for everything I did to you. I turned you into this untrustworthy, bitter person, and I am so fucking sorry. I wish I could take it back. Every single day, I wish things could have turned out differently for us. That we had different names. And even though I thought I was doing it to save you, I know now that I fucking ruined you.

"So go back to Lincoln. Go back to your perfect life where you can shut off and not feel because I can't give you that. I will always love you even when you don't love yourself. And I will continue to love you until my heart stops beating.

"I will never make apologies for loving you because you are a part of me." He slaps his hand over my name, strengthening his claims. "But it's obviously too late."

I don't even know when the tears began to fall because everything he said was right. I am bitter, and I have turned into someone I hate. I've run away for so long, I don't even know who I am anymore. But being with London, I remember, and that scares the living shit out of me.

Deep down, I believe him. I know there is a rational reason this sweater is in his home, but I jumped to conclusions because it was the easy way out. London makes me feel things I didn't know I was capable of feeling, and I'm scared; I'm scared he will break my heart again.

London has every right to hate me. I hate myself. I got scared because my life suddenly seemed so perfect, and there's got to be a catch. I don't know what it's like to live life loving and being loved eternally in return.

I am broken. I just didn't realize how much.

"How did you know where I lived? Where I worked?" I know it's beating a dead horse, but I have to know. I'm not on social media because what would I post? Pictures of my pretentious house and clothes? Photos of a loveless union to reveal to the world that I'm a sad, detached woman who doesn't deserve this adoring man's affection?

When he's silent, his raspy breathing filling the void between us, I finally lift my eyes to meet his. He is furious at me, but behind that is...guilt. I know he's not my stalker, he's not the one who sent the letters...but he knows who did.

"London?" I pose, the gears shifting once again.

He doesn't have time to answer me, however, because the front door opens and a titter of innocent laughter fills the otherwise stale atmosphere. He lowers his head and runs a hand through his snarled hair.

What's going on?

"Daddy!" The affectionate term holds a whole different meaning when it is used in relation to the man I love.

A little girl with pigtails and rosy red cheeks comes bouncing into the kitchen, eyes only for London. When he sees her, his anger fades and all that's left is utter happiness. "Hey, baby." He crouches low, and she runs into his embrace, throwing her tiny arms around his nape.

I stand absolutely perplexed, not even understanding what I'm witnessing. But what I see next leaves me wheezing and seeking out something to lean on before I pass out.

"Emily, I can't find your book bag. Did you...oh my...god."

They say that before you die, your life flashes before your eyes, so I'm certain I'm seconds away from having a heart attack because every single memory, every single moment that I've shared with Belle comes roaring to the surface because she's here…standing before me.

I slouch against the counter, unable to process everything fast enough.

She looks like the Belle I remembered, but now, there is a heavy burden weighing her down. Her eyes are plagued, no longer carefree and naïve. She guards a solemn secret, and when she meets my stare, she knows I'm not leaving until she tells me what it is.

Her attention flicks to the fallen hoodie on the ground. Her face pales while I feel the blood rise to mine. Why does she look like she's seen a ghost? "Honey, can you go to your room?"

Emily, obviously Belle's daughter, pulls from London's embrace with a frown. She turns to look at her mother and then back at her…father. I cover my mouth. I'm going to be sick.

"Listen to your mom. If you do, I promise to take you out for ice cream, okay?" London's focus never wavers from his daughter as he rubs her slender arm. It's only now she notices me standing in her kitchen, slumped against the kitchen counter, trying to make sense of what I'm seeing.

She steps from London's arms and spins around to face me. Her large, intelligent eyes remind me so much of Belle's when she was her age. At a guess, I'd say Emily is around ten years old. "Hi, I'm Emily."

She continues staring at me, waiting for me to be the grown-up and reply. London rises slowly, glancing at Belle, who bites her lip, avoiding any contact with me. "Hi, Emily. It's nice to meet you. I'm Holland."

Her small mouth parts, and she turns quickly to look at London. "Daddy, she has the same name as your tattoo."

London smiles, but it's so bittersweet, I grieve with him. "Weird, right?" He messes up the top of her hair, but she cocks an inquisitive brow. The fact he doesn't want his daughter knowing who I am cuts me deep, but what was I expecting?

"Emily," Belle presses, wringing her hands in front of her. "Say goodbye to Holland." And just like that, I've suddenly found myself as the third wheel. I don't belong here. Emily nods, but not before she kisses London on the cheek.

She paces past me deliberately, examining me closely. The look she gives me…it is so familiar. "You forgot to put on pants." A blush creeps up my neck as I tug down the edge of the sweater I stole from London's dresser. She skips off upstairs, leaving us alone to deal with whatever this is.

I have dreamed of this moment for years. Me dropping to both knees and begging Belle for forgiveness. I don't care that she kissed Lincoln because what I did was so much worse. But now…this changes everything.

The fact Belle keeps looking at London for support hurts me more than I thought possible. But why wouldn't she? They are obviously a couple and have a beautiful child together. I'm once again the homewrecking whore who can't seem to stop fucking up everyone's life, especially my own.

"Your daughter is beautiful," I whisper, holding back ugly tears.

London sighs, rubbing the back of his neck. "Holland…"

"No, it's fine. I'll go. I understand." Belle pounces forward, attempting to touch me, but I jump so far backward, I stub my toe on the kitchen table.

"Please, don't go," London begs, but I can't stay here a second longer.

"I have to. You told me your life was complicated, but you failed to mention that complication was a daughter and wife!" I snap, lowering my voice, not wanting Emily to hear.

Belle's lower lip trembles, while London shakes his head. "She is not my wife."

"Girlfriend then."

"She isn't that either," he rebukes, but I don't care about the technicalities.

"Well, whatever she is, I'm clearly interrupting." With whatever pride I have left intact, I blindly reach for a pen and a piece of paper from the counter. "Here is my address. Please mail me whatever I've left upstairs."

As I attempt to write out my details, the pen decides to run out of ink, only prolonging my stay, which is not an option. Desperately reaching for another, I press the tip to the pad, but when I see a blood red stroke stain the white paper, a blanket of terror swathes me.

My mind can't seem to play catch-up fast enough, and I dismiss my farfetched notion. But taking a closer look at the writing pad, the pen drops from my fingers, rolling along the polished floor.

The answer is there—it is staring me in the face, but I need validation because I don't trust myself anymore. After ten years, I never thought our reunion would be this. "...Belle, does this mean anything to you?" Bending, I offer her the sweater in my trembling hand. She gnaws her lip, just like she did whenever she was in trouble.

She remains silent, but her silence fills in the blanks.

"You've been following me?"

A small sob escapes her, but she quickly muffles it behind her hand. "Yes, but it's not—"

I don't allow her to finish however. "Why? Surely, you'd know that'd scare the shit out of me. Why wouldn't you just say hello?"

"I needed time..."

"Time for what?" I question, throwing my arms out wide. When she remains quiet, I ask, "Did you send letters?" She averts her gaze, her guilt slapping both my cheeks.

I don't know what to say. I know I hurt her, but those letters, they were absolutely sickening. "Belle, how could you? You knew what they would do. They were awful, downright appalling."

She sniffs, still unable to look at me.

"I know I hurt you, but how could you send them to me? I've been terrified…" But my voice drifts off into the distance when she no longer looks shamefaced but rather confused.

"To you?" she asks in a small voice. "I never sent them to you."

I scoff, unbelieving she's just gone back on her word when she all but admitted it seconds ago. "So you didn't send the letters then?" London shifts his weight, his fists clenching and unclenching. Something is suddenly horribly wrong.

"I did send them…but they weren't for you."

"Belle…" London shakes his head, angered and disappointed.

"Weren't for me?" I scrunch up my nose, sick of her games. "Then who were…?"

Silence.

The final piece of the puzzle falls into place, but what I'm perceiving, it makes no sense. London ambles toward me, placing a hand on my cheek. Five seconds ago, I was pushing him away, but now, he's the only thing stopping me from tumbling to the floor.

"Why didn't you tell me you and Belle had a baby?" I question weakly, tears filling my eyes.

He weighs up what to say, brushing away the wetness which coats my cheeks. "We don't," he finally replies, but I don't understand.

"So she isn't your child?" My breathing begins to climb, and

I slump forward, my feet giving way.

London catches me, his face twisted in pain, not for himself however—for me. "Yes, she is mine."

"I-I don't understand what that means." My voice ricochets across the room, and I wonder if I spoke aloud or if this, all of this is in my head. "Please, someone tell me what's going on."

When London looks at Belle, begging for this to end, I finally discern what he means—this was never his story to tell.

With the walls closing in on me, I use whatever sense I have left to beseech my once best friend to finally, after ten years, tell me the truth. But when she does...I wish that this was all just a bad dream.

"Emily *is* London's child...he's just not her...biological father."

"Then w-who is?"

Time stands still.

They say that regardless of your problems, the world will keep on spinning. The sun will rise in the east, and it'll set in the west. The sky will forever be blue, and the stars will kiss the heavens for an eternity. But what Belle is about to tell me...it'll set my world upside down and life won't ever be as I know it.

"Who, Belle?" I whisper, knowing what her answer will be.

She swallows and blinks once. This is it, but nothing could ever prepare me for what she says next. "...Lincoln."

I defy you, stars, I defy you.

ACKNOWLEDGMENTS

My wonderful husband, Daniel. I love you. Thank you for believing in me even when I didn't believe in myself.

My ever-supporting parents. You guys are the best. I am who I am because of you. I love you.

My agent, Kimberly Whalen from The Whalen Agency.

My publicist—Nina Bocci. Thank you for organizing my life. Your support means the world to me. Thank you for always being there.

My editors, Jenny Sims and Toni Rakestraw. What can I say other than I LOVE YOU! Thank you for everything.

My proof-readers—Rosa Sharon from iScream Proofreading Services and Lisa Edward. You guys are the best!

Sommer Stein, you NAILED this cover! Thank you for being so patient and making the process so fun.

Louise Mercer, Gemma Cawley, Christina and Lauren, Tina Gephart, Lisa Edward, SC Stephens, Vi Keeland, Anna Todd, R.K. Lilley, Colleen Hoover, Sylvain Reynard, Kylie Scott, Mia Sheridan, Lexi Ryan, Helena Hunting, Tijan, Rachel Van Dyken, Geneva Lee, Shannon Shade, Kristin Dwyer (I only listen to you!) Heyne, Random House, Kinneret Zmora, Hugo & Cie, Planeta, Art Eternal, Carbaccio, Fischer, Harper

Brazil, Bookouture, Egmont Bulgaria, USA TODAY/ Happy Ever, Aestas Book Blog, Talkbooks, TotallyBooked Blog, The RockStars Of Romance, Michelle Stoeger, Franziska Kurra, Paula Nascimento, Hugues De Saint Vincent, Benita Rolland, Sylvie Gand, Melusine Huguet, Meire Dias, Nikki McCombe, Romance Writers of Australia, Paris, New York—Thanks for the support and laughs.

To the endless blogs that have supported me since day one—You guys rock my world.

A special shout-out to: Laura Foster Franks, Donna Cooksley Sanderson, Ria Alexander, Kell Donaldson, Anne Christine, Melissa Teo, Nadine Colling, Mindy Guerreiros, Gel Ytayz, Melissa Gill, Ryn Hughes, Beverly Preston, Vanessa Silva Martins, Ellie McLove.

My reader group; My Sinners—sending you all a big kiss.

My beautiful family —Mum, Papa, my sister—Fran, Matt, Samantha, Amelia, Gayle, Peter, Luke, Leah, Shirley, Michael, Rob, Elisa, Evan, Alex, Francesca, and my aunties, uncles, and cousins—I am the luckiest person alive to know each and every one of you. You brighten up my world in ways I honestly cannot express. Samantha and Amelia— I love you both so very much. To my family in Holland and abroad. Sending you guys much love and kisses. Zia Rosetta and Zia Giuseppina—you are in our hearts. Always.

My fur babies— mamma loves you so much! Buckwheat, you are my best buddy. Dacca, I will always protect you from the big bad Bellie. Mitch, refer to Dacca's comment. Jag, you're a wombat in disguise. Bellie, you're a devil in disguise. And Ninja, thanks for watching over me.

To anyone I have missed, I'm sorry! It wasn't intentional!

Last but certainly not least, I want to thank YOU! Thank you for welcoming me into your hearts and homes. My readers are the BEST readers in this entire universe! Love you all!

ABOUT THE AUTHOR

Monica James spent her youth devouring the works of Anne Rice, William Shakespeare, and Emily Dickinson.

When she is not writing, Monica is busy running her own business, but she always finds a balance between the two. She enjoys writing honest, heartfelt, and turbulent stories, hoping to leave an imprint on her readers. She draws her inspiration from life.

She is a bestselling author in the U.S.A., Australia, Canada, France, Germany, Israel, and The U.K.

Monica James resides in Melbourne, Australia, with her wonderful family, and menagerie of animals. She is slightly obsessed with cats, chucks, and lip gloss, and secretly wishes she was a ninja on the weekends.

Connect with
MONICA JAMES

Facebook: facebook.com/authormonicajames
Twitter: twitter.com/monicajames81
Goodreads: goodreads.com/MonicaJames
Instagram: @MonicaJames
Website: monicajamesbooks.blogspot.com

Made in United States
Orlando, FL
20 August 2022

21304374R00225